A Crisis in Cyprus

An Elspeth Duff Mystery

Ann Crew

Cover photographs of Kantara Castle and A Street Scene in the Old Section of Nicosia by Ann Crew © 2006

Author's photograph by Ian Crew

ACE/AC Editions
All rights reserved.
ISBN-13: 9781523756469
ISBN-10: 1523756462

Library of Congress Control Number: 2016902281
CreateSpace Independent Publishing Platform
North Charleston, South Carolina

anncrew.com

elspethduffmysteries.com

Also by Ann Crew

A Murder in Malta

A Scandal in Stresa

A Secret in Singapore

Praise for *A Murder in Malta*:

"Each main character has a rich backstory with enough skeletons in closets to provide grist for a number of future novels.

An often compelling . . . excursion through exotic locales featuring unusual, complex characters." —*Kirkus Review*

To Nancy

Part 1

The Delegation

Prologue

Philippa Allard-Thorpe strove for perfection in all things she did. A child of obese parents, she became anorexic in her youth in order to achieve the perfect figure. She said she had graduated *summa cum laude* from her American university, and occasionally when in America or entertaining American guests, she displayed a Phi Beta Kappa key in her lapel. In marriage she wanted a perfect husband and perfect children. When Ernest Thorpe proved human, she divorced him. When her first child died, her second child became an imperfect replacement. Now, in mid-life, her carefully clothed slender figure, classic high cheekbones, and unnaturally straight white teeth disarmed all who met her. Yet, if one looked closely, nothing hid the rigidity of her soul.

As the new manager of the Kennington Nicosia, she insisted there be no errors in the service to the guests or disruption to their comfort. A mistake by any member of her staff meant instant dismissal. Guests were charmed and became relaxed; the staff muttered but benefitted from being employed by the hotel at above average wages.

The one thing Philippa could not control, however, was the manner of her death. As she confronted her murderer, she could find no perfect way to save herself. She could not make her transition from life to death a perfect affair, although in the end she was perfectly dead.

In her last moments that distressed her.

1

Eric Lord Kennington, mogul of the Kennington hotel empire, sat in the newly redecorated private dining room above his offices in the City of London and was savouring a late breakfast and ruminating over the next assignment for one of his top security advisors, Elspeth Duff. He felt a tinge of guilt that Elspeth, who proved so indomitable in all of her assignments, had suffered grievous bodily harm during her last one in Singapore. After three weeks in hospital, four months at her home in London and an extended fortnight at her aunt's home on the island of Gozo in the Republic of Malta, Elspeth agreed to resume her employment with the Kennington Organisation as long as her first assignment would be a quiet one.

In Singapore, her long-time friend Sir Richard Munro, the British High Commissioner to Malta, had saved Elspeth's life. He brought her back to London from Southeast Asia and was a constant companion when she was at St Mary's Hospital recovering from her head wounds. He had taken a month's leave of absence from his post in the Mediterranean republic. Lord Kennington did not sanction this nor was he pleased by it. He did not want Elspeth to become the future Lady Munro. He needed her on his staff, and besides he had grown personally fond of her.

For the moment he was alone, but he expected Pamela Crumm to arrive at any moment. He swallowed the remains of his lavishly buttered toast, scraped up the last vestige of his scrambled eggs and looked out the floor-to-ceiling glass curtain wall at the River Thames and the London Eye in the distance. He loved the twisting Thames but despised the lumbering wheel.

Pamela bustled in, carrying two files, and declined Eric's offer to take a cup of tea from the buffet. She did not look at the view as it replicated the one from her office one floor below.

"I'm considering sending Elspeth to Buenos Aires," he said and then waited for Pamela's reaction. She was his silent business partner and usually had an opinion on any matter at hand. He knew she took vicarious pleasure in the love life of others, particularly Elspeth's. Pamela's small, twisted frame and ugly face allowed no romantic fulfilment of her own.

"Buenos Aires!" Pamela cried. "Eric, have you no heart?"

"I have a business to run without having to condescend to the romantic entanglements of my employees," he responded, trying to hide a twinkle in his eye. Pamela took the bait.

"When the Kennington Organisation, to which I have devoted my entire working life, ceases to have any feeling for its employees I shall sell all my shares immediately." She held forty-five per cent of the shares of the privately held company. Pamela's vehemence was more severe than he had anticipated, but he did not take her words seriously. She had made this threat many times before but never followed through.

"Do you think Elspeth truly cares for Sir Richard?" Lord Kennington asked.

"Much more than she knows," Pamela said, "but I can't convince her that she does."

"Do you think if I send her to Buenos Aires she will decline?"

"No, I expect she will grudgingly agree."

"So why do you think there is a problem?"

Pamela Crumm looked up at Eric Kennington through her thick round glasses. "Sometimes I doubt that you really do have a heart."

She was the only person in the world who could have spoken to him in this way. His reliance on her was absolute and his trust in her judgment complete.

"All right, Pamela, have it your way," he chuckled, willing to give in to her. "Where can we assign her that is close enough to Malta for her to see Sir Richard on occasion?" He stressed the last two words.

"Cyprus."

"Cyprus? I haven't heard there were any major security issues at the hotel in Nicosia. Have you held something back from me?" he prevaricated. Cyprus was the assignment he was already considering for Elspeth.

The Kennington Nicosia was one of a group of smaller boutique hotels owned by the Kennington Organisation. Eric Kennington had established hotels in some of the bigger cities around the world—London, San Francisco, Cairo, and recently Sydney and Paris—but he had a penchant for picking locations for his smaller and often more exclusive hotels in former British colonies with historic roots. The Kennington Nicosia, the Kennington Valletta, and the Kennington Singapore were among them.

Pamela Crumm sat down and faced him. She moved a large vase of fresh summer flowers from the centre of the table so that she could better see him. "As you know, the Foreign and Commonwealth Office contacted me yesterday with a request that we provide accommodation for four of their negotiators who will be trying to help resolve the issues between the Greek and Turkish Cypriots," she said. "They will be staying for several months. The occupancy of the hotel is down right now because of the recent plane crash, and the FCO is willing to foot the bill for the rooms for their negotiators, at a reduced rate of course. Since their assignment will be a long one, their families will be staying with them. I thought we should give it a go. I've run through the figures."

Pamela rummaged in one of her files and handed him several spread sheets with the figures showing the profitability of the hotel and what the long-term presence of the delegation would mean over the course of the next few months. Lord Kennington took them and skimmed through them. He put them down next to his plate and drew out a large gold watch from the pocket of his expansive waistcoat. The watch was a new acquisition, recently purchased from Asprey's, but he announced to all who would listen that it was a family heirloom. Such boasts he felt, even if they were untrue, enhanced his stature among his business associates.

Lord Kennington glanced at his watch and thought of the practicalities of the FCO's request. "Do we have enough room and staff to accommodate the twelve people involved as well as our other guests?"

Pamela nodded her large, perfectly coiffed head. "Philippa Allard-Thorpe, the new manager out there, assures me her staff are willing to stay on during the coming autumn and winter months. She does not anticipate any difficulty."

Lord Kennington swung his watch back and forth. "And where does Elspeth fit in this picture?"

"Naturally, Eric, I will let you decide how best to use Elspeth, but it worries me that the entire security staff in Nicosia is local. Philippa recently hired a totally new team, consisting of both Greek and Turkish Cypriots, in order to ensure a balance in the staff's composition and avoid any illusion of partisanship."

"I'm not sure I fully approve," Eric said, frowning, as he did when he felt one of his managers went beyond their strict responsibilities. "What was wrong with the old staff?"

"She said she felt it had become too entrenched to be effective any longer."

Lord Kennington lowered his head and looked at Pamela from under his bushy eyebrows. "Do you agree?"

Pamela checked a stylish gold earring although he could not see that it needed to be adjusted.

"I have her word for it," Pamela said. "She is a highly competent person, and I have no reason to doubt her, but back to Elspeth. I think we would be well served to have a security presence in Nicosia that is neither Greek nor Turkish, but rather someone senior like Elspeth, whose function would be overseeing the security of the British delegation. I understand the Cypriots have a love/hate relationship with us, the British I mean, and the delegation's presence may cause some animosity."

Lord Kennington handed the papers back to Pamela Crumm. "Pamela, I've never doubted your judgment about the daily operations in our hotels, although I will not broach the subject of your matchmaking. Get Elspeth in here this afternoon."

Lord Kennington took the last bite of his breakfast and finished his tea. He wiped his mouth and rose, thus ending their conversation.

*

Taking the express lift from the lobby to the twentieth floor of the building that housed the Kennington Organisation, Elspeth Duff rehearsed what she wanted to say. She entered Eric Kennington's office, as she had so many times before, with a mixed sense of duty, familiarity, and dread. Not dread for her assignments but dread that she would be co-opted into something more than her job usually required. Her recent leave of absence and the stress of the trial in Singapore over a month ago had left her more anxious than she wanted to admit. Before her ordeal in Singapore, she had experienced little severe physical injury. The wounds she had received and the mystery she had unravelled there left personal scars that still needed to be healed. She wanted to get back to work, to do the pedestrian sort of thing at which she excelled and forget the last five and a half months.

She had dressed with her usual care, conservatively but richly, but she still felt uncomfortable with her new short haircut, the result of her half-bald condition acquired in the hospital. Her hairstylist had done his best, but Elspeth still felt semi-shorn.

As she entered his office, Eric Kennington looked up from his Chippendale desk, also not a family heirloom, and motioned for Elspeth to sit down. "You look marvellous, Elspeth, and ready for an extended assignment. I wanted to send you to Buenos Aires, but Pamela won't let me, so I am sending you to Nicosia. You will like it there. The climate is like Southern California and the pace, I understand, is slow. And, Pamela assures me, it shares the Mediterranean with Malta."

Elspeth flushed slightly. Both Magdalena Cassar and Richard Munro had urged her to stay longer in Malta at the end of her recovery, but she had insisted to them both that she was ready and eager to return to work. Buenos Aires would have been a complication, but Cyprus was within a few hours reach of Malta, which delighted her.

"What will my assignment be?" she asked.

Eric Kennington came around his desk and took her hand. "Pamela thinks I don't have a heart, but, quite frankly,

Elspeth, as much as I might appear to be an ogre, I cannot be totally insensitive to the last few months of your life."

Elspeth smiled at this. Eric Kennington's attentiveness, when he chose to exercise it, was irresistible, which is one of the many reasons why he was so successful in his business. Elspeth was no more immune to his charm than most of the people with whom he dealt on a daily basis.

"Eric, I want to get back to my job full time, to be professionally involved in events and to be absorbed for as many hours of the day as I can be. I need a way to forget what happened in Singapore."

Eric let go of Elspeth's hand. "Exactly. Just as it should be!"

Elspeth often wondered what sort of life Lord Kennington had beyond the running of his hotel empire, but she did not ask. She knew he was married and his wife and two children lived in Essex. Beyond that Pamela Crumm had shared nothing, although she surely knew the details. The internet was no help in clearing up the mystery.

"Do you know anything about Cyprus?" Eric Kennington asked.

"A bit. My cousin Johnnie was out there in the early seventies, during the problems with the partition of the island and with Archbishop Makarios. Johnnie has told me about the beauty and history of the island and the passions of its divided population."

After she spoke, Elspeth regretted her words. Her cousin Johnnie was the Earl of Tay, but she hated mentioning her aristocratic relations to Lord Kennington, even as poverty-stricken as they were. Elspeth was certain Eric Kennington recognised Johnnie's name.

Lord Kennington smiled. Elspeth knew he liked members of his staff to have distinguished roots, but Elspeth had often cried out that the earldom of Tay was granted by the Butcher of Cumberland in reward for what Elspeth considered an act of treason by her Highland ancestors after the Battle of Culloden. Elspeth loved Johnnie but hated his title.

"Pamela will fill you in on the details, but I want to give you the gist of what you will be required to do. Divided lands are never simple places. Emotions can spring up when least expected. My new manager out there has hired a new staff of both Greek and Turkish Cypriots, but this makes me a bit uneasy. Your job is to protect a Foreign and Commonwealth Office delegation who will be staying at the Kennington Nicosia. Elspeth, the task will be one of quiet diligence, as the delegation's negotiations will not take place in the hotel, but I don't want any Cypriot hotheads taking into their minds that an attack on the Kennington Nicosia or any of its guests could achieve their political ends."

"Understood, chief," she said, knowing the sobriquet annoyed him. "Just the kind of assignment I relish," she said, somewhere between irony and enthusiasm.

Lord Kennington seemed not to notice her flippancy. "The assignment will be a long one, at least a few months, so you should prepare to be in Nicosia for the rest of the summer and into the autumn. Pamela has a stack of reading for you and details on the hotel. But most of all, Elspeth, keep both the delegation and yourself safe. I don't want a repeat of Singapore."

Elspeth smiled and rubbed the back of her head, which still ached when she least expected it.

"Nor do I, Eric," she responded with conviction.

*

Pamela Crumm waited in her office, which was adjacent to Lord Kennington's. She had listened to Elspeth's interview with Lord Kennington through her computer earphones and did not need to catch up on Elspeth's conversation in the next room. Elspeth passed smoothly through the connecting door, which Pamela then shut tightly.

Elspeth let out a long sigh of relief and sat down on a chair that was positioned to look out over the City of London to the London Eye beyond.

"Pamela, I owe you so many thanks for getting me out of Buenos Aires. I've travelled across the continents often enough in the past. Perhaps when I complete my assignment in Cyprus, I will be able to face the inside of a plane for more than a few hours at a time, but not now."

Pamela took a chair beside her. "Relax, my friend. I have ordered some coffee for you, tea for me, and I brought some of those pastries you like from the bakery near my flat. I thought his lordship would badger you, but he seems in a complacent mood this afternoon. Guilt, I suspect, over Singapore."

"Singapore was not his fault," Elspeth said. She thought of all the support Eric Kennington gave to her during her time in the hospital, even coming twice to visit her, an act he would undertake for only a few select employees.

Pamela's eyes, magnified by her thick glasses, sparkled. "Yes, but I've made him think it was his fault, so that he will treat you more civilly in future. Here is our coffee and tea."

A waiter set a tea tray on the table between them and withdrew with solemnity. After Elspeth accepted her coffee, she went back to the assignment in Cyprus.

"Tell me about the Kennington Nicosia," Elspeth said.

"Eric bought the hotel about twenty years ago. Although Nicosia is a divided city, he felt that the history of Cyprus and the lure of the island itself would fill the hotel, at least during the summer tourist season, and he has been proven right. In fact, we seldom have a vacancy from March to October.

We shut down one of the wings during the winter, except at Christmas time, when many people want to go to a place filled with Christian history and close to the Holy Land."

"Tell me about the hotel itself. Have you been there?"

Pamela took a sip of her tea and offered Elspeth a pastry baked with buttery dough and topped with apricot preserves.

"Not yet, although I know it well enough to think I have. The hotel is small, only thirty-five rooms, but each one is specially designed to reflect Cyprus's past. Eric personally saw to that when the reconstruction took place. I'm giving you a small suite, since you will be there for so long. It looks out over the garden, which I understand is magnificent."

Gardens figured large at all the Kennington hotels. In places like Cyprus, where flowers abounded during the wet season, many of the plants were chosen from the local flora. Lord Kennington always supervised the layout of the gardens personally and, even if they included indigenous plants, he had them arranged as if they were in a formal English garden. The effect was always opulent. The sparseness of the semi-arid was replaced by the abundance that a full time gardening staff and a great deal of water could produce. Another signature feature of the Kennington hotels' gardens was the inclusion of discreet niches where guests could meet privately or enjoy moments alone. Elspeth looked forward to seeing how this had been accomplished in Cyprus.

"What and whom I am to protect?" Elspeth knew that the obvious answer was the interests of the Kennington Organisation and the security of the hotel and its guests, but Pamela understood her question.

"The Secretary General of the United Nations has been trying to find a way for the Greek and Turkish Cypriot factions to unite and put the island under one government.

The Greek Cypriots feel the island is theirs, since they have been there since the time of Alexander the Great, but the Turks, who arrived when the Ottoman Empire took control of Cyprus in the fifteen hundreds, feel they have territorial rights as well. The conflict between the Turkish Muslims and the Greek Orthodox Christians dates back to the Crusades and continues until today. And we think *we* have problems in present day Britain between the English and the Scots!"

"If the UN is involved, why is the FCO sending out a delegation?" Elspeth asked.

Pamela smiled at her friend. "That's a very good question. I asked it when the FCO approached me. A large number of Britons live on Cyprus, mostly on the Greek side, and we have multiple trade interests in both sectors. Britain has a large military base on the island as well. Need I say more?"

"Britain may have lost the Empire but has never lost its instinct for empire-building, has it?" Elspeth said. In her travels around the globe, Elspeth was always amazed at the influence such a small island kingdom still had on the world at large. Had she been English she might have swelled with pride, but as a Scotswoman she had mixed feelings.

"What do you want me to do out there, Pamela. I don't want to be on holiday, or even appear to be. I know you have good intentions."

"Not as good as you would think. Eric thinks Philippa Allard-Thorpe, the new manager at the Kennington Nicosia, is one of the rising stars in the Kennington Organisation. How do you Scots put it? *I hae ma doots*. The security of the FCO delegation and their families is important. That's your main mission, but I also want you to watch Philippa. I'm an old woman, seasoned if you will, and I am not completely comfortable with some of the decisions she is making."

2

Unlike times when a crisis was brewing at one of his hotels, Lord Kennington did not offer his personal plane to take Elspeth to Nicosia. Since the flight took only four hours, Pamela booked Elspeth a seat in Club Class on the British Airways flight leaving Heathrow mid-afternoon and arriving at Larnaca International Airport in Cyprus in the evening. Pamela explained first class service was not available, but she thought Elspeth would find the departure and arrival time advantageous. Elspeth prepared herself for a certain amount of discomfort but was anxious to get to Cyprus.

The flight was Elspeth's first since she had gone to Singapore for the trial in June, and she was looking forward to it as a means of re-establishing her independence from hospitals, caring friends, relatives and a courtroom. The act of returning to work energised her. At her flat in Kensington before leaving for the airport, she hummed contentedly but tunelessly as she tried to make wardrobe decisions. Since she was to be gone for so long, she indulged herself and packed two bags. Especially when her assignment might take her from the heat of a Mediterranean summer into the cooler and more inclement weather of autumn, shoes presented the most difficult problem. Bah, she thought, as she put the fifth pair in one of her cases, they sell shoes on Cyprus, don't they? Downtown Nicosia had some of the top European shops.

After take off Elspeth leaned her head against the wall of the aircraft and looked out the window. She practiced her geography as she always did when she had a window seat. The English Channel was easy to identify, and so were the neat fields of France. Next came the snow-capped peaks of Switzerland and northern Italy, which she recognised. Then they flew over the Balkans and Greece, which was uncharted territory to her.

Elspeth accepted the over-cooked meal offered her. After she had finished eating, she dozed as the evening sank into darkness. Shortly afterwards their arrival at Larnaca Airport was announced.

She had no clear idea of what her assignment ahead would entail, but she sincerely hoped that it would prove fulfilling but uneventful and that her mere presence would avert any unwanted incidents. She puzzled at Pamela's warning that Philippa Allard-Thorpe might not be as stellar as Lord Kennington presumed her to be. Pamela and Eric drew swords frequently, and Elspeth judged that by now the score between them was even.

*

Philippa Allard-Thorpe had sent a car for Elspeth and expected it would arrive back at the hotel shortly before ten. This gave her time to catch up with her day's work. Philippa never gave a reason for staying late in her office, but she relished the quiet hours in the back of the hotel when the night manager, Alexander, was on duty and she could fine tune the workings of the establishment without being interrupted.

She had swept clean the last vestiges of her predecessor's furnishings from her office. In her opinion he was dreadfully old-fashioned and had allowed the hotel to sink into desultory staleness. New life and new ideas were needed. Philippa was not entirely comfortable that Lord Kennington was sending out one of his personal advisors from London, but Pamela Crumm told her that Elspeth Duff was coming not only to help with the FCO delegation but also because she needed a bit of rest and recreation after a recent accident.

Philippa considered, as she did with all things, what approach to take with Elspeth. Philippa wanted no detractors. She would persuade Elspeth that everything at the hotel was perfect under the new management, so that Elspeth could report nothing negative to Lord Kennington. That would be best. Philippa felt her future career rested on acknowledgement by London that she was the model for all Kennington hotel managers.

Losing track of time, she tapped away at her computer. Emails had piled up during the day, and she felt she needed to respond to each one in depth. This task often occupied her into the small hours, but she was a person who had always survived on four or five hours sleep. Six hours was a luxury that she seldom allowed herself, even on her occasional day off.

*

The driver of the hotel car was waiting for Elspeth as she descended the long ramp from the secure arrivals area into the main part of the terminal at Larnaca Airport. He took her bags and escorted her to his car, which was parked at the drop-off kerb. Elspeth stopped briefly to take in the pleasant night air and smell the dryness of the Mediterranean summer. It reminded her of Malta. The ride into Nicosia was longer than Elspeth anticipated, but the car was comfortable and she was not feeling particularly tired because the time in Nicosia was two hours ahead of that in London. It was now dark and she could see little of the countryside, so she dozed until the car pulled to a halt outside the Kennington Nicosia.

Philippa Allard-Thorpe came rushing out of the hotel with her arms outstretched in greeting. Elspeth, with Scottish reserve, offered her hand in a business-like way. Philippa took it in both of hers. Not liking such intimacy with strangers, Elspeth gave Philippa a professional nod and withdrew her hand.

Philippa led Elspeth into the hotel and across the lobby, which was deserted except for the night receptionist. A pair of French doors were open to the garden beyond, and soft air penetrated the interior. Philippa motioned to the receptionist, who came to attention with a slight frown on his face. Elspeth wondered why.

"Come in, Elspeth. We have been so looking forward to your arrival, and I have personally inspected your suite as I know your stay here may last for some time. Ms Crumm sent me your most recent personal room preferences, and you will find them already in place. Your suite overlooks the garden and has direct access to it, and I am sure you will enjoy it."

Elspeth smiled. "As little air conditioning as possible, three down pillows, three chocolate mint wafers at night, and carrot juice in the fridge?"

"Exactly." Philippa looked smug.

"Philippa, you are becoming an exemplary Kennington hotel manager."

"I try my best." She looked as if this were a mere trifle, although Elspeth knew it was not.

"You must be tired after your flight from London," Philippa said. "Let's meet over breakfast in the morning. Ring me when you are up and about."

Philippa ushered Elspeth across the garden and under an arcade that surrounded it. The evening was still warm after the intensity of the day's sun, but a breeze had picked up and promised cooling during the night. Elspeth could feel the lingering heat on the stone paths that divided the garden beds. She recognised many of the plants from Malta, brilliant bougainvillea, delicate spiraea, and neatly trimmed olive trees, and smiled at Lord Kennington's efforts to make them flourish in the Mediterranean climate. He had added jasmine for scent and finished it all off with an array of English tea roses. As she mounted the exterior staircase to the first floor, Elspeth still could hear the distant noise of the traffic going to and from the city, which broke into the peacefulness of the space.

Elspeth was glad her journey, as short as it had been, was over and that it had not taxed her unduly.

"I change time zones a great deal in my job, but the first morning I am in a new place, I try to respect the time zone I have just left and not the new one I have recently arrived in," Elspeth said. "To the offices in London, however, I am always in Lord Kennington's time zone, whether I am totally jet lagged or not," she added with a smile.

Philippa chuckled thinly at Elspeth's reference to Lord Kennington and unlocked the door to Elspeth's suite. "There are advantages of having a job such as mine where one stays put and can keep control over a long period of time," she said.

"There are times when I think being in one place or even in a single country for over a week or two at a time would have a definite allure," Elspeth responded.

Elspeth at the moment did not pay attention to Philippa's arrogance, but she did pick it up in later conversations and remembered Philippa's use of the word "control".

3

Elspeth woke at nine, Cyprus time. The sun was pushing through the shutters at the windows and casting diagonal designs across the chequered tile pattern of the floor of her room. Knowing each new city had its own cadence, she had left her window opened a crack during the night in order to hear the noises of the city nearby. By late morning, when the temperature could rise to well over thirty-five degrees centigrade, she would resort to mechanical cooling but not yet. The old buildings in Cyprus, such as the one housing the hotel, had many devices to retain the coolness of the night in the interior on summer days, but modern human beings were less tolerant of the late afternoon heat than their predecessors, Elspeth thought ruefully.

When she finished dressing, she picked up the house phone and rang Philippa, who invited her for breakfast in half an hour. From Philippa's tone Elspeth sensed the manager had eaten much earlier. Elspeth rang room service and ordered coffee to be brought to her room. The coffee was strong, but luckily not sweetened in the Turkish way. Elspeth sipped it with pleasure. She felt it would fortify her for her meeting with Philippa Allard-Thorpe.

Philippa had arranged for breakfast to be served in her office, since she said Elspeth and she needed to talk out of the guests' hearing. On a trolley were the yogurt and fruit that Elspeth preferred at breakfast, although she knew a full English breakfast and both a typical Greek and a Turkish one would be available in the hotel's breakfast room beyond. Lord Kennington insisted that local and English food be served at all his hotels.

Each manager in the Kennington hotel chain had discretion over the decoration of his or her private office, and many chose a sleek twenty-first century decor rather than the historical look that Lord Kennington preferred for the outer spaces of his hotels. Philippa had carried this idea to its utmost degree. The room was almost colourless with white walls, glass and chrome furniture, light grey leather upholstery, and severe silver-coloured blinds over the windows. The only accent of colour in the decor was the slate blue leather executive chair at Philippa's desk. Her thin flat-screened computer, sleek phone console, stainless steel printers and copiers, were all of space-age design. Elspeth sat down in one of the leather-covered chairs and discovered that it was as rigid as it looked. The only bright spot in the room was the trolley containing breakfast and flowers, which looked an anomaly in this futuristic space.

Elspeth noticed that Philippa seemed uncomfortable in her presence, and therefore she attempted to put Philippa at ease.

"Lord Kennington has sent me here specifically to watch over the forthcoming delegation from the Foreign and Commonwealth Office and their families," she said. "I understand they are to be in residence for at least three months. The delegates have already been informed that I will be here for their benefit, so I expect that my role will be centred on their daily and evening activities. Rest assured I am not here to evaluate the running of the hotel. I don't do that sort of thing."

Philippa smiled, showing her full range of white front teeth, which gleamed like a toothpaste advertisement. Her expression was strained.

"I suppose I should be relieved," Philippa said. "Your prowess in getting to the bottom of things is well known among the managers, even a new one like me. I'm glad that what you will be doing here has little to do with me. As a new manager, I'm trying to make a good impression on London in hopes that I may advance in the Kennington Organisation."

Elspeth smiled in return and hoped her expression was more genuine that Philippa's. "I appreciate your honesty, and I hope that as the next months go by you'll continue as if I'm not here."

Philippa, thought Elspeth, has all the disarming qualities required of a Kennington hotel manager but does she have requisite warmth? The stark atmosphere of the office belied that. Elspeth tried to soften the tension in the room. "You seem to have a taste for the modern. What made you choose Cyprus for your first position? Cyprus has, as I understand it, eight thousand years of history and is not really on the cutting edge of our current century."

"I disagree." Passion filled Philippa's voice. "All the Kennington hotels, especially behind the scenes, are on the cutting edge. Comfort and Service." She chanted the motto of the Kennington hotels as if it were a mantra. "As a manager, I'm committed to the comfort and service that twenty-first century travellers require at my hotel. Don't they want to feel they are living in the fifteenth century but also to be able to connect their laptops to the world, receive clear mobile phone service, and have the latest exercise equipment at their fingertips? Don't they expect traditional meals but with the nutritional information available? I love the challenge. I plan to make this one of the best Kennington hotels in the world." Philippa said this with such conviction that Elspeth believed her.

Elspeth tasted her yogurt, which was fresh and tart. She asked for more berries, and Philippa spooned some out for her from the bowl on the breakfast trolley.

"You certainly have a clear agenda," Elspeth said as she sampled her newly laced yogurt.

Philippa returned to her desk chair. "I work hard at it. I think the Kennington Organisation needs to be more forward-thinking."

Elspeth wondered what Eric Kennington and Pamela Crumm would think of this criticism of top management, but she held her tongue. She did not owe any response to Philippa.

"May I call you Philippa? It means lover of horses, doesn't it? I had a friend at university named Philippa, and she was a most proficient rider. Did you grow up riding?"

Philippa was obviously amused. "No, I grew up in a suburb on the shores of Lake Erie, near Cleveland."

Elspeth raised an eyebrow. "But you don't . . ."

"Don't sound American? No. Before I went into hotel management, I studied acting and elocution at the Royal Academy of Dramatic Arts in London. The first thing to go were my nasal mid-western tones. I shed them with pleasure."

Elspeth rose and helped herself to more fruit and yogurt and poured herself more coffee. Elspeth noticed that Philippa was drinking mineral water and eating nothing. Perhaps she had eaten earlier, or, judging by her slimness, she may have skipped breakfast altogether.

Elspeth switched to their current business because she was finding their continued social conversation turgid. "When does the FCO delegation arrive?" she asked.

"Tonight, or rather early tomorrow morning. I've made arrangements for them to stay in the east wing. Each family will have a small suite and there's a large community room there. Typically, Cypriot families provide homes for their daughters when they are married. At the peak of their prosperity, the family who owned this building built several wings off of the main house, and each one almost functions independently. The east wing is beautifully appointed and will give the FCO group privacy from the other guests. The kitchen facilities there have been modernised, so that they can even do some of their own cooking if they wish. When you are finished with your breakfast, I'll show you their quarters to make sure you approve. "

Elspeth shook her head. "That won't be necessary. Your arrangements sound completely suitable, and I'm sure the delegation will be pleased. Before I left London, the list of the delegation members was not available. Have you received any official notification of who the members are?"

Philippa rifled through some papers on her desk, which was strangely cluttered considering the stark furnishings in the room. "I have their names here somewhere." She finally produced a file. "I'll have a copy made for you, but you might want to look it over first."

Elspeth took the file and quickly skimmed its contents: Michael Driscoll, his wife Sophia, and their three children Gregory, Hermione, and Kallista. Elspeth smiled at the children's names. George Colton, his wife Joanna, and their sons Christopher and Charles. Finally, Onan Mitsui, his wife Bitki, and their son Azai. Of Japanese ethnicity? Elspeth could not be sure because she did not recognise the given names of the last three. In all, there were an even dozen. Elspeth carefully examined the names and looked forward to finding out more about them.

She looked up from the list. "What about the support staff?"

Philippa looked mystified and blushed slightly through her fair skin. "Support staff?"

"In my past experience, when a delegation from the FCO travels overseas, they are accompanied by a support staff, especially if they are staying at a Kennington hotel. Our prices are far too high to have low-level bureaucrats staying here, but higher-level types are usually accompanied by at least one security person."

"London has said nothing about this to me." Philippa sounded defensive.

"Let me straighten that out, and I will get back to you. Do you have any other guests arriving today?"

Philippa went to her desk and found another file. "We are not completely full, probably because of recent items in the news including the plane crash," she explained. "I expect a university tour of alumni from the University of Chicago to arrive later this afternoon. There are several individuals and couples coming in from Britain and an amateur but obviously well-heeled archaeological study group from Germany will be here as well. I can give you their names, although some of them are repeats, even in the time I have been here."

"I have been in situations in the past," Elspeth admitted, "where vetting every guest was of the utmost importance, but I can't see it's called for today. The FCO, I'm sure, did their homework, and, if they didn't send any security personnel with their delegation, they must have thought it unnecessary."

Pamela Crumm earlier had told Elspeth the FCO delegation would be working closely with the United Nations representatives on the island. Pamela had said they all were experts in their field, and the British Foreign Secretary hoped they would help break the current deadlock between the Greek and the Turkish Cypriots. Real violence had not erupted recently on Cyprus, but when Cyprus had joined the European Union in two thousand and four, Britain wanted Cyprus to be governed by a single governmental entity. Despite the United Nations Secretary General's intervention, this had not happened. The FCO, Elspeth understood, wanted to help in negotiating the unification of the island, but any talks were to be underplayed for the media because failure would have no political advantage in London.

Elspeth did not dwell on this, as Philippa must be more aware of the political situation on the island than she. Instead she asked, "Can you recommend anyone here who could assist me as a guide to the island?"

"What sort of guide?"

"I have responsibility for three wives and six children who need to be entertained over the next few months. I need someone who is fluent in English, likes children, and has an expert knowledge of the island."

Philippa thought for a moment before answering. "I think the brigadier would be a good choice."

"The brigadier?"

Philippa's confidence returned. "Yes, Brigadier Colin French. He retired to Cyprus a few years ago and spends his days finding out everything there is to know about the island. He also has contacts with just about everyone who will put up with him."

Elspeth smiled at this remark. "Meaning what?"

"He is writing what he describes as the definitive book on Cyprus. He wants the British to understand all the intricacies of living on and visiting both sides of the island. He is quite fluent in Greek and Turkish and has many friends in both sectors."

"Can that actually be done?"

"He thinks so, which is all that counts. I know he could use some extra income, so he seems the right sort of person to help you. I'll set up an appointment for you to meet him— today if possible."

Brigadier Colin French did not match Elspeth's expectations. When he arrived for lunch, which Philippa had arranged in a private corner of the indoor garden dining room, he crossed the space with the stride of a man in full health. Elspeth judged that he could not have been much older than she was, somewhere in his mid to late fifties. She had expected an ageing, white haired man with flowing white moustaches and a full shock of hair. What she saw was a trim man with slightly receding hair, who was sporting fashionable frameless glasses, a short, neatly trimmed beard showing signs of greying, and a broad grin across his deeply tanned face. Philippa was right behind him and made introductions. Elspeth's radar picked up that there was more to Philippa and the brigadier's relationship than a casual acquaintanceship.

Philippa made excuses about work left undone in her office. Colin brushed her cheek with his lips. Elspeth sensed Philippa and Colin had plans for later in the day. Elspeth decided she wanted no part in their relationship and therefore assumed her most professional manner.

"Brigadier, I assume Ms Allard-Thorpe has given you some idea of why I have asked to meet you."

"Colin, please. May I call you Elspeth?"

Elspeth did not want to get on friendly terms with this man, whom she felt had a high opinion of himself and was used to having women succumb to his easy charm.

"If you wish," she said, hoping that he heard the chill in her voice. "Business in the twenty-first century has been polluted by American manners, which I have never completely taken to although I spent many years in America." Elspeth wondered what it was about this man that made her share some of her life's history on such short acquaintance.

"Really. What part? I led a commando training group in Texas one summer. Even the jungles of Vietnam were not that hot."

"In California," Elspeth said but gave him no further explanation. She felt he would want to know all about her past if she shared her ex-husband's connection with the film industry in Hollywood, and this was not any business of his.

Philippa had pre-ordered for them, and the lunch was served with the usual precision of the Kennington hotels' waiters.

"This reminds me of meals I have had in Athens," Elspeth said, as she savoured a vine leaf wrapped morsel.

Colin French looked up at her, his eyes provocative, although his words were not. "You'll find that Cypriot food is very simple, and daily fare mainly consists of bread, yogurt, goats' cheese, olives, tomatoes and cucumbers, and locally made wine. Philippa assures me that the Kennington Nicosia has made a careful effort to include a medley of dishes that are native to Cyprus, especially small dishes, called *mezes*, which you would most likely find at celebrations. She's been particularly careful to include both Greek and Turkish specialties on the menu, though prepared in a much more extravagant manner than you would find in most Cypriot households or at local restaurants."

"You sound as if you disapprove," Elspeth said.

"Not at all. Travellers always want to sample the local cuisine, but if the Kennington Nicosia offered the usual diet of most islanders, I fear guests would instantly demand their money back."

Elspeth resisted liking the brigadier, but his manner eroded her resolve. He chatted easily about the island, shared snippets of local lore, and made life on the island come alive, even in the confines of Lord Kennington's air-conditioned garden dining room.

4

As they left the dining room and went into the lobby of the hotel, Philippa appeared behind them.

"Colin, may we speak a moment in private? Please excuse us, Elspeth," she said.

Elspeth was surprised at the edge in Philippa's voice, so she politely withdrew and walked out into the outdoor garden courtyard. Much of the garden was in sunlight, although several areas were shaded by tall, straight trees that Elspeth recognised as a species of cypress she had seen in Malta. She noticed a young woman standing in the shade of one of these trees, and, not wanting to startle her, Elspeth waved at her. The woman did not respond, and so Elspeth spoke out. "I am sorry if I am disturbing you. I didn't know anyone would be out here when it is so warm."

The young woman turned and faced Elspeth, although her blank eyes looked beyond Elspeth. The woman's voice was low and sweet, unusual qualities for one so young. "Please, you are not disturbing me. Few people come out into the garden during the lunch hour because it is generally too hot here in the summer. That's why I love being here at noontime. The heat brings out the aroma of the flowers and shrubs, and I can enjoy them without having to listen to others' conversations."

Elspeth was struck at the resemblance between the young woman and Philippa Allard-Thorpe and decided to introduce herself. "I am Elspeth Duff. I've just arrived from London."

"Yes, my mother mentioned you were coming. You work for Lord Kennington, don't you?"

"As a matter of fact I do. So you're Philippa's daughter."

The young woman put out her hand in the general direction of Elspeth's voice, and Elspeth moved around to shake it.

"My name is Cinnamon, a rather silly name, but one my mother likes, although I have threatened to change it many times. Cinnamon Allard-Thorpe."

"I hope you don't mind me coming out here and disturbing you. I quite agree that despite the heat the garden is beautiful." Elspeth flushed slightly, knowing her companion in the garden could not see the physical beauty of the courtyard.

Cinnamon made no apology for her lack of sight. "Being blind, I find beauty in the way things smell and feel. And sometimes by the sounds, when the traffic is less noisy. I remember the colours quite well from my childhood, and I frequently attempt to match the colours in my mind with the plants' tactile or olfactory qualities."

Elspeth smiled at Cinnamon's explanation. "Shall we sit down?" Elspeth asked. "Since I'll be staying for several months, I'm glad on my first day to meet some of the people here at the hotel other than the guests."

Elspeth did not notice Cinnamon's white cane at first. Cinnamon had adroitly tucked it among the folds of her colourful skirt. She brought it out to find the edge of a nearby bench. She reached out her hand and touched the bench. "This one is in the shade. Let's sit here." Touch was almost as good as sight, Elspeth thought, or maybe even better at detecting heat.

As they settled on to the seat, Cinnamon lowered her voice. "I understand you work for Lord Kennington's security staff. May I tell you something confidentially?"

Elspeth was surprised at this unexpected request but assented. "You may. Does it have to do with security matters?" In Elspeth's experience, some young woman liked to dramatize their situations, but she did not want to antagonise the manager's daughter.

"In a way it does. My mother wants to change everything here, even the name of the hotel to the Kennington Lefkosia, which is the Greek name for Nicosia. Do you think the change would attract tourists? I don't. Mother thinks, however, that the Kennington Organisation should call the hotel by the local name."

Elspeth did not want to treat Cinnamon like a child or jump feet first into what appeared to be a mother-daughter argument.

"Mummy always does that, you know. She wants everything her way and never will compromise."

Cinnamon was holding her head high, her jaw set, and her light-coloured eyebrows lowered sternly above her unseeing blue-grey eyes.

"I'm not here, Cinnamon, to assess the running of the hotel. That belongs to an entirely different department of the Kennington Organisation," Elspeth said.

Cinnamon did not seem satisfied with Elspeth's answer. "London, as my mother calls it, has been here several times since she has taken over the running of the hotel, but they visited for just a few days, and she purposely let them see what she wanted them to see and nothing else. I thought if someone from London were here for a longer time, a truer picture would emerge, not only the one my mother wants reported back to London."

Elspeth could tell Cinnamon did not agree with her mother's tactics, but Elspeth did not want to take sides in a classic dual between parent and child. She leaned over and took Cinnamon's hand, they way she often did with her own daughter when they were at odds. "I have a daughter, probably five or six years older than you are." Elspeth judged Cinnamon was in her early twenties. "She and I clash often, both being strong Scotswomen, but we usually find ways to resolve our differences."

"Ms Duff . . . "

"Elspeth, please."

"All right, although you sound . . . " Cinnamon suddenly flushed.

"Mature, perhaps? No, don't apologize. Since I have a daughter older than you, I undoubtedly do sound older. I raised my children in Southern California, where everyone is completely informal, which has both its bad and good sides. When I am talking with people your age, I prefer that kind of informality. I hope you don't mind."

"Quite frankly, I'm relieved because now I can talk to you more freely."

"You may, of course. In my line of work, I am used to respecting confidences."

Cinnamon turned towards Elspeth as if to look into her eyes. The gesture was so automatic that Elspeth sensed Cinnamon had not been blind for long. Elspeth sat quietly for a moment and waited for the younger woman to speak.

Elspeth closed her eyes and tried to imagine what Cinnamon was experiencing. The warm, humid air embraced them; the sweet smell of the flowers wafted across the garden, and the *basso continuo* of the traffic outside filled Elspeth's ears.

"Cinnamon, when did you lose your sight? Do you mind that I ask?"

"Not at all. When I was eighteen, four and a half years ago, and I was about to apply to go to university, but, naturally, that got cancelled." The bitterness in her voice was palpable.

Elspeth carefully considered her next words to make them straightforward, not saccharine. "How did it happen?" she asked, disguising any emotion in her voice.

"In a car crash. My father was driving. He wasn't paying attention because we were arguing about the music on the car radio. The last thing I ever saw was a car that came around the bend at a very high speed." Tears filled her eyes. "It changed everything. You see, on that day I became intolerable to my mother, and Daddy did as well. It was an accident. It was! The other driver was drunk, although it was Daddy who crossed the centre line. Mummy banished Daddy from her life. They were divorced a year later. And I . . ." Cinnamon's voice constricted, and she did not attempt to finish her sentence.

Elspeth felt she had touched a nerve that was still raw. "I'm sorry. I didn't mean to bring it all back," she said. She took Cinnamon's hand again and noticed that her fingers were slender and beautifully shaped, but they were trembling.

Cinnamon regained her composure. "I wanted to study fashion. I've always loved colour and textiles. I was good at drawing and loved computer graphics. After I became blind, Daddy sent me to a training course at the army base here where I learned to use computers for the blind. I can't create art on them, but I write constantly."

Elspeth did not consider herself a sentimental person, but she instantly warmed to this beautiful young woman. "Do you ever share your writings?"

Cinnamon's voice lightened. "I try to write poetry. I had one piece published in a poetry magazine in England, which was very exciting. I would love to share what I have written with you."

Elspeth, who had studied at Cambridge, remembered the days of turgid poetry readings by her fellow students but somehow doubted that Cinnamon's poetry would be so earnestly dull. "I would be delighted. Once I am settled in, let's find a quiet moment. Shall it be over tea or first thing in the morning?"

Cinnamon's smile could have lit half the city of Nicosia during a blackout. "How about lemonade at my favourite café tomorrow afternoon?"

Elspeth's encounter with Philippa Allard-Thorpe's daughter left her unsettled. In spite of her disability, Cinnamon was a beautiful woman and obviously an intelligent one. She had her mother's erect carriage but also had a softness that Philippa did not possess. Elspeth speculated that this came from Cinnamon's father. She wanted to meet him to see if it were true. Cinnamon's words also reminded Elspeth of Pamela Crumm's concerns about the current management of the Kennington Nicosia. Innovation had its place in the running of the Kennington hotels, and most employees of the Kennington Organisation knew that changes came from the top and not from the field. Philippa Allard-Thorpe was treading on dangerous ground if she had not learned this.

To be fair, Eric Kennington always considered his managers held the pulse of their local environments, but London, as Cinnamon put it, was definitely the policy setter.

Elspeth left Cinnamon sitting on the bench and returned to the lobby. She was relieved at its coolness and crossed to the reception desk to ask if anything had arrived in the post for her. The receptionist held out a formal looking envelope.

"This came for you, Ms Duff, while you were at lunch. A driver from the British High Commission brought it."

Elspeth suspected Richard Munro was already at work to make her stay in Nicosia a pleasant one, since it would stretch out over several months. The envelope contained a heavy card with the seal of the British High Commission at the top. The contents of the missive were handwritten.

Dear Ms Duff,

Sir Richard Munro has made us aware that you will be staying in Nicosia for the next month or two and has asked that we introduce you to some of the diplomatic and local community here. Richard is an old friend from our service the was at Oxford. We would be delighted if you would join us for a small reception tomorrow evening at the British Residency at six. We are entertaining an American trade envoy and his wife and would enjoy having you among our guests. I understand you spent many years in America. Please ring my secretary at the High Commission and let her know if you will be able to join us.

Yours sincerely,
Thomas Wellborne

Elspeth slowly replaced the invitation in its envelope and wondered how she felt about Richard's intervention. Her relationship with Richard had progressed from the gladness of old acquaintance when they had met in Malta over a year ago to ambivalence at his stated devotion, and then, after he saved her life in Singapore, to something much deeper. Elspeth had tried for a long time to ignore her feelings towards Richard but was increasingly aware she could not do so forever. She knew she could not replace his late wife, Lady Marjorie, but, now that the tragedy in Singapore had been resolved, Elspeth knew she could no longer avoid addressing Richard's loving attention. If Thomas Wellborne were the British High Commissioner to Cyprus, as Elspeth assumed he was, he would be an excellent contact to have, especially if she had a personal link to him. Elspeth knew far too well that the diplomatic community did revolve around "having served together in Lahore", as Thomas Wellborne put it. Elspeth also noted wryly her own confusion as to what would be advantageous for her job and what would be socially enjoyable for her. With a sigh, she acknowledged that the diplomatic service offered both work and social rewards to its members. To be involved on the fringes of that life in the next few months had its appeal, but she was certain she did not want to become a diplomatic wife. Taking Thomas Wellborne's note with her, she returned to her rooms where she planned to ring the High Commission and accept the invitation.

Having experienced the heat of the day during her visit to the hotel gardens, Elspeth decided she would first lie down for a rest, as her head was throbbing. The delegation would be arriving late that night, and Elspeth wanted to be ready to meet them in the morning without appearing debilitated, a quality she had never experienced until the attempt on her life in Singapore. When she returned to her suite, the light on her phone was blinking, and her voice mail contained a message from Richard Munro.

"Elspeth, my dear. By now you know I am interfering in your life in Cyprus, but I think you will like Thomas and Carolyn Wellborne. They may also be able to open some doors for you. When you have a moment to talk, I have learned a bit about your delegation. I'll be in my office this afternoon until about six, seven your time. Call this number and you will get a secure line," the disembodied voice said.

Elspeth dug into her handbag and pulled out her satellite phone. She shed her shoes, settled on the sofa, and dialled Richard's number. His personal assistant answered and passed Elspeth on to him without any indication she knew who Elspeth was, although they had met in Malta the year before.

Richard's voice was filled with humour and concern. "Are you angry with me? I hope not. Thomas and Carolyn can help you in Cyprus, but they are not the type to meddle when they are not wanted."

"No, Dickie, I'm not angry. Actually I'm quite appreciative, because normally I am in and out of a hotel quickly while on assignment and never before have been assigned to stay several months in the same place. I think some social diversion may be enjoyable, and I'm looking forward to learning more about Cyprus other than from the innards of a Kennington hotel."

"I'm relieved, my dearest. When I was in London last week I met one of the chaps who is going out to Cyprus, George Colton. He served under me in Ceylon and is a solid person, if not an overly exciting one. You will like Joanna, his wife, who keeps him from being dull. She considers herself a connoisseur of the arts and probably will find local poets and artists to join together in what she calls her 'special gatherings'. George said they were travelling with their two boys, but they had not yet come along when I knew the Coltons first."

"Did he tell you anything about the others?" Elspeth was eager to know as much as possible about the members of the delegation and their families.

"He doesn't know Michael Driscoll or his wife but understands she is a Greek Cypriot and he speaks Greek fluently. Driscoll has the reputation of being a scholar of Greek history and modern Cypriot politics. Colton said Driscoll was chosen for the delegation because of his level head, scholarly ways, and depth of knowledge about Greek-Turkish animosities."

"So far it sounds a harmless group, but what about Onan Mitsui? Is he Japanese?" Elspeth asked.

"The surname would imply that, but Onan is a Turkish given name. Colton said Mitsui was one of the upcoming Turkish specialists at the FCO, with a specialty on the Turkish government's involvement in Cyprus. George has met him and his wife, Bitki, on several occasions. I was not blunt enough to ask about Mitsui's family background, but George told me Mitsui was a growing force in the affairs of the Eastern Mediterranean and his wife, a member of the diplomatic corps as well, is as competent as he is."

This puzzled Elspeth. "But if they are in the FCO, they must be British."

"Yes, but there is probably a complex story there, and I look forward to you filling me in about it at a later date."

"You telling me this makes my assignment seem much less daunting, although I never thought it very threatening in the first place. I hope it doesn't deteriorate into baby sitting for the children."

"I seriously doubt it will. I wouldn't expect any of the excitement of the last three adventures you and I shared together, where people have been seriously harmed."

"Or died. No, Dickie, I think Eric chose this assignment for me because it may border on the benign."

5

Joanna Colton was fond of organising both people and things. Consequently she took on the task of seeing to the comforts of the FCO delegation on their flight to Cyprus. No one spoke of the recent tragic plane crash, but Joanna was convinced that everyone had the news story in mind, so she decided to pontificate on the safety of air travel over all other forms of modern transportation. Joanna's enthusiastic statements were so convincing that soon she saw people relax.

The delegation was seated together in the front section of economy class, since the group was travelling on government stipends and did not hold enough status in the FCO to fly more comfortably. Being summer, the back of the plane was full. The travel department of the FCO had booked a block of seats, and therefore the delegation spent their time between London and Larnaca without disturbing or being disturbed by the other travellers. The children were all diplomatic "brats" and were unfazed by this shuttling to and fro between countries. Christopher and Charles Colton, her twins, would be returning to Winchester in the autumn. The Driscoll children, who ranged in age from eight to twelve, were a self-contained trio and babbled together in a polyglot language made up of English, Greek and Arabic, as the Driscolls had last been posted to Damascus, and they spoke all three languages with the fluency of children. Azai Mitsui, a boy of seven, was involved with a hand-held computer game and disturbed no one because his parents had the foresight to make him turn off the sound.

The parents arranged themselves around their respective children, as travelling parents do. They had met formally for the first time over the last weekend, and the FCO had given the families a day together to get to know each other. All the adults were seasoned diplomats or diplomatic spouses and joined in the camaraderie that typified their profession.

George Colton dozed while Joanna stood and surveyed the group to see that everyone was comfortable. They were not scheduled to land until midnight, Cyprus time, and she wanted to make sure they all remained on good terms before they arrived at the Kennington Nicosia. Joanna had never stayed in a Kennington hotel before but knew the hotels by reputation and was looking forward to her time at one.

Michael Driscoll was chatting with his wife about a book that he said he had discovered in the University College London library that was written by a nineteenth century Greek archaeologist, discussing the removal of the precious marbles from the frieze of the Parthenon in Athens. Michael pontificated on the book's unique point of view, having been written by a Greek who approved of the protection of the antiquities in London and who had been instrumental in their transfer to the British Museum. Sophia Driscoll listened with only half an ear as she watched her children. They appeared to be happy and probably would soon be off to sleep. She looked lovingly at her bookish husband and turned away. She took the headset the flight attendant offered and wrapped it around her head.

Azai Mitsui drifted off to sleep, and his mother took the video game from his hands and drew a blanket over him. She looked up at Joanna Colton and smiled. Joanna wondered what Bitki was thinking. She, being a younger woman and a career diplomat, might be impatient with the other wives. Would the negotiators respect her for her knowledge and intelligence and not just her dark, good looks?

Onan Mitsui looked anxious. George Colton had told his wife that being appointed to the delegation could be a step up for Onan into the higher ranks of the diplomatic service. George suspected Onan's ultimate goal was to become the British Ambassador to Turkey, a place where his grandmother had been shunned two generations before because she had a Japanese partner. Joanna could see the excitement in Onan's eyes as he squeezed his wife's hand.

"So we are finally on our way," Joanna heard Bitki whisper in response to Onan's touch.

"Bitki, I have a premonition that the next few months will be some of the most important ones in our lives."

Bitki leaned over and put her head on her husband's shoulder. "I think, Onan, you may be right."

*

Elspeth knew enough about the violence between the Turks and the Greeks to be cautious. She went for the third time to check the room arrangements for the delegation. Being on a raised part of the hotel site, the wing where they were to be housed had windows that looked out through trees in the gardens and over the wall that surrounded the hotel to the city beyond. Elspeth had walked around the central part of the Greek sector of Nicosia that afternoon and was able to orientate herself from the windows. If one looked hard enough, one could just make out the barbed wire on top of the barrier between the two sectors and the taller buildings in the city centre.

Security for the delegation in the hotel presented several problems. Although the meetings would take place elsewhere, the possibility always remained that hostility to the talks would arise, and members of the British delegation might be pursued by unwanted elements into the hotel. With Philippa's help, Elspeth had already briefed the day staff and later the night staff about being wary of strangers who did not seem to be in the hotel for legitimate reasons. The staff of the Kennington Nicosia all lived in this divided city and seemed unperturbed by Elspeth's instruction.

Elspeth had met with Philippa and discussed the selection of the staff for the delegations rooms. Philippa had picked room attendants whom she said she particularly trusted, although they were not the most senior, and had chosen three members of the new security staff, whom she personally had hired, to monitor the cameras in the wing where the delegation was staying. This dedicated staff would be on eight hour rotating shifts. Philippa introduced Elspeth to them and instructed them that Elspeth was ultimately in charge of security and they would report directly to her if they saw anything unusual.

Later Elspeth replayed this meeting in her mind and felt uneasy. Why had Philippa abrogated all responsibility for the security of the delegates and their families? In the past, Elspeth always worked closely with hotel managers when security was an issue. Was it that Philippa did not want to be blamed if something went wrong? Initially Elspeth put it down to Philippa's inexperience as a manager of a Kennington hotel, but it kept gnawing away at her. Elspeth looked at the time and hoped Pamela Crumm would still be in the office in London.

Pamela picked up on the first ring. "What is it, Elspeth, my friend?" Elspeth knew that the space age phone console on Pamela's desk displayed Elspeth's name in large LCD letters when she called.

Elspeth considered her words. "I keep trying to forgive Philippa for her unconventional ways of running a Kennington hotel, but I'm uncomfortable because I can't seem to forge an alliance with her. She says the right words, but the implications are always twisted somehow. I don't know why."

Pamela chuckled. "You have hit it exactly on the head. Oh, sorry, ducks. I was speaking metaphorically not literally."

Putting her hand to the place on her skull where she had been struck, Elspeth burst out laughing. "But I am concerned," she said and went on to explain her arrangements with Philippa. "What I find most odd is that the security force here is all new. Philippa employed them but has put full responsibility for their performance on me. I always prefer staff members who have been in place for a long time because they understand how our hotels work. Like Eric, I put a high reliance on a staff's longevity, as I know you do. Philippa seems to want to shake things up and trusts her own people, not the ones here in Georgios's time." Georgios Konstantinidis was the previous manager of the Kennington Nicosia.

"When I spoke to him recently about the Kennington Nicosia, Eric said he had complete confidence in Philippa, but I don't," Pamela said. "You already know that. I don't want to disagree with Eric right now because of other things going on here, but I do want you to document to me privately and in writing what you think of Philippa. Emails are OK. Just make them an informal day-to-day log. Eric wants me to handle the minutiae of your visit to the hotel, so your log should seem casual until it needs to be something more formal."

Elspeth cleared her throat and wondered, as she had many times before, how far she should venture into the running commentary between Lord Kennington and Pamela Crumm, the two business partners of the Kennington Organisation. "Shall I encrypt the messages for your eyes only?" she asked.

"No. Write them straightforwardly but send them to me only. If there is a problem later, you can plead ignorance of the disagreement between Eric and me on Philippa's management skills."

"I'll start tonight. I understand the delegation left Heathrow several hours ago; they are due in Cyprus just after midnight. I plan to meet them in the morning and will keep faithful notes, I promise."

Pamela's voice became less serious. "And how is Sir Richard?"

"He is setting me up with the powers that be in the British High Commission here. The High Commissioner and Richard are old chums. I think Richard wants to introduce me to the charms of diplomatic life. Quite frankly, diplomatic life sounds deadly dull. Everyone seems to know everyone, and their lives seem boringly routine, even in times of crisis."

"Elspeth, you have lived far too long solving crises. Perhaps you should take a look at another way to live."

Elspeth set her jaw. "I'm quite content with my life, thank you, except for the occasional bang on my head."

*

Philippa Allard-Thorpe had made carefully arrangements for the delegation, knowing they would be staying for several months and wanting them to take news of the comfort of the hotel and the efficiency of the manager back to the FCO and to Lord Kennington. Because the British government was paying far less than normal Kennington guests, she had calculated what economies she would have to make while still offering suitable accommodation. Her first effort was to organise the delegation's meals in a small dining room in the wing where they were staying. This way she could limit the number of choices by bringing in the food not consumed earlier in the breakfast or dining rooms. The delegation should not suffer undue hardship at this setup because all the food at the hotel was routinely excellent.

The breakfast put out for the delegation was no exception. Knowing they were not settled into their rooms until after two that morning, Philippa waited to have breakfast set up for them until most of the other guests in the hotel had left for their day's activities, be they tourism, study, or business. Philippa surveyed the buffet table and wondered why the cherry pastries, low fat granola, and fresh oranges had not been popular in the main breakfast room that morning. She would have to speak to the chef.

When Elspeth entered the delegation's dining room, she broke Philippa's concentration.

"I assume everyone arrived safely last night," Elspeth said.

Philippa reassured Elspeth. "I personally helped everyone to their rooms and saw to it they had the basic essentials for the night. The children were a bit grumpy but that should not last once they have had a good sleep and a proper breakfast. Mr Colton, the head of the delegation, assured me we had provided everything they needed, but we would have without question."

Elspeth wondered why Philippa had not left the settling of the guests to the night manager but did not ask. Instead Elspeth turned the conversation to the day ahead. "Did they give you any idea as to their schedule today?"

"I didn't ask," Philippa said with a frown. "When Mr Colton is ready, I am sure he will want to meet me, or rather meet us, to discuss his requirements while they are here."

Philippa always spoke with pre-emptive authority. Elspeth vowed to herself that she would not let this bother her. The more she had Philippa's confidence, the more likely she would be able to understand what exactly was going on at the hotel.

The first member of the delegation to burst into the breakfast room was a small, dark boy with an impish grin and a towel draping from his shoulders. "I am Azai, and I'm a superhero. I can see through walls."

Elspeth and Philippa both laughed, Elspeth remembering her son Peter at the same age.

"Azai will be a great help to MI-5 when he gets older but now he needs to eat his breakfast," a cheerful voice said behind them. They turned to see a tall man of indeterminate ethnicity. From a distance he looked Middle Eastern but as he approached his facial features were clearly East Asian.

"I am Onan Mitsui," he said simply, extending his hand first to Elspeth and then to Philippa.

Elspeth introduced herself. "I am Elspeth Duff from the London office of the Kennington Organisation. I believe you've met the manager of the hotel, Philippa Allard-Thorpe."

Philippa held out her hand and assured Mr Mitsui he was welcome to partake of anything he wanted from the breakfast buffet. Onan and Azai were soon joined by Bitki Mitsui, who was as tall as her husband and was startlingly beautiful, with dark hair and eyes and blemish-free olive skin. The Mitsuis made an exotic pair, but they both spoke and acted as well-educated but ordinary British citizens. Azai made noises in a language of his own and wrinkled his nose when his mother peeled an orange for him, emptied some Weetabix and milk into a bowl and put it in front of him.

Philippa made sure the adults got drinks, tea for him and coffee for her, and showed them the hot food table. This gave Elspeth a moment to watch this curious pair. She wanted to know their full story and was glad she would have the time to do so over the coming weeks.

The Driscolls' entrance was noisier, the three children dashing to the buffet to serve themselves. The waiter offered them toast, which they ordered with lots of butter and strawberry jam, and they all wanted hot chocolate. Azai eyed them from over his cereal bowl and asked for hot chocolate too. Sophia Driscoll spoke rapidly to her children in Greek, and they quietened down and took their seats at one of the long tables. Michael Driscoll ignored his family, took his coffee to a spot away from them and began reading *The Cyprus Mail*, which had been left at his door at his request.

The Coltons came last and without their sons, who, according to their parents, had chosen to stay in bed and seldom got up before noon. Joanna Colton invited Philippa and Elspeth to join them. Philippa declined, citing hotel business, but Elspeth accepted. She asked the waiter for coffee and sat down next to Joanna.

"Mrs Colton, I'm Elspeth Duff," she said.

"When I talked to Lord Kennington, he told me you would be here," Joanna responded. "He assured me that, with you in residence, we should have no fears for our safety while we are at the hotel."

Elspeth wondered why Joanna had called Eric Kennington but did not ask. Without a doubt Joanna would tell her later. George Colton sipped his coffee in a way that made Elspeth suspect that, like his sons, he was not a morning person.

Joanna, however, was filled with plans for the day, which involved organising everyone for a trip to Mount Olympus in the Troodos Mountains.

George Colton entered Philippa's office shortly before lunch. Elspeth and Philippa were waiting for him.

Although dressed casually, his manner was formal and serious. "Ms Allard-Thorpe, I appreciate all the trouble you have taken to welcome us here, particularly last evening, or should I say early this morning. The arrangements are quite satisfactory. Since the children can be a bit of a handful, I appreciate your giving us our own corner of the hotel. As parents, we are concerned that our children should not be in any danger from outside hostile elements. Our mission here is delicate. Rather than meeting at the United Nations headquarters here in Nicosia, we will hold our sessions at the British High Commission, which I understand is heavily barricaded. Michael Driscoll, Onan and Bitki Mitsui, and I will be at the meetings every weekday, leaving the children to Joanna and Sophia."

"Is there anyone from the FCO other than your wives to protect the children when they go outside of the hotel?" Elspeth asked.

"London didn't consider that necessary. Things have quietened down recently between the two sides here in Cyprus, and the children will only be allowed in safe places. The High Commission wives organise events for their offspring, and we hope our children will be included. Sophia and my wife seem keen on joining the other diplomatic families, but my boys are being rebellious. They're well able to amuse themselves, but Joanna will get them involved somehow. She has a genius for that sort of thing."

Elspeth could not decide if George Colton's last statement contained a hint of cynicism or not. She sympathised with the twins and hoped she had been more relaxed with her own teen-aged children than George Colton was with his.

George Colton continued. "We don't start our talks for two more days, so those of us who have not been here before would like to explore Cyprus. I haven't visited for more than thirty years, nineteen seventy-three in fact, the year before Turkey's invasion of the north. I'm interested to see how much has changed."

When he had left, Philippa looked at Elspeth and said, "Has the Kennington Organisation really done the right thing, inviting the families here? They're staying at a much-reduced rate. Our summer bookings are a bit down, probably because of the recent plane crash and troubles in the Middle East, and the revenue generated from them being here will be helpful, but I want to keep up the hotel's profitability without letting down our standards. Lord Kennington has asked that I let him know if any trouble arises because of their stay, and I certainly plan to do so." Hardness had replaced the politeness and warmth that filled Philippa's voice when talking to the families earlier. Why?

6

Elspeth lunched in her room. She ordered a Greek salad and fresh lemonade. Sipping the cold, sweet liquid, she walked out on her balcony and looked out at the garden beyond. Her assignment seemed simple, so much so that she wondered why Eric Kennington had sent her here. Surely a junior member of the Kennington Organisation security staff could have done the job. She hoped Eric Kennington was not putting her out to pasture, as her work sustained her and she treasured the independence and the benefits her job gave her. She lay down on the sofa and dozed, trying to think what her future was with the Kennington Organisation. The warmth of the afternoon quelled her misgivings, and the lemonade reminded her of Cinnamon Allard-Thorpe and the promise she had made to Cinnamon to visit the café to hear her poetry.

After her nap, Elspeth rang Philippa to find out where to find the café. The response to her call to Philippa was unexpected.

"Elspeth, I can't condone Cinnamon going to that place again. She mixes with the most terrible riffraff there, the worst sort of university students, both Greeks and Turks, all of whom have dangerously radical ideas that could get them, and Cinnamon as well, in trouble with the authorities. I really believe they take advantage of her blindness. They always make her pay for the drinks, which basically means I do."

The venom in Philippa's perfectly articulated words cut through the phone line. "Her father encourages her, you know, to mix with the students. He's responsible for her blindness and cannot be trusted with her best interests."

Elspeth's interest was piqued. "I didn't realise he was in her life."

"Unfortunately he is. He lives in Paphos and skulks around here on occasion. I have told security to escort him off the premises any time he appears. He isn't good for Cinnamon. She needs to be protected now that she has lost her sight."

Elspeth wanted to point out that blind people these days could be totally self-reliant, but that did not seem the right thing to say. The breach between Philippa and Cinnamon's father obviously was irreparable.

Elspeth was now faced with the dilemma of getting in touch with Cinnamon. She was not sure if Philippa and Cinnamon lived on the hotel premises but, if they did, the front desk would know. Elspeth ventured out from her suite and found a receptionist at the front desk busy at his computer, as the lobby was free of guests in the early afternoon.

As Elspeth approached the receptionist, he looked up.

"Can you tell me how I can reach Cinnamon Allard-Thorpe?" Elspeth asked.

"No need to ask, Elspeth," a voice behind her said. "I was just coming in from the garden."

Elspeth turned towards Cinnamon and spoke to her quietly. "Well met," she said

"The pleasure is mine," Cinnamon responded.

Elspeth was at first startled that Cinnamon recognised her voice and then realised that voices were as clear for the blind as visual images for the sighted.

"I am usually here or in the garden after lunch, if you need to find me," Cinnamon added.

Today Cinnamon wore even more brightly coloured clothes, a long floral skirt and a tight bright yellow top that showed off her slimness and emphasised her fairness. Elspeth wondered who chose her clothes for her because they matched so perfectly. Was it her mother's doing?

"Do you live here?" Elspeth asked.

Cinnamon shook her head of long and silky blonde hair. "No, just around the corner, but Mummy likes to keep an eye on me and always gets me to come to the hotel at lunchtime. She often gets busy and forgets to check on me, but I come anyway. I'm always afraid if she discovers I'm not here, she'll get angry."

"I hope that isn't a burden."

"Sometimes it is, but I always get a good meal." Cinnamon seemed reconciled to the arrangement.

"Do I still have an invitation for this afternoon?" Elspeth asked.

Cinnamon grinned widely, showing the same straight white teeth that her mother had. Was it American dentistry or heredity?

"Definitely. Please come. I've been working on a new poem, a modified double haiku. It's almost in place, and I want to read it this afternoon. I'd like you to meet my friends as well. Mummy thinks they are all ruffians, but they aren't really. They're students and free thinkers who find life exciting. For me it makes a wonderful change from these stuffy walls. I hope I don't offend you by saying so."

It was Elspeth's turn to smile, which she hoped was conveyed in her voice. "No, not at all. The Kennington Organisation works hard at being stuffy. Lord Kennington would be flattered."

Cinnamon held out her hand, which Elspeth took. "I wish Mummy had your understanding, Elspeth. How many children do you have? They must love you."

"I have a son and a daughter, and I believe they do love me. I've always tried to find a gentle path between what they want from their lives and my parental obligations. So far it seems to have worked because I continue on excellent terms with them both. But tell me, what is a modified double haiku? Isn't a haiku a fourteen syllable Japanese poem?"

"You're very close, but actually it is a seventeen syllable poem with lines of five, seven and then five syllables. In Japan it's a very refined art. In English, I think I may be corrupting it a bit, but I like the discipline of the syllables. I'm writing a double haiku, that is two seventeen-syllable stanzas. You will hear it this afternoon." Cinnamon's excitement was palpable.

"When and where can I meet you?" Elspeth asked.

"Mummy would be quite upset if she knew I'd invited you, so meet me at the café, not here. Do you have a piece of paper? You can write down the name in the Roman alphabet, and they can translate it into Greek at the desk for you. Let's meet at the café at half-past four."

Elspeth was grateful that the Kennington receptionists were required to be multi-lingual and wrote down the address Cinnamon gave her phonetically. Elspeth did not tell Cinnamon that she had mentioned the café to Philippa.

Cinnamon turned to go and only then did her white cane appear from under her skirt. "Bye for now, Elspeth. I'm so glad you are coming. Maybe I will adopt you as my fairy godmother. You sound quite wonderful."

With those words Cinnamon was off, navigating the lobby with only the slightest use of her cane.

Elspeth crossed to the reception desk, where the young man looked up from his duties. He watched Cinnamon go through the doors with a long, admiring look. As Elspeth approached, he spoke to her.

"Cinnamon is truly a lovely girl, but, y'know, she doesn't know it." His accent was purely American.

Elspeth looked surprised. "Are you an American?"

He laughed and his dark eyes sparkled. "No, Cypriot, but I spent my childhood in LA."

His black hair was cut short in the European fashion favoured by young men on the Continent, but his stiff buttoned-down white shirt under his hotel jacket had an all-American cut to it. His long, full nose, square face, and bushy black brows, however, were definitely Cypriot.

"I thought I recognised the accent. What part of LA?" Elspeth asked.

"Pasadena. My father was a professor of Greek at the University of Southern California, and I went to school there."

Elspeth like this young man instantly, as he reminded her of many of her son's friends in the Los Angeles area. Her curiosity grew. "Why did you come back to Cyprus?"

"A Cypriot girl I met at USC who came back here after graduating, but she ended up marrying someone else, the person chosen by her family."

"I'm sorry." Elspeth's empathy was real. She had lived through several of her son's failed romances, holding him in her arms as he grieved and comforting him in a way only a mother could do. Those memories were precious to her.

"You don't need to be sorry. After I came back home, I found out I didn't really love her after all," the young man said.

Elspeth held out her hand over the top of the reception desk. "My name is Elspeth Duff. What is yours?"

He shook her hand heartily. "We all know you, Ms Duff. Ms Allard-Thorpe has been very clear about your status with the top people in the Kennington Organisation. I am Christos. Christos Leonidou. According to Ms Allard-Thorpe we are to treat you with utmost respect."

"I'm not the 'wicked witch of the west', you know, despite any words to the contrary," she said with a laugh.

Christos said, almost under his breath, "No, but she is sometimes." Then he added, "You weren't supposed to hear that."

Elspeth frowned and looked severely at him. "I have good ears, Christos."

"Will you report me?" he asked, his intense eyes now wary.

Elspeth had no intention of reporting him but feigned displeasure. After a long minute, she said, "No, I won't, not if you tell me about Cinnamon Allard-Thorpe and write down this address for me in Greek."

Christos let out his breath, relieved. He raised his eyes in adoration. "Cinnamon is one of the most beautiful creatures on Earth. Did you know Cyprus is the birthplace of Aphrodite? Well, Cinnamon is the sightless Aphrodite, one who cannot see her own beauty. Sometimes when I am on my lunch hour I go out to the garden and talk to her. Her voice alone would make me fall in love with her because it is so deep and clear. We talk about poetry, especially world poetry. She loves the Japanese forms. I studied Classics and Greek Linguistics at USC, and so she is always quizzing me about the structure of language. I guess she was pretty visually oriented before her accident, and so left-brained that non-visual stuff like language is harder for her."

"Does she speak Greek?"

"Not very well. She was raised in the expat community," he said with a protracted sigh. "Would that I could speak to her in the words of the ancient poets. I've read her some of the ancient verses and translated them in a clumsy way. She laughs at me but then asks if she could help me translate them into poetic English. I relish doing this with her, but she tells me we will have to find a place to do so where her mother won't get wind of it. We have a date to meet at the library of the Cyprus Museum next Sunday, when I am off work, but if her mother finds out, I think she might wonder why someone who can't see would want to go to a library. You see the difficulty."

Although Christos amused Elspeth, she was hesitant about recruiting him as her ally. Lord Kennington discouraged the practice of pitting employee against employee or staff against management. Any obvious collusion on Elspeth's part with Christos against Philippa would not do. Elspeth felt that her biggest problem in Cyprus so far was not the protection of the British delegation but rather the growing tensions she was discovering among Philippa Allard-Thorpe, her daughter, and the staff of the Kennington Nicosia.

"Christos, I really came to ask you to write out the name and address of the café where Cinnamon has asked me to join her this afternoon. Cinnamon helped me write it out phonetically."

Christos took the piece of paper and read what was written there. He puzzled out the phonetics and suddenly grinned. "I get it. I don't need to write it out for you because it's very close, and you can walk there. What time do you need to be there?"

"Half past four."

"OK. Then I will take you there myself," he volunteered. "I am off at four, when my replacement comes on duty."

"Have you ever been to one of Cinnamon's poetry readings at the café?" Elspeth asked.

Christos shook his head. "No, I understand the participants are university students who sometimes get very political. Because I like my job here and since it helps support my grandmother, y'know, I try to stay away from any event that might erupt into chaos." Christos hesitated. "I'll take you there, but I'm not sure I want to come in with you. I can't afford to be associated with any radical activity, particularly in Ms Allard-Thorpe's eyes."

Elspeth was glad no one was in the lobby so that her conversation with Christos would not be overheard. "Do you think Cinnamon is safe going there?"

"Now that she is blind, Cinnamon thinks she is protected by a special aura of some sort. We've talked about this, but I can't convince her to stay away from the rowdies at the café. She enjoys their noise and their iconoclastic enthusiasms. She says they worship her as one who has known real suffering." Christos expression was filled with real disgust. "I think they are manipulating her to get her to pay for the drinks and they don't care a rap for her otherwise."

Philippa had said the same thing.

Elspeth left the reception desk filled with misgivings. A beautiful young woman like Cinnamon, one who could not see, might not be able to anticipate any danger in her association with others. Elspeth heard Christos's warning and did not feel comfortable disregarding it. She was torn by the maternal instincts that she would have felt for her own daughter and now felt for Cinnamon and if it would be appropriate to intervene in the private family affairs of one of the Kennington hotel managers. Cinnamon Allard-Thorpe certainly complicated things when sharing with Elspeth her feelings towards her mother. Elspeth was undecided as to what her best course of action would be. She hoped Pamela Crumm in London would take her call before four o'clock and her appointment with Christos to go to the café.

Pamela rang back half an hour after Elspeth left a message for her.

"The urgency of your voice mail, Elspeth, ducks, has aroused my curiosity. You're supposed to be in Cyprus resting, but the delegation has hardly arrived in Nicosia before you ring here with a tone of concern in your voice. What is happening there?"

Elspeth bristled. "Resting? I thought I was on assignment, but I have found myself in a terrible dilemma. I thought if I could talk it out with you, you could give me some sage advice." Elspeth often used her friend as a sounding board.

"Sage advice and thyme. Sorry for the pun. His lordship and I have just had a disagreeable hour with the accountant at one of the hotels who is accusing our offices of charging him falsely with cooking the books. I do actually have a bit of time because, for a short while anyway, Eric has gone off in a bit of a huff. I expect he has retreated to the bar upstairs." Pamela gave a short snort, they way she always did when provoked by Lord Kennington.

Elspeth was glad Pamela could not see the grin on her face at hearing the latest foray among the decades-long disagreements between the head of the Kennington Organisation and his business partner.

"I don't really want to be involved with what's going on here," Elspeth said, changing the subject, "but Cinnamon is truly lovely and possibly vulnerable. Her mother is annoyed with her because Cinnamon is trying to be her own person even though she is blind. I think this places unwanted demands on Philippa. She clearly wants to run the hotel full time and not be constantly looking after her daughter. I'm undecided between staying neutral, which I'm no longer feeling, and turning my back on Cinnamon, who may be in danger."

"Why do you think Cinnamon is in danger?" asked Pamela. "It sounds as if she goes to the café all the time and Christos is a bit jealous of the group taking Cinnamon's attention away from him."

"Perhaps you are right. What do you advise?"

"What would you do if Cinnamon were your daughter?"

"I'd go to the café, listen to Cinnamon's poem and find out what the students were about. They may be completely harmless."

"Elspeth, I would urge you to take your own advice, but do let me know what happens. If you do think there's harm, then let's talk about the circumstances in a different light. Tell me why does all this make you nervous? I've always trusted your instincts, so what more is going on?"

Elspeth thought for a moment. "I'm not sure. The feeling here is different from most of our hotels. When Philippa comes into a room everyone on the staff stiffens. Christos alluded to her as the 'wicked witch of the west', a term that I'm afraid I used first. Perhaps the staff picks up her ruthlessness, which she cannot seem to hide when dealing with them, although her interface with the guests is gracious and appropriate. I've heard one dowager gush about Philippa's warmth towards her."

Pamela did not reply at once. Finally she said, "Yes, I picked up the tension too, despite all the good things that she reported she has done at the hotel. She writes lengthy reports more frequently than I want to read them. Elspeth, I asked you to give me your impressions of Philippa Allard-Thorpe, but now I am asking more urgently. Although one guest may gush, we don't want any of our guests or the delegation to pick up the bad feelings of the staff towards the manager."

Elspeth knew Lord Kennington's dictates far too well about the welfare of the guests to misunderstand what Pamela was requesting her to do.

7

"Christos," Elspeth said as they strolled along the dusty street, "I was concerned that you earlier expressed discontent with Philippa Allard-Thorpe's management style, and I want to ask you something bluntly. Were you just referring to her way of running the hotel or her parenting skills as well?"

They were on the way to the café after crossing a bridge that spanned the almost dry riverbed of the River Pedieos on the west side of the old section of Nicosia. Elspeth could sense that Christos was anxious.

Christos flushed and whistled at the air. "I shouldn't have said anything, even flippantly. I don't want to imply anything that could endanger my job."

Elspeth knew she had to tread lightly, so she carefully phrased her next words. "Let me assure you that anything you say will stay with me alone. Part of my job is knowing how to keep confidences when necessary."

He turned towards her. "Then may I speak to you without Ms Allard-Thorpe becoming aware of what I have said to you?"

"You have my word."

He drew her onto a path that led to the gardens bordering the pavement, and they found a bench under a large, flowering tree that Elspeth did not recognise.

"She makes life hell for all of us, Cinnamon and the staff included," Christos said. "Nothing is ever quite good enough by her standards, at the hotel or for Cinnamon. Cinnamon caves in most of the time, but once I found her crying and clenching her fists and saying over and over 'Why can't I please her? Why can't I please her?' After that I noticed the staff felt the same way. We just can't please her. I feel sorry mostly for Cinnamon." His voice deepened as he said this.

"I see," Elspeth said. "What about Cinnamon's father?"

Christos looked over at an exotic flowering cactus in the garden beyond. He seemed to be gathering his thoughts.

"Ernest Thorpe? I've never met him, although I've seen him. He's an archaeologist who works on the western side of the island. He came to lecture at USC when I was a student there, and my father dragged me to hear him. I rather enjoyed the talk, but I didn't admit it to my father."

"Does he ever come to the hotel?"

Christos looked confused. "My father? No, he's still back in LA."

"I meant Ernest Thorpe."

"I've never seen him there."

"Would you recognise him if he did?"

"Absolutely. He's quite distinguished. He looks exactly like a movie version of an archaeologist, y'know, the Gregory Peck type. All the girls at USC went gaga over him."

Elspeth rose and touched Christos's arm. As they walked on, she assured Christos that she would keep the conversation between the two of them confidential. He seemed relieved.

When Christos and Elspeth entered the cafe, the students inside were banging their glasses on their tables. Finally the students quietened down, and Cinnamon was helped on to a chair they had put up on one of the tables. She stood gripping the back of the chair like a statue of Aphrodite and spoke with the voice of a young Medea. Her deep, slow, warm tones caressed each word carefully.

> *Hanging by a thread,*
> *a spider fashions her web*
> *of sunlit spun lace.*
>
> *Her pattern soon gone,*
> *torn asunder by the wind.*
> *Broken illusions.*

Because the poem was so short, someone behind Elspeth spoke out and asked her to read it again. Elspeth turned and saw that the voice belonged to Christos, who had lingered at the door of the café.

Cinnamon reached for the back of the chair to steady herself and turned in Christos's direction, but not before the students around her started clapping, congratulating Cinnamon and calling for a round of drinks to celebrate the occasion of her latest offering. One student, a lean young man with long hair and a black goatee on an unshaven jaw, helped Cinnamon off the table, and she spoke quietly to him. Elspeth could barely hear.

"Thank you, Demetrius," Cinnamon said among the hubbub of the other voices.

"My pleasure always, Cinnamon," he replied, equally quietly, as if he did not want the others to hear.

One of the louder students, who slurred his words slightly, said. "I'm not too sure I get it."

Another answered, "It's supposed to be Zen. You aren't supposed to get it, just sit quietly and contemplate it."

"Like my navel?" asked the first and belched.

Everyone, except Elspeth, Christos and the man who had helped Cinnamon down, burst out laughing at this and toasted their goddess Cinnamon. She was smiling slightly and said weakly, "I can explain the form if you like." No one seemed interested; they were too busy enjoying the new round of beer.

Christos fled from the café, leaving Elspeth without an escort back to the hotel.

8

During the next few days Elspeth only saw Cinnamon from afar because other matters intervened. Shortly after returning from the café, Elspeth found a message waiting for her from Bitki Mitsui. She rang the number Bitki had given and reached the voice mailbox on her mobile. When Bitki returned her call, the ache in Elspeth's heart that had lingered since watching the reaction to Cinnamon's poem vanished.

"May I meet you privately, Ms Duff? I want to discuss a security issue that I think not only affects our job here but also the safety of my family."

Elspeth's could feel her internal antennae rise. "Where can we meet? Do you want to come to my room?"

"No, I would rather speak to you away from the hotel. Do you know the island at all?" Bitki's sounded hopeful.

"Actually not, but you tell me where a good place would be." Elspeth had studied the map of Cyprus on the plane out from London, but she only had a general idea of the shape of the island and the jagged green line between the Greek and Turkish sectors.

Bitki lowered her voice, barely within Elspeth's hearing range. "I want to meet you on the Turkish side of the island. I know a small village there. Let me give you directions. I think it best if you cross over at the main United Nations checkpoint in Nicosia tomorrow morning. I'll hire a taxi to pick you up and bring you to the village once you get on the Turkish side."

Had Bitki sounded less serious, Elspeth might have made light of this clandestine meeting, but she sensed Bitki's anxiousness.

"Can you tell me anything more about this now?"

"No, not until tomorrow," Bitki said, distress in her voice. "Things should not have come to this."

So much for a quiet assignment to help me recover from my injury, Elspeth thought after she rang off.

Elspeth expected the crossing at the checkpoint to be difficult, but the UN patrol seemed bored with their task. She pulled her British passport from her bag. The guard took a cursory glance at it, handed her a stamped pass and waved her through. A taxi was waiting, as promised. Elspeth had learned from past experience that taxi drivers were extremely well informed about the daily happenings in any city or area, and therefore she asked if her driver spoke any English.

"I spent ten years in Manhattan driving a cab that belonged to my brother," he responded in a form of English that is only spoken in New York. "I hated it. New Yorkers are too pushy and too prejudiced. What do they say to me? You come from India? Like I wore a turban or something? But I learned something from them. Money doesn't make happiness, so I came back to Cyprus to find a nice woman and now we are married and have three wonderful sons."

Elspeth had heard that Cypriot families measured their family size in sons and therefore asked, "Do you have any daughters?"

"Fatima, the love of my life and my wife's as well. We are building a house next to ours for her, a big house with all the money I saved and invested in America. We have found a good husband for her."

"Did you return to New York after your marriage and was your daughter raised there?" Elspeth asked, carefully avoiding her strong feelings that a woman should have the right to select a husband on their own.

"She was there only as a young child, but even then we shielded her from the corrupt influence of an infidel society." He turned away from the centre of Turkish Nicosia and soon they were heading east out of the city. Elspeth held tightly to the handle on the door as the taxi driver increased his speed.

"You are Muslim," Elspeth said somewhere between a question and a statement.

"Allah be praised. My Fatima is a devout daughter of Islam. Her husband is the nephew of my closest friend."

As they raced through the countryside along the road that was bordered by the startling blue Mediterranean on one side and the dry hills on the other, Elspeth asked more. She was always curious about the customs of the countries she visited.

Having determined her driver's name was Kahlil and that he liked to talk about himself, she asked if he was a Turkish Cypriot.

"My wife's family came to Cyprus when the Ottoman Turks took control of the island in the fifteenth century. My family is from Syria, and they immigrated after World War Two, although I was born here and consider myself a Cypriot."

He looked at her in his rear view mirror, and Elspeth could see the pride in his eyes.

"How do you feel about the partition of Cyprus?" she asked.

Kahlil bristled and narrowly missed an oncoming van. "The Greeks, they won't give us freedom, so we had to take it for ourselves."

Feeling the vehemence in Kahlil's voice, she decided to redirect the topic of their conversation to the beauty of the island and the country through which they were travelling. Kahlil seemed equally happy to talk about this although his New York accent seemed strangely out of place as they passed a pristine white beach with the azure sea beyond and a crystal clear sky above. As they drove further along the coast Elspeth sat back and enjoyed the scenery without paying attention to his twisted tones.

Finally they arrived at a small village that had little more than a few small houses and a brightly painted tourist restaurant with green plastic chairs outside. Elspeth wondered why Bitki had chosen this spot.

"Did Mrs Mitsui say she would meet me here?" Elspeth asked.

"No, not here. Up there at the house above the village." Kahlil waved his hand towards the window.

Elspeth craned her neck in the direction he was pointing and saw a palatial villa perched on the hill.

"Up there? But that's huge!"

"Miss Bitki's parents live there. It's a grand villa and the gardens are the most beautiful that ever was. Just wait, you'll see."

Kahlil sped on up the narrow, curving dusty drive that led to the house. Elspeth clung more tightly to the handrail on the door of the taxi and hoped the car would not have a puncture or other failure that would send them over the edge, but Kahlil seemed familiar with curves, and they arrived intact at the gates of the massive stone walls that surrounded the house. Kahlil jumped from the car and punched a code into a box by the gates. They swung open with well-oiled ease.

Elspeth did not know what to expect at the villa but what she saw totally surprised her. A tall and distinguished man, whom Elspeth assumed was close to her own age and who looked very British, was standing by the front door waiting for her. He came around to the car door and opened it for her.

"Mrs Duff, I'm so glad you accepted Bitki's invitation to join us today. My name is Jonathan Westwood. I'm Bitki's father."

Elspeth looked to see if she could find any resemblance between father and daughter. Jonathan's eyes were dark, like Bitki's, and he had black hair, now greying, but there the likeness stopped.

Jonathan Westwood must have seen her puzzlement. "Bitki favours her mother, who is a Cypriot. I came out here from the UK in the fifties, before Cyprus became independent, and I fell in love with the island and subsequently with Bitki's mother. I never left. Bitki was raised in England and educated there. She came home during holidays, but she always preferred the English to the Cypriot side of the family. I can't understand why because I find Cyprus just short of Paradise, despite all the political troubles."

By this time, they had entered the main hallway in the house, which Elspeth found cavernous and badly lit but blessedly cool after the heat of the day outside.

"We built the house around the ruins of a Crusader's castle," Jonathan Westwood said. "As an architectural historian, I insisted that the original buildings, such as this one, remain intact and everything we built around them not damage the integrity of the original medieval ruins. I also wanted to use local methods to construct our home. You will find that the walls are coated with plaster, the roofs and floors are tiled, and the main structure heavy timber. I researched the local materials as thoroughly as I could, choosing the best I could find, and my wife helped me design everything to suit our personal tastes. She'll give you a tour of the house if you even hint you are interested. Do come in and meet everybody. Onan, Bitki, and Azai are already here and are in the garden house with my wife."

They turned the corner, where the room suddenly became filled with light coming through a wall of French doors that led out to the garden. Kahlil had been right; the gardens were magnificent. Elspeth was saddened that her Uncle Frederick, an avid gardener who had died many years before, could not be here to see the plethora of blooming plants that filled the vast open space behind the walls of the villa. Lord Kennington, who considered himself a garden designer, would have considered this garden far too out of control, but Elspeth loved it. "I really do feel in Paradise!" she exclaimed.

"Here we are at the garden house. We nestled it into the ruins of one of the small chambers in the original castle walls, which probably was an armoury, and therefore it stays cool during the heat of the day. Come meet my wife, Cari."

Cari Westwood rose as they entered the small room. It was filled with comfortable looking wicker furniture, and in the centre of the room a glass table was spread with lunch—meats, cheeses, salads of various sorts, fresh bread and several bottles of wine in cooling terra-cotta sleeves.

As Cari approached them, Elspeth was aware of the grace with which she walked, a bearing that many wealthy Middle Eastern women had but which Elspeth had seldom seen in an American or British woman. Cari greeted Elspeth with a warm handshake and showed her to a small sofa filled with brightly coloured cushions.

Bitki, who was sitting in a chair beside the sofa, did not rise because Azai was sitting on her lap and playing with an electronic toy, but Onan Mitsui came over and greeted Elspeth. Finally Bitki lifted Azai down to the floor and summoned someone outside. A woman came and fetched him, and he hardly noticed the transfer from one person to another.

"Ms Duff," Bitki began, "I apologise for having to bring you all the way out here, although I thought you might enjoy seeing my parents' home."

"It truly is beautiful. I would have come under any pretext," Elspeth said.

"Onan and I didn't want to speak to you at the hotel because we are worried about a security breach that we believe originated in the hotel itself. I spoke with Daddy first, and he said I should tell you what happened there. He checked and found out you have a security clearance from Scotland Yard. "

Elspeth looked over at Jonathan Westwood, who grinned at her. Elspeth had been given a low level of clearance when she was handling the murder at the Kennington Valletta the year before.

"I've told Bitki she could use my services when needed, and no sooner did she arrive in Cyprus than I had a call from her," Jonathan said. "Let me explain. Over my lifetime, I've established myself as an architectural historian with expertise in the architecture of the Greek Islands and Cyprus, but that actually was not my real purpose for being on Cyprus. Early in my career, I was approached by the British Secret Intelligence Service, the SIS. They wanted me to be, how do they put it in novels, their man in Cyprus after Cypriot independence. Cari was my first recruit, and, until I retired several years ago, we lived mostly undetected. I contacted the SIS in London when Bitki asked to use our home as a safe place to meet you and found you had once worked at Scotland Yard and still enjoy their confidence. Detective Superintendent Tony Ketcham spoke very highly of you."

"Tony and I have a long history," Elspeth said, "in fact back to my university days."

"So I understand. Bitki inherited Cari's and my interest in international affairs quite naturally, and we were delighted when she joined the FCO."

"Thank you, Daddy," Bitki said with a smile in her eyes. "Now you see, Ms Duff, why I came to you. Joanna Colton, in her rather domineering way, arranged a tour to Mount Olympus in the Troodos Mountains the day after we arrived. I didn't want to go, as I have been there many times, but Onan argued that we should try to bond with the group before we went into the negotiating sessions. When we returned to our rooms in the hotel, however, Onan and I found that someone had opened one of the briefcases where many of the official papers that dealt with the Turkish cause in Cyprus where stored. None of the documents were classified, but some of them were sensitive."

"Had Jonathan not trained us to pay attention to such things," Onan added, "we probably would not have noticed, but with intelligence officers in the family, both of us are aware of any minor rearrangement of our possessions. At first Bitki was puzzled by this, so she brought it to my attention. We looked to see if there were any fingerprints, but the briefcase's leather was amazingly clean for a bag that had been carried from London by both of us and had travelled in the back of a

Land Rover from the airport. The Cypriot roads are not free of dust at the end of summer, and if there were fingerprints we would have seen them."

Bitki agreed. "When Ms Allard-Thorpe introduced us to you at breakfast our first morning, you mentioned she was in charge of our accommodation but you were there to make sure we felt secure. Our assignment so far has seemed rather a routine one, and both Onan and I thought the Kennington hotels, with their reputation for impeccable hospitality, must offer your services as a matter of course. After finding our briefcase had been tampered with, I rang Daddy and he called London. Afterwards he suggested we invite you here."

Elspeth absorbed the words slowly. She had not expected such a thing to happen at a Kennington hotel.

"Thank you for alerting me," Elspeth said, "but Lord Kennington doesn't send me out unless he has a good reason to do so." Elspeth did not add that the reason might be her earlier head injury. "I'm the high-priced help. Tell me, did you ask any of the other members of the delegation if they had experienced the same problem? After all, they went to Mount Olympus too."

Onan shook his head. "Not all of them went. George Colton pleaded a headache and stayed behind, as did Michael Driscoll. We didn't ask the others if their belongings had been disturbed."

Elspeth pressed her lips together. "I see," she said. "Do you suspect George Colton?"

"No, not really. As head of the delegation, he had already seen all the papers we were carrying. He'd have no reason to disturb them," Bitki said.

"Who then? Michael Driscoll?" Elspeth asked.

Bitki shook her head. "Michael is a dear. He knows almost as much as anyone in the FCO about the situation on the Greek side of Cyprus but carefully hides this behind a bookish exterior. He's perhaps the most valuable member of our team in terms of sheer knowledge."

"His wife, Sophia?"

"She was on the tour with us, and besides she is completely wrapped up with caring for her three children," Bitki said.

Jonathan Westwood broke in. "Not always. Sophia Driscoll is more than she appears to be."

Bitki frowned. "Daddy?"

"Sophia Andropolous has been one of my main agents for many years. She still hears things from her extended family about the Turkish population here and passes them on to me.

They all turned to him with astonishment.

Bitki was the first to find her voice. "But, Daddy, she's Greek," Bitki said.

"No. She's half and half, half Turkish, half Greek. Her father was a Greek Cypriot, but her mother was Turkish. During the nineteen seventy-four invasion, the Greek Cypriots killed her mother and her father. They said her mother and father were Turkish collaborators. Both of Sophia's parents were beheaded in front of her and her brothers. Her father's relatives took Sophia and her brothers in, and, because the family was wealthy, they rushed the children to England, where they were educated and lived during the rest of their childhood. Sophia came back to Cyprus on holiday twelve years ago with her new husband, Michael Driscoll. Owing to his interest in the history of Cyprus, he and I were soon introduced, and Sophia and Michael spent a week with us here. One night, when Cari and I were alone with Sophia here in the garden, she told us her story."

Elspeth cocked an eyebrow and gave a half smile. "Which is when you recruited her, obviously. To which cause?"

Jonathan smiled. "To the British one, of course."

9

"Slow down, ducks, and tell me all that again," Pamela Crumm said in a voice more husky than usual. "I just this minute got off the line with the manager of the hotel in San Francisco, who was anxious to go to bed, and I have been up since half four. I need you to be more precise so that my small brain can take it all in."

Elspeth knew she was walking a fine line talking to Pamela. Pamela had no access to government secrets, and therefore Elspeth felt uneasy disclosing Jonathan Westwood's revelations with her, although Elspeth completely trusted Pamela's sense of discretion. Therefore Elspeth chose non-disclosing phrasing to try to explain the situation at the Kennington Nicosia.

"Pamela, it appears that someone surreptitiously entered one of delegates' rooms and rifled through government papers."

Elspeth could hear Pamela let out her breath.

"It happened the day after they arrived, when most of the delegation, organised by the indomitable Joanna Colton, was herded off to Mount Olympus. As they had just arrived, I suspect they would rather have been sleeping and enjoying the comforts of the Kennington Nicosia garden, tearoom or exercise room, but it's hard to say no to Joanna. George Colton and Michael Driscoll were the only ones who stayed behind.

George had already seen everything in the briefcase, and, when I asked him, Michael said he was off to see a colleague at the university. This brings us to the question of who had access to the room where the papers were kept."

Pamela was quick to catch Elspeth's apprehension. "I assume you suspect someone who had the means to enter the room, such as someone on the staff," she said.

"That's where my mind keeps going. Do you have any idea as to who on the staff might be interested in the papers?"

"Not without going into their personnel files," Pamela said. "But wouldn't it be easier to ask Philippa Allard-Thorpe? You sound hesitant about doing so."

Elspeth could not lie. "I don't trust her, and I can't tell you why. She has a rigorous agenda obviously, which she describes as her plans to make the Kennington Nicosia the best small hotel run by the Kennington Organisation. All the while I sense that her motivation is to make herself a star and not just the leader of the hotel team. She has been extraordinarily polite to me, but I represent upper management. She probably knows that I'm close to Eric and to you. Am I being too harsh?"

"No," Pamela said slowly. "I think you're being very perceptive. I'll try to make time today to go back over the recent hiring in Nicosia, but I trust your instincts. I'll get back to you as soon as I can. In the meantime, update me on Cinnamon."

"I haven't spoken to her since the incident in the café, although she dutifully appears everyday at the hotel and wanders sadly around the garden. When I see her, I wonder what is going on in her mind. Is she really being deceived by the rowdiness of the café crowd, or does she so desperately want to belong somewhere that she would accept any attention?"

Pamela's secret love of romance surfaced. "She needs to have a steady boyfriend. Christos, for example. Can you help promote that?"

"I've always tried to steer clear of promoting the personal love lives of the hotel employees, Pamela." Elspeth was annoyed at being asked to do otherwise. "I know nothing about Christos. Besides, I have no idea how Philippa would react to my meddling in her daughter's life. As much as I'm beginning to mistrust Philippa, at this point I can't afford to alienate her by mentioning her daughter's behaviour."

"You have a point, of course, but you have my permission to encourage Christos! I'll check him first. From what you say, he is a delightful young man."

*

Kennington hotel staff member's curricula vitae always received careful vetting, both locally and in London. Pamela Crumm's first concern was that so many of the staff were new and wondered why Lord Kennington had approved this, although he later denied it. Normally he liked longevity in his staff members, because, in the end, they were known quantities and any unusual activity on their part would be easily identifiable. New staff members' habits were harder to trace. If Christos were correct, at least some of the staff members were not happy with Philippa's management style, but Elspeth did not know which ones. Elspeth had said that for the sake of peace in the hotel she was determined not to approach any of the staff outside Philippa's hearing.

Pamela rose from her desk and, as she often did in the few quiet moments she had during a day, turned to look at the slow turning of the London Eye at the edge of her office window overlooking the River Thames. At first many people had considered the vast wheel an abomination, but in time the

British public had taken to the slow thrills it offered to anyone willing to pay dearly for the thirty minute ride that gave a view of much of central London below, including Buckingham Palace and Houses of Parliament. Pamela loved the wheel and often at weekends paid to ride on it and look out over the city of her birth. She had travelled around the world on hotel business but loved no city more than her own.

Pamela returned to her desk, leaned her small frame back into her chair and considered her life. At her age, she had long come to terms with her circumstance in life. Her physical limitations, being small and bent, had never affected her mind. She had risen alongside Eric Kennington to the pinnacle of his hotel empire and wielded almost as much power as he did in the running of the Kennington Organisation. Together Eric and she shared ninety-five per cent of the stock; he had fifty, she forty-five. His wife owned two per cent; his two children owned one and a half per cent each, the profits of which were put in trust for their education. Being an older father, Eric's relationship with his children was often a bit rocky. Pamela was sometimes called in to keep the peace in the Kennington family, although she never told anyone this. She wondered if he could cajole the family into keeping their shares if she sold out. She had never tested this, nor had she mentioned the possibility of divesting her shares to any other person, including Elspeth Duff.

Pamela's phone rang and she looked at her console. Lord Kennington had arrived for the day, and Pamela was distracted. Therefore she did not immediately follow up on the task Elspeth had requested.

10

Elspeth was tapping the keys on her laptop when her phone rang. She set her jaw, hoping Philippa Allard-Thorpe was not calling her, and was relieved when the person behind the voice at the other end of the line introduced herself.

"It's Carolyn Wellborne here."

Elspeth took a moment to recall the name and finally realised Carolyn was the wife of the British High Commissioner in Cyprus.

"Tom has sent a note, but I wanted to extend the invitation to you as well."

Elspeth warmed to the deep and friendly voice on the line. She replied with honesty. "In my line of work, I seldom get invited to diplomatic events, although many ambassadors and high commissioners pass through our hotels."

"Probably not British ones," Carolyn replied with a chuckle. "They keep us on such a short shoestring these days that we couldn't possibly afford Kennington hotel prices. Few of us are rich anymore. Diplomacy has become a career, not a pastime."

Elspeth wondered if Carolyn used that phrase often but did not care. She sensed that the Wellbornes, like Richard and Marjorie Munro, preferred life reminiscent of the nineteenth century, when diplomats lived on both their charm and personal fortunes.

Carolyn continued. "I want to ask you to come a bit earlier than the other guests so that Tom and I can get to know you before the others arrive. The official dinner begins at seven. Do come at six and have a sherry with us beforehand."

Elspeth accepted the invitation with genuine pleasure. "May I call you Carolyn, or is that too American?"

"Carolyn and Tom and Elspeth seem totally appropriate, especially after the glowing reports from Richard."

Elspeth flushed and was glad that the conversation was taking place over the telephone and not in person. "You mustn't listen to Richard. He and I have been friends for a long time, and we Scots stick together."

"We'll send a car for you. The affair is informal, which means we will not be dressing for the evening."

Elspeth was relieved because she did not have evening clothes with her. As she changed for dinner, she chose carefully from the things that she had brought to Cyprus and decided to wear her most expensive gold jewellery. Richard, she thought, would not be ashamed of her, and then she questioned why this was so important to her.

The British High Commission in Nicosia was a barricaded fortress, situated on the Turkish-Greek boundary, and Carolyn explained they did not entertain there, but rather at the British Residency, which was near the British High Commission, in the Greek sector of Nicosia.

Tom and Carolyn Wellborne welcomed Elspeth into a small sitting room off the main reception area. The room was comfortably appointed and contained what Elspeth supposed were the Wellbornes' personal mementos, items such as an African mask and an Indonesian shadow puppet, which might spark conversation when other topics were exhausted.

Tom Wellborne reminded Elspeth of Richard Munro, and she felt a pang of loneliness.

After Tom dispensed the sherry, they settled down into some over-stuffed armchairs and fell into easy conversation. Naturally they first spoke of Richard.

"I was delighted when Richard told me you were coming to Cyprus. Tom and I were relieved when he decided to take up the post in Malta. I was quite worried that he would not recover from Marjorie's death," Carolyn confided.

"All of us who knew Marjorie sensed how hard it would be for him," Elspeth responded, wanting to make it clear that she had known Lady Marjorie Munro as well. Elspeth did not want the Wellbornes to think that she was anything other than a friend of both Richard and Marjorie. "Richard and I have known each other since we were teenagers, when he came up from Oxford for two summers to stay with my cousins in Perthshire. He helped me out of several bad jams, particularly when I was at Cambridge. Marjorie and he visited us in Hollywood many times. I think they were fascinated with the life we led there, which was so different from their own. Once we introduced them to several of the stars who were acting in an historic film in which Alistair, my husband at the time, was choreographing the duelling, and they spent a day on set. Most people don't know how long an actor's day lasts. Richard and Marjorie claimed they were quite exhausted at the end of it."

Like most people, the Wellbornes asked more about Hollywood, and Elspeth shared some of her more amusing stories. The hour passed quickly, and at seven they were ushered into the main reception area of the Residency. Elspeth counted twelve guests, but she only recognised one, Brigadier Colin French. Carolyn introduced the others. Soon Elspeth found herself standing beside the brigadier, who was as charming as he was the first time they had met.

"You didn't tell me you knew the Wellbornes," he said, as if she had purposely kept a secret from him.

"I didn't until an hour ago, but we share a common friend."

"So you were asked into the inner sanctum. You should be flattered. Many of the leaders of British expat society in Cyprus would sell half their souls for the same privilege, Philippa being among them. Who is your common friend?"

Elspeth did not like to be questioned like this and so answered blandly, "A friend of my cousin. They were at Oxford together."

The brigadier pressed the connection. "Oh? Who is your cousin? Is he in the FCO?"

"No, simply a farmer in Scotland." Elspeth did not mention that her cousin was the Earl of Tay, a small businessman who inherited the family farm that had been impoverished for several generations until his sister and her husband had taken over the everyday running of affairs there. The farm now prospered, but Colin did not need to know that either. She felt the brigadier would have immediately latched on to the mention of a title in her family and become more attentive to her than she wanted him to be. Thankfully the American trade envoy, who had heard Elspeth had spent time in California, interrupted them. Colin French drifted apart from them, much to Elspeth's relief. Even discussing the latest natural disaster in America seemed better than being probed about her family background.

Her relief, however, was short lived. Elspeth was seated next to Colin at dinner, but by now he seemed less inquisitive, perhaps because of the influence of drink. During dinner

Elspeth turned the topic to Cyprus and asked his advice on local activities that might amuse teenaged boys. She would pass on to Joanna Colton any tips he might offer in hopes that she would turn her energy into entertaining her own boys and not the entire delegation. He was filled with suggestions, including one that he meet her tomorrow for lunch at one of the local Nicosian restaurants that had exceptional Turkish food, which would serve as a contrast to the Greek meal they had shared at the hotel earlier. Caught off guard, Elspeth accepted before she considered the invitation might carry more meaning than him merely trying to be helpful. Although during their lunch at the Kennington Nicosia she had indicated that he might work with her over the next several months, they had come to no formal agreement. However, as the dinner progressed, the brigadier subtly intimated that he would like to know Elspeth better on a personal basis.

The meal ended shortly before ten, the American envoy claiming jet lag and the need to prepare for talks next day. Polite diplomatic noises were made and soon everyone took their departure. Carolyn Wellborne drew Elspeth aside. "Come in for a final nightcap. Habitually I make mine Perrier, but Tom prefers a brandy. Then I'll get the car to take you back to the hotel."

The High Commissioner was saying the required farewells to his guests as Elspeth and Carolyn retreated into the library.

Carolyn spoke first. "I am terribly sorry to have paired you with the brigadier. He seemed quite set on capturing your attention."

"Perhaps. I met him earlier at the hotel. He was introduced as someone who could help me learn about Cyprus and provide information to the families of the British delegation staying there."

"The brigadier has quite an eye for any unattached female of our age."

"A fortune hunter? Then I've nothing to fear because I have no fortune."

"You can be sure he will be looking you up on the internet as soon as he gets home this evening."

Elspeth laughed. "I don't think there is anything to look up."

Carolyn Wellborne frowned. "Does he know about your connections with Richard or with Hollywood?"

"I shouldn't think so. Who would have told him?" Elspeth was certain that her past was a total unknown on Cyprus.

"That irksome manager at the hotel?"

Elspeth wondered at Carolyn's description of Philippa and how Carolyn knew her. Her face must have registered confusion because Carolyn replied, "Nicosia has a tightly knit expat community. One cannot even brush alongside it without becoming known. Be careful with Colin French, Elspeth, and most of all with Philippa Allard-Thorpe."

*

After Elspeth took her leave, Carolyn Wellborne turned to her husband. "So that is who Richard has chosen to take Marjorie's place."

"What makes you say that, my dear? Elspeth seems pleasant enough, but, of course, Marjorie was very special."

"Elspeth is definitely amusing and sophisticated, and she dresses beautifully. She is not at all bad looking, really, although her nose is a bit too pointed and her jaw definitely too firmly set, and short hair, even as well cut as hers, does not suit her. But, in the end, she is definitely too fiercely independent and that will not do for Richard. He needs someone to take care of him." Having made her pronouncement, Carolyn Wellborne excused herself and set off to bed.

11

When Colin French picked Elspeth up outside the Kennington Nicosia, he told her he had carefully chosen a small restaurant on the Turkish side of Nicosia. He had warned her to bring her passport, and they passed through the checkpoint with the briefest of formalities. "Enjoy your lunch, Brigadier," one of the United Nations guards said and winked.

Once over the Green Line, they passed several well-occupied and busy restaurants but did not stop. Finally they came to the outskirts of the city centre. The restaurant Colin had selected was unpretentious, having only a few tables inside and several more outside. The cloths on the tables were clean but obviously had seen many years of use. A lopsided sunscreen shielded the outdoor area.

The proprietor greeted the brigadier loudly and warmly in Turkish and then turned towards Elspeth, taking her hand in his huge one.

"So you are the brigadier's new lady and a very beautiful one too."

Elspeth grinned widely, which Richard always said gave a touch of beauty to her face, but she decried his description.

"No, I am not. The brigadier is helping me out on a business matter, and, because I am visiting Cyprus for the first time, he promised me some excellent Turkish food," she said.

"We have the best in all Northern Nicosia," the proprietor assured her. "You must come again and bring all your English friends."

The brigadier clapped the proprietor on the shoulder. "You must be careful, my friend. Mrs Duff is from Scotland, and sometimes the Scottish and English are like the Greek and Turkish Cypriots, from a nation divided by history and tradition."

"Fair lady, I mean no offence." The proprietor put his hands together as if in prayer and bowed deeply to her several times.

Elspeth laughed at the boastful Turk, whose enthusiasm for life was contagious. "Don't worry. I actually live most of the time in London and have no strong political feelings about Scottish separatism, which we call devolution."

He led them through the main restaurant and onto a patio beyond to a secluded table in a far corner. Elspeth wondered if Colin had requested this.

"Come and sit. I will order for you, as today we have a special dish that cannot be resisted," the proprietor said." He described in detail the marinade for the skewered lamb, the delicate way the rice was prepared and the variety of fresh vegetables. "And you will have wine from my cousin's winery. A special wine I only share with my favourite guests."

The proprietor moved on to greet new guests coming through the door. Elspeth and Colin took seats opposite each other. Colin smiled at her seductively, but she did not return his smile. She searched for something to say that would lead into the intended purpose of their lunch together.

"I expected Cyprus to be like Malta, where I have family, but the scale here is quite different," she said.

Now serious, Colin said he knew Malta and soon was enthusing about the ancient history of both the Maltese and Cypriots, the times of the Crusades, and the various colonisers of both islands. Elspeth was diverted by his dialogue, which she found fascinating, until she saw two guests arrive at the other end of the patio, one of whom she recognised—Michael Driscoll.

Michael's lunch companion was tall and handsome and reminded Elspeth of Gregory Peck, and she tried to remember who recently had mentioned the actor. She and Colin French were sitting at the back of the patio, sheltered partially by an arbour. Elspeth suspected that the new arrivals could not see them, so she felt comfortable asking Colin who the distinguished-looking man was.

"Trouble," Colin said through his teeth. "The tall one, that is. I don't know the other man."

"He is Michael Driscoll from the British delegation staying at the hotel, but why do you say trouble?"

"The other man is Ernest Thorpe, Philippa Allard-Thorpe's ex-husband. I would prefer that he does not see me, as he didn't take kindly to the fact that I dated Philippa after their divorce. He blames Philippa for breaking up the family, and she blames him for causing the accident that blinded their daughter. When Ernest and I have met in the past, he has been distinctly cool, if not downright rude."

"I'm sorry for Cinnamon's sake," Elspeth said. She knew the difficulty her own children had when Alistair Craig and she legally terminated their marriage, even though it ended quietly and without bitterness. How difficult it must have been when things became acrimonious and spilled over into the family relationships afterwards.

The brigadier motioned the waiter to bring the wine and pour two glasses for them.

"You have met Cinnamon," the brigadier said. "Philippa's heart wrenches every time she catches sight of her daughter. Cinnamon is so beautiful, but Philippa can only see her disability. I bleed for Cinnamon, but Philippa won't give up in her hatred towards Ernest, the man she sees as ruining her perfect child." Colin shook his head. "I never had children, but I can't imagine being so rigid about perfection that I could be so unkind to a child."

Although Elspeth already knew the answer to the question she was going to ask, she wanted to hear the reply from a new perspective. "Does Cinnamon ever see her father? Certainly she has limited access to transportation here on the island."

"Philippa attempts to watch her but somehow Cinnamon coerces friends into giving her lifts when she wants to meet her father. Philippa has tried to put a stop to any relationship between them. She has given orders that Ernest should not be allowed in the hotel, and I've heard her berate Cinnamon about contacting Ernest."

Elspeth shook her head and frowned in sorrow. "What an unfortunate situation."

"Yes, I know," said her companion. "I've fought with Philippa many times over this, but she won't budge. In the end, I think, that's the chief reason I no longer enjoy seeing her."

Elspeth looked up at Colin French. She could not make out if he was being honest about making a final break from Philippa or not. Elspeth remembered Philippa's possessive look when she had met her and Colin after they had had lunch together in the hotel. Elspeth did not want to be a voyeur into the past affair between them but felt that Colin might be drawing her into it by his flattering attentions to her. She carefully retracted her hand from the one he had gently laid on top of hers. Carolyn's warning after the party at the Residency about Philippa and Colin came back to Elspeth, and she inwardly cringed. She was confused though because Philippa was the one who recommended Colin as a source of help with the delegation. What could be the reason behind it?

"Tell me more about Ernest Thorpe," Elspeth said.

Colin apparently enjoyed gossiping about people he knew, and as they ate he poured out the Allard-Thorpes' story.

"Ernest has gained international recognition among the archaeologists and ancient historians here, in London, and around the academic world," Colin said. "He has been researching the pre-Hellenic inhabitants of Cyprus since he was a university student in the nineteen seventies, and after his mentor died, he became head of a major excavation near Paphos and a visiting professor at University College London. He has published a number of learned papers and is considered the leading expert in the world on his topic. Philippa came out to Cyprus from America in the mid-nineteen eighties claiming to be a graduate student from an American mid-Western university, although later she told us all she had also trained to be an actress. They met, and she fell for him. He has matured into a striking looking man, but at the time he was all elbows and knees. Philippa decided to take him on as the primary topic of her research, and they were married within the year. A daughter, not Cinnamon, arrived shortly afterwards, although only some of the expat ladies counted the months. Ernest and Philippa became fixtures in the British community, although Ernest still had his head in the first millennium BC."

"How did Ernest react to this?"

"Philippa made him presentable, if that is what you mean, because she wanted the status he brought to their marriage. Unfortunately their daughter died as a toddler. A year later Cinnamon was born. She grew into the beauty you see now, and by the time she was sixteen every young male in the expat community or visiting from Britain made their way to her doorstep."

"I can see why."

"Philippa in the meantime was tiring of Ernest, who from reports other than Philippa's, increasingly disliked his social-climbing wife. Philippa found a position at a small hotel that had once had an excellent reputation but was falling into disrepair. The doyennes of British society on the island said Philippa seduced the owner, who died of a heart attack within a year and left the hotel to her. Ernest, by this time, was the one who was caring for Cinnamon because Philippa had deserted them. Philippa went on to revamp the hotel and make it a fashionable and expensive place where people wanted to be seen. After the accident when Cinnamon was blinded, however, Philippa changed. I only knew her vaguely at the time, but those who seemed to know said she had abandoned her family for bigger pastures. She went abroad, to New York or London, I forget which, and came back six months later waving papers around, proclaiming her accomplishments in the international world of hotel management. Whatever was in those papers held some sort of magic. Philippa was made assistant manager of one of the biggest high-end hotels here. The gossips contended that she had tried to oust the manager there but she was caught at it. Her next stop was the Kennington Nicosia. She stepped in as temporary manager when the original one became ill, and she was promoted to the manager's position when he died. That was about a year ago."

Elspeth listened carefully, taking mental notes. She wanted to corroborate with Pamela what Colin told her about Philippa. Lord Kennington did not hire managers who had less than impeccable credentials. Colin, like all people fond of passing on scandal, might be exaggerating the facts for the sake of a good story, but even gossip contained kernels of truth. An immediate phone call to Pamela Crumm was in order once Elspeth returned to the hotel.

Elspeth debated going over to speak to Michael Driscoll and introducing herself to Ernest Thorpe, but the arrival of Turkish style coffee and a specially prepared baklava delayed her decision. The proprietor waxed eloquently about why his dessert surpassed any other on the island. Elspeth bit into the sweetness of the pastry containing honey, raisins, and nuts and proclaimed it truly magnificent, although she disliked its sugary intensity. Michael Driscoll and Ernest Thorpe left before Elspeth forced down the last saccharine bite.

Colin French remained attentive to the end and, as he dropped Elspeth off at the hotel, asked if she would join him for dinner the following evening. She racked her brain for an excuse to say no but could not think of a ready one. She pleaded the need for an early night instead. Colin was amusing and informative, but Elspeth suspected he wanted a far closer friendship than she did.

Returning to her suite, she turned on her satellite phone and found a voicemail message from Pamela asking her to call London. Elspeth complied hastily.

"Pamela, tell me about Philippa. I have just had a distressing lunch with her one-time male friend, who seems to want to become intimate with me. Ugh. I don't want this happening. Philippa introduced me to a retired brigadier whose name is Colin French. She said Colin was a resource who knew everything worth knowing about Cyprus and who could provide information for ways to entertain the delegation's families. I'm finding that he continually wants to poke into my background, but he has offered to lead a tour of the delegation this weekend to Kantara, a medieval castle on the Turkish side of the island. I can hardly back out."

"What about Philippa?" Pamela asked. "Is she involved?"

"Involved in what?"

"You tell me. What is it that you want to know about Philippa and what does this have to do with the brigadier?"

Elspeth groaned. "I'm rambling, aren't I? Let me clarify because there are really two issues here. Colin, the brigadier, filled me in on the local tittle-tattle concerning Philippa. I know Eric well enough to know he didn't hire Philippa because of her attractive face and manner. Colin implied she has weaselled her way into her management position at the hotel. Please, Pamela, can you find out the real facts for me? I suspect expat gossip is always filled with half-truths, and I know enough to disregard most of it."

"What do you want to know?"

"Why Philippa is now manager of the hotel here."

"That sounds straightforward enough. I'll have to be back in touch because I don't remember the particulars. In fact, I don't remember being involved at all, which is highly unusual."

"Pamela, I'd particularly like to know about the transition between the old manager and the new one. Something happened when Philippa took control. The staff seem rigidly correct, which is not unusual for a Kennington

A Crisis in Cyprus

hotel, but I'm finding them all particularly tense, far beyond what I would expect."

"I see," said the owlish part owner of the Kennington Organisation. "I think I need to pay more attention to the Kennington Nicosia. In the meanwhile, Elspeth, don't let yourself get too entangled with the brigadier or Philippa."

With these words, Elspeth one again recalled Carolyn Wellborne's warning of the night before, and she wondered why Colin French and Philippa Allard-Thorpe evoked such toxic reactions in others.

99

12

The events of the last few days had given Elspeth a headache reminiscent of her days in the hospital in London after she was attacked in Singapore. She thought of ringing Carolyn Wellborne to find the name of a doctor in Nicosia but was afraid Carolyn would ask what Elspeth's symptoms were. Elspeth did not want to become fodder for the British expatriate tongue-waggers in Cyprus, so instead she dug into her papers and found the card that her doctor in London had given her before she left for Cyprus. Elspeth opened her laptop and typed in the email address. She set the volume of her incoming alert on high and prepared a cool, wet facecloth, which she applied to her temples. Refreshing the cloth, she lay down on her bed and hoped the doctor would be in touch soon. An hour passed before her computer let out its characteristic ping signifying a new email. Relief being in sight, she rose and hoped the message was not an auto-response. She was grateful it was not. Her doctor recommended a Cypriot doctor with whom he had corresponded many times on the subject of lingering trauma. Elspeth rang the number, and the doctor ordered a prescription for her, which was soon delivered to the hotel. She spent the rest of the day in bed and ordered room service in the evening. She surveyed the DVDs left in her suite for her use and chose the classic Hitchcock film

Thirty-nine Steps, which she had seen many times before and would not tax her attention or intellect.

In the morning she felt refreshed and considered contacting Colin French to cancel their dinner engagement for that evening. She could use her headache as an excuse, but again she did not want anyone on Cyprus to know about her previous injury. She decided she was neglecting the delegation, so she made her way to their dining room. It was still early, and Michael Driscoll was alone there. Elspeth poured herself some coffee, served herself a bowl of fresh fruit from the sideboard and took a seat next to him.

"I saw you at lunch yesterday," she said, as she took a bite of melon. "Was that Ernest Thorpe you were talking to? I browsed through one of his books before coming out here and recognised his photograph from the back cover. I've visited my aunt many times in Malta, whose history has always fascinated me. The history here has similarities but is also so different."

Michael Driscoll looked startled at her forwardness. He put down the newspaper he was reading and turned his attention to her.

"Yes, Ernest and I go back a long way. His writings, as you must have noted, are highly literate as well as accurately researched. His long residence on the island and his intense devotion to his work is apparent in his writing. I think the only thing he loves more than his work is his daughter."

Elspeth sensed that Michael Driscoll was not one to make light conversation, but he had brought up the subject of Cinnamon so Elspeth decided to pursue the topic.

She took a large sip of her coffee and, hoping to appear off-handed, asked, "Does he see his daughter often? I've met her several times here at the hotel, and she seems quite bound to her mother."

"You've chosen an appropriate word, Ms Duff. You said 'bound' and that is exactly the word Ernest used with me yesterday. His ex-wife forbids him to see Cinnamon and has barred him from entering the hotel. He asked me to keep an eye on Cinnamon. What a silly name. Ernest says it was Philippa's idea. Ernest preferred Ariadne, Artemis, or Athena, but he was overruled. Overruling is a habit with Philippa, according to Ernest. I obligingly listened to his complaints yesterday because he seemed to need to talk. We're good friends, you see. His situation with his ex-wife and daughter is worthy of an ancient Greek drama."

Elspeth nodded. "What a tragedy it must be for him as well as for Cinnamon."

"He has suffered the worst tragedies a man could have, first the death of his first daughter and then the accident with Cinnamon. By his inattention, he was the cause of his second child's blindness, although he was not officially charged. Do you know the story?"

"I've heard the gist," Elspeth acknowledged, "but tell me more."

"He was driving but not paying attention to the road. He'd lived here long enough to know what a dangerous practice that is. Drivers make their own rules, but it was Ernest who carelessly crossed over into the other driver's lane. Cinnamon lost her sight and Ernest lost his marriage. Philippa blamed him. She is a heartless . . . well, 'you know what'. Sophia doesn't like expletives, so I try to avoid them." Michael's voice was constrained. "Ernest was heartbroken and still is. His work suffered for several years, but recently he has gone back to it with gusto. Homer was blind as were other figures in the ancient world. Ernest wants to find evidence that even before the Greeks blindness was considered to give people deeper insight into the world. That's his current research."

Elspeth had not expected Michael to speak so openly. She seized the opportunity this gave her. "I would like to meet Ernest Thorpe. Can you arrange it for me?"

"With pleasure. I plan to see him tomorrow and will ask him. He has a new section of his archaeological dig he wants to show me. He's picking me up at nine, since we have no morning session tomorrow. I'll tell him you would like to meet him."

"I'm not presuming, am I?"

"Absolutely not. One thing you will learn is that Ernest loves to talk about his work. He will also be delighted to have another person who can fill him in on Cinnamon."

"Do you know if he ever sees Cinnamon despite Philippa's ban?"

"Whenever he can, or whenever he can release her from, how did you put it, Philippa's bondage."

Their private conversation was abruptly interrupted by Sophia and her children, whose enthusiasm took their father's attention. Elspeth bid Michael goodbye, and he promised to leave her a message regarding her request to meet Ernest Thorpe.

As Elspeth left the dining room, a voice called out to her. Bitki Mitsui touched Elspeth's shoulder and asked in a quiet voice if they might go out in the garden together.

The morning was cool, and the low rays of the sun invaded the garden and touched the flowers and leaves there.

Bitki hugged herself. "When I was young, I used to go into our garden when the sun first came up. I imagined I was

Queen Berengaria come to wed King Richard the Lionheart. Did you know Berengaria was crowned on Cyprus and was the only English queen ever crowned outside Britain? I didn't know at the time what a sad life she had. He was possibly gay according to careful reading of history. Their marriage probably was never consummated, and, as you must know, they had no children. What a royal crisis that caused. I didn't know about such things at the time, so the idea of coming out to Cyprus to be crowned the Queen of England seemed magical to me. I didn't, however, ask you out here to tell you my childhood fantasies."

Elspeth raised her now clear head and smelled the perfume of the morning, cool and crisp and fragrant with the flowers. Soon the heat would surround them but for now Elspeth enjoyed the coolness. She smiled at Bitki in the way she would have with her own daughter.

"I assumed not, although thank you for telling me about Queen Berengaria," she said. "I didn't realise she had a connection with Cyprus. I find it remarkable how many of history's most famed warriors were gay or bisexual, Julius Caesar, Alexander and many others, but, Bitki, tell me what is on your mind. You seem worried."

Bitki screwed up her dark face. "I am. Onan tells me that I am jittery for no reason, but because of my father's profession I am more sensitive than he is to any irregularities in our daily routine. I decided it would be best if we stored some of the more sensitive papers in the hotel safe, and, at Father's advice, I put them in a folder in an unusual way. When I recovered them last evening, the sheet I had put upside down was right side up. Someone had been through the file. How many people, Elspeth, have access to the safe?"

Elspeth stiffened when she heard this. "Hotel safes, even in our hotels, are not fool proof. The numerical combination to the lock is available to the staff at the reception desk. The manager and assistant manager and the head of hotel security know it as well. In most of our hotels, and I can't think that the Kennington Nicosia would be an exception, the combination is changed frequently, and always when an employee with access to the safe leaves our employment."

"Does anyone else have access?" Bitki asked.

"No, not to my knowledge, so your concern is a real one. You're intimating that not only was your file taken out of the safe, but it was also read. Bitki, can you tell me what consequences this might have?"

"When I put the documents in the safe, I made sure nothing contained in them was classified. Father asked me to include some information that was untrue, what he calls 'misinformation'. That way if that item surfaced later, we could find out who received it and trace it back. I was reluctant to do this, so instead I changed the spelling of the name of one of the people at the FCO. I am waiting to see if this spelling ever surfaces."

Elspeth laughed. "Your father has trained you well."

Bitki crinkled up her black eyes, attractively outlined with a thin line of kohl. "Perhaps too well. I'm always suspicious. Onan laughs at me about it. I think because his grandmother's life was one of such great humiliation, he considers the petty nuances of diplomacy a bit ridiculous."

Elspeth's curiosity was peaked. "Am I being forward in asking about his background? Onan is a Turkish name but surely Mitsui is Japanese."

"You're right. Onan's grandfather was a member of the Japanese ambassadorial delegation to Ankara in the Second

World War. If you remember, Turkey remained neutral during the war until it was obvious the Allies would win, and therefore the Japanese had an embassy in Ankara throughout most of the war. The story is like *Madama Butterfly*. Onan's mother thought she had married one of the Japanese consuls, but when Turkey declared for the Allies, he returned to his Japanese wife. Later they were both killed in the bombings over Tokyo. According to Onan's grandmother, her so-called husband was hedging both his bets. Had the Axis won, he would have returned to Japan and claimed an indiscretion. If the Allies won, he would declare he had a Turkish family and denounce his Japanese wife. Unfortunately he got caught in the middle. Onan's grandmother was disgraced nonetheless. She was taken under the wing of a British officer's wife, who took her to England, where Onan's father was born. You could imagine what it was like for a half-caste illegitimate Turkish-Japanese child in Britain in the late nineteen forties. The officer's wife, however, was wealthy and had influence in high places. She circulated the story that Onan's father was the son of a Turkish pasha and his mother a geisha, which was totally untrue, and soon had the child enrolled in one of the best preparatory schools in London and later Harrow and Oxford. Onan's father, rather than being ashamed of his roots, was delighted with the deception. My father and he are a pair, believe me. They met in London at a conference on Cyprus in nineteen seventy-four, the year of the Turkish invasion, and immediately became friends. The rest you can guess."

"It all sounds Shakespearean to me," Elspeth said smiling. "I must admit I love good stories, and this is one of the most interesting I have heard in a long time. Thank you for sharing it with me."

It was Bitki's turn to smile. "I love the story too, and I love Onan's father, and also his mother, who, is Irish—from Belfast. What an odd mixture we bring to our child, but, in naming him, we have chosen to remind him most of all of his Turkish roots. He is half Turkish on my side and a quarter Turkish on his father's side. The rest is a jumble."

Elspeth nodded. "I applaud you for that. You could have given him an English name."

"Nowadays foreign names have a certain panache, but we didn't do it for that reason. Azai must be proud of his heritage. The twenty-first century is about the world and the mixed up mixture of people in it, not the ethnic purity of the British Isles a hundred years ago. I'm delighted to be a member of that mixture, and I want Azai to be so as well. Onan, Azai, and I are British by nationality and loyalty, but we are also citizens of the world."

Elspeth looked into Bitki's eyes and saw the intense passion in them. Elspeth admired what she saw because it transcended national prejudice. She had seen too much bigotry in her travels around the world and times at Kennington hotels. Bitki and Onan were members of the rising stars in the FCO, and they did belong to the world and would make a difference there. Elspeth, however, needed to focus on the more immediate problem of the compromised documents.

"Bitki, the main reason I am here is for your safety. If there is anyone who has violated your request for the secure storage of your documents, I'll make it my priority to find out who that person is. Thank you for sharing your concern and also the history of Onan's family."

Bitki looked up and with a nod acknowledged her appreciation of Elspeth's concern.

Bitki left Elspeth alone in the garden. The sun had moved higher in the sky and the warmth of the day followed behind it. Elspeth found a bench in the shade and considered what she had heard from Michael Driscoll and Bitki Mitsui. Both had cast, perhaps inadvertently, aspersions as to the seamless running of the Kennington Nicosia. Philippa's unresolved relationship with Cinnamon's father and the unsecured condition of Bitki's documents buzzed inside Elspeth's head like an annoying wasp.

Elspeth sat back and decided to enjoy a moment of the morning sun before she returned to puzzle over the problem she had just uncovered. She must have fallen asleep, because she suddenly became aware of loud voices coming from an open window in Philippa's office.

"I forbid you to see her any more!"

Elspeth recognised Philippa's voice, but she could not identify the voice of the other person in the room. The second voice was choked with anger.

"You can't forbid me to do anything," a low baritone voice growled.

"I can see to it that you never come here again. I have my ways!"

"You do, Philippa, you bitch! Can't you stay out of anyone's life? Do you need to control everyone, even her?"

"You can leave now! Get out! Go!" Philippa's voice was hysterical.

"I will leave, but I want you to know this. Someday someone will murder you for your controlling, vicious ways!"

A door slammed. Elspeth hurried from the garden into the lobby to see if she could identify the owner of the second voice. No one came out of the office area into the public areas of the hotel, and so she assumed he had gone out the back way.

Elspeth decided retreating was her best course and immediately fled to her suite. The rage in Philippa's voice had been bloodcurdling, and Elspeth wanted to avoid meeting her at all costs.

Elspeth sat at her desk and wondered what to make of the conversation she had overheard. First she must record it in her log and send it to Pamela in London. She grabbed a note pad and scribbled down the words as closely as she could remember them. The man's voice had been irate, although Elspeth considered his murderous threat was only uttered in the rage of the moment. Calm and cool Philippa clearly aroused great passion in others, particularly this man. Fear spread through Elspeth. Was the man Ernest Thorpe? That would be the logical assumption. He must have slipped into Philippa's office without being detected. Elspeth wanted to find Michael Driscoll again and ask him if Ernest Thorpe was the sort of person who was likely to make threats like the one she had just heard.

She took up her written notes, and, opening her laptop, transcribed them into an email, which she sent both to Pamela and to herself. She followed with a copy to her son in San Francisco, asking in the covering email that he relegate it to a backup file he had on his computer for the noted items she sent him. She knew he never read her confidential correspondence, both at her request and because he had little interest in his mother's work life.

Then she returned to the situation at hand. How long had it been since she had spoken to Pamela directly in London? Less than forty-eight hours, although it seemed an eternity. Her notes did not yet contain the information she had learned about Ernest Thorpe from Colin French and from Michael Driscoll, nor Bitki's concerns about the material in the safe. She wondered if she should share her misgivings about the conversation between Philippa and the unknown man. Elspeth picked up her satellite phone, tapped in the security code, and rang through to London. She left a voice mail message asking Pamela to read her email and said they needed to talk.

13

Pamela Crumm had not been neglecting Elspeth's request to find out more about Philippa Allard-Thorpe. The selection of a manager of a Kennington hotel was a lengthy process, always involving the personal approval of Lord Kennington. Managers were, for the most part, chosen from among the ranks of the assistant managers who had caught his lordship's attention. Pamela often added her endorsement, but the final selection ultimately belonged to Eric. She knew the reason for this and accepted it. If anything went wrong, he took full responsibility.

He seldom made a mistake in choosing his managers, but Pamela had suspected for some time that he had in the case of Philippa Allard-Thorpe. Pamela tapped a password into her computer and brought up Philippa's confidential personnel file. Philippa did not have as many years experience as most of the Kennington managers, but her references were first-rate and her training impeccable. Besides, she had served with distinction as Georgios Konstantinidis's assistant manager at the Kennington Nicosia. Nothing in her file should have aroused Elspeth's uneasiness nor justified Pamela's sense that something was wrong.

Still Pamela was not satisfied. Instead of reading the entire file on the computer, she rang down to the personnel department and had a hard copy of the documents in the archives sent up to her. She decided she needed a quiet time alone to review them. She rang the head of personnel and told him she would be taking the file home with her that night. The Kennington Organisation's file tracking system was cast in stone, even for a business partner in the organisation, and Pamela was required to follow the set routine to sign out the file.

Business kept Pamela at her desk until just before ten o'clock. The summer night was creeping up to the twentieth floor where she worked, and she paused a minute to watch strings of lights on the boats plying up and down the Thames and the soothing motion of the illuminated pods of the London Eye. She rang the security guard to say she was leaving. She took advantage of a privilege she seldom evoked and requested the company Jaguar to take her home rather than taking a taxi. The driver had driven her many times and knew she preferred a silent trip. He greeted her and held the door for her and then allowed her to submerge herself into her own thoughts. Settling into the back of the Jaguar, she slipped off her fashionable shoes and rubbed her fingers along the fine leather upholstery. The driver might have been surprised had he known she was contemplating what microwavable meal her housekeeper might have left for her in the freezer.

The car swung into an underground car park under the South Bank block of flats where she lived, and the driver made sure she entered the lift safely. Her garden penthouse was one of the real luxuries, other than clothing, that Pamela allowed herself. She had bought it well before apartments in Central London became unaffordable and the South Bank fashionable. She had poured a handsome amount of money and effort into making her new home an ultra-modern space. She had incorporated every device that her architect had recommended or that she had seen in design magazines. The entire house was programmed so that she only needed to touch a button and her bath would begin to fill, her bed would be warmed, and the music she had selected would be played at exactly the volume she wanted. Lights and window blinds were controlled for the time of day and season of the year. Pamela was a small person and consequently all the counters, appliances and fixtures fitted her diminutive stature. In the public spaces she allowed some of the furniture to be at the normal height, but in her private spaces all the furniture was made to match her small size and tastes in physical comfort. She had made the space her own, as she had long ago realised she would not be sharing it with another person. Few people were invited into this place, Elspeth Duff being among the few who were privileged to do so.

Pamela pushed several buttons and the lighting came up, one of Alicia de la Rocha's Mozart piano concerti softly filled the sitting room, and the curtains were silently drawn. Her bath was automatically being poured, and her housekeeper had laid out her silk nightgown and new fleece dressing gown. She emerged from the bath refreshed and made her way to her kitchen. A tray was waiting for her and a note from Jack suggested she might try the vegetarian Moroccan stew he had left in the fridge and required only two and a half minutes warming in the microwave. She found a bottle of Sancerre resting on the bottom rack next to a chilling wine glass. Pamela chuckled and was glad that out of all the applicants for housekeeper she had chosen Jack, who by night was the bartender in a gay bar.

The screw top on the wine bottle was loosened and the stew was in a microwavable bowl covered with cling film. A dish of freshly sliced fruit ready to eat was beside them.

Pamela made her quick preparations and settled into her favourite armchair.

Savouring the complex flavours of the stew and sipping the cold wine, she drew Philippa's personnel file from her briefcase and opened it with both anticipation and anxiety. She turned the pages slowly, searching each one for some hint of impropriety. Georgios Konstantinidis, the original manager of the hotel, had written glowingly of how Philippa helped him in the last year of his tenure as manager at the Kennington Nicosia. The letter was dated two weeks before he retired and was on Kennington Nicosia stationery. The signature was rather shaky, but Georgios was leaving his job because of a minor stroke he had suffered, and such handwriting was to be expected.

Next Pamela turned to the transcript from the Cornell University School of Hotel Administration, where Philippa reported she had received a degree in hotel management and had graduated with the highest of honours, but Pamela noticed that the transcript was not embossed with the school seal but simply rubberstamped. She would check on the authenticity of the transcript in the morning.

She went on to the recommendations. One was from a manager at the Plaza Hotel in New York on stiff hotel letter-headed stationery and another from the Waldorf Astoria. The recommendations for Philippa Allard-Thorpe, who had served as an intern at both places, were outstanding. Pamela wondered, however, how she could verify these, since she knew that both of the writers of these letters were now dead. She felt she might be feeling overly suspicious but decided to call the current managers of both hotels to make sure that Philippa had actually trained at each one and that the recommendations were genuine. Fortunately she knew both the current managers and had the numbers of their direct lines on her laptop computer. She first called the Plaza, but the manager had left for the day. She would phone him the following afternoon, London time. She knew, however, that the manager of the Waldorf often stayed late in order to enjoy the evening events at his hotel and greet the celebrities who dined there. He might still be available.

She used his direct line and reached his personal assistant, who recognised her voice and put her straight through.

"Franz, Pamela Crumm here."

"Pamela, good to hear your voice. How is Eric?"

"Completely involved in a new acquisition, and revelling in it. I have a favour to ask."

"Ask away," the slightly accented voice said.

"When did your last manager retire?"

"Shortly before nine eleven."

"Was he at the hotel full time before that?"

"No, he was in a small plane accident that summer, in July, I think, and his right side was paralyzed. He was never able to return to duty here. Our loss was a great one."

"Do you recall if he was right handed?"

"Certainly. He always made a joke about not being able to do anything with his left hand, which was true."

Pamela looked down at the recommendation in her hand. The letter was dated the fifteenth of August two thousand and one, and the signature was firm and slanted to the left. She thanked Franz and sat for a moment staring at the thick piece of paper in front of her.

Who, thought Pamela, can I contact who might be still alive and who knew Philippa before she came to the Kennington Nicosia? Hadn't Elspeth mentioned something about Philippa taking over a hotel in Nicosia before she was employed at the

Kennington Nicosia? Pamela ruffled through the pages to see if she could find any mention of this. She found nothing in the file. She went back to Georgios Konstantinidis's letter and read it carefully. No matter how good a report, every letter of recommendation that she had ever read had some caveat, no matter how small. No employee was perfect, but there was no hint of any fault in Georgios' letter criticising Philippa. This puzzled her. Suddenly she remembered Georgios' eyesight had been affected by his stroke. Could the letter have been doctored before he signed it and if so, had Philippa herself done it? Pamela was beginning to suspect so. She wondered if Georgios was still alive and whether he was competent enough to remember.

Pamela now knew that all the references would need checking. She did not look forward this job, but most of all she did not relish confronting Eric Kennington if her suppositions proved true.

*

In Malta Richard was experiencing his own doubts. Carolyn Wellborne had rung from Nicosia and invited him to pay a visit to them, but he felt uncomfortable with the invitation. Although he had known Tom Wellborne for many years and they had worked together in Pakistan, neither Richard nor his late wife, Marjorie, had been close to the Wellbornes outside of official duties. Marjorie was a kind woman, but she often said Carolyn was not, despite her outward friendliness. Richard had not heard from the Wellbornes when Lady Marjorie died. In his zeal to make Elspeth feel comfortable and connected in Nicosia, Richard had contacted them, but now he thought that might have been a mistake.

He sat on the fourth floor terrace of Marjorie's cousin's house in Sliema, where he had made his home in Malta, and looked out over the Mediterranean. The wind was coming up from the northeast, and he feared it would gain strength and bring heavy rains by morning, which would upset his plans to go sailing with an old friend visiting from Devon.

In his mind he replayed a conversation with Carolyn about Elspeth's visit to the Residency. She gushed. She and Tom had loved Elspeth at first sight, Carolyn had said, which Richard sincerely doubted. Elspeth could be engaging, a skill she used at the hotels, but her innate Scottish reserve, even though tempered by many years of living in California, did not inspire instant love, although it might be met with admiration. Carolyn implied that Elspeth was breaking the hearts of all the eligible bachelors of a certain age in Cyprus and that, if Richard really valued his relationship with Elspeth, he should come to Nicosia immediately to stake his claim. He ground his teeth at this suggestion. He had known Elspeth for over forty years, loving her most of that time, but she always kept herself just beyond his reach except in that rare moment when she revealed to him who murdered Malcolm Buchanan. Richard had loved Marjorie, too, but in a different way. Marjorie made a suitable diplomat's wife. She had grace and good manners, and her independent wealth had meant she and Richard could always live in comfort beyond the means of a diplomat's salary. Elspeth was filled with life, had a remarkable intellect, and had craved out her independence, even as a young woman. She would not have settled for the life Richard Munro had chosen to live, and, knowing this, he never had the courage to ask her directly to do so after he had met her in Malta.

During the days he sat beside Elspeth's bed in the hospital in London, when she was recovering from her head wounds, and he watched her slip in and out of consciousness, he thought of all the ways he might persuade Elspeth to love him. He added up his assets. He was an aging diplomat, still slender both through genetics and an active life. He particularly enjoyed sailing, which he knew Elspeth did not like because she was prone to seasickness. His hair was now becoming steely and he had it cut short. His face was thin and his nose was a bit too long and narrow, characteristic of his mother's aristocratic family. His wrinkles were a bit too deep, thanks to many years in the tropical sun and on the ocean. He was a good conversationalist and loved to tell stories about people whom he had encountered in his life. He had the skills of calm negotiation and careful management, which benefitted him professionally, and had earned him a knighthood, one generally given to successful career diplomats. He doubted, however, that any of these qualities would rate high on Elspeth's scale of romantic material. She had chosen to become engaged to a vivacious and quixotic student at Cambridge, who was murdered on the day of their engagement. She worked for Scotland Yard briefly and later eloped to Hollywood and married a fight and weapons choreographer in the film industry there. She had spent many years in the social set of film stars and dabbled in their petty mysteries. After her marriage fell apart, she had returned to detection full-time and had spent the last seven years dealing with undesirable characters who came into the Kennington hotels. What role would he be able to play in her life? And now, if Carolyn were right, she was seeking attention elsewhere.

How could he, as Carolyn Wellborne put it, make his claim? The words rankled him, but the thought that Elspeth might find someone else worried him. He thought that in the last year and a half she was growing fonder of him, and he had been able to provide her with support that he felt she had begun to value. She had said so many kind words to him, had implied her warming feelings towards him, had asked his help in seeking Malcolm's murderer and had clung to him when she had learned the truth. She had kissed him tenderly more than once and touched him endearingly many times, but she had never spoken of love. He told her of his love for her and even obliquely mentioned marriage. She had acknowledged his intentions with a smile but demurred from giving him an answer. Would going to Cyprus give him any advantage? Was it worth the risk? But if he did not make an attempt, what future, if any, would he have with Elspeth?

Perhaps the increasing force of the wind had led him to these pessimistic thoughts. He went inside to the over-furnished drawing room, which contained numerous treasures that Marjorie's cousin had accumulated over the years. The atmosphere was stifling, and the multitude of things crowded around him as if mocking his loneliness. He thought about Marjorie and wondered what she would advise him to do. She had never been possessive and, as she lay dying, urged him not to spend the rest of his life alone. Her death had left him empty, until he had met Elspeth in Malta over sixteen months ago, where he had fallen in love with her all over again, the way he had in the Scottish Highlands when they were both teenagers.

He poured a single malt whisky from an ornate cut glass decanter into a crystal glass and settled into a musty armchair complete with a yellowing antimacassar of intricate Maltese lace. He knew he loved Elspeth more than any other living person, and he could no longer settle loving her from afar. If Carolyn wanted to be a matchmaker, let her be. He was going to Cyprus and the sooner the better.

14

Elspeth was making her way across the lobby to her suite to prepare for her dinner with Colin when Sophia Driscoll came rushing towards her. Since Sophia usually had her three children in tow and now was childless, Elspeth suspected that some crisis was at hand.

"Ms Duff, I was hoping to find you," Sophia said rather breathlessly. "May we talk?" Her eyes were pleading.

"Come up to my rooms. I have a dinner engagement in about an hour, but we can talk before then," Elspeth said.

Rather than using the hallway, they crossed the garden to the private set of stairs that led to Elspeth's suite because she did not want any of the staff to report Sophia's dismay to Philippa Allard-Thorpe.

A large bouquet of yellow roses edged with red greeted them in Elspeth's sitting room. She did not stop to read the note with it but instead offered a chair to Sophia, who collapsed into it as if the burden she was carrying was too heavy for her to stand much longer.

"I've convinced Joanna to take the children for half an hour, so I can't stay long, but I had to tell you something, since I understand you are here for us and not for her." Sophia said in one breath.

"Who? Joanna?" Elspeth knew Joanna could be overbearing, but Elspeth did not want to become involved in personality clashes among members of the delegation and their families.

"No, not Joanna, the high and mighty Ms Allard-Thorpe."

"What's the difficulty?"

Sophia ground her teeth and growled. "She's always snooping around, watching the children and me. She's critical of anything the children do. Gregory can be spirited at times, but there is no harm in him. Hermione and Kallista are usually self-contained but occasionally they can be a bit noisy, especially when playing with their brother. I keep them confined to our area of the hotel to the greatest extent possible, but several times they have gone into the lobby. *She* is always right there, berating them. I'll not tell you what the children call her, but I have admonished them for using language like that for people outside the Harry Potter books!"

Elspeth looked closely at Sophia and wondered what she was like when she started working for Bitki's father before she had children. Sophia had strong Hellenic features and beautiful deep brown eyes, but she now verged on overweight. Her jet-black hair had whispers of grey, which she did not try to disguise. As she talked, she spoke beautiful English, but her gestures reminded Elspeth of the local women she had watched on the streets of Nicosia. Elspeth wondered what this lively woman had seen in the bookish Michael Driscoll and why she had married him, but years before Elspeth had come to the conclusion that she was no expert on marriage and did not hazard a guess.

Elspeth came to from her reverie to hear Sophia say, " . . . and there are times when I could strangle Ms Allard-Thorpe!"

This second threat on Philippa's life in as many days startled Elspeth. Wasn't there an ancient Greek play where a mother had murdered someone to protect her children?

She always got the Greek tragedies muddled. She must ask Michael Driscoll when she next saw him, without mentioning Sophia, of course. More disturbing, however, was the animosity Philippa stirred up in the people around her.

Elspeth tried to soothe Sophia by saying Philippa was a new manager and needed to hone her skills in dealing with children in the hotel, since usually there were none. Elspeth also suggested that once the children were enrolled in the British School in Nicosia for the autumn term, they probably would be spending most of their time away from the hotel, which might alleviate the situation altogether. She hoped Sophia and Joanna would find more activities for the children away from the hotel for the rest of the summer months. She made Sophia a cup of tea and found a packet of shortbread, which she opened and offered to Sophia, who took one without seeming to notice. The tea seemed to calm her, and she departed in a better mood. As she left, Elspeth reiterated her willingness to continue her conversation with Sophia at any time.

Elspeth went over to the bouquet and opened the card. The message was short. "*With love, Richard.*" Elspeth flushed and tried not to admit how much the message, however brief, pleased her. Yellow roses fringed with red were her favourite flowers.

As she dressed, she took unusual care with her makeup and accessories, and wondered why. Tonight she needed to find out more about Philippa from Colin but did not want to imply that she had any feelings towards him other than appreciation of his usefulness to her. Richard's offering had made Elspeth feel more feminine, and she smiled inwardly at the thought of him.

*

Brigadier Colin French had retired from the Commandos five years before. He had seen service in most of the hot spots of the world, the last being in the Balkans, but he chose to retire to Cyprus because it had been his favourite posting. As a young lieutenant he had served at the British Sovereign Base in Akrotiri during the Turkish invasion and subsequent violence in the mid nineteen-seventies, and he was assigned here in the nineteen-nineties, when he commanded a large group of British forces being trained for hazardous duty elsewhere. He was a born soldier and was proud of every day he had spent in the military, even in the most uncomfortable and dangerous places. Some days he wished he were in Iraq or Afghanistan, but his body had sustained too many injuries and he no longer was fit for active combat duty. After Sandhurst, he trained rigorously for a position in the Commandos and never stopped daily training after that. Even now, he ran six miles a day and did an hour of calisthenics. He prided himself on his trim body and acute mind.

Colin never married, perhaps out of fear that his work was too dangerous to ask a woman to accept its risks, but he liked women and usually had a special lady friend in his life. Hostesses invited him to parties as a desirable single man, and he had his choice of the most attractive women, married or single, at any gathering. His own sense of honour kept him from affairs with married woman, with rare exceptions, but he courted and was courted by single and divorced women and widows both local and worldwide.

His last fling of any duration was with Philippa Allard-Thorpe, who exhibited all her many charms whenever he was present. They were an item for over a year, but Colin had tired of her. Eventually she became possessive, and he did not want to be possessed. He also became aware of how controlling she was over anyone close to her, particularly Cinnamon. No man, not even one as old as Colin, was impervious to Cinnamon's beauty or the tragedy of her blindness. Cinnamon deserved better treatment than Philippa gave her.

Colin was amazed when Philippa suggested he work with Elspeth Duff. Didn't Philippa see Elspeth's appeal? Colin knew by this time that Philippa seldom did anything without forethought. What was her motive, particularly when his feelings towards her had already waned? Was he being too suspicious? Philippa told him Elspeth Duff had the ear of Lord Kennington, and Philippa wanted to make a lasting impression on the owner of the Kennington Organisation. She might sacrifice her relationship with Colin for her own advancement, but it would be uncharacteristic of her to give up an admirer. Or was she setting Colin up? These days Colin wanted desperately to be rid of Philippa, but he also felt protective of Cinnamon. Tonight he was grateful he would have some diversion with Elspeth and bade his cook select one of the finest bottles of wine from his cellar and to take special care with the dinner.

*

Elspeth arrived by taxi exactly on time, an ingrained childhood habit that she could not break. A manservant showed her into the house and led her to the garden where Colin was waiting. He came up to her and offered a hug, but she brushed past him with only a smile.

The garden was filled with the aromas of the summer evening, jasmine, roses and other fragrances that Colin said his gardener had selected especially for their scent. Low lights marked the walkway, leading through the shade of small trees to a table tucked close by a wall and set with a bright cloth and numerous tiny candleholders. The candle flames flickered in the soft breeze.

"I had the wall built here so that I could dine out of the wind in the evening," Colin said as he handed her a glass of chilled wine. "Even in a gale, I can find shelter here. They are forecasting strong southerly winds tomorrow, which will bring the sand from the Sahara, but tonight gentle westerlies are blowing, and we should be comfortable. Come, let me show you round the garden."

The garden was small and Colin spoke of each plant as if it were a friend. "Barnabas, my gardener, fusses over every bloom, as do I. I spent my life facing the prospect of killing and being killed, but in retirement I hate to neglect even the smallest thing in my garden. Years ago an old woman gave me a shoot from a flowering plant when I went to buy vegetables. She blessed me, and I felt her gift was a blessing that I carry with me even now. The plant still grows here and is quite large now."

Elspeth turned to Colin with a slightly arched eyebrow. Was this simply a new form of seduction? He sounded sincere, but Elspeth was not easily persuaded by his words.

"You don't believe me, do you?" he said.

Elspeth smiled. "For that you must forgive me. I'm a bit ignorant about gardening, probably because I've never tended a garden of my own. My father in Scotland potters about in his garden at the edge of the loch, but, when faced with annual disasters, he simply states that the first law of gardening is that plants die. I did not inherit his horticultural sensibilities."

Colin put back his head and laughed. "I should have suspected that the name Elspeth Duff brought with it some sensibilities common to the Scots."

Elspeth snorted, remembering Richard constantly teasing her about her Scottish sensibilities. "Not when it comes to gardening," she said. Then she chastised herself for enjoying the banter. As they sat down to dinner and the food was served, she quickly changed the tone.

"Brigadier," she said, purposely choosing to address him by his title, "I hope I have not accepted your invitation under false pretences. I need your help with several things."

"My attention is all yours, my fair Scottish lass. Fire away." He grinned at her over the rim of his wineglass.

Elspeth laid out her agenda.

"First, I need you to organise an expedition."

"Just tell me where."

"I thought Kantara Castle. You mentioned it in passing yesterday. I understand it has enough history to enchant both children and adults. Isn't it one of the better preserved castles in Northern Cyprus?"

"It hasn't been spoiled over the years and has stood up well to the harshness of the sun, rain and wind for over a millennium. Consider the expedition arranged," he said and snapped his fingers, "but tell me what the other things are."

"I want you to tell me more of what you know about Philippa Allard-Thorpe between the time Cinnamon was hurt and the time Philippa became manager of the Kennington Nicosia."

Colin's face twisted, and the candlelight distorted it even more. "That may prove more difficult."

Elspeth looked up from her food. "Difficult? How?"

Colin sipped his wine. He pushed his food around his plate politely but did not eat. "Because much of what I know is gossip and may not be accurate."

Elspeth took a bite of her food, swallowed and then asked, "Did you know her at that time?"

Colin looked away into the twilight of the garden. "No, I didn't but I knew of her, as I told you yesterday. She was Ernest Thorpe's wife, and he was well known even then. After Cinnamon was injured, Philippa left Ernest and supposedly took Cinnamon with her to New York for some sort of treatment. The two of them did not come back to Cyprus until some time later. That must have been three or four years ago. On her return, Philippa morphed into Ms Allard-Thorpe, hotel manager extraordinaire."

Elspeth put down her knife and fork and raised her glass without drinking from it. She looked directly at Colin. "Do you know anything about her life before she worked at the Kennington hotel?"

"Not anything for sure. I only know what others said."

"All right, tell me the gossip."

"Hearsay evidence?"

"I suppose so. You're not on trial."

"I'm relieved. Did anyone ever tell you how deeply blue your eyes are?" he said. "And doesn't your London office have this information?"

Annoyed at his compliment, Elspeth lowered her eyes and concentrated on her food. "I don't have access to personnel files unless some incident at one of the hotels has occurred involving the staff."

"And has one now?"

Uncomfortable with her host's words, Elspeth pleaded innocence. "Not that I'm aware of. I'm trying to find out why Philippa is such a catalyst for other people's emotions."

Colin laughed and leaned back on the legs of his chair. "Perhaps because she has so few of her own."

"You are harsh, Brigadier."

"Mmm. Perhaps too much so. I care for Cinnamon, and I am aware of the hurt Philippa inflicts on her."

"Didn't you see Philippa for a while?"

"See? If you mean date her, yes, for over a year."

"Do you still?"

He set his glass down and propped his elbows on the table, looking straight at Elspeth. "Ms Duff, now you are prying."

"I don't mean to, but I am curious about who Philippa is."

"You and everyone else."

Elspeth could not decide if Colin was purposely evading her questions, but she decided to test him further. "Where exactly did she work before the Kennington Nicosia?"

Colin shrugged and gave in. "I understand she wheedled her way into the management staff of the Cypriot Britannia, which was a famous hotel when the British were still in control here. It was very run down by the time she began working there, and the owner was totally demented. Philippa reportedly seduced him and, dying in a fit of ecstasy, he left the hotel to her. All vicious gossip, of course. He neglected to leave her any money, however, so she soon negotiated with a Greek developer, who financed a complete overhaul of the hotel. Later she sold the hotel to him, and he threatened to raze it to the ground in favour of a larger and more modern hotel. Philippa did not ingratiate herself with the historical preservationists or traditionalist British expats on the island by selling off this historic hotel."

"Did she make much money from the sale?"

"I understand it was in the range of seven hundred and fifty thousand Cypriot pounds, quite a fortune for the little girl from Ohio. Most members of the British establishment on the island were not amused when she profited from the loss of a favourite place for expats to gather."

Elspeth frowned. "I still wonder how she got her job at the Kennington Nicosia?"

"Georgios Konstantinidis, the manager at your hotel, was taken with Philippa. He, like the owner of the Cypriot Britannia, was an old man, and Philippa has an unmatched facility for feigned seduction when it benefits her. Believe me, I know."

Elspeth didn't press the point. "I find a real disconnection between the two Philippas I hear about. On one hand there is the warm, capable, charismatic manager of the hotel; on the other hand there is the scheming, cold, self-serving person who needs to dominate. Which is true?"

The brigadier laughed and finally turned to his meal. "Strange as it may seem, she's both. Her goal is to be perfect and she needs the people around her to mirror back her perfection, but, as is inevitable, she always finds ways that others have failed her. Cinnamon is the prime example."

"Beautiful and talented Cinnamon. What a dreadful shame." Elspeth could feel tears rise in her eyes.

"I think," Colin said, "you will find that Cinnamon has a group of invisible supporters, unseen because of Cinnamon's disability and because Philippa dislikes feeling that her daughter needs any support but hers. I've noticed, for example, a young man behind the reception desk at the hotel who is particularly attentive."

"That's Christos. I'm certain he's in love with Cinnamon."

"Has he told her so?"

"No. I think he fears for his job. He helps support his grandmother. He's a funny combination of a kid who grew up in Los Angeles and a devoted Cypriot grandson. His job's important both to him and to his family. I'm going to make it my business to bring Christos to Lord Kennington's attention, although I won't tell Philippa. He's a fine young man."

Colin put his hand over Elspeth's. "Matchmaking?"

Elspeth withdrew her hand gently but firmly.

"Now, Elspeth, I think you are beginning to understand Philippa," he said as if he had not noticed her gesture.

Elspeth thought there was little more to be gained from this discussion and changed the topic abruptly. "Now let's talk about the trip to Kantara Castle."

They passed the rest of the evening in desultory conversation, first about the historical significance of the castle and then on to personal anecdotes. Colin told Elspeth about some of the more colourful and exciting moments of his career, and Elspeth shared amusing stories of her recent travels for the Kennington hotels. She did not mention Hollywood or Scotland Yard or her more perilous assignments at the hotels around the world. Elspeth needed the brigadier's help with the delegation, but at the end of the evening she hoped she had left the impression that she did not want to be involved with him on a romantic basis. She suspected that having been seen with him three times over the last few days had already set the expat rumour mill buzzing.

As she left, however, she asked if he would come to the hotel next day to help arrange the expedition to Kantara Castle. Elspeth knew Joanna Colton would want to organise the details because she always did. Elspeth stepped into the waiting taxi with relief that the evening was over and that she had evaded the increasingly warm advances that Brigadier Colin French made towards her.

When she returned to her room, it was filled with the scent of Richard's roses. Thank you, Dickie, she thought silently. Thank you for being there for me. As she lay back on the sofa in her sitting room, she could feel the dull ache coming back into her head.

15

The following morning Elspeth ordered a light breakfast in her suite. When the knock came at her door, she bade the person enter and was given, not her breakfast, but an ornate flower arrangement in a large glass vase. Thanking the hall attendant, she put the vase on the opposite side of the room from the roses she received from Richard the night before and opened the card. *With fond remembrance of last night. C.,* the card read. Elspeth growled. She suspected Philippa had already opened the card and this irritated Elspeth further. Another knock came almost immediately, and Elspeth was relieved to find her breakfast and on the tray a single flower in a discreet bud vase supplied on the standing order of Lord Kennington for all his guests and visiting staff.

After breakfast, Elspeth decided she would approach Philippa Allard-Thorpe and tell her Colin French was coming to the hotel to discuss the excursion to Kantara Castle. She found the manager in her office. Philippa rose and greeted Elspeth with warmth, taking her hand and gushing praise for her care of the delegation.

"It is such a relief to me to have you here," Philippa purred, "because I don't have to worry about the members of the delegation or their families. The political situation here always puts one on edge. I know that anyone from the Foreign Office can be trusted, but I never am sure if elements from outside might come into the hotel to disrupt our peace here. Lord Kennington would not like that at all."

Ya betcha, sweetheart, like I didn't know, Elspeth thought in Mae West tones, and then she cursed herself for being so judgmental. Curb your thoughts, Elspeth, she said to herself.

Philippa made arrangements for Elspeth to use one of the smaller conference rooms where she could meet Colin French and Joanna Colton and walked with Elspeth into the lobby just as Colin entered the hotel. Philippa rushed up to him and put her arms around him in greeting. Colin responded with a tepid hug. Elspeth simply put out her hand and shook his, thanking him for coming. Shortly afterwards Joanna bustled in from the garden, declaring that she hoped she was not too late. Colin introduced himself before Elspeth or Philippa had time to do so, and soon Colin, Elspeth, and Joanna were hard at work. Philippa retreated to her office without another glance at Colin.

*

Having slept badly after her conversation with the Waldorf Astoria manager, Pamela Crumm arrived at her office at half past six. With all the careful checks into Kennington Organisation staff members' backgrounds, how had Philippa's presumably false reference from the Plaza been missed? Pamela went on the internet to find out more about Cornell University School of Hotel Administration's trainee program. Her search results made her wonder why, when Cornell had its own hotel facility in Ithaca for training its students, Philippa would have done two internships in New York City. She called down to the personnel office and asked if anyone on the Kennington staff in London had attended Cornell four years before, and she was promised as immediate a response as possible.

For a brief moment she looked out her window and saw the sun had broken through the clouds over London and the Thames, but she soon was immersed in the complex tasks of running the day-to-day operations of a worldwide hotel chain. She expected Eric Kennington back from Paris, where he was coordinating the opening of a new Kennington hotel. She wanted to have everything in order for his arrival, as he had been gone for the last two days. As she tapped out the list of things that needed his immediate attention, she knew she was dreading bringing up the subject of their manager in Nicosia.

Lord Kennington arrived in a flurry just before ten and was immediately immersed in the priorities of the day. He consulted with Pamela on several of the more critical items and signed the papers she had prepared for him earlier that required his signature. She assured him that she had read them all carefully and he did not have to worry about them.

Finally he raised his head and looked at her. "Pamela, you are hovering. Why on earth are you doing so?"

Clearing her throat she said, "There seems to be a slight complication in Cyprus."

Eric Kennington looked up with an expression somewhere between puzzlement and annoyance. "Not Elspeth Duff again? Surely her assignment in Nicosia couldn't be more benign. Has anything happened to her?"

"No. Elspeth is quite well, although she did bring this situation to my attention."

"Intrepid Elspeth," Lord Kennington said with a grin. "She couldn't just rest in Cyprus, could she? She would have to dig something up. Well, that is why I pay her such an outrageous salary and give her far more latitude in her assignments than I should. What has she found now?"

He often fumed about Elspeth, but Pamela knew he trusted and admired her.

"Do you remember Philippa Allard-Thorpe, Eric?"

"What a silly question, Pamela. Of course I know all my managers."

"Did you interview her before she became manager in Nicosia?"

His lordship now was definitely annoyed. "You must remember that I even flew out there, as I had not been to the hotel for quite some time. Georgios Konstantinidis ran the hotel with such unseen efficiency that I seldom worried, but after his stroke things began to slip. He knew it and so did I. When he recommended Philippa Allard-Thorpe, I had to bow to his suggestion. Normally I wouldn't have picked someone so young or untried, but everything about her impressed me. Have you met her?"

"Only in passing at one of the managers' conferences here. She's quite attractive."

Lord Kennington deflected Pamela's irony. "Definitely. I consider that a great asset. Why are you asking all these questions?"

"Because I think she doctored her CV."

Eric Kennington stopped, his Dunhill fountain pen in mid-air. "What makes you think that? Surely the personnel department would have checked."

"Surely or not, I took her file home last night to review her references."

Lord Kennington capped his pen. "Did Elspeth put you up to this?" he said, his eyes narrowing.

Pamela looked innocently away. "Not exactly. She simply implied Philippa was less than she would have us believe."

"Have the guests complained?" he demanded.

"On the contrary, many guests have sent complimentary notes."

Eric Kennington looked over his gold-rimmed reading glasses and scrutinized his business partner. "Then what is Elspeth's problem? Have any members of the FCO delegation complained?"

"Not that I'm aware of, although Sophia Driscoll said Philippa doesn't like her children in the lobby."

"Philippa's right. Didn't we give the FCO delegation a whole wing to themselves?"

Pamela would not be deterred. "Elspeth feels the members of the staff don't like Philippa."

"I thought Philippa replaced most of the staff. Georgios's staff was getting on a bit, or so she said, and fresh blood was needed. After visiting the hotel, I believed her."

Pamela banged the flat of her hand on his desk, which was real Chippendale but not a Kennington family heirloom, as Eric sometimes asserted.

"Eric, you are not listening to me. When I went through Philippa's personnel file last night, I discovered that every reference she gave us was from someone who was already dead or dying at the time. Personnel could not have read them very carefully." She did not add that there was a note from Eric approving Philippa's position as manager without further checks.

Lord Kennington was not a fool, nor did he want to appear to be, so he turned his full attention to Pamela and demanded, "I want you to authenticate every reference and document in her file. I also want you to alert Elspeth to report any dissatisfaction with Philippa in the field, from any source, guests, staff, visitors to the hotel, or, most of all, from the FCO delegates. The delegation is Elspeth's charge, and she needs to keep them secure and happy. We don't want word to get out that the Kennington Organisation mistreats diplomats, even ones staying at one of our hotels at a vastly discounted rate. I don't want the countries that treat their higher-up officials with more generosity than HM's government to hear we are slipping in our service to the diplomatic corps of the world. Now let me tell you about the arrangements in France."

An hour later Pamela retreated into her own office and rang Elspeth in Nicosia.

"I think Eric tacitly approves of you watching Philippa Allard-Thorpe, but we both need to tread cautiously. At the recommendation of Georgios Konstantinidis, Eric personally overrode a thorough investigation into her CV before she was elevated to the post of manager. I am going back to verify the references, but your task is more immediate. Can you quietly interview both the staff and the delegation on their reactions to Philippa? I know Sophia Driscoll has already voiced concern, but Eric agrees with Philippa that the children do not belong in the public areas of the hotel."

Elspeth was on a secured line but still answered circumspectly. "Interviewing the staff, even on a casual basis, will alert Philippa, if I'm not careful. She rules with the tentacles of a sleepless octopus, but tell Eric I will do my best. She still is trying to flatter me because she thinks I have a special relationship with the two of you. Yuck, as my children used to say, I hate this, but it's my job, isn't it?"

Pamela tutted, as she always did when Elspeth grumbled about her job. "Do your best, my friend, and try to remember you are still recovering from your head wounds and aren't Superwoman. Don't take any risks that will put you in harm's way."

"I hate the headaches. They still happen, but I'm not an invalid."

Pamela tutted one more time and asked, "And how is Sir Richard?"

"Pamela, I'll do as you ask, but Richard Munro is none of your business," Elspeth replied curtly.

When Elspeth rang off, Pamela thought. "So this relationship with Her Majesty's High Commissioner to the Republic of Malta is becoming a touchy one for Elspeth." Pamela smiled for the first time all morning.

*

Her Majesty's High Commissioner to the Republic of Malta was planning his final arrangements for his trip to Cyprus, but, just as he was asking his personal assistant to book his flight, he had an incoming call from the FCO in London, requesting that he cut short his long weekend in order to be in Brussels for a meeting on Tuesday afternoon. Some days he felt that he should retire again, but he knew his work with the FCO after Marjorie's death had sustained him, and he was at least obligated to finish his tour in Malta. Besides, he enjoyed diplomatic life and wondered what he would do, other than sailing and marrying Elspeth, if he retired completely. He needed to resolve their relationship once and for all. How could he be clearer with Elspeth? He hoped that during his upcoming trip to Cyprus he would find an occasion to talk without her being distracted by her job.

Once he knew his flight schedule, he picked up the phone and rang Thomas Wellborne in order to confirm his arrival time. Then he called Elspeth.

Richard sensed her disappointment when he said he would be staying for three days only. Elspeth told him her difficulty. "On Saturday I have arranged for an excursion for the FCO delegates and their families to one of the Crusaders' castles on the Turkish side of the island. I regret I can't bow out now. Dickie, why don't you come along? Only the FCO people and our tour leader, a retired British brigadier recommended by the hotel manager, will be in the group. Fourteen of us in all. Colin, the brigadier, that is, has hired a coach to take us. I'm sure one more person can squeeze in. He says the road to the castle is a hair-raising one, so be prepared."

Richard was delighted and said so. "It would be my greatest pleasure, my dear one, if indeed there is room. Since I've been in Malta, I've read a great deal about the Crusades and the Knights of St. John, who were expelled from Cyprus and as a result came to Malta. A Crusader's castle sounds exciting, and I'm certain I'll enjoy myself thoroughly." Especially being with you, my dearest and elusive Elspeth, he thought to himself.

*

Elspeth rubbed the sore spot at the back of her skull and wondered how she could best approach the staff without Philippa's knowledge. Perhaps she could start with Christos, since she had already made a personal connection with him. Elspeth checked the schedule board outside the staff room and saw Christos would be on the desk that afternoon and early evening. It was now just past eleven.

She decided to talk privately to Joanna Colton, who, after their meeting with Colin French, said she was returning to the delegation's rooms in the east wing. Elspeth wanted to approach Joanna in person, so she took a route to the delegation's wing that avoided crossing the lobby or passing by the staff offices. If she felt anxious about her movements through the hotel, how did the permanent staff feel? Philippa needed Elspeth's good word in London, which put the hotel staff members at Philippa's mercy if Elspeth found them wanting. In retrospect Elspeth could not pinpoint a single instance where Philippa had directly caused uneasiness among them. Elspeth could find no fault with Philippa's handling of her job but sensed the tension that spread through the workings of the hotel. The hotel ran as smoothly as any other Kennington hotel, and the high Kennington standards were manifest throughout the hotel itself. Why such uneasiness? Elspeth was unsure if it was the product of her imagination or caused by the sensibility that Richard teased her about and that had blessed or cursed her all her life.

She found Joanna in the common area of the delegation's wing. A stack of guidebooks surrounded her at the table where she sat.

"I love castles, especially old ones," Joanna said, looking up at Elspeth. "Kantara is a good choice, even if we have to go over to the Turkish side. Bitki told me that you have already crossed the Green Line to visit her parents' home and garden. Did you have any trouble?"

"The UN guards hardly looked at my passport. They simply handed me a stamped piece of paper so that there would be no permanent record of my being in Turkish Cyprus. I sensed this was their standard procedure."

"Mmm," said Joanna. "I think even the twins might like this excursion. At least it may get them away from their computers or the satellite television for a while. They used to play at being Richard the Lionheart, so to visit somewhere he actually had been should intrigue them. They have put on their bored look this morning, which will make my day difficult. Did your children do that?"

Having become accustomed to Joanna's style of conversation, Elspeth had no qualms about interrupting her rambling. "Mrs Colton, I've been meaning to ask you something, in confidence if I may?"

"What is it? Nothing about the boys, I hope. Or is it Bitki or Sophia? They sometimes resent me taking charge."

Elspeth laughed. "No, I want to ask you about the hotel."

"The hotel? Wonderful place! Wish the FCO always chose places like this."

"I am concerned about the level of service."

"Jolly excellent. There always seems to be someone about, asking if we are comfortable. I'm delighted the manager is so concerned."

"Is she about often?"

"Yes. I assume it's hotel policy for the manager to check the rooms when they are not occupied because I usually find her in our wing when we are returning from some excursion or other."

Elspeth nearly said there was no such hotel policy, but she caught herself in time. Joanna did not need to know why Elspeth was asking questions.

"While you are here, there's something I'd like to mention to you, Ms Duff, because it has my husband worried. George has been with the FCO a long time and is rather set in his ways about women in diplomatic positions, so perhaps his attitude is a bit biased, but he thinks Bitki Mitsui might be passing information to the Turks."

Unable to hide her surprise, Elspeth turned to Joanna Colton with great concern. "Why does your husband think that?"

"We saw Bitki talking to a scruffy young man in the garden. George served briefly at our consulate in Istanbul and got to know a bit of Turkish. He said Bitki and this man were definitely speaking Turkish. I've seen him here before as well, talking to the beautiful, blind girl who comes to the hotel everyday. I asked Bitki who the young man was, and she brushed me off. No one of importance, she said, just one of Cinnamon's student friends. Cinnamon, I gather is the blind girl."

Elspeth nodded. "The young woman is Cinnamon Allard-Thorpe, the manager's daughter. She comes here for lunch and strolls in the garden afterwards. I've met her there too."

"Do you know who the young man is?"

"Since I haven't seen him, I can't be sure. Her blindness prevents her from attending university, but she has a number of university student friends, both Greek and Turkish. It could very well be that Bitki was talking to one of those students."

"I'm amazed that someone as precise as Ms Allard-Thorpe at checking everything at the hotel would allow her daughter to come here so frequently and, what's more, bring some rather unkempt and radical-looking students with her."

"Mrs Colton, I think you've just cleared up a mystery bothering me since I accidentally overheard a conversation the other day when I was in the garden. I'm sure Ms Allard-Thorpe knew the student was here that day but now she's taken measures to see that he will not come again."

Elspeth felt an enormous sense of relief at having possibly identified the unknown baritone voice arguing with Philippa through the louvres of her office window.

Joanna Colton was not easily put off. "I still find it strange that Bitki met him, not once but twice. I wouldn't put it past the Turks to use the poor blind girl as a way to get one of their spies close to our delegation. I don't trust Bitki or Onan Mitsui. They say they are British but they look foreign to me. George says I mustn't be so bigoted, that Britain is a multi-ethnic country now, but I still don't like it."

Elspeth left her interview with Joanna Colton with mixed feelings. She made her way to the garden in hopes of meeting Cinnamon there. Fortunately Cinnamon was sitting under one of the flame trees and waving one of her fingers up and down in the air. She turned as Elspeth approached.

"It's Elspeth Duff here, Cinnamon."

Cinnamon smiled in Elspeth's general direction and said, "Please don't mind me. I am counting syllables in my new poem. In the haiku form, syllables are very important. After I get it right, I'll ask someone to write the poem down for me. Often if Christos is off duty, he comes out and helps. Otherwise one of my student friends does it for me."

"Do they come here?"

"Once Demetrius came, but I asked him not to come again. My mother doesn't like my friends coming to visit me at the hotel. She finds them too poor."

"Poor? That seems an odd word." Elspeth remembered Joanna Colton's use of the words unkempt and radical looking, but those were visual terms and not ones Cinnamon would be likely to use.

"Many of *my* friends couldn't afford to be a guest here, and most disapprove of the hotel's pampering of the rich," Elspeth said with a chuckle. She wondered if she were belittling the hotels with these words, true as they might be.

"Really?" Cinnamon said with a baffled look on her face. Her mother most certainly would not utter such words, even in private.

"What are you writing today, Cinnamon? I was impressed by your spider web imagery."

"I am writing a poem in honour of my father. Next Saturday is his fiftieth birthday."

"Quite venerable, indeed."

"No," said Cinnamon, "he's the youngest person I know. He's asked that I invite my friends to join him for a picnic."

"You do see your father then?" Elspeth asked shamelessly.

"Every time I can. *She* doesn't like me to, you know, but I love my father. She blames him for my blindness, but it wasn't his fault." Cinnamon spoke these last words through clenched teeth. "Perhaps I am being an unloving and ungrateful daughter, Elspeth, but there are days when I just wish *she* were dead!"

Elspeth did not need to ask who *she* was.

16

After thanking the Wellbornes for their hospitality, Richard left the Residency and arrived at the Kennington Nicosia just as the delegation was convening on the steps at the entrance. He paused for a moment before descending from the taxi and announcing himself. He saw Elspeth leaning against one of the columns at the doorway. She was dressed in a loose open-necked white shirt with a Nehru collar and light tan trousers, and she stood with one knee bent. On the column behind her she was resting a sandalled foot, its thongs wrapped around her shapely ankle. She held a floppy straw hat in one hand, and the other, which was resting on her knee, held dark glasses. Her short light brown hair ruffled in the slight breeze, and she looked more relaxed than he had seen her since before her brush with death the winter before. Cyprus must be treating her well. With amusement in her intense cobalt blue eyes, she was watching an older woman marshal a gaggle of children into the waiting coach. Two couples, one dark and the other dark and fair, looked on from each side of the porte-cochère. They seemed unrelated to each other and appeared as if they were not attached to the children and did not condone their clamour. An impish child turned to the dark couple and called to them to hurry. Richard was filled with a burst of joy at seeing Elspeth again. Her casual dress reminded him of their halcyon days in Scotland before the murder in Cambridge that had changed her life. As he approached her, she raised her cheek, which he brushed with his lips, and with her eyes she pointed to the delegation.

"Welcome," she whispered with a wry smile. "Here they are, the whole kit and caboodle. Are you up to a day of this?"

"With you among them, my dear, I promise it will be all pleasure."

*

Lingering by an ancient BMW, Brigadier Colin French chatted with the UN troops at the guard post on the Green Line. The brigadier had earlier advised the delegation to use their non-diplomatic passports in order to keep a low profile. After the group cleared the gate without any difficulty, Colin gave directions in rapid Turkish to the driver of the coach, in response to which the driver kept shaking his head. Finally Colin motioned impatiently towards the driver indicating he should follow his BMW. As they waited for this exchange to take place, Joanna dispensed bottles of water to the children but warned them that the road might be rough and twisty and to drink sparingly so they would not get sick. The two older boys scowled, but the others nodded obediently.

The day was bright and promised to be hot on the plain below the peaks, but the breeze off the Mediterranean would keep the mountaintop cool. Colin manoeuvred along the flat roads by the coast and then began the steep ascent up the mountain towards Kantara Castle. The road narrowed significantly, and he slowed in order to keep an eye on the coach behind him. They wound up the road that in places became a rough single track. His car scraped stones along the way, and he hoped there would be no damage to its underside. He watched the coach, which in some places had difficulty negotiating the turns. Finally, unscathed, they arrived at the car park under the steep bastions of the castle. The high stone walls dwarfed the vehicles and people below, and a rough and narrow path led up to the derelict fortress above.

After parking his car under a tree, the brigadier directed the coach driver round to a spot that would protect his vehicle from the midday heat. First the children and then the adults filed out onto the gravelly, dusty soil of the car park. Colin French announced that he would lead a tour of the castle in half an hour but that in the meantime they were free to climb up the steep, rocky stairs and roam through the ruins. He did not relish his task ahead.

*

Wishing to guard Elspeth in case she slipped, Richard climbed the stairs behind her. When they reached the centre courtyard of the castle, he drew Elspeth aside. The others had scattered.

"Do I sense some tension among the members of our party? Or have we been in enough difficult scraps together that when I'm with you I automatically become suspicious, much like one of Pavlov's dogs?" he asked.

Elspeth laughed and took his arm. "Oh, Dickie, I'm so glad you are here. How quickly you pick up hidden dissention, but I'm sure this derives from your work more than our adventures together."

Richard led her to a shady bench made from stones that had fallen from the castle walls. "In diplomacy we are naturally wary of our adversaries but always try to trust those on our side. That doesn't seem to be the case here, or am I mistaken?"

"No, you're right," she said. "The group has not bonded together as well as the FCO might have hoped, I suspect. I wonder what the FCO's rationale was letting the delegation live together with their families as well as working together."

"Cost, I expect," said Richard, knowing too well the increasing frugality of the Budget Office at the FCO.

"If cost is a consideration, then why let them stay at a Kennington hotel?"

"Did Eric Kennington give them a tremendous discount?"

Elspeth leaned back. She drew a spiral in the soil by the bench with the toe of her sandal, which caused dust to swirl around it. "He did, but one has always to be aware that Eric usually has an ulterior motive, such as marketing when the hotel's bookings are down. *Important British Delegation Stays at Kennington Nicosia* headlines might read. One can almost see that scrolled on the banner at the bottom of the BBC News channel."

Richard laughed. "Elspeth, are you being unkind to your employer?"

Elspeth looked at him under an arched brow. "Dickie, are you being avuncular the way you used to be when we were young?" she countered.

His eyes softened. "No, my dearest, I don't want to be that at all. Why don't you tell me where the tensions lie? And also who the brigadier is?"

For Richard, the second question was the more important one, and he was glad when Elspeth chose to answer it first.

"Brigadier Colin French is an old flame of the hotel manager, Philippa Allard-Thorpe. When I first arrived, Philippa told me he was a person who knew a great deal about Cyprus and who could help me learn about the island, its people, and the best places to visit. He also could suggest ways to amuse the younger members of the delegation. It seems Philippa and Colin were an item for over a year, and I think her concern was more for him than us. She says he is stretched financially, but he has . . . ," Elspeth paused and bit her lower lip.

Richard wondered what her next thought was.

"He does seem well connected," she finished. "The discontent you picked up centres around Philippa Allard-Thorpe. Philippa's story is a long one, which will fill an evening when we are alone. Will you have any spare time during your stay with the Wellbornes for a private evening with an old friend?"

"Why, my dearest Elspeth, do you suppose I came to Cyprus? Carolyn Wellborne has my days and nights organised, but I insisted on dinner alone with you tonight." Richard did not add that Carolyn had winked at him when he had made his request.

"I shall have to confirm with my social secretary if I am free tonight," Elspeth said in falsetto tones fit only for royalty, and she pretended to flip through the pages of a diary. "She has confirmed my calendar is quite clear. Oh Dickie, I have so much to tell you."

Richard drew in a deep breath of sea air that rose from below and slowly blew it out. He could think of no nicer experience in the world than to be sitting on the stones of a medieval fortress close to Elspeth. He touched her hand, which she did not pull away.

"You seem filled with intrigue," he said. "Pamela Crumm said you had been sent here to rest."

"Did she?" Elspeth cried with sham indignity. "I was led to believe that I came here on assignment."

"Have I let the cat out of the bag?" he asked with a grin. "You seem to have made your trip out here an assignment despite Eric Kennington's duplicity about its importance. I'll wait for the details, but give me an overview. Let's find a place to go where no one will hear us."

They hunted through the crumbling walls of the castle and discovered a secluded recess off what looked like the one-time stables. They found a small ledge and took a precarious seat. Elspeth lowered her voice so that that there was no chance she could be overheard.

"Philippa Allard-Thorpe, who has been manager of the hotel for the last year, was recommended by the former manager, Georgios Konstantinidis, whom Eric hired when the Kennington Nicosia was first opened about twenty years ago. About a year ago Georgios suffered a stroke and had to retire. Philippa was his assistant, and Eric promoted her to manager. On the surface she appears to have both the ability and manners required for such a position, but she has stirred up a curious unrest in the hotel staff. I haven't yet been able to pinpoint what it is. Pamela told me that Philippa hired most of the current hotel staff in order that there would be no comparisons made by them between her running of the hotel and Giorgio's. Eric agreed to Philippa's request, but Pamela is wary and has asked me to watch Philippa. I've discovered a number of disturbing things, but as yet they have not formed into enough of a pattern that I can send in an official report to Eric. Every day, however, I email my hunches, observations, and whatever else I think might be important to Pamela."

"Was it Pamela who asked you to do this?"

"We're old friends."

"And co-conspirators."

"Dickie! Whose side are you on?"

"Yours, my dear, always."

"Then you can help me today. I want someone other than me to watch the interactions among the people here. I need your independent judgment."

"Do you expect any problems?"

"No, not really. Everyone will be relaxed today. What better time to observe what is happening?"

What better time indeed, Richard thought.

Part 2

The Murder

17

Elspeth and Richard were interrupted by the arrival of Colin French.

"There you are, Elspeth. May I be introduced?" the brigadier asked.

Elspeth rose and made a formal introduction. "Brigadier, this is an old friend of mine from Scotland who is visiting the Wellbornes at the British High Commission. Sir Richard, this is Brigadier French."

Richard stood, held out his hand and filled in the gap. "Richard Munro. I've come over from Malta to stay with the Wellbornes, and I knew Elspeth was here. She invited me along today because she thought I might like to see a bit of historical Cyprus."

"Then come and join us. "I'm going to give a brief guided tour later, and afterwards the Kennington Nicosia has arranged a picnic that is at this moment being laid out on the other side of the castle, but first let me show you the way to the tower of the keep, which is my favourite part of the castle."

"My pleasure, brigadier. Lead on," Richard said.

Richard took Elspeth's arm in his and spoke a bit too loudly. "Come along, Elspeth. I understand the view from the top is excellent. I'll help you over the rough spots going up.

No use letting your fear of heights interfere with us seeing the view."

Elspeth looked curiously at Richard. She had no fear of heights; in fact she enjoyed scaling the rocky highlands in Scotland where she had grown up. Richard knew that, so why would he imply otherwise? And how did he know there were places up to the keep of the castle that had rough spots? Had he been reading the guidebooks or was he simply making assumptions by looking at the ruins?

When they started climbing the stairs of the tower, Richard whispered to Elspeth. "If we want to keep up this façade, take my arm and appear to be unsteady."

"I really want to get to the edge of the wall and see the view, but you have insisted I am acrophobic. Now I can't waltz over to the edge without a seeming care. Why the deception, Dickie?" she whispered.

Elspeth wondered if he had made up this ruse in order to get closer to her and show that she favoured him, not Colin.

Richard sniggered wickedly, which was uncharacteristic. Colin left them once they reached the top and said he had go back down to organise the tour. Richard put his arm around her waist. So that was his intent, she thought, smiling inwardly and leaning against him. She looked down the many metres of sharp cliff below, across the plain and beyond to the Mediterranean Sea. She turned around and tried to look unsteady in case anyone was watching. She suddenly gasped at what she saw.

Richard heard her. He tightened his grip around her and glanced down at her questioningly.

"Do you see the group climbing the stairs below?" Elspeth pointed, although her aristocratic grandmother had trained her that pointing was impolite.

Richard looked in the direction indicated. "The tall, distinguished looking man with the group of scruffy young people and the girl with the cane?"

She nodded. "He's Ernest Thorpe, Philippa Allard-Thorpe's ex-husband. I recognise the others as well. They're friends of Cinnamon Allard-Thorpe, Philippa and Ernest's daughter. But, worse, Cinnamon is among them. She's blind and this seems an odd place to bring her."

"Is their presence here a problem?" Richard asked.

"I'm not sure, but I think it might be," Elspeth said. "One member of the FCO delegation, Sophia Driscoll, earlier confided to me that another member might be colluding with someone who might be one of the students below. That is too many mights, isn't it? Dickie, this is a tangled spider's web. Paradoxically, Cinnamon wrote a poignant poem about a spider's web being destroyed in the wind. I'll ask her for a copy and show it to you."

"I sense you feel the poem is significant."

"There are so many interwoven things going on here, as in a spider's web, and I have no idea what's insignificant and what's not."

Richard and Elspeth watched the group below. Ernest Thorpe gestured up at the castle and seemed to be enjoying the reactions of the students. One student stepped forward and seemed to be challenging him. Ernest's head went up. He smiled as if delighted and continued his discourse. The students gathered more closely around him. They moved out of Richard and Elspeth's view as they climbed up the steps into the main part of the castle.

"Let's go around to where we can see the party from the hotel. I wonder what's going to happen when everyone meets." Elspeth took Richard's arm again as she spoke.

"Elspeth," he said, "I believe you love the intricate complexities of the human condition."

"Without a doubt. I can't imagine leading a life that discounted human interaction. I'd make a terrible nuclear physicist or mathematician. So let's see what happens next." Elspeth's words were bantering, but she suddenly changed her tone. "Dickie, I think we *do* have a real difficulty here."

Richard went to the parapet and looked down. "The hotel staff who came with us seem to be setting up a picnic. I don't see a problem"

"The problem is Philippa Allard-Thorpe."

"Is she the woman directing things?"

"Uh huh. The same. I can't understand why she is here and not at the hotel in Nicosia."

"Keeping tabs on the brigadier and you?"

Elspeth flushed. She had not mentioned anything about having lunch and dinner alone with the brigadier, so what exactly was Richard implying?

"I think she is keeping an eye on the delegation. Both Bitki Mitsui and Joanna Colton said she has been snooping around the delegation's quarters. Philippa is what my son would call a 'control freak'. Don't you love young people's vocabulary?"

Richard put his arms back around Elspeth's waist. "Not particularly," he replied dryly as he lowered his cheek to hers. Elspeth felt her body warm but turned back to the matter at hand.

"Dickie, I'm concerned that Philippa and Ernest will clash. Several days ago, I heard Philippa ranting at someone about staying clear of *her*. I suspected at the time that the '*her*' was Cinnamon. I could only vaguely hear the person in the room with Philippa. He had a muffled baritone voice. If the voice belonged to Ernest Thorpe, then we may be headed for an unpleasant confrontation."

"And she shall cause trouble wherever she goes," Richard said, paraphrasing the nursery rhyme.

"Exactly. I never thought we'd be in another crisis together. I think I'm a curse."

Richard leaned over and kissed her cheek and said in a falsetto. "And a lovely one at that."

"Dickie, be serious. I'm at work."

"I'll try to remember," he said with mock gravity, at which she laughed.

The inevitable happened as Elspeth and Richard were coming down from the top of the keep. Out of sight of Colin and the hotel party, Elspeth jumped easily down the uneven steps. She rounded a corner that brought her in full view of the courtyard below. Ernest Thorpe's group of students had found a flat spot well out of sight of the place where the hotel staff were putting up tables. Several of the students were laying out travel rugs, and Ernest was holding Cinnamon's arm and whispering in her ear. Cinnamon was smiling and laughing. One of the students brought out a rucksack and pulled several gaily-wrapped gifts from it. Ernest looked surprised, and Cinnamon threw her arms wide to the air and said, "Happy Birthday, Daddy."

Without warning, Philippa Allard-Thorpe was upon them. She began to yell at Ernest. Elspeth could hear only a few of her words, but the content was clear.

"How dare you! . . . Don't you know she's blind, you fool? . . . What if she stumbled?"

Philippa pointed to the steep cliff at the edge of the students' picnic spot.

Ernest drew Cinnamon towards him protectively, and she clung to him. Elspeth couldn't hear Ernest's responses to Philippa, as his voice was less shrill than hers. The only words that drifted up to where Elspeth and Richard were standing were "stay out of this, you . . ."

Elspeth could fill in the rest.

*

They watched Colin French start the tour of the castle but did not join him. The only participants were Joanna Colton and her two boys. Richard and Elspeth arrived at the picnic area to find three long tables set out with salads, stuffed pitta breads of various kinds, kebabs, cucumbers and tomatoes, and fruit juices. Local beers and wines were cooling in an ice-filled barrel. Elspeth knew that the simple appearance of the food belied the delicious flavours that the Kennington Nicosia's chefs had skilfully put together for the picnic. The FCO group formed a queue, helped themselves to lunch and seated themselves at the small tables with parasols that circled the buffet.

Elspeth was surprised to see Christos Leonides among the waiters and wondered why Philippa had chosen him to come to Kantara. Elspeth introduced Christos to Richard, and Richard spoke warmly to the young man. Christos blushed with pleasure.

Philippa appeared from nowhere and intervened.

"Ms Duff, Christos should not be idly talking to you. He has a task to do. Christos, you are needed to help at the dessert table."

Philippa looked cool and collected, not as if she had just had a shouting match with her ex-husband. She introduced herself to Richard, who simply put out his hand and said, "I am Richard Munro, an old friend from Elspeth's past. I understand you are manager of the Kennington Nicosia. My experience of Kennington hotels has always been one of great pleasure. Thank you for providing such an elegant picnic for us." He turned his back to her, as if she were a servant. Philippa bridled.

The members of the delegation spread out among the picnic tables and soon were absorbed in consuming their food and drink. The day grew hotter, and after lunch the brigadier suggested that everyone be left on their own to rest or wander among the ruins. The party dispersed, mostly to areas of shade.

Elspeth went quiet as Richard came up to her, led her over to a secluded alcove and, touching her cheek gently, asked if she were still feeling any effects from the incident in Singapore.

"A bit. My headache comes back now and again, but let's not talk about it."

Their conversation became languid and finally they sat without speaking. The silence between them was comforting.

Richard reached over and took her hand in his. She turned it over and, smiling, looked at the long fingers that always touched her so tenderly. She knew she had crossed the boundary between doubting her emotions for him and trusting them. Now she needed to find a way to tell him, wondering if this was the right moment. Then she remembered she was on duty.

Suddenly an anguished cry cut through the hot air. "Oh . . . God! No! Philippa! No!"

They rushed from the alcove to find the brigadier holding the limp body of Philippa Allard-Thorpe in his arms. Her head hung at an unnatural angle.

Colin French looked up at them with pain in his eyes. "She must have fallen," he said. "I'm afraid she's dead.

18

Thomas Wellborne did not relish the task of dealing with the death of a British citizen on the Turkish side of the island. Britain did not officially recognise the Turkish Republic of Cyprus, although the British High Commission did have a small office in northern Nicosia to handle consular matters there. Ultimately Thomas was in charge. The current negotiations for Turkey's entry into the EU made relations strained between Turkey and the UK, especially on the subject of Turkish Cyprus. The British delegation staying at the Kennington Nicosia was here to negotiate with the Turkish and Greek Cypriots, but the death of a private citizen was not in their remit.

Thomas sincerely hoped that Philippa Allard-Thorpe had retained her American passport, leaving handling her death to the US Embassy, and he was sadly disappointed to find otherwise. She had taken British citizenship as soon as the law would allow after her marriage to Ernest Thorpe. Matters were made worse by Elspeth Duff's suspicion that Philippa's death might not have been accidental. There were no witnesses to the fall or reasons to explain why Philippa was on the battlements of the castle rather than supervising the clear up of the hotel's picnic. Besides, Elspeth, backed by Richard Munro, had earlier brought up the possibility that

Philippa's fall could have been murder, perpetrated by any one of the people who were present at Kantara Castle at the time of her death.

The removal of Philippa Allard-Thorpe's body from the Turkish side had been irregular. Without consulting the British High Commission or reporting anything to the Turkish Cypriot police, Brigadier Colin French had negotiated with the UN border patrol, whom he seemed to know, to drive the body back across into the Greek sector. Once there he called an ambulance and had the body taken to a British hospital nearby and, at their instruction, on to a morgue. Had matters stopped there, Thomas Wellborne would have been relieved.

Elspeth Duff, however, had demanded an interview with the High Commissioner and was determined that there should be an autopsy, much to Thomas's consternation.

"Philippa Allard-Thorpe was an employee of the Kennington Organisation, and Lord Kennington has directed me to take every measure possible to determine the reason for the fall," she said.

The High Commissioner wanted to dismiss Elspeth Duff, but Richard Munro was with her and assured Thomas that Elspeth's request was in order. Thomas found them both meddlesome. Cyprus would be his last post, and he wanted his career to end on a high note, with the Greek/Turkish crisis resolved and Cyprus united in the way it had been under British rule. He was one of the strongest proponents of the quiet negotiations now underway and did not need the awkwardness of the death of Philippa Allard-Thorpe, whom he knew slightly and mistrusted completely, to interfere with the successful end of his diplomatic career.

Had Richard not been present, Thomas Wellborne would have been inclined to give Elspeth Duff a pat on the hand and an assurance that the High Commission would do everything possible.

Normally the body would have been sent back to Britain for burial, but Philippa presented a conundrum. She technically was British, but all her current ties were on Cyprus. She had no apparent next of kin, other than Cinnamon Allard-Thorpe, her beautiful blind daughter.

Richard Munro came back into Thomas Wellborne's office when Elspeth left after explaining that her presence was needed at the hotel.

"Tom," Richard said, brushing away the offer of a gin and tonic, "you may find Elspeth a nuisance, but her instincts are seldom wrong. If she thinks Philippa's death may be murder, you should take her seriously."

Thomas poured himself a drink, doubling his usual amount of gin. He did not like Richard's tone.

"Richard, surely you aren't letting your personal feelings for Ms Duff interfere with your judgment? Do you know how complicated a murder investigation would be at this point? I don't even want to imagine what consequences might arise if suddenly it appears that there was foul play on the Turkish side involving one British citizen and possibly others."

Richard acknowledged Thomas Wellborne's point with a condescending nod but did not agree. "If Philippa Allard-Thorpe was murdered, we can't just ignore the fact."

Thomas banged his glass down on the desk, stood up suddenly, and walked towards the window. "Wouldn't we all benefit if we let the matter lie? We can't interrupt the good work the delegation has done so far by having the Turkish

Cypriot police poking around into their activities at Kantara Castle. The situation is too delicate for that."

Richard would not be placated. "What about the girl Cinnamon? Shouldn't she know the truth about her mother's death?"

"Richard, what would she feel if she found out that her father was the murderer. What then?"

Richard responded quietly. "At least she would know the truth."

"Are you implying that the truth will set her free?" Anger filled Tom Wellborne as he said this.

Richard rose and faced Tom. Richard's eye level was slightly above Tom's, which annoyed him. "If the truth is not discovered, Ernest Thorpe will always be under suspicion, and Cinnamon will always have doubts. If by denying a more thorough investigation, do you want to be responsible for that happening?" Richard tone was now challenging.

Thomas turned suddenly on Richard. "Does Elspeth mean this much to you?"

"Damn you, Tom. Leave Elspeth out of this. I was with her when Philippa fell and no suspicion can be pinned on her. She's doing her job to ensure the security of the hotel, its guests, and the FCO delegation, and Philippa was part of that charge. You can't blame Elspeth for insisting on an inquiry." His voice was low but his colour heightened.

"I didn't ask you to become involved, Richard. Cyprus is my turf, not yours." Thomas returned to his desk, picked up his glass and took a long drink.

"I'm well aware of that, Tom, but I can't leave Nicosia feeling that one of my colleagues reneged on his responsibilities towards a British family and a British international corporation for the sake of low-level negotiations, which probably will come to nothing anyway."

Richard's allegations hurt. Thomas Wellborne wanted to leave the FCO with a degree of distinction. Richard, who had garnered greater recognition in the FCO than Thomas, still held sway in London despite his semi-retired status. Tom remembered the animosity he had felt towards him in Lahore when Richard had been promoted over him, although it was an old hurt and was forgotten until this moment.

"Richard, I have jurisdiction here."

"I'm not asking anything other than that you treat Cinnamon Allard-Thorpe decently. Certainly she has suffered more than most of us, especially at her young age."

"A blind girl cannot come between the success or failure of our delegation."

"She's not just a blind girl. She's the daughter of one of Britain's most noted archaeologists and manager of one of Britain's premier hotels, owned by a man who has great influence in business circles in London. Do you truly think this matter can be brushed under the carpet?"

"It may have to be until the delegation has completed its work."

"You seem to be suggesting that one of the delegation is involved."

The two men's voices were now both raised in their determination to take command of the situation. "This is my mission, Richard. I'd appreciate it if you would leave," Thomas said between his teeth.

Richard stiffened. "My pleasure," he said, and he turned and strode from Thomas Wellborne's office. Thomas glared at Richard's departing back.

*

Richard returned to his bedroom at the Residency. He was still shaking. He fished his mobile phone out of his briefcase and rang Elspeth.

"What's wrong, Dickie? Aren't you at the Residency?"

"Not for much longer. I've been defending your investigation into Philippa's death, and I fear I have just been undiplomatically kicked out."

"That bad?"

"Indeed."

"Why not come here? We are in a state of chaos, with Philippa not being here, but the night manager is trying to take control, and the delegation has withdrawn to their quarters. I must admit I'm glad you are coming. I'll arrange for a room for you."

Once settled in his room at the hotel, Richard made his way to Elspeth's suite. She told him she had dinner ordered for the two of them. She handed him a whisky and poured herself a glass of white wine.

"To better times," he said, fatigue now in his voice. "And to Tom Wellborne's speedy retirement."

Elspeth sat down on the sofa beside Richard and placed her hand on his arm.

"Dickie, why do you suppose Tom Wellborne is so opposed to the autopsy?"

"Possibly because of Philippa's reputation here as being an overly ambitious harridan, and her death is interfering with his success as High Commissioner. Do you think, now that we have time, you can fill me in on all the details of what is going on here?"

"If we can do it over dinner. The kitchen staff function somewhat independently from the rest of the hotel. I sense that the head chef and the others in the kitchen were not terribly fond of Philippa. When I went there to order our dinner, the chef's mouth kept trying to suppress a smile. They are serving *mezes* in the dining room, which I thought you would enjoy. It's a Cypriot smorgasbord, as you probably know."

Dinner arrived shortly afterwards. Elspeth dismissed the waiter after making sure everything on the trolley was ready for serving. She laid the food out on the warm plates and set them on the table.

As they ate, she told Richard about her stay in Nicosia. Each time she reached a point where different people had told her different things, he asked for clarification.

Finally she stopped with an apology. "Now that I'm telling you all of this, Dickie, I'm aware I haven't sat down and done my homework. As you can see, I'm not really clear on the many intertwined feelings forming among the members of the delegation or what tensions already exist there." She told him of her trip to Bitki's parents' home and promised him to secrecy. "Besides, I'm not particularly clear about the timeline of Philippa's career in hotel management. Pamela Crumm is looking into this, but I think I have let my judgment become clouded with my growing dislike of Philippa."

"My dearest Elspeth, since I've been dismissed from the official residence, I have this evening and tomorrow to help you, if you are willing to accept my assistance. I must be in Brussels day after tomorrow, but until that time, I am yours to use as you will."

Elspeth grinned. He caught the look and said stoically, "Within limits." They both burst out laughing.

"Oh, Dickie, I'm so pleased Tom Wellborne kicked you out. Let's get to work in the morning, but for the rest of the evening I think I would rather let my head rest and enjoy your company.

19

After dinner they left the hotel. Elspeth felt distinctly relieved that the hotel manager was no longer watching them. They wandered out on to the streets of Nicosia. The evening was still warm and light, and Elspeth took Richard's hand and pressed his arm to her. They crossed the bridge over the bed of the River Pedieos, which had only a trickle of water running through it, and entered the old part of the city. The narrow streets were lined with tourist shops and restaurants with outdoor seating.

They passed the café where Cinnamon performed her poetry reading and were strolling down the bustling street, when a voice called out to them. They turned to find Christos with Cinnamon on his arm. Cinnamon clung to him tightly with her head resting on his shoulder. She obviously had been crying.

"Is that you, Elspeth?" she asked. "Christos, can we go somewhere where we can talk to Elspeth?"

"My cousin has a restaurant close to here. I'm sure he can provide us with a private corner to talk in." Christos's voice was filled with a desire to look after Cinnamon.

"Do you mind, Elspeth?" Cinnamon asked.

"No, dear Cinnamon, of course not. I want you to meet an old friend of mine, who has helped me over some very difficult times on my life. I think he can help you as well." She introduced Richard without using his title or position.

Christos winked at Elspeth and whispered to Cinnamon. "I'm sure they can help."

Once they were seated, Cinnamon's tears began to flow again. "I wanted to go to the café and asked Christos to take me, but when I heard the noise and the gaiety inside, I couldn't go in. So I asked Christos to walk with me around the streets. I felt I needed to talk with someone about my mother's death. It still feels unreal." Her blind eyes searched around the room as if hoping to find some sort of bearing. "My mother would have told me that crying in public was 'not the done thing'. What would she say now if she knew the tears were for her?"

Christos handed her a handkerchief and put his arm around her shoulders as if to shield her even from Richard and Elspeth.

Elspeth spoke gently, thinking of her own daughter. "Cinnamon, where is your father?"

"He's coming tomorrow morning to take me to his home in Paphos. Do you know I've been there only a few times in all the years since the accident. He tried so hard to protect me. Mother didn't want me to visit him, but I met him whenever I could. She blamed him, you know, for my blindness." Her blank blue-grey eyes blinked as if hoping to see where she was. "It wasn't his fault. It was mine. Mother could not accept that. Oh, why should this all have happened?" The tears came again, more abundantly this time.

Richard broke in with a sweetness Elspeth had not heard from him before. "I lost my wife two years ago. I know what grief is like, and how long it takes to heal. It does, although the love never goes away. Cinnamon, please be assured that we can help you, not with your grief, but with finding out what happened at Kantara Castle yesterday. You may not want to know now, but eventually you will find it is important."

"Mr Munro . . ."

"Please call me Richard."

"Richard, on the contrary, I do want to know what happened as soon as I can. You see, my mother wouldn't listen to the details of the accident that took my sight, and therefore she made all of our lives unbearable with her worst assumptions. I don't want anything like that to happen again. Please find out the truth and quickly."

"Let me help, too," Christos pleaded. "I want to do everything I can for Cinnamon."

"Elspeth, Richard," Cinnamon said turning in the direction where they both were sitting, "Thank you. When I became blind, I thought nothing worse could happen to me. I was wrong. This is worse. I am going to Paphos tomorrow to stay with my father, but please keep in touch with me." She asked Christos to write out her mobile phone number and give it to them.

Christos's cousin brought tea, and they continued to talk quietly. Cinnamon shared moments from her early life on Cyprus as if needing to be in touch with happier times. She turned back to Elspeth and Richard. "Did you know that my father and I were at Kantara Castle yesterday?"

Elspeth looked around at Richard before speaking. "Actually we did know. We saw you from the top of the keep before lunch."

"I didn't know Mummy would be there. When I asked Daddy what he wanted for his fiftieth birthday, he said he wanted to have a picnic with me, and he laughed, saying he also wanted me to invite 'my radical friends'. Calling them my radical friends was a bit of a joke between us, because that's what Mummy called them. They do have political opinions but most of them are rather naïve, and they profess the standard idealistic notions that so many university students have. Mummy didn't like them because she said they were unkempt and unruly. She said she thought I could do better." Cinnamon's voice had a bitter sadness in it. "Oh, why couldn't she have been less critical?"

Elspeth laid her hand over Cinnamon's. "I've always felt the gravest omission parents can make is not being able to express their love but only their misgivings."

"My mother expressing her love? I often wondered if she loved me at all. My parents had another daughter before I was born, you know. She died. I could never be as perfect as she was, even before I became blind." Cinnamon began to cry again, this time in short gulping sobs without tears.

"I don't understand why my mother was on top of the castle when she fell," she continued. "She hated high places. When we used to go to Kantara when I was small, she always let Daddy and me climb up to the top, insisting she liked the view from the level just as well. In fact, why would she be at Kantara Castle at all? It was not her day off; that would have been today. She was going to take me to a reading at the Cultural Centre at the university, if she could get away from the hotel, but our excursions were usually cancelled because of hotel business."

Christos rose and touched Cinnamon's arm.

"It's time to get you back home so you can prepare for your move tomorrow. Since your father is taking you to Paphos, you will need to pack. Let me help you," he said.

Left alone, Elspeth and Richard sat quietly together.

Finally Elspeth broke the silence. "I can't imagine the terrible mixture of feelings Cinnamon is experiencing right now. Love, grief, dismay, and even the stigma of being 'the replacement child'. Who was it that used that term? How hard her healing process is going to be."

Richard sat with sadness in his eyes. "Yes, how terribly hard. My sincere hope is that we can clear away all suspicion that her father was somehow involved. How unfortunate that Cinnamon and her father were at Kantara at the same moment Philippa decided to come and check up on the delegation's picnic. Elspeth, if your fears are true, we have a lot of work to do to unravel this mess, especially how Philippa died and why."

Elspeth looked up at Richard, her face pinched "I thought we might relax this evening, but now I think we should go back to the hotel and begin our investigation. Do you mind, Dickie?"

20

They walked back to the hotel arm in arm. The comfort of Richard's loving hold calmed Elspeth.

"Poor Cinnamon," she said. "Should I have shared my misery over Malcolm's murder with her? Somehow a parent's death is different from a fiancé's, and therefore I didn't. Had I known the truth at the time, I'd have been spared years of grief and led my life quite differently."

"Have you had such thoughts before, Elspeth?"

"I thought about it a great deal when I was recovering in hospital and at home in London. Had I learned earlier who murdered Malcolm and why, I would not have gone to work at Scotland Yard, and I'd never have met Alistair. Instead I would have joined my father's solicitor's office in Pitlochry and probably by now be a batty old spinster solicitor whom people greeted politely on the street and said quietly, 'She could have been so much more considering her education'."

Richard laughed out loud. "I rather think you would have married well, had three sons who were at Fettes College and Oxbridge, a brilliant daughter with whom you constantly sparred and who was at the Sorbonne, and enjoyed a daily romp with your four Labrador retrievers before your highly successful and wealthy husband returned home to the castle."

Elspeth joined his laughter but scolded him. "Dickie, how passé! I should have become an advocate and QC and then a judge of great distinction and looked much better in my wig than any other member of the court, but I'd have missed Lizzie and Peter, and they wouldn't have had the pleasure of me as a mother. I hope they like me being their mother. I think they do, although after talking to Cinnamon, I have many doubts as to whether I was a good parent or not."

Richard squeezed her arm gently. "Every time I've talked to your children they have a delightful way of being concerned about your wellbeing but are fully confident that you are in charge of your own life without them needing to be involved."

"Dear Lizzie and Peter." Elspeth sighed, knowing that her motherly relationships stood on solid ground.

"Dickie, may I ask you a personal question?"

"Of course, but, if it is too personal, I may not answer."

"Did you mind not having children?"

Elspeth could feel Richard becoming tense.

"Yes and no. Marjorie said she didn't want children. It was a sadness I carried for a long time, but I came to terms with it. I decided our niece and nephews would take the place of children we might have had, and, considering my career, I formed as close bonds as possible with them. There are three of them, my brother's son and daughter and Marjorie's brother's son, Fergus. All are wonderful. I hope the next time we're in Scotland together you can meet them all."

"Tell me about them," Elspeth asked. His telling lasted until they arrived back at the hotel.

"Dickie, I know it's getting late, but do come to my suite and let's begin our work. Am I being too much of a martinet?"

"Lead on, slave mistress," he said grinning broadly.

They ordered coffee and brandy from room service and set about reviewing the information Elspeth had already gathered, outlining their activities for the next twenty-four hours.

"Have you made notes so far?" Richard asked, using his professional voice.

"I have the emails I sent to Pamela, but I fear I have not been diligent in compiling the data they contained into a coherent whole and doing cross checks. Until now there seemed no reason to do so. Pamela suspected Philippa might be a problem, but no one expected she would die."

"How do you usually track this sort of thing?"

"When necessary I print out my notes and look for the obvious discrepancies, often using a timeline."

Richard held up his brandy snifter, twirled the liquid in it so it caught the lights in the room and said, "Shall we begin?"

It took her almost two hours to compile the emails and for them to read them together. Then she told him everything she could remember that was not in the emails. She tried not to leave out anything of importance, including her meals with Colin French and his attention to her.

Richard asked questions as she spoke but made no comments otherwise. When Elspeth had finished, he sat quietly sipping his brandy before speaking.

"Everything you've told me seems to revolve around Philippa, even your conversations with the members of the delegation," he said.

"Surely not the issues Bitki told me about when I was at her parents' home."

"I think Philippa was the person reading the papers. You said she had to control everything. Surely she, more than anyone else, had easy access to the papers and would want to know what the delegation was about. If I am reading her character correctly, it would be like her to tamper with the papers."

"To what end, Dickie? Do you think she might have been spying for one side or the other?"

"That's a possibility but I think that she may have wanted somehow to manipulate the delegation's situation in the hotel to her own advantage."

"Are you suggesting that she was trying to find things in the papers that might prove that Bitki or Onan Mitsui are collaborating with the Turks? I can't see how Philippa would benefit from knowing this."

Richard frowned and said, " Let's go back over Philippa's advancement in hotel management. I'm still unclear about the sequence of events. Do you think we can work out the timeline? Don't you have information from three sources, your lunch with the brigadier, Pamela Crumm's review of Philippa's personnel file, and your subsequent dinner with Colin?"

Elspeth tried to remember. "At lunch Colin told me Philippa had tired of Ernest and started working at the hotel that she finally inherited. She turned the hotel around and made it a great success, and later sold it at a huge profit. Afterwards Philippa went to the States and later returned, proclaiming herself an expert on international hotel management, and she became assistant manager of one of the big hotels here. From what Colin said she transferred laterally to the Kennington Nicosia, and on Georgios Konstantinidis's death she became manager."

"What did Pamela Crumm tell you? Think now in terms of dates."

"She said Philippa studied at the Cornell School of Hotel Administration and afterwards trained at the Waldorf Astoria and Plaza in New York City before coming back to Cyprus. Pamela said the recommendations from the Waldorf and Plaza were supposedly written shortly before the disaster in New York on September eleventh, two thousand and one."

"When was Cinnamon's accident?"

"She told me it was four years ago."

"In two thousand and one. Do you know what month?"

"No, but I am sure Cinnamon will tell us if we ask."

"Has Pamela verified any of the information in Philippa's personnel file?" he asked. "I think we need to get dates other than those on the letters of recommendation."

"I'll call Pamela first thing in the morning."

"Now," Richard said, "tell me what Colin French told you the night you had dinner at his home."

Elspeth rubbed her forehead, trying to recall the exact words. "He said that after the accident, Philippa took Cinnamon to the States for treatment and came back to become, how did he put it, 'Ms Allard-Thorpe, hotel manager extraordinaire'."

"We have three different stories. Why didn't Colin mention at dinner the things he had mentioned at lunch, specifically that Philippa had studied hotel management and owned and run a hotel before Cinnamon's accident?"

"In his defence, both at lunch and dinner he did mention that he only knew these things through gossip."

"But he did change his story."

Elspeth agreed. "We'll get the Kennington Organisation's side of the story in the morning. Dickie, it's after midnight. Shall we call it a day?"

Richard rose and took Elspeth gently in his arms. "Good night, sweet Elspeth," he whispered.

After she showed him out, she stood leaning against the doorframe. Intense physical sensations circulated through her body. She squeezed her eyes together in order to let go the fire burning inside her. "This isn't the time, Dickie," she said firmly to the air and wished she meant it.

The phone in her sitting room rang as Elspeth was dressing. She checked her watch and found it already was nine o'clock. Despite the brainstorming Richard and she had done the night before and the many questions raised, Elspeth had slept soundly and dreamed of her Aunt Magdelena's garden on the island of Gozo in Malta. When she was a child, Elspeth thought of it as her secret garden, known to no one else, and in her dream she floated above it and felt great peace.

"This is the reception desk, Ms Duff. There's someone here who would like to speak to you."

Elspeth took the call.

"Ms Duff, Ernest Thorpe speaking," a deep voice said. Cinnamon obviously had inherited her rich voice from her father. "Is there somewhere I can speak to you in private?"

"Does Cinnamon know you are here, Mr Thorpe?"

"I told her I would come round at ten. I expect she's in her room at Phil's gathering her things together, so I have a few moments free."

"Then I'll meet you in the lobby in about twenty minutes. In the meantime I'll arrange for a private room where we can speak." And I'll also finish putting on my clothes, she thought, grinning at the thought of greeting him in her red silk pyjamas.

Ernest Thorpe was waiting in the lobby for Elspeth, who was now fully and fashionably dressed. On close examination Ernest Thorpe resembled his daughter. Although Cinnamon had inherited her mother's strong bones, she had the same softness in her face her father had. Elspeth had ordered coffee, tea, and breakfast rolls to be delivered to the private room. After she poured a cup of coffee for each of them, she took a seat opposite him.

"First of all, I want to thank you for all your kindness to Cinnamon, both before and after Philippa's fall. Cinnamon told me you and your friend met her last evening and were so kind," he said.

"The pleasure was ours, truly. I have a daughter who is only slightly older than Cinnamon."

"So she told me. Ms Duff, may I ask you to help the two of us?"

"Of course."

He sipped his coffee tentatively. "Cinnamon is extremely vulnerable right now. She has spoken to me about wanting to know everything about her mother's death. As much as I love her, I feel I know her only slightly these days. Her mother made every effort to keep us apart. We stole times together, but they were always short. I don't know how much the facts of Phil's death will affect her, and therefore I am asking you to use your best instincts in the way you tell her what you learn."

"I shall. Right now there is little to report, only a great deal of speculation. Perhaps, Mr Thorpe, you could clear up some of the mysteries about what happened at Kantara Castle yesterday."

He put his cup down and selected a croissant. "I don't think I can tell you much. Cinnamon asked me what I would like to have for my fiftieth birthday. I wanted to ask her to come live with me and leave her mother, but Cinnamon was strangely bonded to her mother, and I knew she would not be able to break that hold. So I asked to meet her friends. She suggested Kantara Castle because we loved going there together when she was a girl. I had no idea Phil would be there on the same day."

"Do you think Cinnamon told her mother you would be there?"

"I have no idea. Most likely Phil weaselled it out of her." Deep bitterness filled Ernest Thorpe's voice.

Elspeth looked up at Ernest. At the picnic Philippa had said she had come to Kantara Castle because she wanted to make sure the delegation's outing was a success. This had surprised Elspeth, as the duties of hotel managers did not usually extend to supervising activities outside the hotel. The kitchen always managed catered events including picnics. Cinnamon said Philippa had been on duty that day and the following day was her day off. Initially Elspeth assumed Philippa was trying to show what diligence and care she was showing the delegation, but now that seemed doubtful. Had Philippa gone there instead to spy on Cinnamon at her father's party?

"Mr Thorpe, did you talk to Philippa that day?"

"No, actually, I saw her but did not want to meet her, so I rounded up my bunch and promised them beer at a tavern in Kyrenia. We left shortly before one o'clock. I don't know what time Phil fell, but we neither saw nor heard anything."

Elspeth knew this was a lie. Richard and she had both heard the altercation between Philippa and Ernest. Why did he not tell Elspeth the truth?

"Mmm," Elspeth said, not knowing how to respond but not wanting to challenge him. "May I ask you a bit about Philippa's past? I hope I am not being intrusive." Elspeth continued without waiting for his assent. "When did Philippa go to America to study hotel management?"

Ernest Thorpe looked at her curiously. "After Cinnamon's accident, Phil took her to New York supposedly to see if the blindness could be corrected. I wasn't aware that she did a course there, but she might have. They were gone for about six months."

"When was that?"

"The accident was in early February of two thousand and one. They must have left about a month after that."

"And when did they come back?"

"Just before September the eleventh. I was relieved that they had arrived here safely before the terrorist attack in New York."

"Can you tell me anything about the hotel that Philippa ran before the accident?"

"The old Cypriot Britannia? Quite frankly, Ms Duff, that was one of the biggest embarrassments of my life. Phil decided that living around my dig was dreadfully boring, and one day she simply left."

Why? Elspeth wondered. Was there someone else? Ernest did not seem to notice Elspeth's bewilderment.

"I found out several weeks later she had taken a job at the hotel," he continued. "Rumours flew that she also had taken up residence with the owner of the hotel, who was old enough to be her grandfather. You can imagine how difficult I found it to explain this to Cinnamon, who was twelve at the time, and, although a budding beauty, was quite shy about her sexuality.

The old man died of a heart attack in about six months, and Phil, as she had a way of doing, took over the hotel."

"Was Cinnamon still living with you when this happened?"

"Yes. Because Phil had ambitions of her own, she wanted nothing to do with our daughter."

"But recently Philippa seemed to have custody. What happened?" Elspeth hoped she could ask this question without getting a lie for an answer.

Ernest Thorpe's mouth twisted in distress. "The accident," he said almost under his breath. "You see, it gave her control, which was the most important thing in the world to her. She was in the process of selling the old hotel when the accident happened. Shortly afterwards she came into a great deal of money. The accident meant she could demand control of Cinnamon. Phil filed for custody, making the case I was an unfit parent, and took her to New York under the pretence of getting treatment for her eyes."

"Pretence?"

"Cinnamon told me later they had lived most of the time at the Plaza Hotel there. Phil was gone much of the time, leaving Cinnamon alone in the care of a nurse, who took her out into Central Park on most days. The nurse spoke little English, but Cinnamon picked up enough Spanish to be able to chatter away with her."

"Do you know if they went to Ithaca?" Elspeth asked, without elaborating.

"No, they stayed the whole time in the States. I don't think they ever were in Greece."

Elspeth smiled inwardly at her deception. A scholar of archaeology and classical history would associate Ithaca with ancient Greece and not with Cornell University.

"When Philippa came back to Cyprus, where did she go?"

"Briefly to one of the bigger hotels in Nicosia and soon afterwards to the Kennington hotel."

"You're sure about that?"

"Quite sure, but you must know that."

"I'm sorry to have been so inquisitive, Mr Thorpe. It's an occupational hazard."

"I fully understand. I ask a lot questions, too, but most of them are about the first millennium BCE."

"Cinnamon said you are taking her to Paphos today. Will you give me your contact details, so that I can keep you informed? Would you prefer I email you about my investigation into Philippa's death, since Cinnamon would not be able to see what I have to say?"

"That would be best, although I know she wants you to stay in contact with her."

"I promise I'll stay in touch. Ask the reception desk to call me in my suite when you are ready to go. I'll come and say goodbye to you both."

Elspeth rang Richard's room and arranged to meet him in time to take leave of Cinnamon. Afterwards, she decided to go to the delegates' common room to see if any of them were about. She found Sophia Driscoll there, her children around her. They were gobbling down heaps of unhealthy foods and shunning the fruit, yoghurt and whole grain breads.

Sophia drew Elspeth aside. "I saw you with Ernest Thorpe this morning in the lobby. One wonders if all the gossip about him and Philippa has any basis of truth. She fled from him, you know, when she found out he was having an affair with one of his graduate students. She tried to get Cinnamon to come with her, but Ernest spread rumours that Philippa had deserted the family. How terribly odd that Philippa and Ernest were at the castle the day she fell."

Her implication was clear.

Elspeth said as blandly as she could, "Do you think there is a connection?"

"Of course, Ms Duff. They hated each other. He obviously pushed her over the brink."

"Did you see him?"

"No, he is far too clever for that. All of us on Cyprus knew that after Philippa had changed him from the gawky twenty-something archaeologist into the dishy person he is today, and every woman who came in contact with him fell in love with him."

"Including you?" Elspeth asked with a mischievous grin.

"Yes, a bit I suppose, but I had just met Michael, who, for all his pedantry, captured my heart. "And," she said with a flourish, "I have never looked back."

Elspeth laughed. Because no one else was in the room, Elspeth withdrew and left Sophia to her brood. Elspeth wondered where Sophia had heard this gossip about Philippa. Elspeth preferred Ernest Thorpe's version of the story.

21

After assuring Cinnamon that they would stay in daily touch, Richard and Elspeth retired to her suite.

Elspeth sank down onto one of the sofas in her sitting room, drew her hand through her short hair with a grimace and blew out her breath. "Dickie, are expat communities always so filled with rumour and gossip?"

Richard sat opposite her, and smiled at her with admiration. Her clothes that morning were more formal than they had been at the picnic, tailored beige trousers, bright blue silk shirt, and gold jewellery. They set off her cobalt blue eyes, one of her few physical assets she liked. By his look, she knew he approved and it warmed her.

"That is a given," he said in answer to her question. "Any pettiness of humankind is magnified ten times over in the small communities the British Empire left behind."

Elspeth cocked her head at him and decided his long face suited him. "Have you enjoyed the company of expats over your career?"

"Not really, but Marjorie always said expat life was a microcosm of the real world only much more vicious."

Elspeth laughed. "Marjorie never put a foot wrong, did she?"

"Seldom. She was raised in the Commonwealth and so grew up in that culture. She always said there was no real harm in it."

Elspeth remembered Lady Marjorie, her aristocratic manner and her icy charm. To Elspeth's knowledge Marjorie never did put her foot wrong. Elspeth was envious of people with qualities like Marjorie's. Elspeth had heard it said that Marjorie made Richard's career a success. She may have helped, although Elspeth knew Richard was abundantly talented in matters of diplomacy.

If Elspeth were to join Richard's life, she knew she would have to change and to face her unruly edges, which all her adult life she had tried to keep under tight bounds. Over the last year, Elspeth was slowly coming to grips with how Marjorie's long shadow was cast over her new relationship with Richard. Yet, if there were to be a deeper relationship between the two of them, she would have to accept their past together and be comfortable with it. Why now did Elspeth feel jealous? After all, Marjorie had been an integral part of Richard's life for over thirty years, and Elspeth had already rejected Richard's two proposals of marriage to her many years before.

"Dickie, let's get to work," Elspeth said, putting away her thoughts. "Let's leave Philippa's hotel background for now. I propose we talk to Colin French again about the fall. Did he see it? He never said. Also, we need to question the delegation as to where they were when Philippa fell."

Richard looked at her lovingly, and at that minute she almost gave in to admitting her growing need of his affection. No, she said again to herself, not now.

"Let's set up a plan to do this," she said, masking her feelings.

"Later today?" he suggested, to which she agreed.

"If Ernest Thorpe is the killer," she went on, "should we have allowed Cinnamon to go with him?"

"Do you think he would harm her? I don't think he would."

"You're probably right. We should learn more about him, however. Who else in the rumour mill would know about him and his life with Philippa and afterwards?"

Richard frowned. "Your brigadier has already helped but his information is somewhat contradictory." Richard stressed the word your, which annoyed Elspeth.

"Certainly the Wellbornes are out," Richard continued, "which is of little relevance as they have only been here for several years. I'm *persona non grata* with them anyway. I'm trying to think if we knew anyone who retired to Cyprus. Give me a moment."

Despite her resolve, Elspeth flinched at the use of the word "we" meaning Richard and Marjorie. Naturally he would think of Marjorie when speaking of his past life in the diplomatic service.

"Let's Google Ernest Thorpe," she suggested, "and see if he has any university connections here. Academicians, in my experience, are often more truthful than others." Elspeth found her reading glasses, which she perched at the end of her nose, and booted up her computer. Information on Ernest Thorpe came up on numerous sites. His main academic relationship appeared to be with University College London.

"Dickie, do you remember Amanda Bell?"

He came to look over her shoulder, putting his hand lightly on her shoulder. She let it rest there but resisted putting her hand over his.

"In Stresa? Amanda would be hard to forget," he said with a chuckle. Amanda, a six-foot-three redheaded beauty, was badly injured in a car crash when working for Lord Kennington in Stresa the year before. Yet, despite her broken leg, she skilfully manoeuvred herself around in a wheelchair, and, toting a concealed and probably illegal handgun, she cornered a kidnapper. She was hard to forget.

"Have I updated you on Amanda?" Elspeth asked. "Eric Kennington was so impressed with her work with us in Stresa that he hired her part time while she is finishing her degree at University College London. I wonder if I still have her email address. Perhaps she can help us find links to Ernest Thorpe and people who know him outside of the confines of the expat community."

Elspeth scrolled down her contacts list. She pushed her glasses higher up her nose and said, "I have her address. I'll type a quick email to her and let's hope she is at home studying and not off on some assignment for Eric."

Elspeth tapped away at the keyboard.

"Elspeth, may I use your mobile? I want to ring Margaret, my PA in Malta, who has access to my address book. Don't worry, she is quite used to me ringing her at all hours. She has a flat close to the High Commission, and, since she lives alone, she appreciates having something to do when she is not at work. It helps with the loneliness, she says."

Without looking up, Elspeth waved her hand at the sideboard, where her mobile phone lay beside the hotel's daily offering of flowers.

"I keep thinking there is someone we knew who retired here," Richard said as he dialled. "If Margaret reads down the list, I think I'll remember who it is. She should be at her desk at this hour, but if not, it takes her less than fifteen minutes to get to the High Commission."

Elspeth nodded and smiled. She had met Margaret, a fussy middle-aged woman and had no reason to fear competition. "I do love communications in the twenty-first century," she said. "Do you realise that in the last ten minutes we have accessed the internet and used email, and you are about to make a call relayed by satellite? What would the Crusaders have thought?"

"Or even ourselves thirty years ago. Elspeth, I love and hate these times. We have lost the art of leisurely living in a civilised world."

"But gained more connections in virtual time. It's brilliant."

"Is it? I wonder if personal relations these days through the machine you are banging away at and the one I have in my hand are better than the handwritten letters and face-to-face encounters of our youth. I like the old ways, not the new ones. We expected less urgency and were definitely more polite."

Elspeth looked over her glasses at Richard. "My more progressive friends in California would say we were truer to ourselves because we can be totally divorced from those who were different from us, but that is another discussion altogether."

A beep sounded from Elspeth's computer, which signalled she had an email message. Mandy Bell must have been at her computer when Elspeth's email arrived.

To: eduff@kenningtonhotels.com
From: a.bell@archaelogy.ucl.ac.uk.
Dear Elspeth,

Hello to Sir Richard!! I am glad you two are working together on another case. I enjoyed collaborating with you both in Italy. All my wounds are now healed except for the occasional ache in my leg on very wet days. Will Tuttle and I still see each other when he is in town, which isn't often enough!

In response to your question, Ernest Thorpe is on the faculty here, although he has been on site in Cyprus forever and does not venture back to the northern climes other than once or twice a year to deliver a lecture. Daddy knows him slightly, having visited Cyprus on trips to and from Egypt. I've left a message for Daddy, who luckily is here in London, and I will let you know when I hear from him.

Best regards to you both. I am wrapped up in my final papers but at Christmastime could be diverted by a trip to Cyprus if you need me.

Warmest regards to you both,
Mandy

Richard came over to where Elspeth was sitting and read over her shoulder.

"It doesn't sound as if the romance between Will and Mandy is progressing very quickly," Elspeth said.

Richard chuckled. "They're destined for each other, I think. Give them time. But do you think her father can help us?"

"We'll find out. If Mandy perseveres with her parent the way she did during the murder investigation and kidnapping in Stresa, then help is on the way. Maybe Sir Collingwood Bell can clear up the mystery of the two sides of Ernest Thorpe."

The satellite phone's ring interrupted them. Richard's PA was on the line. He retreated to the sofa and took a note pad and pen with him. He kept saying, "No. No. Haven't heard from them in years. Start with names beginning with M." Finally he heard something that seemed to please him. "Yes, that's it. Give me the address."

He scribbled something down. "Is there a phone number or an email address? Well, no matter. Cyprus is small and I am sure we can find them."

He turned to Elspeth. "The military attaché who was at the British High Commission in Kuala Lumpur when we were there retired to Cyprus ten years ago. Marjorie was quite fond of his wife, and they kept in touch. As of two years ago they were living here in Nicosia. I wonder if we can find a way to contact them."

"Personal letter?" she suggested with an arched eyebrow.

"Touché," he said, his eyes twinkling. "Point well taken."

She grimaced and then laughed in return. "Let me see if Christos is here," she said. "He may be able help us."

Elspeth rang down to the staff room and was told that Christos had been out of the hotel all morning and was not on duty until noon, but half an hour later, Christos rang Elspeth and agreed to come to her suite.

"Do you know this address?" Elspeth asked, as she handed Christos Richard's note.

"The street is in a district where a lot of British expatriates live. Most of the houses there are villas, which they could not afford elsewhere," Christos said.

Elspeth dug out her map of Nicosia and asked Christos to show her where the street was. He quickly found it and circled it.

"How could we find out if the major has a phone line?" Sir Richard asked.

"I would suggest it would be easiest if you sent a note around to your friend."

"Ah ha," Richard said, suppressing a smile. "I'll write a note."

Elspeth burst out laughing.

"Christos, when you go back to the front desk, will you ask the concierge to call me. I'll need someone to deliver the note," Elspeth said.

"I want to help Cinnamon in any way possible." Christos's black brows lowered over his dark passionate eyes. "She protests whenever I offer and keeps telling me to be careful to keep my job here."

Elspeth thought of the contrast between this young man and the woman he so ardently wanted to protect. Ebony versus gold.

"I promise you things will be different in the hotel from now on," Elspeth said. "I'll probably be calling on you a great deal in the next few days. What time are you off work?

"I have a break at four but am taking the evening shift for a friend who covered for me this morning."

"Christos, can you get your schedule to me for the next week and let me know how I can reach you when you are not at the hotel?" she asked.

"Yes. I'll send it up to you. I must go. It's nearly noon."

*

Major Bruce Ogilvy was surprised to receive a letter from Richard Munro written on the expensive stationery provided to guests at the Kennington Nicosia. His wife had written to Richard on Marjorie's death and received a short note back, but that was their last communication. The major called Katherine, his wife, in from the conservatory and showed her Richard's letter.

"Richard says he will be here until early tomorrow morning and wonders if he might see us on a 'half-business, half-pleasure' basis, as he puts it. Are we engaged this afternoon? He's invited us for tea at the Kennington hotel. They have jolly good teas there as I recall."

Katherine Ogilvy took the note and read it. "I would give up all other engagements for the chance of a tea at the Kennington, but as it happens we are free."

"I'll ring him then and accept. I wonder what he means by half-business, half-pleasure. Do you suppose it has anything to do with the death of Philippa Allard-Thorpe? She always was a rather unpleasant sort, don't you think?"

The news of Philippa's death had been in *The Cyprus Mail* that morning.

The major rang the hotel and left a message accepting Richard's invitation with pleasure.

*

Elspeth rang room service and had lunch delivered to her suite. She asked for copies of the morning papers and spread out *The Cyprus Mail* in front of her. The article on Philippa's death was discreet but politicised.

Elspeth read the article to Richard.

> *Tragedy strikes once again at Kantara Castle, leaving one to question why Turkish authorities have not put up proper protective barriers at one of North Cyprus's famous sites. Long time Cyprus resident, Philippa Allard-Thorpe, manager of the Kennington Nicosia hotel and ex-wife of the famed archaeologist Ernest Thorpe, fell from the top of the keep at the castle yesterday and was killed instantly. The incident has been determined to be an accident, and no police*

*investigation is expected. Her daughter, Cinnamon,
and her ex-husband survive her. Funeral arrangements
are pending.*

Richard helped himself to a breadstick and absently waved it at Elspeth. "The article, despite its anti-Turkish bias, mentions a critical point. *The incident has been determined to be an accident, and no police investigation is expected.*"

Elspeth raised one eyebrow slightly, which she often did when thinking. "The brigadier must have been devilishly clever in contriving to get Philippa's body across the Green Line. How can we confirm when and if he actually did report the fall to the police? If he did, I suspect it was after he brought Philippa's body across to this side of the Green Line. I hope the North Cypriot police won't stir up an international incident over something they undoubtedly would prefer to forget. Dickie, I still can't rule out foul play. Many of the important people in Philippa's life were there. Most of them disliked her, some more adamantly than others. Besides, Cinnamon told us her mother didn't like heights, so what was Philippa doing at the top of the keep? The only reason she would climb up there, I think, was because she was going to meet someone on top, someone who may have pushed her over."

"And," said Richard as he took a bite off the end of breadstick, "we all had spread out to our various postprandial spots to relax after the meal. I think our plan to discover everyone's whereabouts grows in importance."

"Something has been bothering me ever since her fall," Elspeth said. "Why didn't any of us hear it?"

"Hear it, my dearest? A person falling on the ground doesn't make much noise, especially a person as slight as Philippa."

"But why didn't she scream?" Elspeth said.

"Like the Hound of the Baskervilles?" he relied. "Why didn't the dog bark?"

"Exactly. Perhaps I lived too long in Hollywood, but no producer would have let someone fall from a tower without a bloodcurdling scream."

22

After lunch Elspeth and Richard made their way to the east wing of the hotel and found most of the delegation having lunch in the common room. The twin boys were looking bored as they sat in front of plates heaped with food. The Driscoll children were sitting stiffly in front of their plates and appeared to have just been disciplined. Azai was nowhere in site, but his parents sat in a corner eating companionably, their attitude relaxed.

Elspeth spoke to them all generally.

"I wonder if Sir Richard and I might talk to each one of you after you've finished lunch? It has to do with Philippa Allard-Thorpe."

Heads turned around. Glad of their attention, Elspeth continued. "Let's start with the twins first, and then Joanna, followed by you, George. Michael and Sophia, it won't be necessary to talk to your children at this point, but we would like to talk to each of you individually. Bitki next and Onan last."

Elspeth purposely used the delegation members' given names. This technique had been taught to her at Scotland Yard. Using people's given names relegated them to a position of lesser status than if their titles and surnames were used. She also assumed her most authoritarian voice.

Elspeth had commandeered a small room off the delegation's common area where they could do their questioning. The twins' ennui evaporated as they came in the room.

"Was she murdered?" one of the twins asked. Elspeth thought it was Christopher.

"Not to my knowledge, but Lord Kennington wants to know what actually happened at the picnic. Sir Richard and I thought you might be the two people who could give us the most information. That is why we asked to see you first."

"This is awesome, Charles," said one twin who now identified the other. "We are involved in a real investigation! You're a detective, aren't you, Mrs Duff?"

"I was when I was at Scotland Yard. Now I handle security investigations for Lord Kennington," she said, trying to keep back a grin.

The boys seemed impressed. "Have you solved a lot of crimes?" Charles asked.

"Quite a few," Elspeth admitted blandly, knowing by saying so she had caught the twins' attention. "In the past Sir Richard and I have solved three murder cases together."

"Cool!" It was Christopher this time. "Were they bloody?"

Richard looked sternly down his long nose, which caused Elspeth to choke back a giggle.

"We are not here to talk about that," Richard said. "We want to know what you boys were doing after lunch at the castle."

Charles took the lead. "Brigadier French told us that King Richard the Lionheart laid siege against his enemies who were hiding in the castle and that terrible things went on in the dungeon. We thought we would go down there and find out how creepy it was."

"Did you see Ms Allard-Thorpe after lunch?" Elspeth asked.

Both boys thought. Finally Charles answered. "No. I remember seeing her earlier when she went over to speak to a bloke who was with a group of guys and that blind girl that wanders around the gardens at the hotel, but that was before lunch."

"Did you see that too, Christopher?" Richard used the avuncular tone that always annoyed Elspeth.

"No, but Charles told me about it. I went and found a rock to spread out the map of the castle that the brigadier had given us. I was trying to find the way into the dungeon. Charles went off on his own."

"Charles, did you hear what Ms Allard-Thorpe said when she spoke to the man?" Elspeth asked.

"Not exactly. Actually, he looked up and saw her coming and turned his back. She may have said something to him. If she did, I couldn't hear. I heard him call to the others in his group, and they quickly moved away. They were all laughing and nodding their heads. One of them gave a high sign."

"Then Ms Allard-Thorpe never spoke to the man?" Richard asked.

"Not that I heard," Charles said again, "but she looked really miffed when he turned away."

"Where did you go then?" Elspeth asked.

"I went back and found Chris, who said he knew how to get into the dungeon. After lunch, we were trying to get down there when Daddy came to fetch us. He said there had been an accident and we were going back to Nicosia straight away."

Richard smiled at them. "You two have been very useful. I'm leaving Nicosia in the morning, but I want you to try to remember anything else you saw or heard and report it to Ms Duff immediately."

"Wow!" said Christopher, "wait until we tell the others at school about this." His voice became squeaky. "And what did you do during your summer hols?" Then he spoke deeply, "Oh, actually, not much. We were helping an ex-Scotland Yard detective and a Knight of the Realm in the investigation of a murder at a castle where King Richard the Lionheart held siege during the Crusades. How cool it that!"

They all laughed. Elspeth broke in. "Charles and Christopher, there is no evidence Ms Allard-Thorpe's death was a murder, as exciting as that may seem. She fell from the battlements of the keep. There were no guardrails. We think it probably was an accident, but we still have to question everything."

"Off you go," Richard said. "And thanks for your information. It was most helpful."

The boys left with a conspiratorial look on their faces. Their expressions were livelier than Elspeth had seen them since they had arrived in Cyprus.

Joanna Colton came next. "What have my boys been telling you? They seemed positively elated."

Elspeth shook her head in sympathy. "Basically they said they were trying to find a way into the dungeon and did not see Ms Allard-Thorpe fall. I'm glad. Death may seem exciting to teenagers but the reality of it is never easy."

"We swept them out of there as soon as I heard about the accident. A young man, one of the waiters, was wonderful. He was clearing up but immediately took charge of us, shuttling us into the coaches and supervising the other waiters who were putting the remains of the picnic in the back, although he looked rather scared. You should keep your eyes on that young man. He's very clever. As a matter of course, I did everything I could to help him."

Elspeth acknowledged Joanna's contribution with an appreciative nod. It was what she would have expected. "Mrs Colton, I admire your ability to take charge when needed. We are aware that Christos is a valuable asset to the Kennington Nicosia. But the reason we are here is to try and determine where everyone was at the time of the fall. We still haven't found any witnesses."

"George, my husband, was napping near the entrance to the castle. He'd found a bench in the shade, planted himself there, opened up his book and dozed off. Poor dear, he doesn't have the energy he used to have. I was helping with the clear up, an old habit of mine, although I'm sure the Kennington hotels would never expect a guest to do such a thing."

"Where was Ms Allard-Thorpe at this point?" Elspeth kept her voice bland.

"High-handed Philippa? Sorry, we all called her that. Speak no ill of the dead. She was so bossy most of the time. She was probably off directing the activities of one or the other of our delegation before she fell."

"Did you see her during the tidying up?" Elspeth asked.

"I was so busy that I didn't any pay attention to her. I was glad she wasn't managing the clear up and demanding this, that and the other thing. When she was around, everything had to be her way."

Elspeth resisted making any comment.

Luckily Richard came to the rescue. "Did you see the blind girl and her friends?"

"Actually not, although Michael Driscoll mentioned he had seen his friend, Ernest Thorpe, Philippa's ex-husband.

Michael wondered why Ernest had chosen to come to Kantara Castle on the same day as our picnic."

"It is a mystery to both of us," Richard said. "We'll ask Mr Driscoll about that, but can you tell us about anything you saw personally, particularly involving Ms Allard-Thorpe?"

"The waiters all seemed surprised when she arrived and, when they saw her charging up the stairs to the castle, there was a low groan from most of them. Under his breath, one said, "Not her here. What'll we do wrong this time?" I had a feeling that Ms Allard-Thorpe was not much liked by her staff."

Elspeth glanced over at Richard. "Did you know any of the waiters other than Christos?" she asked.

Joanna nodded. "Several of them have waited on us here at the hotel. I don't know their names but I could identify them."

"I may ask you to identify them later," Elspeth said. "Mrs Colton, others in the delegation have expressed the same concern you have about Ms Allard-Thorpe's interference. Have any of your personal belongings been tampered with or gone through?"

Joanna frowned. "Unlike Bitki, who is always suspicious, I don't pay much heed to that sort of thing. If you are asking if anything of ours has been stolen, no, absolutely not."

"Normally when I conduct inquiries for the Kennington Organisation, I try to stay with the facts, but throughout my stay here, I have a sense that Philippa Allard-Thorpe stirred up a great number of emotions among your group. Even you have labelled her, what was it, 'high-handed Philippa'. What do you mean by that?" Elspeth asked.

Joanna Colton smiled weakly. "I've been accused of over organising things, but I seldom have met anyone like Philippa before. She would walk into the room and immediately find seven things wrong with her staff's performance. George and I have lived all over the world and stayed in many hotels. This is by far the nicest one, even with Philippa's constant butting in all the time. She criticized things I couldn't see, and I do notice things."

Elspeth did not want to defend Philippa, but she wanted to appease Joanna Colton. "Ms Allard-Thorpe was a new manager in our organisation, and perhaps she was a bit overzealous. A longer tenure in her job probably would have solved that." As she spoke, Elspeth knew her words were not true.

"The problem with Ms Philippa Allard-Thorpe was that she had absolutely no sense of humour. I may be bossy in my own way, but I can laugh at myself when I get out of hand. Ask George."

Elspeth believed it, and it amused her. "I shall. May we talk again?"

"I'm here and always willing to oblige."

Richard followed Joanna as she swept from the room and invited her husband to join them.

George Colton sat down and greeted Richard as a colleague and then Elspeth.

"Damnable way to end a picnic. I was just having a nice nap under a shady tree when Joanna came and woke me. She was afraid the twins might have seen what had happened. I don't think she will ever come to terms with their ghoulishness. I'm afraid I was a bit like that myself at their age."

"George, you and I have been around a long time. What do you make of the whole situation?" Richard asked.

George Colton looked surprised. "I suppose I've been so focussed on the talks that I've been in my own cocoon. I leave all the outside organising to Joanna, who in her loving way usually overdoes it."

"Tell me," Richard asked, "What did you make of Ms Allard-Thorpe?"

"The manager who fell?"

"Exactly."

"Attractive woman. She was a bit aggressive for my taste. American, I understand, although she didn't sound like it. I suppose I didn't pay much attention to her. She was one of those people in the background who make things happen. Isn't that what a hotel manager is supposed to do?"

"They should, but the Kennington Organisation is not used to having one of their managers fall from the top of a castle keep," Elspeth said.

"Unfortunate," George Colton sniffed. "The boys will love telling the story at Winchester when they go back in the autumn, but quite frankly the sooner you can clear this up, the better. I wouldn't want this sort of thing complicating our talks."

Richard looked sympathetically at George. "I understand. We're sorry to have disturbed you, George."

"Didn't disturb anything really except my nap."

George Colton left the room with a nod to Richard and a smile towards Elspeth.

Michael Driscoll was next but before he came into the room, Elspeth turned to Richard. "Because Michael Driscoll's a friend of Ernest Thorpe, we may get more information from him than the rest, but let's limit our conversation with him to the things that happened yesterday. After you leave for

Brussels, I'll try to get him to tell to me more about Ernest Thorpe."

"Whatever you say, my dearest, on one promise, that you will keep me thoroughly informed when I'm away."

"I promise," said Elspeth. How comfortable it was to have Richard at her side. "I wouldn't think of leaving you out."

Michael Driscoll entered the room, his face filled with intelligence and intensity instead of his normal abstracted expression. This is the real Michael Driscoll, Elspeth thought.

He sat across from to his two inquisitors and took charge of the conversation. "Ernest Thorpe and I have been friends and colleagues for many years. I hope in your investigation of Philippa's death you realise that Ernest is one of the most honourable and trustworthy people on earth and has more integrity than any other person I've ever met. I saw Ernest and Cinnamon at the castle yesterday, and I think they were as surprised at Philippa's arrival as anyone else. I spoke briefly with Ernest just before he took Cinnamon and her friends away. Seeing Philippa, he decided his best course of action was to leave as quickly as possible, even if it spoiled the outing Cinnamon had arranged for his birthday. The lads were delighted to go to Kyrenia for beer at a tavern there, but Cinnamon was definitely upset. She said to me, 'Why does she always want to spoil everything?' What can one say to such a beautiful child and one so wounded by the hatred between her parents?"

Elspeth agreed. "Yes, more than anyone Cinnamon is the victim of their squabbling. What a pity for her. Did Philippa speak to Cinnamon or Ernest Thorpe yesterday?"

"Ernest told me he saw her coming and scrupulously tried to avoid her, but Cinnamon could not ignore her mother.

Cinnamon inherited her warm heart from her father. I don't know exactly what Philippa said to Cinnamon, but Ernest said after speaking to her mother, tears came to her beautiful blind eyes. My description, not his. Philippa was a bitch. If you will forgive me saying so, she deserved to die."

Richard sat up, startled. "Surely, Michael, no person deserves to die ahead of her time."

"Richard, Philippa's time should have come long ago. She did nothing but cause misery for her family," Michael Driscoll said with real vehemence.

"That's one of the sad things about modern life. We don't know how to muddle along any more," Richard said, regret in his voice. "Did Ernest hear what Cinnamon said to her mother?"

"He said she appealed to her mother to leave them alone."

"And how did Ms Allard-Thorpe reply?"

"Viciously, but that was not unusual."

"Did Ernest actually hear Philippa's words?"

Michael Driscoll thought for a moment. "He said he heard only the occasional word. 'I'm doing my duty' was one phrase; 'guests from the hotel' was another; 'protect you from your father' was a third."

"Do you know what happened after Philippa spoke to her daughter?" Elspeth asked.

"Ernest told me that one of the young students came up to Cinnamon and took her arm. The student nodded coldly to Philippa and escorted Cinnamon back to the group. Philippa spun around and marched angrily away."

"Did she go round to the other side of the castle or into the keep?"

Michael Driscoll thought and said, "I don't know, but from what Ernest said she disappeared around the keep.

He couldn't swear to that in a court of law; it was just his impression. After meeting Ernest, I joined Sophia and my children, and we went directly to the picnic."

"As an employee of the hotel, let me express my regret at this unfortunate situation. I hope you'll be willing to talk with me again," Elspeth said.

"Ms Duff, the pleasure will be mine. I certainly would like to clear all this up for the good of the delegation but most of all for Ernest and Cinnamon."

"We would like to ask your wife some questions as well. Will you ask her to come in here in about five minutes?"

In that short hiatus, Elspeth spoke to Richard.

"We heard Ernest speak to Philippa, but Michael said his friend did not. Why?"

"Perhaps Michael Driscoll is covering up what he knew for Ernest Thorpe's sake."

Sophia Driscoll's reaction to Philippa's death was not as intense as her husband's, but she had her own way of expressing what she thought of Philippa Allard-Thorpe.

"Ms Duff, this whole situation is very unfortunate, and I do appreciate your trying to discover what actually happened. I take my hat off to the brigadier for getting Philippa's body over to the Greek side. No one has mentioned what a fiasco it would be if the Turkish Cypriot police got involved. It would probably cause an international incident, and that's not what we need right now. I'm extremely worried about Michael and my children. Ernest Thorpe and he are such close friends, and Michael hated to see what was happening to Cinnamon. My concern is for the children. Unlike the Colton boys, my children are young enough that the concept of death upsets them terribly. The girls have become very silent, and they keep asking me if everything is going to be all right. Gregory cried in his sleep last night and, when I went to comfort him, he told me he was scared that he might fall off a castle wall too."

"Mrs Driscoll, I totally understand. My children were raised in the Los Angeles area and, when they were young, whenever there was gang violence or a particularly gruesome murder, they would cling to me. I was never good at explaining to them what death was about," Elspeth said.

Richard spoke with equal sincerely. "When I was a boy, a ghillie who was a gaemekeeper on a nearby estate in Aberdeenshire where I grew up was shot by poachers. I knew this ghillie, who had always been kind to the boys in the area, and it took me several years to feel safe wandering alone through the woods around my home."

Sophia smiled at both of them. "Before marrying Michael, I spent time here in Nicosia and know first-hand the violence that took place between the Greek forces and the Turkish ones. In those days, however, people here considered the British to be above the violence. I was easily persuaded that Anglo-Saxon ways were a model worth adopting. What an outmoded notion nowadays! Now there's this incident with Ms Allard-Thorpe, and I can't stay so detached."

"Are you suggesting what happened was more than an accident?" Richard asked.

"Of course it wasn't an accident. Practically every person there would have beendelighted to push Philippa Allard-Thorpe over the ramparts."

Elspeth tried to look surprised, but her words came out archly. "Including yourself, Mrs Driscoll?"

"I was with the children the whole time. Surely, I couldn't have thrown her off the tower with them in tow."

23

Elspeth did not ask Bitki or Onan Mitsui to come into the room immediately. She sat instead and put her index fingers together and knotted her other fingers.

"Here's the church and here's the steeple. Open the door and see all the people. I think when we get finished here, Dickie, we will see all the people. They all seem to have reasonable explanations as to their whereabouts when Philippa fell. What surprises me, however, is that so many people have made the assumption that she was pushed over the edge rather than falling, but they didn't blame anyone for committing the crime."

Richard looked over at Elspeth and thought she was particularly striking when her wide brow, now exposed by her short haircut, was furrowed in thought. But he did not think it was an appropriate time to tell her so. He simply sat quietly as she tried to work things out.

"After we finished lunch at the castle," she said, "I saw Bitki, Onan, and Azai playing ball together. I'm sure they will corroborate this story when they come in. To date it appears as if none of the delegation could have been responsible for Philippa's fall. Perhaps I should leave it there."

Knowing her so well, Richard challenged her. "Can you?"

"Probably not, and besides, Eric wouldn't let me. I wonder why Philippa was such a polarising person? Superficially she was stellar, but when anyone, except the guests got near her, intense feelings boiled up."

"Since I only met her once and then so fleetingly, I'll take your word for it. I did watch her at the picnic, as you asked. She seemed all sweetness and helpfulness, but she held her body rigidly the whole time, almost as if she was playing a part that she had not completely learned."

"That was characteristic of her. Why do you suppose she came to Kantara Castle? One doesn't just chance by a place so difficult to get to. I'm sure she came deliberately, and I'm not completely convinced it was to check up on the staff." Elspeth spoke to the air more than to Richard. "Why the coincidence that our picnic was scheduled for the same place and time as Ernest Thorpe's birthday excursion?"

"Do you remember who suggested Kantara Castle for the delegation's picnic originally?"

"Colin, I think."

"Could he have known about the birthday party?"

"He may have," Elspeth said slowly. "I wonder if Cinnamon told her mother about going to the castle?"

"Are you suggesting that Philippa put the idea of a trip to Kantara Castle into the brigadier's head after hearing Cinnamon and her father would be there?"

He watched her frown and press her lips together, her expression puzzled.

"The suggestion might not have been that direct," she said. "If Philippa did know about the excursion to honour Ernest's birthday, she might have casually mentioned Kantara Castle to the brigadier. Then shortly afterwards, when I asked him about a place for a delegation outing, Kantara came into his head."

Such were the powers of suggestion, he thought. "The relationship between the brigadier and Philippa seems unclear to me. Did you understand it?" he asked.

Elspeth slowly shook her head. "It felt like their affair was breaking apart but was not completely broken. Colin told me he wanted out of it, but, when he said this to me, I wasn't certain whether he was simply using it as an approach to invite me out." Elspeth reddened slightly as she said this. Richard said nothing.

"Every time I saw the two of them together," Elspeth continued, "Philippa seemed possessive, but he looked as if he didn't want to be possessed. According to the brigadier they'd been seeing each other for over a year, but I assumed he didn't consider this an exclusive arrangement. At the dinner party at the Residency several woman seemed to have well-established and affectionate relationships with him."

"Are you implying that Philippa considered Colin her special territory? Do you think she knew about the others?" he asked.

Elspeth shook her head again, more as a gesture of doubt than denial. "From what I can make out, Philippa was not part of the diplomatic social set here. She probably considered most of the women in it idle and therefore of little consequence. The brigadier is retired and reasonably handsome. He seemed quite at home at the Residency. Did I tell you Carolyn Wellborne warned me about both Philippa and Colin."

Richard wished for a moment he had not left the Residency or Thomas Wellborne in such high dudgeon. An interview with Tom and Carolyn at this point might prove useful. He hoped Elspeth might re-establish a connection with them, for, although she had been the subject of Richard's disagreement with Thomas Wellborne, she had not taken a part in it. He thought better of asking her to contact them, however.

"Why do you suppose the warning?" he asked.

She bit her lower lip. "Let me try to remember. At the time I had no idea what Carolyn meant, since the comment had no context and I had only recently met Philippa and Colin. I wasn't quite certain if she was warning me against them as individuals or as a couple. Now I'm totally perplexed. What I'd give to be rid of the problem of Philippa Allard-Thorpe and all the trouble she has caused. My head is pounding."

Richard took her hand. Tenderly she put her other hand over his and then withdrew both. Her gesture was not unkind but it hurt him.

"Do you suppose we could put Bitki and Onan off for a while?" she asked. "I could use a break. Dickie, be a dear and tell them we will see them later. I really need a wee bit of a lie-down right now."

Richard did as bidden but with some concern. In London a month ago, before coming out to Cyprus, Elspeth claimed she was fully recovered from the head wounds she had received during her last assignment, but the sudden onset of her headache troubled him.

He always tried to handle even the most chaotic events in his career with calm and reasoned discourse. In his first and only meeting with Philippa, he decided he did not like her intense nature despite her outward intelligence and good looks. He felt angry with Philippa because her actions and subsequent death were causing a relapse in Elspeth's health. He once had to deal with a young man under his authority who affected those around him in a similar manner to that of Philippa Allard-Thorpe. The man tried to orchestrate everything in Richard's office and was surprised when the

FCO, at Richard's request, stepped in and removed him from future overseas duty. If Philippa had not died at Kantara Castle, would Elspeth possibly have had the unpleasant task of informing the Kennington Organisation about Philippa's lack of suitability for her position? Richard thought Elspeth would not under any circumstances because she would claim that was not part of her job. He rued her stubbornness.

What if Philippa had been pushed? Who would have gained from this? Any number of people. The staff did not like her. Ernest Thorpe had been deprived of his daughter's company for a number of years and probably resented Philippa's interference in his relationship with his daughter. The members of the delegation, no matter how well accounted for at the picnic, suspected she was rifling through their things or criticising their children's activities. Cinnamon was constantly subjected to Philippa's controlling parental supervision. Had any of these relationships been so intense that someone resorted to murder? Human emotions were hard to quantify, but the urge to kill another person meant the murderer felt such desperation or hatred that it seemed the only way out. Yet none of the people at Kantara Castle seemed to fit the profile of a killer nor did their motivations seem strong enough to result in homicide.

With these troubling thoughts, Richard went to find Onan and Bitki Mitsui. They were alone in the common room. Onan looked worried as he stood up and greeted Richard. Bitki was obviously keeping her emotions in check but her eyes looked pleading.

"If possible, Bitki and I would like to talk to you alone, Sir Richard, somewhere where we won't be overheard. We've discovered a small place to sit on the rooftop above our quarters. Today is quite cool for a summer's day, and we thought you wouldn't mind going up there with us. We feel we could talk there in confidence because we will be able see if anyone is approaching. We'd like to discuss something with you before we talk to Ms Duff."

With Richard's agreement, they led him to a corner of the wall outside of the east wing where a hidden staircase led to the roof. They released the cordon that blocked it and climbed up the three storeys of the building without speaking. Richard watched the view unfold beneath him and wondered how many people took the trouble to climb the old stairway. When they reached their destination, they were treated to a view of the jumble of buildings in Nicosia in the distance. To the north a large Turkish flag flew from a mosque, a token of the divided city.

As they stood at the parapet, Richard asked, "Now tell me, why all the intrigue?"

Onan answered. "Bitki and I think someone is trying to subvert our talks here."

"Why do you think that?"

"As Ms Duff may have mentioned, when we first got here, some of the papers we had left in our room were disturbed," Bitki said. "Later, we arranged for some of our papers to be stored in the hotel safe and purposely set a trap to see if they were handled by anyone but us. We put one sheet upside down, but when we got the papers back, that sheet was right side up. Sir Richard, do you know who my father is?"

"Elspeth told me. I know of him but have never met him."

"I talked to Daddy, and he advised me to put the piece of paper that was tampered with in a protective sleeve and send it back to the Secret Intelligence Service in London to see whose fingerprints might be on it. They found three sets of prints other than ours. One set belongs to Onan's secretary in

London, one set belonged to Philippa Allard-Thorpe, and the third set belonged to one of the richest and most unscrupulous men here on the Greek side of the island, someone who would have every reason to prefer the work of the delegation was discredited."

Surprised, Richard turned away from the view and faced Bitki. "How did they have Philippa and this man's fingerprints?"

"They must have taken Philippa's when she became a British citizen," Onan said. "As to the man, he's been charged in London with drug trafficking several times. The cases were always dropped."

"I see, but why have you come to me about this?"

"We are dealing directly with the Secret Intelligence Service but, if this becomes common knowledge, anyone who has meddled into Philippa Allard-Thorpe's affairs might be in danger, Ms Duff included. Let's call the man 'Aristotle', because this nickname is often used among law enforcement officials here. This current Aristotle has strong underground connections here in Cyprus, throughout the eastern Mediterranean area and in southern Italy," Onan said.

"You seem to know Ms Duff well, Sir Richard," Bitki said. "We thought you might advise her to let us handle this situation behind closed doors and not interfere."

"Are you suggesting Philippa Allard-Thorpe was involved in a relationship with this 'Aristotle' that might have resulted in her death?" Richard asked.

"We've no idea, but we don't want anyone hurt. We also don't want the work we are trying to do here compromised. My father suggested he might talk to both you and Ms Duff and warn you of the dangers of pursuing an inquiry into Philippa Allard-Thorpe's death."

"Unfortunately I'm leaving Cyprus tomorrow morning for Brussels. I don't know when . . ."

Bitki interrupted him. "My father has suggested the sooner he sees the two of you the better. He's proposed dinner this evening at his home, where we can all talk confidentially. We fear that anywhere in the hotel, even up here, we might be overheard."

"Mrs Mitsui, if you and your husband think the situation is this serious, I'm certain I can persuade Elspeth to go with the three of us this evening to visit your father. We have an engagement with an ex-colleague of mine for tea here at the hotel, but we could be ready to join you by half past six."

They made arrangements to meet outside the hotel, and Richard left them on the rooftop.

Richard pondered the best way to approach Elspeth. He had imagined a quiet evening with her after the Ogilvys left the hotel and made inquiries at the concierge's desk to find an intimate restaurant where they might dine alone. Now it appeared they would be whisked off to the Turkish side of the island for a clandestine meeting. He smiled wryly. So much for a calm and romantic weekend with the woman whom he loved so well, and so much for Lord Kennington and Pamela Crumm's scheme to send Elspeth to Cyprus for some rest.

*

Elspeth was stirring when Richard knocked at her door. No amount of positive thinking could drive her headache away during the interviews with the delegation, but an hour's rest with cold towels round her head and several tablets prescribed by the local doctor had reduced the pain to a bearable level.

When she heard what had transpired while she was tending her headache, she regretted the unexpected change in their weekend plans that Philippa's death had caused. Perhaps it was the opportune time to tell Richard that her feelings towards him had reached a point where she must deal with them, and with him, honestly. She was not, however, prepared for the news Richard brought her when he entered her room.

He spoke softly but hardness filled his voice. He told her Jonathan Westwood wanted to see them but only briefly why.

"Dickie, you couldn't have done anything else but accept, although I'm sorry we can't dine in peace and leave Philippa to her heavenly rest. What mystifies me, however, is that when we were at Kantara Castle our group and Ernest Thorpe's were the only ones there. Nobody from this Aristotle's bunch was around. How could they be responsible?"

Richard blew his breath through his teeth. "The more one touches Philippa, the stickier things become. We have no idea if one of the students, for example, could have been in his pay."

"I'm sorry you have to run off to Brussels on Her Majesty's business. Could you ring her and tell her Elspeth Duff needs your help more than she does?" Elspeth said with a weak smile.

Richard grinned in return. "As Her Majesty is such a gracious lady, I'm sure she would agree, but her government might see things differently."

"Dickie, when might you be able to come back to Cyprus?"

"I think by Friday if all goes well in Brussels. I can at least stay for the rest of the weekend."

"Is there any chance you could pull strings and stay longer?"

"I'll contact London as soon as I get to Brussels. I'm certain they will relieve me of my post in Malta and attach me to the Secret Intelligence Service with a special assignment to assist Ms Elspeth Duff. You always seem to be getting me into these things." He sighed and winked as he said this. Their adventures always brought them closer together.

Elspeth laughed. "I think that would be a super idea, as long as they assign you to me exclusively."

These bantering words would linger in his mind long after the afternoon was over.

24

Richard entered the lobby with a fully restored Elspeth on his arm. As they passed the reception desk new arrivals were checking in. An older woman with a commanding presence found her arrangements slightly different from what she said she had requested. The woman behind the desk assured her everything she wanted would be taken care of immediately, although her room arrangement matched the list of preferences compiled by the Kennington Organisation for repeat guests. Another traveller had confused the dates of his arrival, but a room was made available.

The Ogilvys, sitting in the lobby, were watching the activity at the desk with obvious amusement, and the major whispered something in his wife's ear. She was overdressed and looked frumpy, Richard thought, but then no one could match Elspeth's taste in clothes, and her dress was always appropriate. Richard and Elspeth approached his friends.

"Richard, good to see you," the major said with gusto. "So nice of you to invite us to enjoy a famous Kennington cream tea."

When Richard introduced Elspeth, Mrs Ogilvy simpered and the major shook Elspeth's hand robustly. Richard wondered if he and Elspeth would now become an item in the expat community's gossip.

When the four of them entered the tearoom, the Ogilvys looked sufficiently impressed. A waiter led them to a reserved table that looked onto the garden. Richard ordered cream teas for them all and told the waiter to put it on his bill.

"Jolly nice of you," the major said, and his wife looked relieved.

After they had dispensed with appropriate small talk, Richard turned to business.

"I appreciate you coming round, and it is marvellous to catch up," he said, "but I think I said in my note that this is only half pleasure. I assume you know about the death of Philippa Allard-Thorpe, who was the manager here. Ms Duff represents the interests of the Kennington Organisation, and, as her friend, I am assisting her. She asked if I knew anyone who might know about the affairs of the expat community here, and since both of you have been here for quite some time, I wonder if you could give us an unbiased view of Ms Allard-Thorpe. Did you know her?"

Katherine Ogilvy said, "We were not quite part of her set although the circles in the British community here in Cyprus often overlap. One does hear things."

"Quite," the major concurred.

Elspeth hid a grin behind her teacup and nodded in the friendliest manner that she could muster. "We've heard several different stories from people who are closely involved, but we'd hoped to find some people who heard what happened but had no agenda, so to speak. Do you know anything about Ms Allard-Thorpe's relationship with Ernest Thorpe over the last few years?"

Katherine Ogilvy apparently enjoyed the gossip that circulated in the expat community more than her husband. "When we first got here," she said, "the Thorpes were at the centre of the social whirl. She was so outgoing and attractive and he scholarly but handsome enough to turn heads. They moved in society as favoured ones, but about four or five years ago something changed. Philippa moved out of their house in Paphos and found employment in Nicosia at the old Cypriot Britannia Hotel. Two stories circulated. One was that Ernest Thorpe had begun an affair with one of his graduate students and another that Philippa was becoming tired of the boredom at an archaeological dig and had taken up with a business man who had promised her some sort of personal advancement away from Ernest Thorpe."

"Was either rumour substantiated?" Elspeth asked.

The major furtively glanced over at his wife. He smiled conspiratorially. "No one knew the real truth. Some said Philippa left for better fields; others that Ernest got weary of his wife's harshness and sought softer and kinder companionship."

Richard raised his eyebrows. "Who was the business man, do you know?"

"Nikki Amasis. His enemies call him Aristotle, not after the philosopher but after the shipping magnate, with whom he shares many characteristics and a similar sounding name, although I've never heard that Ari Onassis was involved in any illegal dealings."

Richard tried to hide any sign of recognition that he knew who Amasis was and let Elspeth ask the next question.

"Did they have an affair?"

The major shook his head doubtfully. "They may have briefly, but we all got the impression that theirs was a strictly business relationship. The gossip was that Philippa Allard-Thorpe seduced the owner of Cypriot Britannia who was three times her age if a day. Damned attractive woman! One can't imagine her having an affair with the old man unless she had an ulterior motive. It turned out he left the hotel to her when he died."

"I met both Philippa and Ernest several times before they parted company, and I have met him on many occasions since," Katherine Ogilvy added. "His kindness is so much a part of him, and her ambition, particularly later, became so apparent that one can see why they separated. She's an American, you know, and American women abroad can act, as my mother used to say, 'above themselves'. Ms Allard-Thorpe, as she asked to be called when she started at Cypriot Britannia, took the brilliance she had tried to achieve in the social set and turned it to earning money."

"Why do you suppose that happened?" Elspeth asked.

"I expect that Nikki Amasis, which by the way is not his original name, had a lot to do with it," Katherine said. "Some said he approached Ernest Thorpe with a proposition to turn the dig into a tourist attraction, but Ernest didn't want people tramping over his site and refused him. Mr Amasis does not like to be rebuffed and may have found a way to extract his revenge. He's not a nice person."

"Why do you think Philippa Allard-Thorpe was attracted to him?" Richard asked.

The major laughed. "Money and power. He probably promised both. It's a damned shame, because the Thorpes have a beautiful daughter named Cinnamon, who I understand was devastated at her parents' breakup."

"Did Cinnamon stay with her father or go with her mother initially?"

Elspeth's question made Richard wonder if the ambitious Ms Allard-Thorpe really did want a child in tow and why she recently insisted on Cinnamon staying close to the hotel.

"She lived with her father before the car accident," Katherine Ogilvy said. " Ms Allard-Thorpe showed no interest in her daughter until then. She probably found Cinnamon an inconvenience, but Philippa suddenly wanted to protect her daughter after she became blind. Poor, poor girl. Such a pity. She became the pawn of both her parents."

"Mrs Ogilvy," Elspeth asked, "you seemed better acquainted with Ernest Thorpe than his ex-wife, but do you know if Philippa was close to anyone who might be able to share more light on her feelings at the time?"

"Try the aggressive Mr Amasis," Mrs Ogilvy snorted.

"Katherine, be generous," her husband chimed in. "Amasis holds a great deal of sway on the Greek side of Cyprus, and Philippa Allard-Thorpe wouldn't be the first woman who fell under his spell, especially if he offered her something she felt she was missing in her own life."

The Ogilvys' position on the breakup of the marriage of Philippa and Ernest Thorpe was so divergent that it startled Richard. He did not remember them disagreeing on anything before. Marjorie would have known more about them than he did, however. He found the major's sympathy towards Philippa interesting but out of character. Before this Richard would have believed that the major supported the crown, the church and a strong, solid, old-fashioned marriage like his to Katherine.

25

The Ogilvys left the Kennington Nicosia filled with cream tea and obvious satisfaction. On their departure Elspeth and Richard returned to her suite.

"We have a new player, Nikki Amasis" Elspeth mused, as she sat down on one of the sofas.

"Unfortunately not," he said.

"Not?"

"One of the reasons we are off to Bitki's parents' home this evening involves Nikki Amasis."

"All right, Dickie." Elspeth sounded gently annoyed. "What are you keeping from me?"

Richard recounted the details of his meeting with Bitki and Onan on the rooftop. Elspeth listened intently before she spoke.

"It looks like Philippa was involved with Nikki Amasis to the end. Does the name Amasis have some significance that I don't know about?"

Richard considered himself a bit of a history buff and had read all the ancient Greek texts. "It's from Herodotus. He tells us that Amasis was the last truly Egyptian pharaoh. And, as I remember, Amasis demanded tribute from Cyprus. It seems our Nikki was careful when he chose a new name. What do you suppose his original one was?"

Elspeth chuckled. "I should've known you would know about the ancient Amasis. To most people the name would mean nothing. Do you think he knows its origins?"

"I'm sure he does. Now, dearest Elspeth, before you go rushing off trying to see Amasis about Philippa, will you listen to what we hear tonight from Jonathan Westwood?"

"Are you suggesting I should err on the side of caution?"

"Doesn't your head, physically not mentally, tell you that?"

Elspeth rubbed the spot at the back of her head where she had been hit in Singapore and nodded sadly. "Too much. Why did Eric and Pamela think this assignment would be simple?"

"Because Philippa Allard-Thorpe wanted everyone to think that her management of the Kennington Nicosia was seamless and effortless. The unfortunate thing is that she could not escape from all the elements she couldn't control and that ultimately led to her death. My dearest one, my greatest regret is that I have to leave in the morning. I know you well enough to imagine you will go off in pursuit of Nikki Amasis without the least thought of any danger to yourself."

"What threat could I pose to him?" Elspeth asked with feigned innocence in her voice.

"Let's ask Bitki's father that question tonight."

"You are a hard man, Sir Richard Munro."

Richard's heart constricted until Elspeth smiled.

"Elspeth," he said in a schoolmaster's voice, "have you given any consideration of the possible risks that might be involved?"

She shifted her eyes back and forth from one side to the other, and then they both burst out laughing. Richard, with calculation, threw his arms about her and she responded in kind.

"What a bunch of silliness," she said, breaking away when their laughter had subsided.

He wished it were really so.

*

The same taxi driver who had taken Elspeth to the Westwood home previously was waiting for them on the Turkish side of the Green Line. The summer sun was still bright, although the day had cooled slightly. They drove along the northern coast of the island with its beaches and rocky shore. Richard occasionally murmured appreciative words about the scenery but mainly seemed content to sit beside Elspeth and take her hand in his. The Mitsuis had gone on ahead of them, and they were alone with Kahlil, who chatted on about Turkey's problems in getting membership in the EU because of the Cyprus situation, his feelings about Cypriot politics, and the state of village affairs. Elspeth let him ramble without interrupting him and wondered what Richard was thinking. He sat smiling contentedly in a way that made her heart beat a little faster.

Suddenly Richard broke his reverie and spoke to the taxi driver. "Mr Kahlil, do you know anything about Nikki Amasis?"

Kahlil swerved wildly around a lorry, pulled ahead at great speed and turned to look at his passengers, unmindful of the curving road ahead. A passing car hooted its horn, making Kahlil turn his attention back to the road.

Kahlil spoke through his teeth. "Amasis is a crook. Don't let his manners or position in the business community fool you."

"Have you met him?" Elspeth asked.

"No, and I never want to. He would steal from his own mother and convince the world she was wrong to complain."

"Tell us what you do know about him," Richard said.

"He has his fingers into everything in Cyprus. He started poor, but he made money by smuggling arms to the Greek forces during the troubles in nineteen seventy-four. After that he had enough money to buy ships and drugs. He now runs a big shipping enterprise, which may be legitimate, but it's only a way to cover his drug running. He's careful not to push the drugs on Cyprus. They come from Afghanistan, and he puts them in his warehouses all over the island, on both sides, then sends them to Italy, France and Britain. He is what they call in New York 'street smart' and can pay for big, corrupt lawyers if anything goes wrong. No one has ever been able to get anything to stick on him. He makes a bad name for Cyprus, Greek or Turkish. He's the manure at the bottom of a camel's dung heap!" Kahlil opened the window and spat.

"Not a nice person, it seems," Elspeth observed.

"Ask Mr Westwood. He will tell you," Kahlil said. "Mr Westwood is a wise and good man, even if he is not Muslim."

Kahlil turned his attention back to the road and muttered to himself as he drove on. His vitriolic statements seemed to have exhausted him, and he stopped his commentary on the ills of the world.

Jonathan Westwood was waiting for them at the door. He showed them in and took Elspeth's wrap. He led them into a large drawing room rather than into the garden. The room was cool, and Elspeth was glad she had chosen a long-sleeved dress.

"It's too windy to sit outside," Jonathan explained. "Come and meet everyone here."

Cari Westwood, Bitki, and Onan sat by the fire, and each held a glass of wine. When asked, Elspeth chose chardonnay, but Richard said he preferred claret. Jonathan poured their drinks and took a seat. They settled into polite conversation until the doors burst open and Azai came pelting into the room to bid his parents and grandparents good night. Hugs and assurances of Weetabix with bananas in the morning seemed to convince the young boy that he should go to bed. He ran out and grabbed the hand of the waiting servant whom Elspeth had seen with him during her last visit to the Westwoods.

Jonathan Westwood refreshed their glasses and then settled down to business.

"I thought we would deal with the issue of the tampered papers before dinner and then put it aside before we serve you a typical Turkish Cypriot meal. Cari has specially seen to its preparation. Sir Richard, I know you have dealt with sensitive issues throughout your career at the FCO. Ms Duff, I understand from Detective Superintendent Tony Ketcham that you have handled sensitive issues too, but your concerns in your current job are those of the smooth running of the Kennington hotels and not international security per se. I don't need to dwell on the intricacies of Cypriot politics or even fully brief you on the complexities of Onan and Bitki's delegation's mission here. What we need to explore is the involvement of Philippa Allard-Thorpe with Nikki Amasis and her possible handling of the papers that Bitki put in the safe."

"Our delegation's discussions are not top secret but they are sensitive," Onan said. "The outcome of the negotiations might very well affect the policing of Mr Amasis's many interests here in Cyprus. Some of what he does is completely legal, some not, but the authorities frequently overlook his illicit activities because of the money he brings to the island.

We know he is involved in international drug trafficking, but no court in Cyprus or in Britain has ever been able to convict him of it. You both can appreciate what we are trying to do here. In our efforts to unite the two sides of Cyprus, we must be highly sensitive to the animosity of the poorer Turkish Cypriots towards the more prosperous Greeks. Bitki and I were chosen for the delegation because of our expertise in Turkish Cyprus affairs and the Turkish government's issues involving Cyprus. My father-in-law still holds on to his British viewpoint. We have different ideas, but we seldom are in disagreement over the substantive matters that affect the politics of the future of Cyprus. I know I'm being a bit heavy here." Onan smiled and looked towards his wife. "Help me out, Bitki."

Bitki glance over at him and returned his smile. "Daddy trained me to be suspicious of anything that seems dodgy, but I think every member of the delegation is truly pledged to the success of our mission, although each of us has our own point of view. Michael Driscoll is as expert on the Greek Cypriot side as Onan and I are on the Turkish, but I hope his scholarly ways give him an open mind, and we try to stay neutral as well. We all want the best for Cyprus, Greece, Turkey and the European Union, and most of all we want political and economic stability in Cyprus. Britain's interest is to have a strong trading partner here and a continued agreement on our military bases, which we think are vital in keeping the eastern Mediterranean region free from all-out war. We do not want special interest groups, like Nikki Amasis's enterprises, interfering in what we are doing. He demeans Cyprus by his disdain of the law and legal commerce."

Elspeth listened intently before addressing Jonathan Westwood. "You're correct in assuming that one of my main reasons for joining you today is to discover how

Philippa Allard-Thorpe was connected to Amasis and if her involvement with him resulted in her death. The allegation she might have been sharing information with Amasis is indeed serious. If her actions affected the reputation of the Kennington Nicosia, I'll need to convey that to Lord Kennington in London, but the details can remain secret if you think it wise. I can assure you we don't want to get in the way of the delegation's mission. If, however, our hotel manager was implicated in disclosing sensitive information about the FCO delegation to unwanted elements, our security staff both here and in London will make it their top priority to correct this. Tomorrow I'll be in touch with London as quickly as possible. Please let us know anything we can do to assist you."

Bitki and Onan Mitsui accepted her offer, but Jonathan Westwood would not let the matter lie. "Ms Duff, you are in some danger if you challenge the position of Nikki Amasis. I want you to leave that to us."

Elspeth felt marginalized. "Why is that, Mr Westwood?"

"The Secret Intelligence Service has been called in. You need not know why, but we need you to concentrate your efforts on the affairs at the hotel and not the affairs of state."

"But aren't the investigations intertwined?" Elspeth asked.

Jonathan Westwood looked as if he was not used to having his dictates questioned and stared at Elspeth, half with alarm and half with incredulity. "Ms Duff, your wellbeing could be seriously threatened here. I cannot command you to be cautious, but I highly suggest it to you. You can contribute to our investigation in many significant ways, but, please, realise that many matters here are bigger than the death of Philippa Allard-Thorpe."

Elspeth remained silent for a moment, not because she wished to cause obstruction but because she truly could not differentiate in her mind how she could investigate Philippa's death, its impact on the Kennington Nicosia, and the reputation of the Kennington hotels but ignore all the other issues surrounding Philippa's activities beyond the boundaries of the hotel.

"Mr Westwood, I will, of course, work as carefully as possible, but I know our London office will not be satisfied with a cover-up of Philippa's death. You probably already know her tenure as manager of the Kennington Nicosia was not as straightforward as Lord Kennington would have liked. Her death brought up issues within our own organisation that need to be resolved. Can we work together on this? I promise to tread lightly when dealing with Nikki Amasis, but I want to be free to explore Philippa's past. Right now there are many unanswered questions, and the answers to these directly concern both the Kennington Organisation and me as its agent. I can understand the greater ramifications that the answers to these questions may have, and therefore I would like to keep in contact with you to let you know what I learn at my end. I would also like to request the name of someone in your service with whom I can meet on a daily basis. Does that seem unreasonable?"

*

Richard sat back and let this discourse happen. His interactions with Elspeth seldom allowed him to see her in her strictly business capacity, and watching her now made him admire not only her clarity and toughness but also her honesty as she spoke. He wondered how this might work out in a marriage. He was aware of Elspeth's hesitancy in her relationship with him, and he began to suspect that part of this was the result of the commitment and unshakable integrity that she showed in her job. He looked at the set of her jaw and the fierceness in her eyes. Could he endure that in a marriage? He thought of Marjorie. Her strength was in the innate courtesy that she showed to every person she met, be it a prince or an Outback aborigine. Marjorie was born to her role. Elspeth, unlike Marjorie, had sculpted her life using her own competence and intelligence. Elspeth's character was derived from the independence that both her parents instilled in her as a young girl, and he knew she had not disappointed them. He thought back to the first time he had seen her, striding across the fields in an old kilt and pullover, dogs at her heels and the tomboyish grin on her face. She personified the joy of being alive. Marjorie, he was sure, had never savoured freedom like that and she probably had not regretted it. Life had treated Elspeth somewhat unfairly, but she had emerged to become a graceful but direct woman. She was a woman of the twenty-first century where Marjorie had not been. Could Richard accept that in a future relationship with her?

His thoughts having wandered, he did not at first realise that Jonathan Westwood was addressing him directly.

"Sir Richard, how would you advise us in this matter?"

Since he was not sure what this matter was, he assumed it was the conflict between Elspeth's desires to find the reason for Philippa's death and the Secret Intelligence Service's need to control the situation. He tried to answer as diplomatically as possible.

"I've worked with Elspeth on several cases, and I think you will find her discreet, fair, and fully cooperative," he said.

Jonathan Westwood looked a little puzzled at the reply. "I hoped you would caution her about the dangers she might face."

Richard cleared his throat and tried to hide his embarrassment.

"Terribly sorry," he stammered. "I was thinking of the times she and I have handled sensitive cases together. Only once has she encountered physical danger and that, unfortunately, was from a Kennington hotel employee. You definitely can count on Elspeth to be cautious where necessary, but I haven't heard anything here that might suggest imminent danger."

"Nikki Amasis has a great deal to lose if Cyprus is reunited, as he plays a shell game with his warehouses and illegal shipments between the Turkish and Greek sides of the island'" Onan said. "Despite the barbed wire barriers, the Green Line is very porous and when things get difficult on one side, he simply slips his goods over to the other. Millions of pounds are involved and human lives have been lost on several occasions. All this seems beyond the realm of the posh atmosphere of the Kennington hotel, but since Philippa was involved with Amasis, the ugly reality of his world suffused her life and therefore the affairs of the Kennington Nicosia."

"Can we find an acceptable way to deal with all this?" Elspeth asked. "The Kennington Organisation wants to have minimal fallout from Philippa's death. If the Secret Intelligence Service takes over the investigation, Lord Kennington will most certainly want to know how Philippa's actions might have disrupted the smooth running of the Kennington Nicosia. Right now everything we know points to Philippa having fallen accidentally from the keep, but many of the people whom Richard and I interviewed assumed she was pushed. Mr Westwood, I want to find out if her death was indeed murder. As you would suspect, the Kennington Organisation would like to keep such an accusation as secret as possible, and consequently your request for secrecy is highly appreciated. We don't want false rumours spread about, but we want to know how Philippa Allard-Thorpe really died and if the repercussions resulting from her death will hurt the reputation of the hotel. We want the dirty details to be kept quiet. Does that sound callous?"

Jonathan Westwood smiled. "To evoke an old cliché, 'it sounds like we have the beginning of a beautiful friendship'. Have you ever thought of joining the SIS?"

Elspeth brushed off his last remark with a brief smile. "Since I need a contact with the SIS, I propose that either it be Onan or Bitki or that you put one of your people at the hotel posing as a guest. I can make the arrangements."

Jonathan Westwood considered this. "Let me get back to you on that. Bitki and Onan would be obvious choices, but I don't want their mission for the FCO compromised. I think I prefer someone else, who might naturally be a guest at the hotel."

Cari Westwood had remained quiet throughout the discussion but finally spoke. "I've always wanted to stay at the Kennington Nicosia. Would this be a good chance for me to do so?"

Jonathan Westwood sighed, as if he did not expect to win this argument with his wife. "Cari, didn't you say you wanted to retire from the service?" he said hopefully.

Cari looked blandly at him and said, "My stay could serve two purposes. I can be the liaison and also will have time to be with my grandson. No one will question that."

26

When they returned to the hotel, Richard suggested to Elspeth that they take a walk in the garden. He wanted to speak to her but was not certain if he could do so easily as his heart and mind were in conflict.

"Normally I would love to stroll with you, Dickie, but tonight I'm cold. My ancestors would find me an unworthy daughter of the Highlands, but I am shivering when it's over twenty degrees centigrade outside. Would you settle instead for a drink in the bar?"

Richard looked oddly at her because Elspeth was seldom cold, and the obvious alternative would have been to go to her suite or his room. Was she purposely trying to keep him in a public place? He felt unnerved but agreed to her request. Several guests were gathered round a table near the bar, but Richard saw an unoccupied corner and suggested they sit there. Richard ordered a whisky for himself and a small brandy for Elspeth. They settled into comfortable chairs near two of Lord Kennington's carefully chosen landscape planters, which reminded Richard of ancient Greek relics in the British Museum. They sat without speaking and sipped their drinks.

Richard cleared his throat and his voice cracked. "Elspeth, my dear, I leave Cyprus in the morning with every regret in the world that I can't be here to support you over the next week. I worry about you, but I suppose you know that."

Elspeth smiled up at him. "Yes, dear Dickie, I know. I'm too sorry a person for you to waste so much of your concern over, but I can't back out of this assignment now, however risky Jonathan Westwood thinks it may be. I promised Jonathan I'd be careful. Besides, I like Cari Westwood and am looking forward to having her here in the hotel, although she will not replace you. Will you really be able to come back next weekend? "

Richard's heart bumped, and he hoped Elspeth truly did want him back for more reasons than one. "My dearest, I'll get here as soon as I can." He discerned a slight frown on her face, perhaps because she was finding him patronising, and therefore he modified his tone. "We make a good team, don't we?"

"The best. When do you hope to be back?" Her words restored his confidence.

"I'll book the flight at the airport tomorrow morning and let you know. Let's talk a bit about the week ahead."

Elspeth took a small sip of her brandy and swirled the liquid around in her glass for a long moment. Then she abandoned it. "I'll need to get more information from London. I'll call Pamela in the morning and see if she has tracked down the truth about Philippa's trip to the US and her academic pretensions. Her record has some obvious flaws. I'm also curious what the autopsy will tell us."

"Because she didn't scream?"

"Exactly. Her death was too convenient for a great number of people. I wonder if Nikki Amasis is among them."

Richard felt alarmed. "Elspeth, you promised to leave that one alone."

Elspeth looked askance at him. "So I did. He is so tantalizing."

"And much too dangerous. Stay away from him, Elspeth." Richard hoped she heard him and would heed his warning.

"All right, I promise, or rather I promise to do nothing without the SIS's approval."

Their conversation drifted on to other things, most of them reminiscent of their earlier times together. Richard noticed Elspeth seemed distracted, and she soon fell into silence. They stayed in the lounge for another half hour and then made their way up to their rooms. Richard was surprised when they got to her suite that she invited him in. As she closed the door behind them, she raised her hand to his face gently and put her lips to his. At first she kissed him tentatively, then more warmly, and finally, with a great laugh, passionately. He responded in full, finding her action unexpected but exceedingly agreeable. Finally she whispered in his ear.

He held her back and looked at her. Her face was beaming but her eyes shy. He drew her to him.

"Are you sure, Elspeth?" he said into her hair.

"Yes, I'm sure. I've wanted to ask for a very long time but didn't know how. And I did ask nicely."

He pleasured her for a long time before they made love. He could feel the fire slowly rise in her at the same time it took hold of him.

In the morning before leaving the hotel, he arranged with the hotel florist to have two perfect yellow roses with a touch of red at the edges sent round to her suite. A note was attached.

> *My most precious one,*
> *Stay well until this coming weekend. Do take care*
> *of yourself as you are so dear to me, and remember to*

call if you need anything. You have my secure mobile number.

With all my love and thank you for last night,

R

*

Elspeth woke late the next morning from a deep sleep and was acutely aware the pillow next to her was empty. Lovingly she traced the indentation made by Richard's head with her finger and knew her heart was full. She spent a long time arguing herself out of feeling lightheaded.

Finally she rose and ordered breakfast from room service.

A waiter whom she recognised from the picnic brought her breakfast and Richard's flowers. She put away the note to read later.

"Stay a minute, please," she said to the waiter. "I don't know your name."

"I am Theo," he responded.

"Theo, you were at the picnic on Saturday, weren't you?"

"Yes, Ms Duff, unfortunately. We've all been rather under a cloud since then."

Elspeth was grateful the young man spoke such fluent English and continued. "Under a cloud? Why? I'll speak to whoever is causing it if you like."

"It's the chef who runs the kitchen."

"What's his name?"

"Chef Marcus Antonius. That is his professional name, not his real one."

"Please, Theo, you may speak freely here. I assure you nothing you say will go beyond this room. Tell me about the atmosphere in the kitchen. The security office in London has asked me to find out as much as possible about Ms Allard-Thorpe's death. Please don't fear for your job because it's not my intent to judge the staff's performance. I'll defend you if necessary. The more I know about how you all are doing, the better I'll understand what might have happened last Saturday."

"The chef told us to talk to no one."

"I see. Then I'll have a word with him later this morning. Thank you for breakfast and the flowers. What time do you get off work?"

"When lunch is finished. Usually about half past two."

"After I speak to the chef, I may ask you to talk to me again. Would you be willing?"

"Yes, Ms Duff. Christos says you are the best."

Elspeth acknowledged the compliment, recognising Christos's slangy expression.

"I've great respect for Christos' opinion. Tell him so."

After Theo had left, Elspeth opened Richard's note and read it through several times. She wished it had been longer but smiled happily nonetheless. She tucked it in a zipped pocket of one of her cases to savour it again.

Elspeth brought her mind back to work. She looked at her watch and calculated the time in London, which was two hours behind Nicosia. She expected Pamela Crumm would be in her office by now and rang her.

Pamela's cheerful voice answered on the first ring. "And how is my Aphrodite in Cyprus this morning?"

Elspeth was glad Pamela could not see her blush. "Pamela, you are far too cheerful for a Tuesday morning," she said evasively.

"A definite personality disorder on my part, and for that you must forgive me. What's up, ducks?"

Elspeth briefly filled Pamela in on her visit to the Westwoods with Richard the night before and assiduously avoided any mention of the conclusion of the evening. She felt compelled to let Pamela know that a certain security department in Her Majesty's Government had become involved and let Pamela draw her own conclusions.

"Richard was a bit harsh with me and said I mustn't get too involved with issues that go beyond how Philippa's death affects the hotel. I'll try."

"Sir Richard has the right instinct, and I'm sure his lordship will concur, as do I." Pamela always referred to Eric Kennington as "his lordship" when she deferred to his position as the ultimate authority at the Kennington Organisation. "Elspeth, it's important that we uncover all the facts around Philippa's death, but I don't want to put you in danger again after Singapore. I don't particularly relish going to the hospital every day for three weeks to make sure you are still alive, the way I did last winter."

Elspeth felt admonished and grudgingly agreed to be careful. "Pamela, I expect to get the results of the autopsy today. Richard thinks I'm being obsessive, but I'm concerned that no one heard Philippa fall. She was uptight for sure, but almost anyone would scream if they plunged from a tower."

"I agree with you, but let's wait until we know how Philippa died. She may have had a fainting spell."

Elspeth was doubtful. "Strange you should say that. I forgot to mention that Cinnamon confided to me that her mother didn't like heights. Have you actually heard of anyone, however, fainting when they looked over a precipice? Vertigo, perhaps, but never actual unconsciousness. Most people would have the sense to step back from the edge, especially someone as intelligent as Philippa. I called to ask you if you have heard anything from the school in Ithaca, New York and if you have found out whether Philippa actually studied there or not. Richard and I have spoken to several people here, and the timeline doesn't seem feasible. I think most courses of study at universities in the States take several years. By all reports Philippa wasn't absent from Cyprus for more that six or seven months."

Pamela chuckled. "You and I are beginning to think too much alike. I've ferreted out the name of the Cornell School of Hotel Administration's dean. The manager of the Waldorf Astoria has already telephoned the dean to set up a phone call between him and me, and I'm frothing at the mouth because of the five-hour time difference. You'd think after all these years I'd accept that the sun rotates around the world and not all people live on London time."

"You are both incorrigible and indomitable, Pamela. Tell Her Majesty that she, like the Red Queen, should decree that the entire world should be on London time. I've another request, however. Can you find out what crimes Nikki Amasis was charged with in the UK?"

"I thought you weren't going down that path, Elspeth."

"I agreed not to deal with him directly, but I want to know what he is about and why the manager of the Kennington Nicosia was possibly sharing the contents of the hotel safe with him."

Pamela growled. "Are you sure of that? Tread lightly, Elspeth."

Elspeth was annoyed. "I can't give up my job completely because you've all become overly protective of me. What kind of a security advisor can I be if I'm warned that every inquiry I make has the potential of a slight bash on the head and I should steer clear of risks? Besides, the incident in Singapore was caused by one of our own, not someone from outside. By the way, has he been sentenced yet?"

"He has asked for mercy but they gave him twenty years."

"I hear the prisons in Singapore are harsh. Poor man."

"Do you really think so? Harming you was his choice to make. Tell me what are your plans for this week? I'm sure Eric will want to know."

"I'm going to contact Ernest Thorpe and Cinnamon in Paphos. I know things may be difficult for them right now, but I suspect they would like to get this whole thing over with as soon as possible. I also have concerns about what's happening at the hotel. My room service waiter this morning implied all was not well in the kitchen, and I know we can't afford to let the quality of the meals and food service slip even slightly."

"Eric asked the night manager to take Philippa's place temporarily. Have you met him?"

"Alexander Woolsey? Yes, briefly. Tell me his background."

"His father was in the British Army and his mother a Greek Cypriot. They met during the troubles in Cyprus in the nineteen seventies, married shortly afterwards, and Alexander was born on the military base there on the island. He speaks English, of course, and Greek, French, German, Italian, Arabic and Turkish as well. He worked at our hotel in Cairo, and Eric had plans for him to become night manager there, but Alexander said that after his father died his mother wanted her son to return to Cyprus. He asked to be assigned to Nicosia, although the hotel is much smaller."

"Did he know about Philippa's style of management when he requested this transfer?"

"Probably only in a general way, but Cypriot sons have a loyalty to their parents that British offspring could well emulate. Eric's been pleased with Alexander's job performance although Philippa was mute on the subject. Perhaps she was too involved in her own intrigues to notice."

"That doesn't sound like her but now we'll never know. I look forward to meeting Alexander again this morning. Does he know about the delegation's importance?"

"Philippa was in charge of keeping the top staff at the hotel informed, so one must assume he does. Elspeth, I still think it's essential for you to tell him in a most general way why you are there. I don't think we should involve him in the thick of things right now, but we need him to be diligent with regards to the safety of the delegation."

"I'll go down to his office as soon as we ring off, and I'll let you know."

"Thanks, my friend. I'll let his lordship know you are on the case as usual, but heed Sir Richard's warning. He has his, your, and our concerns at heart."

Pamela disconnected the call before Elspeth could protest. Elspeth put down the phone and felt ganged up on by all concerned. She also knew she was letting personal feelings distract her from her work. Damn, she thought, and set her jaw. I appreciate Pamela and Richard wanting to protect me, but I'm the trained investigator. When she left her suite, Elspeth tried to leave her heightened emotions behind.

Alexander Woolsey was expecting her. Elspeth estimated from his looks that he was only slightly older than her son, but she tried not to let this affect her judgment of him. She soon discovered that his boyish appearance belied his seriousness of intent.

"Ms Duff, please come in. I have coffee, freshly squeezed juice and some warm crescent buns, if you would like something."

Elspeth had already consumed two cups of coffee but accepted the juice and a roll. She noticed that the office already looked less harsh than it had under Philippa's regime. Alexander had added several photographs of his family and a large vase of flowers, which must have come in with the morning's shipment from the Kennington gardens in Morocco. As she surveyed the room, Elspeth commented on the changes.

"My wife already has ideas on how to make this office less stark, but I've warned her that the Kennington Organisation are very particular about its hotel's interior decoration. Besides, my elevation to manager may only be temporary. Lord Kennington didn't say for sure."

"Every manager I've known has put his or her personal touch on the manager's office. That way when guests come into the office, they get a sense that they are dealing with a human being, not an automaton." She stopped short of saying that Philippa's office was the least comfortable she had ever seen.

"Mr Woolsey . . ."

"Alexander, please."

"Then please call me Elspeth. Tell me a little about your background and how you feel about running the hotel here, at least for the time being."

"I feel privileged to be given this opportunity. Ms Allard-Thorpe ran the hotel with an iron hand. I sensed that caused resentment among some of the staff, and I'd like to get rid of any lingering feelings of discontent. Although many members of the staff are new, they are all hardworking and want to succeed. A job at a Kennington hotel is considered highly desirable in the hotel world, as you must already know." He said this last statement with a smile.

"Did you get any training outside of the Kennington Organisation, Alexander?"

"At Cornell in Ithaca, in the States. Then I spent a year at the Dorchester in London before moving on to Cairo."

Elspeth tried to keep her voice even, but her mind jumped at the mention of Ithaca. "I hear such good things about Cornell. When were you there?"

Alexander gave the dates, which Elspeth calculated were about the same time as Philippa said she had studied there.

"Did you ever discuss your training with Ms Allard-Thorpe?" Elspeth asked.

Alexander thought for a moment and replied, "No, the subject never came up. I transferred from Cairo at Lord Kennington's personal behest. She seemed to think I had some connection to him and always alluded to my impeccable credentials within the Kennington hierarchy."

"I see," Elspeth said, wondering what the real dynamic had been between Philippa and Alexander. "Please tell me a bit more about the morale here. When I spoke to London this morning, they said they wanted the transition in the management of the hotel to be seamless. Any guest who did not see Philippa's obituary in the local newspaper yesterday should have no idea that anything changed behind the scenes here."

Elspeth noticed that Alexander's Adam's apple moved up and down nervously as he swallowed several times.

She continued. "I'd like you to arrange small meetings between the two of us and the staff. We may have to spread this over several shifts, but, by the end of the day, I want to have talked to each staff member who is on duty today. I'd also like to speak to the head of each department separately, including a private meeting with the chef. I understand he's a bit temperamental."

"Marcus Antonius? Yes, he is, but aren't many chefs? I'll set up the meetings for you and let you know."

"Alexander, I am going to take you into my confidence and want you to give me your word that what I say to you now will not go beyond this office."

He nodded in agreement, although his reply was awkward and reflected his level of inexperience. "We're trained to know there are many secrets that must be respected by hotel management."

"First, I want your uncensored opinion of Philippa Allard-Thorpe."

He looked increasingly uncomfortable. Under similar circumstances Elspeth's son at age six would have whined, "Do I have to?"

His reply was more honest than she expected it to be.

"She wanted everything her own way," he said. "Her standards were very precise. We all tried to follow them, but sometimes they were contradictory. She would ask for one thing and then, when things didn't work out well, she would deny she had asked for it. We all trod lightly around her. Her first reactions were often angry, but later she would give an apology, which, if you will please forgive me for saying so, was usually rather insincere."

"Did you find her hard to work with?"

"Do you want me to be completely frank?"

Elspeth nodded.

"It was difficult, but, luckily, I was on duty during the night shift, and our time together usually overlapped for only a short time at the end of the dinner hour. She always stayed for the meal, but usually left me alone after that and often went to do paperwork in her office."

"Did she have days off?"

"Supposedly, but she frequently came in anyway. The staff didn't like this because they felt she was spying on them. Personally I found it intolerable, since I took over her duties on her days away and her presence reflected badly on my management. She was a controlling b . . . she was very controlling."

Elspeth looked up in surprise. She had not expected Alexander Woolsey to express himself so forcefully.

"I think we need to talk more, after I interview the staff." She said. "I'd like you to be in the meetings with me, which I hope you take as a compliment. I sense a certain wisdom in you that is beyond your age."

Alexander swallowed with pleasure. "I will do all I can."

"Then let's discuss the details," Elspeth said, "and I'll rely on you to arrange the interviews as quickly as possible."

27

Dr Robson, the pathologist at the hospital, did not get in until noon, but he promised Elspeth he would call as soon as he had finished the autopsy on Philippa Allard-Thorpe's body. Elspeth paced her sitting room while waiting for the call. She berated herself for her impatience, a trait she had learned too well when living in California. Cypriots had their own time, and she suspected the doctor might have learned Cypriot ways during his tenure on the island. He proved her wrong.

The phone rang at two o'clock, and Elspeth immediately recognised the burr of her native Highlands.

"Mrs Duff, are you there?"

"I am. What did you find?"

"I've rather alarming news for you in regard to Mrs Allard-Thorpe," the doctor said. "She didn't die from the fall. She appears to have been strangled and died from asphyxia. There are severe bruises on her throat."

Elspeth drew in her breath in surprise. "Are you saying, Dr Robson, she was dead when she fell from the tower?"

"Almost certainly. The body had numerous broken bones, but there was virtually no bleeding, which suggests the heart was no longer beating when she landed from her fall. The brain shows evidence of lack of oxygen."

"Are you suggesting that she was assaulted before she fell?"

"That would be a good assumption."

Elspeth was amazed at the Scottish doctor's words. "Did you find any signs of a struggle?" she asked.

"You are the security person, Mrs Duff, and I'm not a police coroner, only a simple pathologist. What do you want me to look for?"

"Anything like skin under her fingernails, hair on her clothing that isn't hers, and any scratches or other abrasions on her body? I'm also not skilled in forensics, doctor, but that would be a start."

"Would you like to examine the body with me when I look for these things?"

She had seen several corpses in the course of her career, but the experience had always been unpleasant. "I will, if I must. I've only seen one autopsy, when I was at Scotland Yard. I didn't faint like so many young police officers, but afterwards I rushed to the loo and was horribly sick. Luckily no one saw me. I would prefer you do your examination without me."

Elspeth heard Dr Robson chuckle.

"If you wish," he said, "but there's another matter—informing the police."

"My superiors at the Kennington Organisation would prefer not to involve the police at this point," she said. She had made this statement often enough in her work.

"But," said Dr Robson, "the cause of death is most likely murder."

Elspeth scrambled for a good excuse to prevent the police from being informed immediately. "It happened on the Turkish side, which I believe is outside the Greek Cypriot police force's jurisdiction."

"That does present a wee problem, doesn't it?"

"Yes," conceded Elspeth, "and perhaps a bit of a conundrum. Ms Allard-Thorpe was a British citizen of American origins living on the Greek side of the island. She was killed on the Turkish side and brought back to the Greek side by another British citizen in a somewhat unconventional manner. Do you see difficulties in this scenario?"

Dr Robson reverted to a scientist's point of view. "I can only give you the bare facts. I could perhaps ease the situation by reporting the circumstance of Ms Allard-Thorpe's death to the British High Commission, and they could deal with the police."

Which would further exacerbate Tom Wellborne, thought Elspeth. She recalled Richard saying her relationship with Tom was not severed, although his was. She might be able to work with Tom. Would he be willing to suppress the report to the Greek Cypriot police?

"Dr Robson, can you hold your report for twenty-four hours? You can recognise the difficulty with the surreptitious transportation of Ms Allard-Thorpe's body across the Green Line."

"You have twenty-four hours," the doctor said, "but I will notify the High Commission.

"I'll get back to you as soon as I can," she said and rang off.

Elspeth lay back in her chair. The result of the autopsy did not surprise her, considering all that she knew about Philippa, but the consequences of its findings raised issues that she wished she could avoid.

She called room service and ordered a late lunch. She hoped food would help her clear her mind. Theo brought her Greek salad, filled with fresh greens and vegetables, pungent olives and local Feta cheese, a glass of cold lemonade and bread still warm from the oven. He greeted her with a wide smile and told her that he was asking around and had some information for her if she was still available to see him when his shift was over. Elspeth agreed.

After finishing her meal, she had no idea how correctly to handle contacting the High Commission, so she simply decided to call Thomas Wellborne. She found his private number and rang through. His personal assistant said she would see if he was available, and in a few seconds he was on the line.

"Elspeth, how nice to hear from you. I regret the spat with Richard but hope you will not take it personally. He's very protective of you."

Elspeth paused before answering and then said in a controlled voice, "I'm quite aware he is. He is such an old and respected friend," she added, trying to allay any suspicions that she harboured any deeper feelings for him. "On my last assignment, I was struck on the head, and Richard found me lying in a pool of blood. Not a happy thing for either one of us, so please be indulgent of his concern for me. But, Tom, I have called you about another matter—Philippa Allard-Thorpe's death."

"Tragic, tragic," the High Commissioner said, although his tone did not echo his words.

Tragic for him or for her? she thought. She said, "At the insistence of our office in London, I asked for an autopsy to be performed on Pamela Allard-Thorpe's body. The pathologist reported to me a short while ago and gave me startling news. Philippa died from strangulation and not from the fall."

Thomas Wellborne took a moment to digest this information. Finally he said, "Are you still suggesting murder?"

"There can be no other conclusion. As you know, Philippa attracted controversy in her life, and her death seems even more problematic. I think you and I need to talk in private. Can we meet later this afternoon?"

"I have a meeting with the head of the United Nations Forces here at three, which should be over by four. Will you come to the High Commission for tea at half past four? I'll let the guards at the gate know. We've very tight security because our building sits right on the Green Line."

"I don't think this will be a social visit but a cup of tea is always welcome."

"Then I will have it sent up to my private office."

"Tom, I want this meeting to be confidential. Would it be possible for the two of us to meet alone?"

"Everything will be hush-hush, I promise," he said.

Theo knocked discreetly on her door a few moments later. Christos was with him. Elspeth invited them in and offered them a seat. Both sat perched on the edge of their chairs, as if they were uncomfortable being asked to relax in a guest room.

Christos began. "Theo wanted me to come with him because, y'know, we've been in this together from the start."

Elspeth smiled at Christos's modern turn of phrase.

"We were both serving at the picnic and saw a bit of what happened," Christos continued. "Since then we have talked to the other waiters who were there, and we all agree."

"All agree on what, Christos? Did you see where Ms Allard-Thorpe went after the rest of us left the picnic area?"

Both Theo and Christos nodded. Theo spoke this time although he appeared somewhat anxious. "She followed you and your friend."

Elspeth was surprised. "Can you be a bit more specific?"

Christos confirmed what Theo had said. "She was watching the two of you all through lunch, not openly but out of the side of her eyes. When lunch was over, she turned and saw you going around to the other side of the castle. She gave us orders to finish clearing up and then she followed you, keeping behind you, y'know, so that you wouldn't see her."

"Where was she when you last saw her?"

Christos seemed a bit nervous but admitted what he did next. "I didn't want her to mess up your visit with your friend, so I tailed her. You two went into one of the ruined sections of the castle, and she stood at the base of the tower watching you. After that you disappeared from view. Ms Allard-Thorpe suddenly turned away from the direction you had gone in. It looked like someone called out to her, because she put her hand up to her ear and said something like, "Is that you?" Then she turned and went in towards the stairs that went up the tower where she must have seen or heard someone she knew."

"Did you see who that was?"

"No," said Christos, "I was afraid she might see me, so I went back to the picnic area and helped with the clearing up."

"Theo, did Christos say anything to you when he got back from following Ms Allard-Thorpe?"

Theo flushed. "I won't say what he called her, but he said she'd met someone and he hoped she wouldn't be back to pester us soon."

"Christos, can you tell me anything more about the person who called out to her?"

"No, but now I wish I'd kept following her. I might've seen who it was and who might've been with her when she fell."

"It is a pity, although I shouldn't be condoning what you did."

Christos looked contrite.

"I know," he said. "You heard me say the other day she was like the 'wicked witch of the west'. I probably shouldn't have said that to you, but that's how most of us felt."

Elspeth admired his frankness.

"Ms Allard-Thorpe was a complicated individual and raised many strong feelings in those around her, but any person's sudden death is regrettable," she said. "My task is to discover how she fell. You've been very helpful in telling me what you saw. I want both of you to think carefully about the rest of the afternoon at Kantara Castle. You don't need to answer right now, but it would help me to know what happened afterwards. With this type of investigation, even the smallest detail can offer insight into what really went on at the castle after the picnic. Ask the others what they did too. I'm relying on the two of you to gather as much information as possible. Most importantly, I want you both to keep whatever you discover to yourselves. Let me know tomorrow what you find out."

As they left the room, Christos turned back to her. "Have you seen Cinnamon since she left the hotel?" he asked.

"No, but I plan to visit her in the next day or two."

"Tell her I am thinking of her," he said, "and please say it in a way that will let her know how much I . . . " he stumbled on the next words " . . . like her."

28

When Elspeth arrived at the fortified British High Commission compound, the guard at the gate rang the High Commissioner's office, and Tom Wellborne came through the barricaded fence at the entrance to greet her and take her to his private office. Before they began their conversation, he served tea and said he was eager to know more about what Dr Robson had reported. When she had finished telling him, he ran his hand across the top of his head and let out a long puff of air.

"Tell me again what happened after Philippa's body fell."

"Richard and I had wandered off and were sitting in a secluded corner of the castle talking about old times, when we heard Colin French's cry. We rushed out and found the brigadier holding Philippa's body. She was obviously dead. It looked as if her neck was broken. We all assumed she had died as the result of her fall."

The High Commissioner glowered. "And after that?" he asked.

"No one responded to the brigadier's cry except the two of us. As I remember, we ran forward but knew immediately there was nothing we could do to help. The brigadier was overwrought, but one can only assume his combat training clicked into place. He laid Philippa's body on the ground. He took off his shirt and spread it over the upper part of her body and her face. Then he requested, or rather ordered, us to make sure the others didn't come round to see the body. He said he would take charge of getting the body back to Nicosia if we could divert the attention of everyone who was at the picnic. Neither Richard nor I questioned his command, as his task was much more difficult than ours, and he had pulled himself together after his initial cry of surprise."

"And then?"

"We left the brigadier with Philippa's body and went back to the picnic area to see if we could assemble the members of the delegation and hotel staff in order to let them know what happened. Richard went back to the brigadier, who wanted to commandeer the hotel's kitchen van. After giving his car keys to Richard, the brigadier put Philippa's body into the van, so the rest of us had to make do with the brigadier's car and the two coaches that were left. We all crowded together around the remnants of the picnic but no one complained. Our trip back to Nicosia was made in silence."

"Was there anyone else at the castle when you were there?"

Elspeth had not anticipated Tom's question but could not dodge it.

"Unfortunately, yes. Ernest Thorpe, his daughter Cinnamon, and a number of her friends were having a party at the castle to celebrate his fiftieth birthday."

"Where were they when Philippa Allard-Thorpe fell?"

"I think they had left." Elspeth wished she were more certain of this. "Philippa hadn't been expected at the picnic, so we were all puzzled when she arrived. There was no reason for her to be there. As was her way, she immediately began to re-organise the way the picnic was laid out. The people from the kitchen staff gave in, not too gracefully I must add, to Philippa's instructions. When the picnic arrangements were changed to her satisfaction, she walked over to where Cinnamon and her ex-husband were setting up their meal. According to one of the people we questioned, Ernest Thorpe turned his back on Philippa, although just before that Richard and I had heard them having words."

"Do you know exactly when Ernest Thorpe left the castle?"

"No, but I didn't see him after the brigadier found the body."

Thomas Wellborne shook his head and said, "I hope it isn't Thorpe who killed her. He's a frequent visitor here at the High Commission, and he keeps up good relations with the British on both sides of the island. What concerns me is that no one knows exactly how Philippa fell. Thorpe may have strangled her and pushed her over the parapet, walked calmly down from the tower and escorted his daughter and her friends away. It could all have happened very quickly, long before the brigadier found the body and raised the alarm."

"I could ask Dr Robson if he has any idea about the time of death, but he would probably only give me a general answer, between the hours of one and three, that sort of thing. The sun was warm, and Colin French was holding the body in a sunny area when we first saw him. The heat would affect the calculated time of death even more. So you see, Tom, we have a bit of a conundrum."

The High Commissioner rose from his chair and began pacing. "The division of this island makes things so damned awkward. The police on the Turkish side should have been brought in, I suppose. The brigadier will be in great trouble if the Turkish Cypriots learn he transported a dead body across the Green Line. How long do you think we can keep

Dr Robson from reporting this to the police here on the Greek side? Do you think he will honour the twenty-four hours you requested?"

"It might be wisest for you to contact him. I assume he's still a British citizen."

Elspeth wondered if Thomas Wellborne knew about the SIS's investigation into Nikki Amasis's dealings with Philippa. He must, but Elspeth did not want to bring it up. She did not think it would significantly help in solving Philippa's murder, and therefore she took another tack.

"Tom, I'm trying to find out what happened at the picnic, and more importantly if anyone from the hotel was responsible for Philippa's death. Beyond that I'd be exceeding my capacity and interfering in a police and/or High Commission matter. After our talk today, I feel I must pass the reins over to you. Naturally I will keep you informed if I discover anything that might be of use to you. You know better than I the formalities that need to take place between your office and the Cypriot authorities."

"Unfortunately, those formalities are fraught with multiple layers of bureaucracy, but, as you say, that is my job."

Tom Wellborne seemed anxious to end the interview, and Elspeth made a polite retreat as quickly as she could without awkwardness. She thought of walking the short distance back to the hotel, but the extreme security measures at the High Commission daunted her, and she asked for a taxi to the hotel instead. Once out of the compound, she changed her mind and directed the taxi driver to take her to Colin French's home. Perhaps the brigadier might have some answers to her problem.

29

Colin French was dressing for dinner with one of the army widows who had settled on Cyprus and who always offered the brigadier excellent food, wine, conversation, and occasionally something more. She was comforting rather than possessive, which pleased him. Tonight he needed to forget Philippa Allard-Thorpe, the hotel, the delegation, and Elspeth Duff. He had been annoyed when Elspeth called and said she needed to talk to him urgently. He checked his watch and saw he had an hour before the widow expected him. Besides he could phone and say he would be late. She was the forgiving sort and would not complain.

Colin asked his cook to set out a bottle of wine, but not one of the better ones in his cellar, and some peanuts. He waited at the gate and watched her alight from a battered taxi.

Elspeth responded to the questioning in his eyes. "I didn't expect to come here. I was on my way back from an interview with the High Commissioner when I thought it only fair to you to bring you news of the autopsy, particularly since you discovered Philippa after the fall and did so much to get the body to this side of Cyprus."

Colin French smiled just enough to be polite and asked her into the garden. "I'm sure Mr Thomas Wellborne was not pleased with my stunt. Undoubtedly I have upset his desire for a quiet end to his tour of duty here. Am I in trouble?"

"I'll leave that issue to be settled between the two of you," Elspeth said as she came through the gate of his compound.

He led her to a part of the garden away from the house. Elspeth took a seat on a bench alongside a bed of flowers that his gardener had recently planted. Their blossoms gave off a light scent, which Colin thought complemented Elspeth's presence.

He sat down next to her and turned serious. "I hope you understand why I had little or no choice but to get Philippa back on the Greek side after her fall. Can you imagine how much more difficulty there would have been if I had admitted to the UN guards at the checkpoint that my passenger, a British citizen, had died of a broken neck when she fell off the top of one of the Turks' tourist attractions. We would still be over there now negotiating our release from jail." He laid his arm casually across the back of the bench, and Elspeth withdrew almost imperceptibly.

"She didn't die of a broken neck," Elspeth said.

Colin jerked back, horror in his face. "Of course she did. It was patently obvious when I found her. I had a terribly hard time steadying her head on the headrest of the van's passenger seat before I reached the Green Line. I wanted to make it look like she was asleep and not dead."

"Numerous bones were broken, but she died of asphyxia. The pathologist suspected she was strangled," Elspeth said. She searched his face and tried to judge his reaction.

Colin shook his head regretfully and then rose and walked to the end of the bench, clenching his hands over its back. "Surely, the pathologist must be wrong. I saw no evidence of strangulation when I found her. It looked like her neck was broken when she landed from the fall."

"Dr Robson said her neck was badly bruised. She died from lack of oxygen to the brain."

Colin hit his hand of the back of the bench, not once but several times. "Bloody hell. Are you trying to tell me she was murdered?"

Elspeth did not move. "It looks that way." Her voice was dry. "Thomas Wellborne wants to let the matter lie for a day or two while he decides to which government body on which side of Cyprus to report the crime."

Colin smiled at this. "I bet old Thomas is in a lather, but I'm also in a precarious position. I'm not sure if I actually committed a crime, but one or the other of the police authorities, or maybe both, could raise a terrible rumpus if they know I removed the body from a murder scene. I suppose I'll have to go up to the High Commission in the morning and see Thomas. What a total disaster. Trust Philippa to make the complications of her death as complex as the ones during her life." Now he was angry.

"She was rather that way," Elspeth agreed.

Colin brought himself under control and bowed stiffly. "Elspeth, you must forgive me. I have an engagement shortly and must be off. I want to thank you for bringing me the news. I thought there would be an autopsy and hoped we could all finally be free and clear of Philippa when we found out the results. That doesn't appear to be the case. There's usually a taxi down the street. May I call it for you?"

As he handed her into the old Mercedes cab, he brushed her cheek with his fingers. "Please keep me posted," he said.

"The case is basically out of my hands, Colin, but I will let you know if I learn anything new."

After the taxi disappeared, he leaned back against his gate and whistled to the air. "Colin, old man, you are definitely in trouble this time." He knew Thomas Wellborne would not let him off lightly. Then he thought of the widow and hoped the conversation over dinner would be centred on any topic but murder and that the evening would end intimately.

*

When Elspeth got back to the hotel, she wanted to talk to Richard, but she suspected he would still be deeply involved with meetings in Brussels. She decided to call Pamela Crumm instead. Pamela did not answer her phone, and Elspeth left a voice mail message.

Elspeth found a light and elegant Indian shawl in deep tones of red, violet, green and yellow, which at one point Richard had admired, wrapped it around herself and ventured out into the coolness of the garden. Several guests had done likewise and were admiring the plants in the late afternoon light. She recognised Cari and Bitki among them. They looked up as she approached.

Cari welcomed Elspeth warmly. "Elspeth, I'm finding your hotel most charming. I've been here to tea many times but have never been a guest before. I've filled out your questionnaire and am assured that by tomorrow morning everything I've asked for will be provided."

"Probably by this evening and the next time you visit as well," Elspeth responded. "Lord Kennington insists."

Cari laughed. "I don't suppose I'll be able to convince Jonathan to stay in a Kennington hotel when we travel next. He is a bit of a penny pincher."

Elspeth felt a burning need to talk with Cari and Bitki in private and invited them into her suite for a sherry before dinner, but she declined their invitation to join them in the delegation's wing for a meal afterwards. She wanted to be free to talk to both Pamela Crumm and Richard Munro as the evening progressed.

As soon as they were seated, Elspeth said, "Cari and Bitki, you need to know the results of the autopsy, but other than conveying them to Jonathan, I want you to keep them under wraps for now." She briefly outlined what Dr Robson had told her.

Bitki looked startled, but Cari simply nodded her head up and down. "Philippa Allard-Thorpe had been on a slippery slope for too far too long. I'm amazed it took so long for someone to murder her."

"Mummy!" Bitki cried out. "You are being cruel."

"No, my love, only honest. Philippa had double dealt for many years. In the end, it seems to have caught up with her."

"What do you know, Cari, that might help us find who did this?" Elspeth asked.

"You must realise that Philippa was a person who would twist any situation to her own advantage. She married Ernest Thorpe because she thought he would propel her into prominence in the world of archaeology and the Cypriot expat community. He did neither. It was she who pushed them into society. They had two children, the first of whom died at age three. Cinnamon was born four years afterwards. The first daughter became the cherished child and Cinnamon the inadequate replacement. Cinnamon, before the accident that blinded her, and even now, is a beautiful young woman, but to Philippa she could not fill the place of her perfect first child. Naturally, a three-year-old does not assume the rough edges of character that one finds in one's offspring as they grow up. Can you imagine Cinnamon living with those feelings from her mother? It must have been crippling."

Elspeth responded with a sympathetic look. "Bitki, you must forgive two older women from speculating on childhood development."

Bitki, who had been listening quietly, smiled lovingly. "Azai is already showing signs of rebellion," she said, "but I think Onan and I are on to his scheming."

An intelligent parent, thought Elspeth. "Cari, please go on. Philippa's treatment of her daughter seems as if it was only the smallest of the problems in her family."

Cari continued. "Philippa had high ambitions and when her husband could, or would, not provide her with the opportunity to exercise them, she branched out. You've heard, I'm sure, about the Cypriot Britannia Hotel, but what you may not know is Nikki Amasis bought the hotel after Philippa inherited it."

This surprised Elspeth, who said, "Is he normally an investor in the tourist industry?"

Cari took a sip of her sherry and pursed her lips. "I can't tell you everything, but Amasis, on a much grander scale than Philippa, uses every opportunity to advance his business enterprises."

"And somehow Philippa was drawn in by him?" Elspeth asked.

"Yes, we believe so, and she probably got in over her head."

Elspeth put down her glass and frowned. "That worries me, because the Kennington Organisation has always operated with the highest standards of integrity, and to have someone like Philippa Allard-Thorpe inveigle her way into our system is anathema to everything we represent."

Cari reassured her. "You are not alone in seeing Philippa's duplicity. She was a master at deception. She had good looks and spoke the Queen's English, and she always had great allure. We were all taken in."

"You knew her personally?"

"Most of the expats did. She tried to dominate our society, but eventually her ambitions became transparent and fell flat. I think that may be why she left Ernest and took up with Amasis. He offered her more clout."

"Clout?" asked Elspeth. "What did that give her?"

"I think it may have been money and a way into a new world."

"Meaning the international hospitality industry?"

"Precisely," Cari said, "but Nikki Amasis never gives anything away without a price."

"Was Philippa so naïve?"

"No, not naïve. I think she was so narcissistic that she found Nikki's attentions flattering rather than manipulative."

Elspeth put her fingers to her temples, rubbed them and let out her breath. "This is troubling news but only corroborates what I already suspected. If any of this gets out, London . . ."

"Have no fear, Elspeth. The SIS wants publicity even less than you do. From now on we would prefer everything be handled behind closed doors. Certainly we'll leak nothing to the press, and I doubt you will either."

"What about Thomas Wellborne?"

"After Jonathan hears about the autopsy, I'm sure he'll meet Thomas and set up a plan for handling Philippa's death and her connections with Amasis. Thomas will be glad to have the problem taken out of his hands. The High Commissioner, for all his charm, does not like controversy on his watch."

"So I gather," said Elspeth dryly.

After Cari and Bitki left her suite, Elspeth checked the time and wondered if it was inappropriate to ring Ernest Thorpe. It was now half past seven, and they might be in the middle of dinner at the Thorpe household. She decided to wait until the next morning. Instead she again tried Pamela Crumm's office in London. This time she reached her.

"Elspeth, I have just rung off from Cornell University in New York. The dean at the hotel school is absolutely delightful, but I fear I've promised an apprenticeship for one of his students at one of our hotels in America. The school is very prestigious, so I assume Eric won't be upset. Or I may not tell him at all."

"You're a wise woman, Pamela."

"I try," said her friend. "But after giving that promise, I extracted what I needed to know about Philippa Allard-Thorpe. She was indeed registered at the school, for an extension course in New York City. It seems she never completed the course but about six months later asked for a transcript, which indicated that her course work was incomplete. The school's registrar duly sent Philippa's paperwork to her with the official stamp of the school."

"And what did she send to the Kennington Organisation when she applied for her job?"

"She gave us a very official-looking transcript that showed her having a degree in hotel management with highest honours, duly stamped. Are you surprised?"

Elspeth snorted. "Not at all. Philippa constantly proves true to form."

"I've spent the afternoon with our personnel department checking all her other references," Pamela said. "It appears they all are manipulated versions of the truth. She had recommendations from the Plaza Hotel and the Waldorf Astoria on crisp stationery, but all the people recommending her are now dead. One was totally incapacitated at the time the letter was supposedly written. I'm totally amazed at Philippa's audacity."

"And," Elspeth ventured, "at her success in fooling us."

Pamela groaned. "Yes, there's that too. His lordship will not be amused when he hears."

"Knowing Eric, I think you may have a tirade in the making. Call me when it's over," Elspeth said.

"I may need sympathy."

"It is yours, dear Pamela. How could I deny a friend?"

30

Elspeth wondered if it was a good time to call Richard but finally decided against it. Suddenly shyness came over her. You are a fool, Elspeth, she thought. You can't handle this closeness to him. Why did you think your relationship with a man would be more successful this time? Since Richard knew the final results of the autopsy would be coming in soon, why didn't he call her rather than the other way round? Berating herself, she now regretted she had turned down the invitation to dine in the delegates' wing. She no longer relished another meal by herself in her rooms. She had not checked the hotel registration list that day and wondered if, on an off chance, one of the guests was someone she knew and might join in the dining room. During the seven years of her job with Lord Kennington she had become acquainted with many of the regular guests. She roused herself, grabbed her handbag in case she decided to go out, and made her way to the reception desk.

As she entered the lobby, she found an altercation going on between the concierge and a young person with spiky hair, a goatee, and baggy clothing. Elspeth drew near and saw the young person was one of Cinnamon's student friends. Elspeth went round to the concierge's desk and interrupted the dispute.

With disdain in his voice, the concierge turned to Elspeth and said, "Ms Duff, this person says he knows you and wishes to see you."

"Yes, I know him," Elspeth said. She turned to the student and suggested they step outside. Before they left, the concierge advised her to take care and offered his help if she needed it.

Once beyond the hearing of the doorman, Elspeth turned to the student. "You are one of Cinnamon Allard-Thorpe's friends, I know. Is there somewhere you and I might go and talk instead of here at the hotel?"

Relief spread across the young man's face. His face was longer and more finely drawn than many of the Cypriots Elspeth had met, and his clothes were trendy rather than dishevelled.

"There's the pub just across the river," he suggested. "It will be a bit noisy. Do you mind?"

"Not at all, as long as it has a place where we can speak without others hearing. Lead on," she said and took his arm as she would have taken her son's. At first he looked surprised and then grinned proudly.

"I doubt anyone could hear over the din, but we can go there and see. My name, by the way, is Demetrius. I saw you the day Cinnamon read her poem at the café and again on Saturday at the castle. Cinnamon asked me to find you. She wants to see you and called to ask me to give you a message. She wonders if you could go out to Paphos." Elspeth noted that his English was fluent but his accent was reminiscent of the north of England.

As they walked into the old section of Nicosia, Elspeth remembered Sophia's concern about the student in the garden at the hotel.

"Demetrius, have you been to the hotel before?"

"Yes, to meet Cinnamon. They threw me out."

"When was that?"

"About a week ago, I think. Cinnamon asked to meet me, but that bloody mother of hers caught sight of me and set her guards on me. She left orders that in future I was to be denied access to the hotel. That was the problem tonight when I came looking for you.

"Then I'm glad I came down into the lobby. I hope to visit Cinnamon and her father tomorrow or the next day, and I'm glad she wants me to stay in touch. Do you have any idea what she wants see me about?"

"Not really. You see, Cinnamon pretends to be all sweetness, but she has a sad and bitter side. With a mother like that, who would blame her?"

"Do you know if Cinnamon spoke to her mother last Saturday at the castle?"

"I saw them talking. Cinnamon seemed upset and told her mother to go away."

"Did Cinnamon's mother speak to Ernest Thorpe?"

"She tried, but after a few words he turned his back and walked away. Bloody awful the things she said to him as he left."

"Did he react?"

"Not really. Later, as we were getting ready to drive away, he apologised to us all for her behaviour."

"Demetrius, when did you learn that Ms Allard-Thorpe had fallen from the tower?"

"Sunday morning. Cinnamon rang me on my mobile. She was crying. I tried to cheer her up and tell her she was better off now, but I don't think she wanted to hear that."

"How long have you known Cinnamon?"

"About six years or so, before her accident anyway. She's a very beautiful girl."

"Are you a Cypriot?"

"Only half. My mother was English, from the north of England. She and my dad met at university."

"You speak English very well."

"I lived with members of my extended family in Manchester and went to school there when I was younger."

They arrived at the pub, which proved to be crowded. Most of the patrons were young and appeared to be regulars. Many greeted Demetrius.

Elspeth was hungry and offered to pay if he would like to order for them both. Demetrius thanked her for her generosity and suggested a local beer. While waiting for their meal, Elspeth turned the conversation back to Demetrius's experience at the hotel.

"Did Ms Allard-Thorpe actually ask you to leave the hotel or did she send a member of the staff to do so?"

"A member of the staff, I suppose. A man in a hotel uniform."

"Did she ever speak to you personally in her office about you not seeing Cinnamon?"

"No. Cinnamon's mother liked to hide behind her authority and sent the man to speak to me and escort me out," Demetrius said with disgust.

Their food came and with it a group of students, several of whom Elspeth recognised from the poetry reading and the picnic.

"Here's to Ms Duff," cried Demetrius. "She's offered to buy us all a round of drinks."

Had Elspeth been paying for the drinks herself, her Scottish thriftiness might have come into play. As it was, she put the tab on her Kennington Organisation credit card and justified it on her expense account as 'information gathering'. Several of the students, who were rather full of drink, corroborated Demetrius's story about the picnic, but they were mainly interested in more beer.

Elspeth pleaded fatigue, although it was only eight o'clock. She hoped to leave quietly, but Demetrius saw her rise and followed her out. "Let me walk you back to the hotel," he said. "It's safer that way."

The doorman at the Kennington Nicosia was occupied with the arrival of a taxi and apparently did not see them. Demetrius left her at the front door and waved cheekily to the doorman's back. Elspeth watched him disappear down the street.

When Elspeth returned to her rooms, there were no messages for her either on her computer or her mobile. Disappointment filled her.

31

Ernest Thorpe had anticipated Elspeth's call and was pleased that it came so quickly. He suggested Elspeth come to Paphos for two reasons. One, he wanted to keep Cinnamon away from the Kennington Nicosia, where memories of Philippa might disturb her, and, two, he wanted Cinnamon to consider his house in Paphos her home, a place where she could be safe and loved. Cinnamon had spoken to him of Elspeth's kindness over the last few weeks, and Ernest thought a mother figure might help Cinnamon through the shock of what had happened at Kantara Castle. Cinnamon smiled warmly at him when he told her Elspeth was coming to Paphos.

Cinnamon and Ernest were waiting by the door as the hotel car pulled through the gates and up the drive. The day was warm but winds were coming off the sea, blowing Cinnamon's hair in the fashion of Botticelli's Venus.

Cinnamon called out, "Is that you, Elspeth?"

Elspeth came forward and took Cinnamon's outstretched hands warmly. "Yes, it's me. Ernest, thank you for your invitation. I have a great deal to tell you both."

Ernest's home had all the trimmings of a bachelor's home, leather chairs, black and white photos of ancient Greek pieces of art, probably from his digs, and local carpets in muted colours on the terra cotta tiled floor. A long wooden table was half filled with books and papers and half set for their lunch.

The only other adornments in the room were pieces of pottery and mosaics, which must also have been found at his sites and be interesting archaeologically, but they were not at all beautiful to Elspeth's eyes.

Ernest offered Elspeth a glass of wine from a large bar cabinet, but she declined. Cinnamon requested sparkling water and Elspeth asked for the same. Ernest poured himself a light whisky soda.

He led them out on to the patio to seats behind a wall under an arbour that sheltered them from the sun and the wind. Cinnamon tapped her way over to a bench and settled into it, folding her stick into her skirts. The gesture reminded Elspeth of the first time she had seen Cinnamon in the gardens of the hotel. Ernest held his hand out to a canvas chair and invited Elspeth to sit down. He took a chair opposite her where he could look directly at her.

"I see Demetrius found you and told you I wanted to see you," Cinnamon said with delight in her voice.

"Yes, he came to the hotel last night and took me to a terribly noisy pub." Elspeth did not mention Demetrius was on the point of being thrown out of the hotel when she found him. "He gave me your message. Cinnamon, I need to talk to you and your father about last Saturday. I know I may raise unpleasant memories, so I thought we might get it over with early. Do you mind terribly? "

Ernest Thorpe shook his head. "Of course not. We expected this and actually would like to know what is happening in Nicosia."

*

Elspeth decided not to tell them about the autopsy. She felt it would upset Cinnamon and, if Ernest Thorpe were involved in the murder, he already would know how Philippa died.

"Cinnamon, Brigadier French was able to get your mother's remains to a hospital on the Greek side, and the Kennington Organisation will handle the funeral arrangements, with input from you if you wish. As far as we can tell, you are her only heir and will inherit all her property. Do you know who her solicitor is and if she had a will?"

Elspeth watched Cinnamon's face harden. "Mummy didn't talk about those things with me. I hated how she treated me like a child, but I do know her solicitor. He came to our home occasionally, and Mummy and he would go off to her study to discuss business. I don't know for sure, but I think Mummy was rather well off. She sometimes talked about her investments, grumbling if they had gone down or getting excited when they went up. She had a program on her computer where she used to track them."

Elspeth wondered if the computer was still in Philippa's home. "Did your mother have a housekeeper in Nicosia?"

"Yes, she's called Maria."

"Is Maria at the house now?"

"I don't know, but I expect so. She lives in a small flat off the kitchen and normally stays in the house unless she's out shopping. She's a widow and doesn't like venturing out otherwise."

"Does she know you are here?"

Ernest nodded. "I telephoned and told her about Phil's accident and that Cinnamon would be going there to pack her thing because I was taking her to live with me. She said she understood and would stay at the house as long as Cinnamon wanted her there. She seemed more concerned about her own future than Cinnamon's. Cypriot widows sometimes have no independent resources and a situation like Maria's is a godsend."

"Cinnamon, may I have your permission to speak to Maria?"

"She's a bit of a sourpuss, but she kept the house well enough to stay in my mother's service, which was a miracle. You may try to speak to her, but she may not be willing to talk. She is very disapproving of most things."

Elspeth smiled, recognising the type. She wondered what she would have to do to get into Philippa's house and particularly to take possession of Philippa's personal computer. "Does Maria read English?" she asked.

"Some. Mummy could leave simple lists for her."

"Will you dictate a note to her?"

Ernest Thorpe intervened. "Let me get Phil's solicitor to call her. He's British but can speak Greek fluently, and Maria will recognise him. Being an old-fashioned Cypriot woman, she will take his word over Cinnamon's."

Elspeth knew her next request would put her on delicate ground, and therefore she chose her words carefully. "Lord Kennington asked me to make inquiries into Philippa's death and requested this be done in as discreet a way as possible. I realise talking about this may be painful for you both, but there're several things I need to know."

They both started speaking at once and then stopped. They laughed, whether from anxiety or anticipation Elspeth did not know.

"You go first, Daddy," Cinnamon said.

Ernest nodded. "Saturday was my fiftieth birthday, and more than anything else I wanted to be with Cinnamon. I met her on the sly at the park near the river about a fortnight ago, and she was delighted when I told her my wish. She asked if she could invite her friends from the university. She told me they would be awed, as she put it, to meet me, as several were studying history and another archaeology. How could I refuse? When Cinnamon was a child, she loved tales of the knights on Cyprus and sometimes imagined she was a fair lady taken by the infidels and rescued by a crusading knight who had come out from England. She loved going to the old castles here on the island, and Kantara was her favourite. The three of us would often go there for a picnic, and after we'd eaten Cinnamon and I would climb the tower where I would tell her stories, most of them straight from my imagination, about the time of the Crusades. Phil would stay below. She always said I was filling Cinnamon's head full of nonsense."

"I loved those stories, Daddy," Cinnamon said.

"I know," he responded and turned back to Elspeth. "When Phil took her away, I used to go to Kantara Castle, climb the tower and remember those magic moments that she and I shared together. Once I even took Cinnamon there secretly. She asked if the two if us could climb the tower together. We did, and, although she could only feel the old stones of the castle under her feet and with her fingers, we had one of those rare times a parent gets to have with an adult child, a reminiscence of their loving relationship during her childhood."

"It was special for me too," Cinnamon said.

"Cinnamon made her way up almost by herself, as if remembering the stairs and passageways from many years ago. As we stood up there, I knew I had just experienced one of the best moments of my life. Therefore when she suggested Kantara Castle for my birthday picnic, I was thrilled."

He smiled at Cinnamon and went on. "I packed several hampers of food, because Cinnamon told me the boys were always ravenous. I brought beer as well, which she insisted was a must. I expected them to be rowdy, so was touched when they all quietened down and brought out a gift for me. The gift was wrapped clumsily in paper with a rather untidy ribbon, but when I opened it, I found a photograph of Cinnamon that was quite exquisite."

He reached over to a side table and picked it up to show to Elspeth. Cinnamon was sitting on the capital of a broken column with her beautiful hair caught in the long rays of the evening sun. Her head was thrown back, a smile spread across her face, and her unseeing eyes caught the sunlight.

The photograph brought tears to Elspeth's eyes, and she lamented that Cinnamon could not see its beauty.

"What happened then?" Elspeth asked.

"Let me tell, Daddy. We all started to eat. My friends were enjoying the meal and Daddy was laughing alongside them, when he suddenly stopped. Then I heard my mother's voice. Daddy growled through his teeth and said to me, "Tell her to go away." I went in the direction of her voice, and she came up to me. Daddy followed me. I begged her not to interrupt the picnic, and she snorted and told me I was in bad company. Mummy always hated it when I was having fun without her, but in the end she did leave us alone. When I got back to the group, I could feel that Daddy had lost all his feeling of joy. He suggested that we pack up and go into Kyrenia. The boys were making a frightful row, kicking a football about until finally the ball went over the cliff. None of them wanted to retrieve it once they saw how far down it had gone. Daddy promised he would buy them all another one when we got to Kyrenia, where we were planning to have dinner. Daddy invited them to his favourite tavern, and they rousingly supported his idea. We left shortly after that."

"Did your mother speak to your father when you went out to meet her?" Elspeth asked.

"She yelled something at him about it being dangerous, but he ignored her."

"Ernest, did you see anyone with Philippa after that?"

Ernest blew out his breath. "I wanted nothing to do with her and turned away after she spoke to me. I think she went back towards the other side of the castle. I didn't see her again."

"Cinnamon, did she come up and speak to you later?"

"No. Daddy asked us to pack up as quickly as possible. My friends seemed to understand and helped put things back in the hampers. They did so quickly because I think they wanted to avoid my mother."

Elspeth tried to imagine the scene. She and Richard had seen Philippa go over to the Thorpe's picnic and heard her shout at Ernest, but they had not seen Cinnamon speaking to her mother. Why would Ernest ask Cinnamon to tell Philippa to go away? It did not make sense. Was Cinnamon covering for her father? Shortly after Richard and Elspeth saw the encounter between Philippa and Ernest, they had gone to the hotel picnic on the other side of the castle and were out of view of Ernest's party. Elspeth and Richard did not see the Thorpe party leave.

"When you left, did you note the time?" Elspeth asked.

"We got to Kyrenia shortly after half past two," Ernest said. "It's about an hour and a half's drive. The roads aren't very good. The students had come to the castle in their own vehicles. I had my car. We drove back separately."

"Did you split up at the castle and did the two of you go alone to the tavern in Kyrenia in your car?"

Ernest Thorpe seemed uncomfortable with the question. "You can imagine that since the accident when Cinnamon was hurt, I've been very protective of her travelling with people I don't know. The two of us went to Kyrenia together, and her friends followed. I'm certain Philippa would have disapproved of my driving Cinnamon. Believe me, I now drive extremely cautiously."

Elspeth nodded at him sympathetically. "Cinnamon, do you remember Demetrius ever coming to the hotel?"

"Oh, yes. I invited him once because he had agreed to pick me up after lunch and take me out to meet Daddy."

"Did your mother see him?"

"Unfortunately. She made a terrible fuss and said I wasn't to invite him to the hotel again."

"And why is that?"

"Mummy didn't like my friendship with him. She said it was dangerous and would lead to no good."

Elspeth was surprised at the answer to her question, particularly the word 'dangerous'. Demetrius looked more reputable than many of the other students. She expressed her confusion. "Why did your mother think he was dangerous?"

"Because of his family connections. Demetrius told me he wanted nothing to do with his family and was trying to distance himself from them. He often expressed his dislike of them and what they stood for."

"Who are his family?"

"His father is Nikki Amasis."

Elspeth was shocked. She hoped her face did not register what she was feeling. Cinnamon could not see it, of course, but Ernest could.

He said, "Phil got involved with Amasis right after she left us. He financed her, I think, when she was running the old Cypriot Britannia Hotel. The owner of the hotel, who took her in when she went to Nicosia, was an old man, and the hotel was failing. She wanted to make a success of it, and it was rumoured she cut a deal with Amasis to find the capital to do so. I don't know the details, but suddenly the hotel was redecorated, the staff changed, a new chef hired, and the fortunes of the hotel turned around dramatically. The old man died and left the hotel to Phil. She sold it soon afterwards to a consortium controlled by Amasis, who sold it on to an international chain of hotels. She took all the credit for revitalising the hotel, but she may have made a bargain with the devil to do so."

Cinnamon sat rigidly as Ernest spoke, and her jaw worked back and forth. Finally in a low voice she said, "Daddy, that was only rumour."

"Yes, my dear, I know that. I'm sure Elspeth can find out the truth."

Elspeth was not certain she could. She had agreed to leave Nikki Amasis alone, but she could not explain this to the Thorpes. She vowed to find out as much as possible from Pamela Crumm in London about the Cypriot Britannia Hotel and Amasis's involvement in it.

On the trip back to Nicosia, Elspeth tried to sit back and enjoy the countryside along the way. Unlike Kahlil, the driver was silent and left her to her own thoughts, which were preoccupied with the information Ernest and Cinnamon had given her before lunch. Much of the countryside was rocky, arid, and uninteresting when they were out of sight of the sea. She thought of Cinnamon's spider's web. Cinnamon had given her a written copy after lunch, and Elspeth took it out and read it again.

Hanging by a thread,
a spider fashions her web
of sunlit spun lace.

Her pattern soon gone,
torn asunder by the wind.
Broken illusions.

In light of the last few days' events, Elspeth found the poem filled with much more meaning than it had before. She imagined Philippa was not only the spider trying to spin the illusion of a perfect hotel manager, presenting herself in sunlit lace, but also she was hanging by a thread, perhaps held by Nikki Amasis. The web became tangled and Philippa was strangled by an unknown assailant and pushed over the edge of the castle wall. Broken illusions. Philippa's own illusions, perhaps, but the ones she had fashioned so carefully to promote her own image and deceive those around her.

Elspeth asked to be set down before they reached the hotel, as she needed to stretch her legs and clear her head. When she arrived at the hotel entrance, she was surprised to find a police car waiting under the porte-cochère.

A man in police uniform stood by the car, watching Elspeth approach. He was obviously in a hostile mood.

"Mrs Duff," he said curtly in stilted English, "I am asking you to accompany me to police headquarters to answer some questions about the murders of Philippa Allard-Thorpe and Demetrius Amasis."

32

Elspeth sat silently in the back of the police Land Rover and tried to take in what the policeman had said. Had she heard him correctly? The murders of Philippa Allard-Thorpe—and Demetrius Amasis? Granted, she had seen Demetrius the evening before, but she had not even known his full name or family affiliation until a few hours ago. Demetrius was so light-hearted at the pub, except perhaps in his concern for Cinnamon. Who would want to murder him? Elspeth wanted to ask where and how he had died, but the policewoman sat taciturnly beside her, looking straight ahead.

They pulled up at the back of the central police station, and Elspeth was led through a side door. The policewoman took her into the outer office of the detective branch. She motioned to a chair and took another nearby. They sat without speaking. Elspeth watched the hands of the clock as fifteen minutes passed by. Finally a door from an adjoining office opened, and a uniformed police officer came out and beckoned her into his room. He was a burly Greek, who appeared taller than he actually was because of his starched uniform and thick-soled shoes.

He introduced himself in excellent but slightly accented English. "I am Ajax Markides, a detective chief inspector in the Cypriot police. I asked that you be brought in for questioning, although you are not under arrest. We understand you are a security officer for the Kennington hotel chain and you were at the picnic where Philippa Allard-Thorpe died. You also had dinner with Demetrius Amasis last evening. Is that true?" His tone was bland and non-accusatory.

Elspeth could not relax completely. Although she had not been directly involved in the transporting of Philippa's body across the Green Line, she was aware that it had happened. She also knew the results of the autopsy and had been instrumental in delaying the findings to the police. Although she knew nothing of Demetrius's murder, she was with him the night before. Fortunately she remembered from her training at Scotland Yard that, when questioned by the police, people frequently revealed more information than the police already knew and often incriminated themselves. Consequently, she decided to say as little as possible and refer the police directly to the British High Commissioner. From her long experience working with police departments around the world, she knew she had this right as a British citizen.

"Yes, that's true," she answered. "How may I help you, Detective Chief Inspector?" She wanted to sound as helpful as possible without telling him anything.

"When did you last see Demetrius Amasis?"

"Last evening."

"Where?"

"At a pub in the old section of Nicosia, across the river from the Kennington Nicosia hotel. I don't know its name."

"When did you leave the pub?"

"It must have been about eight."

"Did Demetrius go with you when you left?"

"Yes, he accompanied me back to the entrance of the Kennington Nicosia."

"Did you go from the pub directly back to the hotel?

"Yes."

"Did you walk or take a taxi?"

"We walked."

"What did you do when you got back to the hotel?"

"I went to my room."

"Did you leave your room after that?"

"No."

"Can anyone corroborate that?"

"No," she said. She did not mention the security cameras in the hotel.

"Is it your habit to go to bed so early?"

"Yes, recently. I had rather a bad head injury earlier this year and require more sleep than normal."

"Can that be confirmed?"

"The injury? Of course."

The detective took another tack. "How well did you know Demetrius Amasis?"

"I've met him only twice, once at a poetry reading, although I did not speak to him at the time, and again last night."

"Mrs Duff, what was your real reason in meeting Demetrius last night. Surely it was not to discuss poetry?"

"No, it was not. He brought me a message from a friend."

"Who was that?"

Elspeth felt he might be leading her into a trap and tried to avoid it. She did not want to give him Cinnamon's name if she could help it, but his questions were very direct. She admired his skill but wondered if she could trust him with the whole truth. Admitting Cinnamon was near the scene on the day of her mother's murder would link her to the crime, even if the link was a weak one. Elspeth decided on a diversionary tactic.

"Chief Inspector," she said, "I know nothing of Demetrius's murder. Can you tell me when it happened and how? He was very much alive when I last saw him, and he said he was returning to the pub to enjoy a beer with friends."

The Chief Inspector surprisingly gave in to request. "His body was found this morning outside the Cyprus Museum in the Municipal Gardens. He had been strangled, and his body had been dragged into the shrubbery."

"Was there any sign of a struggle?"

He looked curiously at Elspeth. "Have you ever worked for the police, Mrs Duff, or were you trained in journalism?"

"I was at Scotland Yard for four years."

"Then that explains your question. At this point we are not at liberty to give out any more information."

"How did you know I was with Demetrius yesterday evening?"

"We found a letter in his pocket addressed to you at the Kennington Nicosia."

She decided not to react to the chief inspector's statement. Instead she said, "I see."

"Where did you go earlier today?"

"How do you know I was not at the hotel?"

"We keep a much closer watch on foreign visitors than most people realise."

"I see," she said again, feeling a bit foolish.

"We know you visited Ernest Thorpe and his daughter. Did you tell them the results of the autopsy on Philippa Allard-Thorpe?"

"No, I . . ."

Elspeth knew she had been trapped by the Chief Inspector by implying she knew about the autopsy, and she struggled to regain her dignity. "Chief Inspector, I'll tell you what you want to know, but naturally my main concern is to protect the hotel guests and staff. That's my job. Ernest Thorpe's daughter was Philippa Allard-Thorpe's as well, and Ms Allard-Thorpe was the manager of our hotel. Perhaps you can appreciate that I have Cinnamon Allard-Thorpe's welfare in mind as the daughter of one of our employees."

"Mrs Duff, you must know that under our laws a pathologist is required to report to us the results of any autopsy that indicates foul play. For the purposes of the investigation into Ms Allard-Thorpe's death as well as that of Demetrius Amasis's, we want to keep the results of the autopsy as close a secret as possible, and therefore I would be grateful if you do not share them with the Thorpes or anyone else. There are two links between you and the murders—your position at the hotel and your meeting with Demetrius last evening. We do not suspect you are guilty of either murder, but you can see why we wanted to talk to you."

"Rest assured, I'll do whatever I can to help with your investigation."

"For the moment, I'm allowing you to go, but I will probably want to talk to you again when we discover more. In the meantime, I suggest you return to the hotel and stay there. I'll warn you that Mr Amasis may try to contact you if he learns of your association with his son. He is a very dangerous man, and I urge you, although I cannot order you, not to speak to him. Please leave that to us. I will have you taken back to the Kennington Nicosia now, in an unmarked car if you prefer."

Dangerous again, she thought. "Yes, please. I would prefer that," she said.

33

Elspeth was shaken by her encounter with the police and was glad when she reached the hotel. Evening was fast approaching, and rain threatened from clouds she could see in the distance. She stood looking out the window of her suite and tried to think of a way to protect not only herself but Cinnamon as well. She went to the phone and rang Cari Westwood, inviting her for drinks. Elspeth hoped her voice would not quaver. Fortunately Cari seemed to find nothing unusual in Elspeth's call and agreed to come along as soon as the Mitsuis returned from their talks and retrieved Azai from his grandmother's care.

Elspeth took seriously the chief inspector's request that she should not leave the hotel, but she wanted something better than the wine in the mini-bar to entertain her guest. She made her way to the dining room to see if the sommelier could recommend a suitable wine. There she found Christos checking the reservation list. He was alone, which gave Elspeth a chance to ask him for the wine and to speak to him without being overheard.

Christos asked if Elspeth had seen Cinnamon and was delighted at Elspeth's response.

"I found her more accepting about her mother's death than I thought she would be," Elspeth confided. "I think being with her father has helped."

"Does she know about Demetrius Amasis's murder?" Christos asked. "He was one of the students she hung out with, y'know, one of the ones we saw at the café when Cinnamon was reading her poem about the spider."

"How did you know about Demetrius?" she asked, curious to know his source.

"I had just come on duty when Mr Woolsey called down to the kitchen for coffee. The head of room service asked me to take it up to the manager's office, although it was not usually my job. Staff assignments are rather chaotic at the moment. Nikki Amasis was in Mr Woolsey's office and was obviously upset. When I entered the room, he was demanding to see you because he said you probably knew who murdered his son. I recognised him because he gets a lot of press in Cyprus, although not the flattering kind. He's a crook with big money, so he gets away with it. If I were you, Ms Duff, I wouldn't agree to talk to him."

Although Christos's concern was real, Elspeth began to feel annoyed that everyone she met was telling her to steer clear of Nikki Amasis. She felt she needed an unbiased opinion of the man and decided she would call the brigadier later and find out what he knew.

Having accepted a bottle of good wine and asking Christos to arrange for some hot hors d'oeuvres to be brought to her room, she left the dining room and skirted the lobby for fear she might meet the infamous Mr Amasis.

"Cari," Elspeth asked as her guest seated herself in one of the comfortable armchairs, "do you know about Demetrius Amasis's death?"

Cari nodded. "The SIS has a contact in the police. He rang Jonathan as soon as Demetrius's body was found. I've been in contact with Jonathan several times this afternoon using a secure phone line, and therefore I'm in the loop. The police are terrified that Nikki Amasis may send his own henchmen out to find the killer. You should be careful if they come to the hotel."

"Why is everyone so intent on warning me against Amasis?" Elspeth said almost to herself. She filled Cari in on the latest happenings. "I seem to be among the last people to have seen his son alive, and Demetrius was found with a letter is his pocket in an envelope addressed to me. I think it may be from Cinnamon who asked Demetrius to contact me at the hotel."

"Don't you find it odd, Elspeth, that Cinnamon didn't just try to telephone you?"

"Perhaps she couldn't, dial I mean."

"Her father or one of his servants could have done it for her, but I suspect that Philippa, who needed such control over her daughter, had probably given her a mobile with either Braille keys or voice recognition. The hotel number would be on the phone."

Elspeth contorted her face in disgust at her own short sightedness. "Of course," she conceded. "I keep forgetting how sophisticated modern communication is, despite the fact I use it everyday. Do you think Demetrius came here to talk to me for some other reason than bringing Cinnamon's note?"

Cari let out her breath. "Whenever Amasis's name comes up, there are complications. Did Demetrius say anything to you about any other reason for his visit?"

Elspeth tried to remember as accurately as possible the private conversation she'd had with Demetrius the evening before. "No, now that you mention it, he didn't say anything. I think I may have made an incorrect assumption that the letter found in his pocket at the murder scene was from Cinnamon. We talked mainly about her and about her relationship with her mother. What else might he have wanted to see to me about? When we got to the pub, he was quickly surrounded by friends, and we didn't get much time to talk."

"Did the police say the letter was from Cinnamon?"

"They didn't. I was trying to protect Cinnamon, and, from the way the Chief Inspector spoke, he seemed to reinforce my initial assumption. Cari, it's essential we find out who wrote the letter found on Demetrius's body and what it said. Do you think your contact in the police department could find out? Certainly, in the light of Amasis's comments to Alexander Woolsey, I'm somehow implicated."

"Unfortunately, it seems so. I'll get Jonathan to do what he can, but you may be in more peril than any of us expected till now." Cari set her jaw and drew in her carefully sculpted dark brows.

"Do you think I'm in physical danger from Amasis?"

"You may be. Can you put the hotel security staff on alert?"

"Yes, certainly, and I may ask for further help from you. Tell me more about Amasis. Why would he target me? Cinnamon told me Demetrius was estranged from his father."

"On the surface Amasis is a crafty international business man with enough wealth to be accepted into the jet set probably because he has a reputation for being slightly dangerous. We've known for years about his smuggling activities. He's been charged several times both in Britain and France, but he has always managed to evade conviction. We know he has contacts in the Mafia. His current wife is the daughter of one of the minor dons in the Cosa Nostra in Sicily. Outwardly he is very suave and extremely handsome in many women's eyes, but people who get in his way in business have been known to disappear. The few who have been found afterwards were dead, and the cause of death was always attributed to suicide or an unexpected heart attack."

"Does he live here with his wife?"

"No, she spends most of her time in Palermo. He's had several wives since Demetrius's mother died giving birth to their son, and most of his new wives married him for his money and deceivingly good looks. One died mysteriously and one divorced him after five week's of marriage and, incidentally, was glad to accept a very small settlement. The current one has enough protection from her family to make any foul play out of the question. "

"Charming," said Elspeth cynically. "But why might he suspect me?"

"The SIS will try to find out," Cari said. "Elspeth, please protect yourself in any way you can."

"Now I finally understand why you all are advising me to stay away from him. Now I hope he stays away from me."

"I think I need to get Jonathan directly involved. Sit tight until I get back to you," Cari said.

She swallowed the last of her wine and left Elspeth to her own thoughts.

*

Jonathan Westwood had retired many times from the SIS, but current events kept calling him back. Two years ago he nearly brought Nikki Amasis's career to a halt, but the defence attorney asked for information that would have led to uncovering several important intelligence sources that Jonathan did not want to compromise. Amasis went free. Now this. Jonathan's daughter, son-in-law and grandson's presence at the Kennington Nicosia and the picnic where Philippa was murdered brought him into a case that he would have preferred to avoid. He thought Cari could handle the details, but that was before Demetrius's murder. He also knew he might need to use his governmental contacts with Thomas Wellborne, for whom he had no respect. Jonathan's immediate worry was for his family, but he could not overlook the more far-reaching aspects of the two murders. He had just stepped into the garden to deadhead some flowers from his bushes when Cari called. After all these years he could not resist the seductive persuasiveness of his wife's voice and gave in to her request.

"Damn vixen!" he thought fondly. He went to his study and unlocked the gun case. Hamud, one of his operatives, would be crossing the Green Line in the morning at a location far out of sight of the border checkpoint, and would take with him the item that Cari requested.

34

The morning found Cari Westwood temporarily relieved of her grandmotherly duties. She settled in the coolness of the garden courtyard on one of the benches under a tree. She sat for a long time staring at a leafy branch that fluttered back and forth in a breeze that promised future showers. She tried to reconstruct the sequence of events leading to the two murders and what the connection might be between them. Nikki Amasis was an easy suspect, particularly because of his many illicit activities on Cyprus and throughout the eastern Mediterranean, but would he murder his own son? Cari knew Amasis was an opportunist, often doing evil to further his commercial interests. She suspected he might have been responsible for numerous activities related to various deaths over the years, but Demetrius was his only child despite his four marriages. There could be the possibility of more children, but he lived apart from his current wife, and it was likely she would not divorce him or allow him to divorce her. The truth must be elsewhere. Ending her musings, Cari went into the lobby and used the house phone to call Elspeth and invite her to come for a quiet talk in the garden.

Elspeth came through the hotel and out into the fresh air. Cari saw the fatigue under Elspeth's eyes and the strain in her jaw muscles but did not question the reason. Elspeth sat down beside her and smiled, her lips making the motion but her eyes filled with concern.

Cari Westwood took a deep breath and began. "Elspeth, I need to talk to you about Amasis, at least to the extent that the SIS will allow. We know he had some kind of hold over Philippa Allard-Thorpe, and, consequently, is more connected to the Kennington Nicosia than I am sure Lord Kennington would like. Amasis's enterprises, both legal and illegal, are too numerous to recount at the moment, but, by using Philippa, I suspect he was trying to make inroads into the high-end hospitality business. The Kennington Nicosia is a gem, and he may have been using his influence with Philippa to make an offer to Lord Kennington for the hotel. He needs a place to house his associates in a certain style when they come to Cyprus, as many of his business contacts are accustomed to the Georges Cinq or the Ritz, and, with few exceptions, the majority of the accommodations on Cyprus don't reach that level. The British Government fears Amasis may be setting up a conference of his colleagues in crime to discuss the establishment of a central drug dealers' collaborative for the eastern Mediterranean. Amasis undoubtedly would be the head of such a consortium."

"How was Philippa involved?"

"Philippa offered a respectable front and could arrange for meetings to take place after the summer tourist season on Cyprus. She could placate the Kennington Organisation by filling the hotel and at the same time pay back some of her obligation to Amasis, but suddenly the London office of the Kennington Organisation decided to house the FCO delegation here. Their residence may well last into the winter months, and then Lord Kennington sent out one of his top hotel security people. Philippa knew you would keep a watchful eye on the activities around the hotel, which would put her in a precarious spot. She wished to advance her status in the Kennington Organisation, but she was beholden to Amasis. Her murder has to be viewed with this in mind."

Elspeth looked towards Cari and blew her breath through her teeth. "She was in a frightful mess, wasn't she, and so are we. No wonder she was always wound up as tensely as an old clock on Saturday night and was usually in a foul mood when she was away from the guests. Now that she is dead, however, one must assume that the threat to the hotel has lessened."

Cari raised a questioning eyebrow. "Didn't you tell me that Philippa had changed most of the staff when she took over? Perhaps I've spent too much of my career being unduly suspicious, but how many of those people are associated with Amasis? Elspeth, does your London office have anything to do with vetting of local staff?"

"The managers generally handle the hiring of the local staff. Only the manager, assistant manager, night manager and head of security are given full scrutiny from London, unless there are problems. Lord Kennington also likes to approve the appointment of chefs at his larger hotels. Cari, I will have to rely on Jonathan or you to give me any information about our local staff's association with Amasis. I'll get Alexander Woolsey, the new temporary manager, to compile a list of all members of our staff."

"Alexander Woolsey?" Cari was startled.

"He was the night manager here before Philippa died."

"I see." Cari's tone was cautious. "Was he cleared by London?"

Elspeth looked disconcerted. "As soon as we are finished here, I'll call the personnel office in London and find out. If they don't give me the information, I'll call Pamela Crumm, who is one of the owners of the Kennington Organisation and oversees the everyday running of the hotels. Tell me, why question the promotion of Alexander Woolsey? He came here from the Kennington Cairo."

"Wasn't this a step down from one of your larger hotels?" Cari asked.

"I understand he requested it for family reasons." Elspeth sounded defensive, and Cari wondered how to tell her the truth.

"When Alexander was a student," Cari said carefully, "he worked for Nikki Amasis as a driver and gofer. Amasis was so impressed with his intelligence that he funded Alexander's education, first in Athens and then in America. No, Elspeth, the Kennington Nicosia is not clear of Amasis's influence. I suspect that Alexander came back here at Nikki's request and not that of his family."

"Do you have any direct evidence of this? If it is true, the Kennington Organisation is in great trouble, and I'll have to get the highest levels involved."

"Direct evidence? No, not exactly. Circumstantial evidence? More than enough."

"I see. Then I need to rethink the situation. Primarily I'm concerned with the hotel and the safety of the guests and also with the security of the delegation. Amasis's other actions don't concern me unless they're related to Philippa's death and consequently the hotel."

I hope that's wise, Cari thought to herself.

Cari took out the object that she had in her pocket. "Elspeth, you should also be mindful of your own safety. Here, I have something for you."

She put the small, cold metal object in Elspeth's hand. "It's a Walther Model 9 pistol, best used at close range. Keep it with you and loaded at all times."

Elspeth looked startled. "I occasionally carried a handgun in my private detective work in California, but I do not like guns and haven't handled one since going to work for Eric Kennington. I'm not at all happy about this. Is it licenced?"

"The police will not be happy either if they learn you have it, but Jonathan and I insist. You're correct. In order to carry a gun in Cyprus one needs to get a licence from the Ministry of Justice or needs to be sworn in as a special constable. Since you have done neither, the police would look askance at finding you with a gun, but they need never know."

A light but steady rain began to fall, and the two women retreated inside. Elspeth made her way back to her suite and Cari to her family.

*

Elspeth took the gun and stowed it in a drawer in her sitting room. She went to the window and watched several flashes of lightning cross the sky. The night before had been unsettling as she drifted in and out of sleep, remembering her last hours with Richard and trying to put them from her mind. He had not called, although she had received a confirming email from British Airways saying he had booked a flight back to Cyprus arriving early Sunday morning, much later than he had told her originally. Why the delay? Finally, with an aching heart, she called Brussels. He answered his mobile with diplomatic crispness. He must have been on his way to a meeting, Elspeth thought, and regretted ringing him. Lady Marjorie, she was sure, would never have done so. His replies were cool, as if he were with someone and could not talk. She told him quickly about Demetrius's murder, her visit to the Thorpes and to the police, and her conversation with Cari Westwood. He gave monosyllabic replies.

Finally he asked, "How many people have actually warned you about him?" He did not mention Nikki Amasis's name.

"Let me see. The Westwoods, the police, and Christos. Cinnamon also told me that her mother thought he was dangerous, and Edward Thorpe concurred."

"I'm sorry but I can't right talk now, but I suggest you listen to them." He rang off with no parting words of affection.

Elspeth would not have been true to her Scottish heritage if she did not have a streak of stubborn defiance. So much for everyone warning her, and besides Richard was back to being avuncular. If Mr Amasis wanted to speak to her, she also wanted to speak to him. Would he be so heartless that the murder of his son was of no consequence? Didn't he come to the hotel because he thought she might know who killed his son? That didn't sound like a hardened criminal; it sounded like a distraught father. Others might think her next act foolhardy, but she thought it necessary considering the circumstances.

Besides, there could be no danger if they met in a public place, somewhere where she would be surrounded by other people.

She looked through the phone directory in the desk drawer and found the number for Amasis Enterprises.

35

Glad to be inside away from the unsettled weather, Elspeth spent the afternoon and early evening in the manager's conference room interviewing the staff. She gleaned little fresh information. If any of them had direct ties to Nikki Amasis, they were not telling. Some, but not all, said they had suffered abusive words from Philippa Allard-Thorpe. One added, "She always came back full of smiles the next time she saw you, although she never apologised. I confronted her once, and she denied that the incident had happened. To her credit she always treated the guests like minor royalty. That's probably why she was so successful."

Yes, successful enough to be killed, Elspeth thought, but said nothing. Several times she thought of the small gun in her suite but was not sure whether she felt safer with or without it.

Her appointment with Nikki Amasis was on Friday afternoon. He asked her to come to his office, and, although she requested a more neutral meeting spot, he did not relent. She was greeted by a security guard at the main entrance to the Amasis Enterprises' corporate compound and was thankful he did not discover her gun. Shortly afterwards a competent and respectable looking middle-aged Cypriot woman came out into the lobby where Elspeth was waiting. She introduced herself as Mr Amasis's personal assistant but did not give her name. She took Elspeth on an express lift to a large office suite on the top floor of one of the buildings. Nikki Amasis was waiting for her.

He grinned and held out his hand. "Are you surprised I'm not an ogre? Has everyone been warning you against me?"

Elspeth flushed as he greeted her. Nikki Amasis had been described to her as suave and worldly, but she had not expected him to be so boyishly handsome. He was tall for a Cypriot, perhaps six foot three, and had darting green eyes, salt and pepper hair, unnaturally white teeth, a clean-shaven face, and heavily tanned skin. His arms below his short shirtsleeves and half-bared chest under his expensive silk shirt had the physique of an athlete. He set this off with several gold chains around his wrists and neck. He would have looked more at home in Monte Carlo than Nicosia.

The office looked out over the city of Nicosia, facing north towards the Turkish side and the great crescent flag on the mosque there, and revealed the jumble of Nicosia's buildings on both sides of the Green Line.

He dismissed his PA and offered Elspeth a seat. "First," he said in fluent American English, "give me your gun. No, I'm not clairvoyant; the security monitor downstairs picked it up on the screen."

Elspeth drew the pistol from her shoulder bag, where she had put it as her business-like short-sleeved suit had no pockets. He took the gun, opened his desk drawer and placed it there.

"I assume you are not a special constable, and I suspect you do not have a licence. I want to thank you for coming. My reputation isn't very good in the expat community, but I assure you my only reason for meeting you here is to ask you about Demetrius. We didn't often agree, he and I, but I loved him and felt if I allowed him free range through his university years he would come back to me. Do you have a son, Mrs Duff?"

"A daughter and a son, but they are well beyond university age, and we did survive teenage rebellion, thank heavens."

"Is there a Mr Duff?"

"My father," she parried, using her standard response to the question, "but aren't we here to talk about Demetrius?"

"Yes, we are. You appear to be the last person known to have seen him alive other than his murderer. Can you tell me about your meeting with him?"

"You have good spies, Mr Amasis."

"That's how I survive, Mrs Duff."

"There's really little to tell." Elspeth related the circumstances of her trip to the pub with Demetrius.

Nikki Amasis listened attentively and when she finished, he drew out a sheet of paper from the drawer where he had put her gun. "Here's a copy of the letter found on Demetrius's body. It is not a note from Cinnamon Allard-Thorpe."

Elspeth took the paper and read it. It was brief, computer generated, and printed on Kennington Nicosia stationery. It said: *I know you saw me. What will buy your silence?* The note was unsigned.

Elspeth licked her lips. "Do you think I wrote this?"

"I don't know. If I did, we wouldn't be having this conversation. The stationery is available to anyone staying at your hotel and therefore does not implicate you specifically. Obviously Demetrius came to you after he received it. He could have been asking for your help in finding who wrote the note or telling you what would buy his silence. Which was it?"

"Would you believe me if I told you I had no idea that Demetrius had this note in his pocket. He told me he came because Cinnamon had asked him to get in touch with me."

"Couldn't she have rung you?"

Elspeth swallowed, no longer charmed. "I suppose so. At the time I didn't ask."

"Mrs Duff, the Kennington Organisation would not have given you your current job if you were stupid. Don't play dumb with me." The politeness in his voice was gone.

She rose. "I don't have anything further to add."

"Then you can't account for the note? Doesn't that make you guilty?"

Elspeth searched for a reply without finding an adequate one. Finally she said, "I wouldn't have come here today if I had killed your son. As you say, I'm not stupid."

"But you brought a gun."

Who said 'the best defence is a good offence'? Sun-tzu, was it? "I truly regret the death of your son, but I can offer nothing more. Please give me my gun. I wish to leave."

He opened the drawer, took out the gun, and handed it to her. As she was returning it in her bag, the door burst open. Three uniformed members of the Cypriot police with Detective Chief Inspector Ajax Markides behind them surged into the room.

The Chief Inspector addressed Nikki Amasis in rapid Greek and one of the uniformed men drew out his handcuffs. Nikki put out his hands with a smirk. Then he said something in Greek that was obviously off-colour.

Then the Chief Inspector swung round and saw Elspeth. "Mrs Duff, what are you doing here? I thought I told you to stay at your hotel. Since you seem to be involved, you had better come along to the station as well."

Elspeth was led into a small, windowless room at the station that was bare except for a table, four straight-backed chairs and a security camera. One of her police escorts told her to wait, then locked the door as he left. The room smelled stale with fear. They had taken her shoulder bag with her wallet, passport, mobile, and the gun in it. Elspeth expected they were examining these items and also looking for any residue from the gun. Her knowledge of ballistics wasn't good enough to know if an unfired gun would leave anything traceable.

She waited for three hours. Would they allow her a call, the way the police did in Britain and the States? Then came the problem of deciding whom to call. Thomas Wellborne came to mind first, after that Colin French, and finally Cari Westwood. Thomas could act in his position as High Commissioner, but could he really intervene if the police accused her of the crime of possessing an illegal firearm? Colin French would know a lawyer who might help her, but did she want to encourage his attention? Cari Westwood, on the other hand, had an inside contact in the police who might be able to pull strings.

Elspeth berated herself for having accepted the pistol from Cari. Elspeth imagined what the prison would be like in Nicosia and shuddered. Could she lie her way out of this by saying Nikki Amasis had offered her the gun? Was the gun registered at all? Had it come from the Turkish side, which Elspeth suspected? Should she tell the truth and admit that she knew she was breaking the law? She was angry with herself because she had indeed acted stupidly. Only so much could be blamed on her head injury.

The hours passed slowly and the temperature in the room cooled. Elspeth stood and wrapped her arms around her body to warm herself. She paced up and down. What would Richard say? It mattered to her. Would he come to her defence or be angry with her enough to throw her over? His lack of communication over the last few days and rescheduling his arrival time distressed her. Certainly, if she were arrested, he would not want to continue his involvement with her despite his protestations of life-long devotion. She could not imagine him condoning her foolishness or lowering herself to criminal levels.

She looked at her watch, which showed six o'clock. Why so long? Wouldn't they have charged her by now if they thought her guilty? The silence grew around her. Once or twice she heard the sound of heavy footsteps outside the door. Each time she hoped someone would come in, but then the feet would move on.

What of her job? She could feel Eric Kennington's rage two thousand miles away. She was certain Pamela Crumm would come to her defence but might not be able to protect Elspeth's position in the Kennington Organisation.

By the time the door opened Elspeth was both hungry and thirsty and needed to go to the loo. A man in civilian clothes whom she did not recognise entered. His stiff manner and sense of command made her believe he might be up in the higher echelon of the police force.

"Mrs Duff," he said, "you are free to go for now, but you are not to leave the Kennington Nicosia hotel until we can question you further. I will get a car to take you to the hotel and will expect you back here at nine in the morning. In the meantime we'll keep your handbag and its contents."

Relief spread through her body and tears came to her eyes.

"Thank you," she whispered. She had not been charged with a crime after all.

The policeman nodded. "You can thank Mr Amasis. He says you are innocent and has arranged for your release."

The evening air smelled sweet but she felt tainted. She knew Nikki Amasis had wound his tentacles around her the way he had with so many other people.

When Elspeth returned to the hotel in an unmarked police car, she greeted no one, not even the doorman, and headed immediately to her rooms. She went into the bathroom and promptly threw up what little was left in her stomach. She wanted to cry, but tears would do no good. She wanted to talk to someone but knew of no one in whom she could confide who had not warned her about Nikki Amasis. Besides, the police still had her mobile phone, which was in her shoulder bag. Damn, she thought, damn, damn, damn, damn. I am a total fool.

The room phone rang, but she let it go on for five rings, knowing it would cut to voicemail after that. Then there was silence, and the message light went on, blinking at her like a one-eyed dragon. It seduced her with its persistence, and she finally lifted the handset and pushed the tormenting button.

"Elspeth, it's Richard here with so many apologies that I've not been in touch. It's been hellish in Brussels with diplomatic tempers flying and long hours going well into the night. I'll explain all when I get there, an occasion I look forward to with all my heart. I love you, my dearest. I'll ring back when I can." The click at the end of the message was like the chop of a guillotine.

Elspeth sat very still, staring out the window but seeing nothing. She could find no way out of the dilemma into which she so stubbornly had walked. She kept shaking her head back and forth but no ideas came. At one point the tears welled up again, but they did not offer a solution. She finally thought 'I shall just have to carry on'. She had not felt this way since her fiancé Malcolm had died over three decades before.

At nine o'clock she felt hungry and rang for room service. When asked what she wanted, she replied, "Whatever is left over from the dining room tonight." Ten minutes passed before a waiter whose name she did not know arrived with the tray. Later she remembered only one thing on the tray, a large white envelope embossed with the Amasis Enterprises logo. Her hunger vanished as she tore open the letter and read its handwritten contents.

Dear Elspeth Duff,

After meeting you, I fully believe you did not kill my son. At my request my lawyers have acted on your behalf. Carrying unlicenced guns is a serious crime in Cyprus. Since I may be busy for a while with the police, I have one favour to ask in return. Please find my son's murderer.

—Nikki

He had signed his name with a flourish.

36

Elspeth sat up suddenly from a deep sleep. The clock by her bedside read four o'clock. The last time she had looked at it, it had read one fifty-five. She had been dreaming that she was chained to a wall in a cell and a large mouth, smelling foully of garlic, was shouting, "The letter was addressed to you! You are guilty as charged! There is no hope for you now! Off with your head!"

"Wait; that's all wrong," she cried out in her dream. When more fully awake she remembered the Chief Inspector had used the words "the envelope was addressed to you" when he had first interviewed her on Tuesday. What had Amasis's copy of the note said? Something like *I know you saw me. What will buy your silence?* That was it. Yet Elspeth hadn't seen anything incriminating as far as she could recall. Who was the note meant for? For her or for Demetrius? Either might be possible. It also could have been for someone else. She must find out if the envelope containing the note was sealed when it was found. That would make all the difference because then Demetrius would not have known what the note said. Suddenly the envelope was as important as its contents. Knowing she could do no more until she talked to the police, she rolled over and slept fitfully until the sun came through the louvres of her bedroom window.

She dressed carefully for her interview with the police. Because she did not know if she would be detained again, she pulled on dark trousers, a loose fitting cotton shirt and a grey tunic, which would give her some protection against the coolness of the interrogation room. She made up lightly and packed a small bag with a change of underwear, a toothbrush and toothpaste, a comb and a small mirror. At the end she added a lipstick and a packet of hand wipes. She took what little jewellery she had brought with her and put it in the hotel safe along with her laptop. The police had her passport, her wallet with her credit cards, and her mobile phone, all of which were in her shoulder bag. The last thing she did before leaving was to write a short note to Richard. She had spent considerable time composing it in her head.

> *Dearest Dickie,*
>
> *I seem to be in some trouble with the police that is totally of my own making. Do not feel obliged to intervene, as I do not know what the consequences of all this will be, and, of course, I want to protect you from any unpleasantness. Cari Westwood can fill you in.*
>
> *As ever,*
>
> *E*

The note was stilted, but Elspeth could think of no other way to write it. She did not want to make it too affectionate because he might soon want to be rid of her.

She walked to the police station, which took her under twenty minutes. She did not know how much longer she would have her freedom and therefore tried to enjoy even the smallest fragments of the street life: a child playing on a doorstep, an old man with a wide toothless grin, the loud call of a street vendor, the garish T-shirts in the tourist shops, a string of straw hats strung up outside a doorway, even the prickly cacti in the public garden. Looking at her watch, she hurried at the end and arrived promptly at nine.

Half an hour passed before she was shown into Detective Chief Inspector Ajax Markides's office. The authoritative man who had released her the evening before was there, although the chief inspector was not. Jonathan Westwood was standing beside the man.

"Mrs Duff, I am the Chief of Police here in Lefkosia," he said, using the Cypriot name for the city. He did not give his name. "Please sit down."

Elspeth turned to Jonathan, who looked away. She did as she was bidden.

The chief continued. "You have put yourself at great risk, and I could easily have you jailed for illegal possession of a firearm. You also are involved in the murders of Philippa Allard-Thorpe and Demetrius Amasis. If it were not for the interference of my friend here, I would not have let you go."

Elspeth wondered if he meant intervention rather than interference, but his English was proficient, and she thought he had chosen the word carefully. Jonathan made no move to correct him.

"Last evening I had my deputy research who you are," the chief continued, "and I have made several phone calls this morning to confirm what he discovered on our secure internet sites. Because you have been vouched for by one of my colleagues at Scotland Yard, I'm not going to detain you, but I am going to warn you. The murderer or murderers of two people are still out there, and we intend to catch him, her, or them. Since you might be able to give us valuable information, I am going to ask Chief Inspector Markides to interview you again. I want you to be thorough. Mr Westwood has asked to be present, and I have granted his request, despite my better judgment. After that, I want you to leave solving the murders to us."

Elspeth sat still for a long time, feeling her life flow back into her. She cleared her throat and said, "Thank you, sir," and nothing more.

The interview went on and on. Ajax Markides proved to be as skilled an interrogator as he had been the first time he had questioned Elspeth. They went over and over the events at the picnic, both those she had seen personally and those later recounted to her by the members of the FCO delegation.

At that point he asked, "Was everyone accounted for?"

"Yes, Sir Richard Munro and I interviewed them all when we got back to the hotel. We only left out the young children."

"Do you think the people you questioned would corroborate their stories if I spoke to them?"

"Although they could plead diplomatic immunity, I'm certain they would, particularly the twins," she said with a tepid smile. She was tired of the endless questions and longed to get back to the hotel among the delegation. "It will make the telling of their summer holiday's adventures even juicier."

The chief inspector did not smile back. "Tell me again about the Thorpes and their recollections of their picnic."

Elspeth recounted all the details that she could remember of Ernest and Cinnamon's description of the picnic. The Chief Inspector hardly responded as she spoke.

Several times he looked in Jonathan's direction, but Jonathan sat woodenly with his arms crossed over his chest. He even appeared to doze occasionally, although Elspeth suspected this was feigned.

Towards the end of the interview Elspeth asked for a break and was escorted to the ladies' room by the policewoman who was taking notes. Why the escort? She no longer was a suspect, or so she thought.

Noon was approaching when they finally reached the time of Elspeth's last meeting with Demetrius. She had waited all morning for that moment. The questioning so far was one-sided, but now Elspeth wanted to know more about the note and particularly the envelope found in Demetrius's pocket. She decided to ask the Chief Inspector directly.

"Chief Inspector, I have answered all your questions as well as I can, but one thing has bothered me since I talked to Nikki Amasis yesterday. When you questioned me the day before yesterday, I assumed that the note Demetrius was carrying was addressed to me and was from Cinnamon Allard-Thorpe. I didn't know what the note actually said until Mr Amasis showed it to me. You implied that the envelope you found on Demetrius's body was addressed to me. Is that true?"

The Chief Inspector's head jerked up, and he looked over at Jonathan, who appeared not to be paying any attention.

"Mrs Duff, I am asking the questions."

"I know, Chief Inspector, but Mr Amasis showed me what he said was a copy of the note, but he didn't have a copy of the envelope. If, indeed, the note asked how the recipient could be silenced, it's important to know to whom the note was addressed. I saw nothing at the picnic that would give me any clue as to who Philippa's murderer was, and therefore I don't think the note could have been meant for me. If it was addressed to Demetrius, however, he might have been coming to ask me for advice but in the end thought better of it. How the envelope was addressed and if Demetrius opened it thus becomes of critical importance." Elspeth hoped the urgency she was feeling was reflected in her voice.

Jonathan broke in for the first time. "Elspeth, you must realise that you are still in danger."

"Yes, I know. If the murderer thinks I saw something, he might resort to killing me. If the note was directed at Demetrius, we know the sad result of that."

Jonathan nodded. "If the murderer thinks Demetrius spoke to you . . ." He let the sentence die in the air.

"Mr Westwood is correct," the Chief Inspector said. "You are in real danger. You must not do anything more to solve this case. You must leave it to us. I also suggest that you consider leaving Cyprus immediately."

"But I still have my job to do."

The chief inspector rose. "You cannot do your job if you are dead. We do not want another murder on our hands. I want to review the transcript of your testimony and will possibly have further questions. I will ask the sergeant to take you back to your hotel. You are not to leave there until I inform you that you may do so. I advise you to stay in your room and let no one come in whom you cannot trust, particularly if that person was at the picnic and in Lefkosia on the night Demetrius was killed."

Elspeth looked to Jonathan for help.

"I'm not officially here," he said. "I'll let Cari know you are coming. I can only recommend you take the chief inspector's advice to heart."

*

Richard Munro stood at the reception desk and asked for a room. He knew he had arrived a day ahead of schedule.

Christos was standing at the desk behind the receptionist, who said, "Your booking isn't until tomorrow, Sir Richard."

"I found I could return a day early. Can you find something for me?"

Christos bowed his head respectfully, and Richard wondered what he was thinking. Christos whispered to the receptionist in Greek. She tried to hide a smile. She skimmed down through the list of unoccupied rooms. Would his room be near Elspeth's suite? Were his feelings for Elspeth so transparent?

"I think we have one that will suit you, although it hasn't been made up yet. Could you wait a short while?" the receptionist said.

"Yes, of course. I'll have a drink in the bar."

"Sir Richard," Christos said as Richard was leaving the reception desk, "Ms Duff left a note for you. She said to give it to you tomorrow, but now that you are here, I don't see there's a problem if we deliver it to you today."

"Thank you. It's Christos, isn't it?"

Christos beamed. "Yes, sir."

Richard ripped open the note. He read through it quickly, and then more slowly. *Not obliged to intervene?* What utter foolishness, Elspeth, my dear, dear doubting one.

"Christos," he said, "See that my room is made up as quickly as possible. Don't let them fuss with the amenities. Whatever is there will do. I need to make some calls in private."

He rang Cari Westwood first and arranged to meet her on the roof in half an hour's time; then he rang Thomas Wellborne.

37

Clutching the strap of her shoulder bag as if it were her lifeline, Elspeth slumped into the back of the police car and asked the driver to leave her at the service entrance to the hotel. The arrival of a senior member of the Kennington Organisation staff in a police car at the main door would arouse the attention of the guests, not to mention that of the staff. When they reached the back of the hotel, the policewoman accompanying Elspeth stepped out of the car and escorted her inside without comment.

Elspeth skirted the manager's office and took the service lift to her floor. She thought of retrieving her possessions from the hotel safe but decided she would leave it until later. She ordered a late lunch while contemplating how precious freedom was, even if she were confined to the hotel. Now that she had access to her satellite phone, she could call London, but right now she wanted time alone to think. How preposterous of the police to assume that she would simply let matters lie. She opened the room service menu and ordered the highest calorie lunch on it, finishing off with the richest chocolate dessert. Her physical activities might be restricted but neither her brain nor appetite was.

Two things bothered her. One was the conversation she had overheard coming from Philippa's office when the man wished her dead. The other was the Chief Inspector's insistence that everyone's whereabouts at the picnic needed to be confirmed.

She could think of only one person whom she could trust implicitly—her father in Perthshire.

On an impulse, she dialled the number of his law firm in Pitlochry, hoping this was one of the days he had decided to eschew retirement and be working in his office at Duff, MacBean and MacRoberts. She found him there.

"Elspeth, how are you, my dear? Your mother and I were talking about you at breakfast and were hoping your stay in Cyprus has been as restful as you hoped, and that you will soon be fully recovered."

"Daddy, unfortunately there has been a bit of a complication here. I felt I needed your common sense to help me deal with it."

"I hope you have come to the right place. Tell me what has happened."

Elspeth decided to omit the full extent of her interviews with the police. She told her father about Amasis's part in Philippa's rise through the hotel business. The more she discovered about Nikki Amasis, the more she was sure the real truth of the murders of both Philippa and Demetrius centred around him.

James Duff listened without interrupting. When Elspeth stopped speaking, he said, "I don't think you are telling me everything, my dear. Tell me about Philippa's family. You mentioned she left them to advance her career. You know murders are generally committed by family members or by partners in romantic liaisons, rather than outsiders."

Elspeth reluctantly related the sad story of Cinnamon, her blindness, and her desperate attempts to establish an on-going relationship with her father.

"I sense you don't think Ernest Thorpe had anything to do with the murder."

"No, he is a gentle man and totally absorbed in the ancient Hellenic era rather than the twenty-first century, although I heard that several gossiping expats insinuated he was too attractive to live without a partner. Wishful thinking on their parts, I suspect. He *is* quite handsome in a professorial sort of way."

She heard the quiet tones of her father's voice, one that had offered her advice ever since her cousin Johnnie had stolen her teddy bear when she was three.

"Something is bothering you, Elspeth, but you're not telling me what it is. I think that whatever the issue may be, it's the thing on which you need to concentrate."

"Although it seems insignificant in the light of Philippa's relationship with Nikki Amasis and his need to control her, one morning shortly before she died I overheard Philippa ordering a man to stop seeing a female who was simply identified as *her*. Afterwards Philippa asked the man to leave the hotel and never return. That small snippet of conversation keeps rattling around my head. I assumed the '*her*' was Cinnamon. Demetrius told me he had once been forcibly escorted from the hotel, but his accent didn't resemble the hushed baritone voice I heard respond to Philippa after her 'eviction order'."

"I've always found in my cases that I pay special attention to the small details that keep nagging at me," James Duff said. "Elspeth, explore that incident as fully as you can. Try to identify the voice. He may not be the murderer, but, whether he is or not, Philippa's interaction with him is important enough that you should not shrug it off if it's still bothering you. Ring me back and let me know what's happening as matters develop there."

"I will, Daddy, as long as you promise not to tell Mother anything."

"As always, your secrets are sacrosanct with me. I don't like to overburden your mother with problems that might worry her. Elspeth, for both our sakes, take care and protect yourself. Now that the police are involved, let them do their work."

"Of course, Daddy," she said, although she had no intention of doing so.

She licked the back of her chocolate covered spoon with a sigh. Her dietary overindulgence and the supportive words from her father cheered her and made her eager to continue working, trying to fill in the missing pieces in the puzzle of the two deaths. She threw off her practical tunic and severe flat shoes and walked barefoot out into the sunshine on her deck. She stretched her arms to the warmth of the sun and was dazzled for a moment by its brightness.

Two shots rang out, grazing the wall behind her and spattering plaster dust in her eyes. My heavens, she thought illogically, target practice, and I seem to be the target. She fell down on her hands and knees behind the balcony parapet and crawled back into her room. Suddenly she craved the safety of the police interrogation room.

Seriously frightened and trying to let her heart settle back to its normal rhythm, she reviewed her options. She could call the police, contact Cari Westwood, or she could deal with this herself. The first two options had their appeal, but she felt either one would only elicit further admonishment from them. She literally had been put in the line of fire, and now it was time to fight back.

The shots gave a different meaning to the note Nikki Amasis had shown her. *I know you saw me. What will it take to buy your silence?* Until now, she thought she had nothing about which to stay silent. Think back, Elspeth, think back. What is it the murderer thinks you know that is so threatening to him? How strange everyone has assumed that the murderer was masculine, but the crime of strangulation did seem like a man's doing. What did she know or what had she seen that had become so vital that it needed to be suppressed by another murder? She rubbed the tender spot on the back of her head and sought the guidance of her greater intelligence. Unfortunately it offered no insight.

*

Richard Munro and Cari Westwood heard the shots from the rooftop. They ran to the edge as a man dressed in a white T-shirt and black trousers, his face hidden by a baseball cap and dark wrap-around glasses, ran down a small alley at the side of the hotel and disappeared. Shortly afterwards they heard a motorbike engine start up and the screech of tyres. Richard stood horrified, focusing on the spot where the bullets had hit the wall, when he saw Elspeth crawling inside her suite from her balcony.

"No, no, Elspeth. No, not again," he cried.

He left Cari standing on the rooftop, stumbled down the stairs and ran towards Elspeth's rooms. He called through her door. She took a moment to unlock it. As he entered, she threw her arms around him and then drew back, surprise and fear in her eyes. Her usually tidy hair and clothing were in disarray. She was shaking violently. He took her back in his arms and comforted her. Finally he led her to the sofa and made her lie down.

"Do you think the shots were meant for you, my dear?" he asked once she appeared comfortable.

"They must have been." She told him why. "Dickie, I can't let this person intimidate me. The police want to solve these crimes without my help, but now I want to get back at him myself."

"You are putting yourself at too great a risk, Elspeth. I care so deeply about your safety, and I want you to as well."

Her eyes blazed. "I don't take kindly to being shot at."

"Of course not. You *should* take it very seriously. You might have been killed. He's killed twice before, and one more death won't make any difference to him in the end. Elspeth, why are you so cavalier about your own wellbeing?"

"Because I believe in justice. I didn't like Philippa and hardly knew Demetrius, but they should not have died the way they did. I will not put up with being imprisoned in this hotel."

Despite her defiance, he could tell she was frightened.

"You should report this to the police," he said.

"I don't want to deal with them again," she said, clenching her jaw. "Besides who's to say the bullets weren't random. No one was hurt. There is no crime to report."

"Attempted murder?"

"I have no proof, nor do you."

He knew Elspeth too well to argue with her. That would only further solidify her stubborn resolve.

"Very well then, but come with me to the Residency tonight," he said.

"The Residency? I thought you and the Wellbornes weren't on speaking terms?"

Richard grinned diffidently. "I couldn't stay on bad terms with Tom forever. Our diplomatic corps is too small, and there is no place in it for animosity. I rang Tom after I got in this morning. He's invited the two of us round for dinner with some of the local people. George and Joanna Colton are going as well. The police don't need to know. It's not as if you will be at risk or get into any trouble with the three of us alongside you. Besides the Residency is on British sovereign territory and you're probably better off there anyway."

Elspeth cocked her head and raised an eyebrow. "In defiance of police warnings?"

"You have nothing to fear, my dearest one."

38

Tom Wellborne knew his wife disliked last minute changes to her carefully arranged plans, and therefore he was amazed when she agreed to add Richard Munro and Elspeth Duff to the evening's guest list.

"I suppose you want me to seat them together?" she said. He could tell she was annoyed.

"No, Carolyn, I think Richard should be seated next to Joanna Colton and Elspeth should be paired with Colin French."

"Tom, you are seldom unkind, but I think there is a bit of cruelty in what you are asking. Why Elspeth with Colin French?"

"Perhaps I am being unkind. I still harbour some resentment towards Richard and, although superficially I want to make it up with him, I'd like him to squirm a bit."

"Do you still think he's so serious about Elspeth that putting her next to Colin will irritate him?"

"No doubt about it. Besides, she's here in Cyprus stirring up one holy mess after another with the police and Nikki Amasis. Jonathan Westwood's been on the phone, repeatedly asking if we can get her to drop the investigation into the two murders. I suspect more is going on than he is telling me."

She blew her breath through her nostrils. "I knew from the first Elspeth was a trouble maker for all her sophisticated airs. I can always tell. Can we advise Richard against her in some way?"

Tom shook his head back and forth slowly. "I'm afraid not. As they put it in Victorian novels, he is indeed smitten."

"Pity," she said and began to rearrange her seating chart. "Elspeth can never replace Marjorie," she said with finality.

*

As much as she relished Richard's company, Elspeth finally begged him to leave her suite. She had experienced few physical threats to her life, other than the attack in Singapore that had put her into hospital and required convalescence for over six months. She had seen numerous shootings on movie sets when she lived in Hollywood where her ex-husband directed the fight scenes in films, but the bullets were never real and were never directed at her. She had no doubt the two shots that hit her balcony wall were missed attempts at her life, and she realised she was frightened. Her protests to Richard about feeling fine were more bravado than a reflection of her true feelings. The shots had terrified her. She did not crawl back into her room because she was afraid the gunman would fire again, but because her whole body acted instinctively to get away from danger. She had dropped to her knees and dragged herself across the balcony to save her life, and she had fallen on the floor inside her sitting room gasping for breath. Even Richard's caresses could not take her fear away. She was now more determined than ever to find out who had shot at her and possibly killed Philippa and Demetrius. Besides she felt a strange need to honour Nikki Amasis's request to find the murderer of his son. Nikki might be an international criminal, but his appeal to her was genuine.

After Richard left, she debated calling London but decided against it. Nothing she could report shed any light on Philippa's murder or provided any benefit to the functioning of the hotel. She decided instead to lie down and rest. Oddly her head hurt less than it had in the last few months. Nothing like a new problem to replace an old one, she thought.

When Richard knocked at six, she was dressed and ready. She wished now she had not surrendered the pistol to Nikki Amasis and subsequently to the police. She would be in the company of a number of people all evening and felt some safety in that. Even if the party moved outdoors during the evening, she would find some excuse to stay in a protected area. At least she would not have to spend the evening alone and terrified.

A driver from the High Commission waited for them at the back of the hotel, as Richard had requested. Elspeth took the centre seat in the back between Joanna and Richard, and George sat upfront with the driver. Elspeth was relieved the back windows were tinted. No one seemed to follow the car, and no dark figure appeared lurking in the streets. By the time they reached the Residency, Elspeth began to relax.

Drinks were served in the main reception area. When they were shown in, Elspeth looked around the room and was pleased to see several familiar faces. Colin French and the Ogilvys were among them. The major was in uniform and Mrs Ogilvy slightly overdressed. Colin's attire was more casual, and he was engaged in conversation with a blowsy middle-aged woman who seemed to hang on his every word. Elspeth also recognised a couple who had been at her first dinner party with the Wellbornes. Carolyn introduced Sir Richard to them all and conversation turned to the weather, items in that morning's *Cyprus Mail*, and the arrest of Nikki Amasis.

"There's no doubt in my mind," Mrs Ogilvy said a bit too loudly "that he is responsible for his son's death." Everyone stopped talking. Murmurs came from several people but no one responded to her statement. Carolyn Wellborne broke the silence. "May I offer another drink, anyone?" Conversation resumed.

Colin French came up to Elspeth, who at the moment was standing alone, and said, "Gossip has it that you know more about Nikki's arrest than the rest of us."

Elspeth looked up at the ceiling and then back at Colin. "Didn't you once tell me gossip is merely gossip and has little truth in it? I don't want you passing on any false statements."

"Then it's true," he said with a laugh. "No hint will ever cross my lips that I have it from the source."

Colin's earlier companion came across the room like a tugboat, took his arm and dragged him away.

A voice behind Elspeth said, "As possessive as ever is Mrs Treadwell. She won't let Colin alone whenever she is around him, poor soul." It was George Colton speaking. "She has been looking for a good catch for years, ever since her husband died out in Capetown when Joanna and I were there. I hear she's bought a large villa on the coast and is hoping to lure Colin into taking up permanent residence there. He's going to have to be even more slippery than usual to get out of it."

Elspeth looked at George curiously. "I'd no idea you were so close to the expat community. Did you know Colin before?" Elspeth asked.

"No, I just met him here, but his reputation as the man who always gets his way with women and then gets away is a well-known fact. Even during the short time we've been in Nicosia, we've heard a lot of juicy tittle-tattle." He grinned and winked.

Elspeth laughed for the first time that day. "Thank you for being so diverting, George. You've brightened my evening."

Richard came over with Elspeth's drink and soon George drifted off. Richard smiled contentedly as he watched Elspeth and sipped his whisky.

"I've been to thousands of parties like this, and they are all the same. I suppose there is comfort in that," he said.

"Or stifling boredom, a condition I would love at the moment. Dickie, I need to pay a visit to the loo. Hold my drink for me, would you? I'll be right back."

Elspeth remembered the ladies' room was down the hallway, but somewhere she took a wrong turn. As she was trying to find her way back, she passed a doorway that was slightly ajar. She heard two people speaking in low tones. In a voice she recognised, the man said, "They'll never know, will they?" in an angry low tone. It sounded as if the woman slapped him.

Elspeth hurried down the hallway, and finding the ladies' room, rushed in and hastily shut and locked the door behind her. She leaned her back against the wall, gasping for breath. Hearing that voice, she suddenly knew who was unaccounted for when Philippa was strangled, and who would kill Demetrius if he thought he had been seen murdering Philippa.

It took her several moments before her heart rate slowed. She was now certain the man behind the voice had tried to kill her that afternoon when she was on her balcony. She was afraid he might try again before she could get back to the reception and Richard. She looked in the mirror to see if she looked reasonably calm. She unclenched her jaw and clutched her handbag to stop her hands from shaking. A few metres back down the hall and she would be in the assembled company again. How could she get Richard aside and let him know what she had discovered. Could they tiptoe out of the room and surreptitiously call Chief Inspector Markides without raising suspicion? Find Richard first; he may have an idea, she thought.

The walk back to the reception area was the longest one she had ever taken. She pinned on her best smile and listened for the sound of someone approaching from behind or hiding in a place where he could trap her. Step by step, past one doorway and then the next. She held her head up and, because she was not looking down, stumbled into a small table, setting the lamp on it rocking. There was still no sound behind her. She let out her breath. She turned the corner and saw the library beyond.

"Elspeth," he said coming up to her. "Come, let me show you the library." He gripped her arm tightly and pushed her through the door.

*

Richard thought Elspeth had been gone too long and feared she might have fallen. He asked the waiter the way to the ladies' room. Suffering a look of disapproval from him, Richard made his way down the hallway. Following the directions given to him, he found the room empty with its door open. Elspeth had disappeared, which made Richard apprehensive. He had warned Elspeth not to be alone. He should have gone down the hallway with her. Where could she be? He did not think she would go into the private areas of the Residency, so she must be in one of the side rooms. All the doors along the corridor were closed. He went by each, putting his ear against it. Inside one he could hear voices, one of which sounded like Elspeth's. With a pang of relief he slowly turned the handle.

*

"Brigadier," Elspeth said with as much lightness as her constricted throat would allow, "how pleasant to see you here this evening. I've been planning to come and consult with you in the next day or two." She forced herself to smile, but she could not look at him.

He swung her around roughly. "You know, don't you, who killed Philippa?"

"What are you suggesting, Brigadier?"

"Do the police know?"

"I have no idea, Colin. Now may I return to the party?"

"I warn you, Elspeth, not to say *anything* to the police, and to leave Cyprus as soon as you can, that is if you are still alive."

Elspeth laughed. She thought it sounded half-hearted. "That's what the police said. Only they didn't suggest that I might not be alive to do so."

"Why did you come here tonight?"

"Because I was invited. Should there be another reason?"

Colin flexed his large hands. "You saw Demetrius just before he died, didn't you?"

"The evening he died, yes."

"Did he show you the note?"

So he knew about the note.

"No, he said he had one, and I assumed it was from Cinnamon," Elspeth answered truthfully.

He put his hands around the back of a wooden chair, his knuckles white. "I'll ask you again. You know who the killer is, don't you?"

Elspeth thought quickly. She did know and now Colin had confirmed it. He hardly could kill her here, or could he? And then hide her body. Would he afterwards return to Mrs Treadwell at the party and claim a place by her side? No one would think it odd. Certainly he had done the same thing with other women in the past. Elspeth wondered if she could goad him into a confession. That would put her life in peril, but she had no doubt that it already was.

"I didn't until just a few moments ago. Now I do," she responded.

He leered at her and began flexing his hands again. "How did you find out? I'm curious to know."

Elspeth no longer had any need to lie. "I recognised your voice when you were speaking to Mrs Treadwell a moment ago. It was the same voice that threatened Philippa in the hotel. She was trying to control you, wasn't she, to keep you from seeing Cinnamon?"

"Not from seeing Cinnamon, from seeing you," he snarled.

Elspeth was surprised. "Me? Surely not."

"Philippa was a controlling bitch. She deserved to die. We're all far better off without her."

"Why did you kill Demetrius? He was an innocent. Or did you have dealings with his father?"

"Touch Amasis? Not on your life. It was Demetrius who saw me with Philippa on the castle tower."

"Was he trying to blackmail you?"

"I didn't wait to find out."

"So it was you who wrote the note. Now it makes sense. Demetrius was coming to show me the note from you and ask my help. I should have seen that. But in the end he was afraid and didn't show me what you had written."

Colin French looked coolly at Elspeth. "Now you know, and I have only one alternative. I'm sure that, unlike Demetrius, you cannot be bought off."

Richard stood outside the door transfixed. Brigadier Colin French was a large man, trained in commando tactics, who had killed many times in the line of duty, and now it seemed he would have no compunction in doing so again, this time to cover his recent crimes. Richard knew he could not overpower Colin. Instead Richard improvised. He threw open the door and said with exasperation in his voice, "Oh, there you are Elspeth. I've looked everywhere for you. Come back to the party. You too, Brigadier. Carolyn has been asking where you'd gone."

Richard doubted that the brigadier would kill them both on the spot.

39

Detective Chief Inspector Markides, in full uniform, stood in Thomas Wellborne's office at the Residency and looked directly at Elspeth, who was seated next to Richard. Tom Wellborne leaned against the wall nearby and looked relieved that there were no longer police cars with flashing lights outside the gate.

Despite her outward composure, Elspeth was still shaken by her encounter with the brigadier but was considerably relieved now that he was in police custody.

The Chief Inspector did not mince words. "Mrs Duff, I warned you to stay at the hotel, but you disobeyed my orders. You put everyone here in grave danger, most of all yourself. The brigadier could easily have killed you."

"I am well aware of that," she responded, "but it would have been extremely difficult for him to get rid of my corpse. Both Sir Richard and I knew that." Silently she wondered if Colin French would have carried out his threat if Richard had not appeared.

The Chief Inspector looked angry. "Your risk was too great."

Elspeth felt both elated and defiant. "If I hadn't come here and confronted him, we probably would never have known what actually happened at Kantara Castle."

Tom Wellborne broke in. "What made you suspect?"

Finally, Elspeth thought, I can explain without the presumption that I was complicit in the murder of Demetrius Amasis.

'"Two things gnawed at me. The first was the Chief Inspector asking me if everyone was accounted for at the picnic, and I answered yes. I thought everyone's location had been vouched for when Sir Richard and I interviewed the members of the delegation and I talked to the hotel staff at the picnic, but when I answered the Chief Inspector during his interrogation of me, something didn't feel right. I assumed that because Colin was at the foot of the castle keep he had been there when Philippa fell. He wanted us all to think so because that gave him accountability. I was fooled just as much as everyone else. Actually, he strangled Philippa, pushed her off the edge and then ran down to 'discover' her body. Colin must have suspected that Demetrius either saw him rushing down the stairs from the tower or talking with Philippa before she fell. Demetrius was the person the brigadier wanted to buy off and the note on hotel letter paper was meant for him. The brigadier must have used the stationery to divert attention from himself. Because Demetrius was estranged from his family he didn't know where to turn. He must have remembered Cinnamon telling him I had helped her and had a background in security. When Nikki Amasis showed me the text of the message, I knew it wasn't meant for me. My initial assumption that the envelope addressed to me was the same one that held the threating note was incorrect. There must have been a note from Cinnamon in an envelope addressed to me, and Demetrius reused it to conceal the note from the brigadier. This was the envelope the police had. I am still not completely sure why Demetrius decided not to tell me about the note.

We were walking alone both to and from the pub. In the end he may not have wanted to involve me, more's the pity."

Richard took her hand in his. "He probably supposed that by sharing Colin's note with you, he would be endangering you. What strange thoughts must have been going through his head as he walked with you."

"You said there were two things that bothered you. What was the other thing?" Tom Wellborne asked, addressing Elspeth.

"It happened well before the picnic. Philippa had a flaming row with a man in her office. I happened to be outside in the garden and overheard the conversation quite by chance. Their argument was vicious. He said he was grateful he wasn't her husband. She told him not to see *her* again. I assumed the *her* was Cinnamon and the man was Ernest Thorpe, since I had not met him at the time. The man's voice was muffled, and therefore I didn't immediately identify it as belonging to Colin French. But when I heard Colin having words with Mrs Treadwell this evening, I recognised his voice; it was the same one threatening Philippa. I imagine Colin didn't want to be tied down and Philippa was trying to do just that. The '*her*' could have been any of the women he was seeing. Their argument must have triggered his determination to get rid of her."

Elspeth thought it was not diplomatic to mention that the *her* was Elspeth herself.

She continued. "It was Colin who planted the idea of having the picnic at Kantara Castle in Cinnamon's head and then proposed the delegation from the hotel have their lunch there as well. The power of suggestion worked well. When Cinnamon chose the location for her father's birthday party, she did so after talking to Colin. Colin wanted Ernest to be at the castle because as Philippa's ex-husband he would be the one most suspected of pushing Philippa over the edge. Colin probably didn't know Philippa disliked heights and would not have gone up to the top of the keep on her own. Colin must have invited Philippa up there, seducing her with an offer she did not want to refuse—perhaps a rekindling of their relationship. We will never know unless he confesses."

The chief inspector glowered at Elspeth. "We do not like outsiders interfering with our internal security," he said.

"Forgive me, Chief Inspector," she snapped with only feigned courtesy, "but Philippa's murder was of great concern to my employer and consequently to me. Me finding her murderer was not exactly interfering with your investigation. Rather it has solved the mystery of who committed the crimes."

"I am not too sure, Mrs Duff, whether you are a very intelligent person or a very stubborn one."

Elspeth now grinned. "I hope I am both when it comes to doing my job."

The chief inspector softened and smiled. "Perhaps rather than scold you, then, I should congratulate you for making our job easier. You are on British sovereign soil here at the Residency. I suggest you stay here until you leave Cyprus."

"Chief Inspector, there's no longer any danger. I plan to return to the hotel and resume my duties there."

Later in Elspeth's suite, Richard sat beside her and shook his head. "Elspeth, Elspeth, Elspeth. Despite all your sophistication, you haven't changed a mite since your childhood. You are as feisty as you were when I first met you despite everything you learned at Cambridge, from your Aunt Magdelena, and from all the requirements the Kennington

Organisation imposes upon you. I loved you then and I love you now. Is there any chance you might consider marrying me?"

Laughing, Elspeth flung herself against the back of the sofa. "I do love you too, and I think I have ever since the FitzRoy affair in Malta, but it took me a long time to admit it to myself." She looked at him seriously. "I hope that after last weekend you have no doubts about my love because I don't have any, yet I'm certain our future together can be possible only if you are willing to accept me as I am, Dickie. I have to be me and not a shadow of Marjorie."

A deep chortle of happiness came from Richard Munro's throat. "I was afraid of that," he said.

Epilogue

Richard and Elspeth finally had their weekend together, uninterrupted by murder or mayhem. They spent it joyfully, with much laughter and a fair share of intimacy. Monday morning would come too soon, and Richard would have to make his way back to Malta. They were having dinner in Elspeth's suite when a knock came at the door. Theo shyly handed Elspeth a pale blue box with a card attached.

Elspeth took the box and looked expectantly at Richard, but he seemed totally mystified. Elspeth removed the card, revealing the Tiffany label on the top of the box, but she had no clue as to the box's origin. She had not seen a Tiffany's in Nicosia. She tore open the envelope. The note was short. *"In gratitude, Nikki."*

She untied the white satin ribbon carefully and opened the box. Inside lay a showy gold and diamond bracelet. She handed the note and box to Richard.

"Definitely out of my league," he said. "You've gathered admirers here, I see. I think I'll need to come back more often if you stay here much longer."

"I'd like that," she said with a huge smile, her eyes sparkling. "Now tell me what I am going to do with this?"

The next morning, after Richard had left for the airport, her fingers lightly caressed the ostentatious beauty of the gold and diamonds, and then she placed the bracelet back in the box, neatly tied the ribbon and put it in a small bag from the hotel gift shop. She penned a short note, which she added to the bag.

> *Mr Amasis,*
>
> *I am most flattered but the greatest gift you could give me would be to find another hotel for your takeover. I did enjoy the bracelet for an evening. It is truly beautiful.*
>
> *Elspeth Duff.*

She called Theo and instructed him to have the bag and note delivered to the offices of Amasis Enterprises because she had heard Nikki's lawyer had already secured his release.

Author's Appreciation

A Crisis in Cyprus is the fourth in the Elspeth Duff mystery series. Its main characters have now become a part of my life. Therefore my apologies go to my relatives and friends who have to put up with me referring to them and the Kennington hotels as if they were real. They are to me.

I want to thank my brother and niece for going to Cyprus with me and helping to research the locations in this book. The three of us had a wonderful day going to Kantara Castle. Antonis G. Antoniou, owner of the Antonis G. Hotel Apartments, where we stayed, drove us to Kantara Castle in his new Mercedes Benz and had much to say about the conditions of the road up to the castle and a great deal more about the division between the two Cypriot countries.

Many thanks go to Jocelyn Jenner for her eagle eyes in reviewing my manuscript and for checking to see that my British English was correct. She verified much of this with her husband Ray, particularly police and government terminology. Some of the corrections may seem strange to North American readers. I also am grateful for the proofreading done by my friend and fellow author Patricia McCairen.

No book is complete without expressing my appreciation and love to Ian Crew, who is my main supporter and constantly encourages me to continue writing and keep publishing.

Read on for an excerpt from the fifth book in the Elspeth Duff mystery series, *A Gamble in Gozo.*

From *A Gamble in Gozo*:

"I can't marry you, Dickie. I just can't. I don't belong here, and you do. Marjorie did, but I don't. Surely you can understand that."

Richard Munro watched the tears run uncontrollably down Elspeth Duff's cheeks and drop off her strong jaw. She did not bother to brush them away when they fell on her silk blouse. His heart was filled with dismay.

"Elspeth, I love you. Try. They're not all that bad. I admit Daphne and Adrian can be a bit pompous, but they'll come round."

"Pompous? Dickie, if they could call out the court executioner and have me dragged out to be hung, drawn and quartered, they would have done so. No, this isn't my world, and I don't want to be a part of it."

She wiped the back of her hand across her chiselled nose and with disgust looked down at the mess she had made. He handed her his handkerchief.

Taking it, she said, "You're asking too much of me. Let me go." She blew her nose and wiped her cheeks.

"Do you love me, Elspeth? In Cyprus you said you did."

"I loved you in Cyprus and even before that. I can't deny that. I still love you, but I cannot marry you and become a part of your world. I'm not Lady This or Lady That. I'm a plain Highland lass who has made a major muddle of most of her life, but I've finally managed to come heads up and happily afloat. Now, just as everything seemed to be going right, you came along, made me fall in love with you and then expected me to morph into your life. I couldn't do that when we were young and I can't now. I don't know why I gave in in Nicosia and agreed to marry you at Christmas."

"You said you loved me," he pleaded.

"I do. I love you more than the earth, the moon and the stars. I love you more than I thought it possible to love another human being, but the price of marrying you is too great. Can't we just stay lovers?"

Richard jerked in displeasure at the word 'lovers'. He found it common.

She must have read his mind. "See, that's just it!" she said, tears gone.

"I told them your cousin was the Earl of Tay. That seemed to please them," he said in Daphne and Adrian's defence.

Elspeth snorted unpleasantly. "Have they checked *Debrett's Peerage* recently? Or is that dusty tome unlikely to reveal what a joke the whole Tay earldom is, granted in seventeen forty-six by the Duke of Cumberland after the Battle of Cullodon to a coward who turned against his own clan. Nowadays the earldom is probably the most impoverished in all Scotland. I've pleaded with Johnnie to drop the title, but he says he can't, and, besides, it helps him in business. Business, your lofty in-laws would say. Trade?"

"Elspeth, why are you so against titles?"

"I always have been as was my mother before me. A title tells so little about a person, unless they have earned it, as you did. And I don't expect to change my opinion, especially after meeting your in-laws." She raised her voice. "Tell the Higher than Almighty Earl and Countess of Glenborough that the riffraff has departed, and you are saved from a descent into hell."

Elspeth spun round and left the room, slamming the door as she did so.

Richard stood there paralysed, unsure how to act. He wanted to grab Elspeth and shake some sense into her, and he also wanted to embrace her and wipe away her anger and tears. Miserable in his indecision, he did neither. He stood and stared at the back of the closed door and hoped no one in other parts of the building had heard their angry words.

Ann Crew is a former architect and now a full time mystery writer who travels the world gathering material for future Elspeth Duff mysteries. She currently lives near Vancouver, British Columbia.

Visit *anncrew.com* or *elspethduffmysteries.com* for more information on the author and the book series.

Made in United States
Orlando, FL
13 October 2024

52590834R00191